Also by Mary Stewart
Published by Fawcett Crest Books:

NINE COACHES WAITING

MY BROTHER MICHAEL

MADAM WILL YOU TALK?

THUNDER ON THE RIGHT

WILDFIRE AT MIDNIGHT

THE IVY TREE

THORNYHOLD

THIS ROUGH MAGIC

AIRS ABOVE THE GROUND

THE GABRIEL HOUNDS

TOUCH NOT THE CAT

A WALK IN WOLF WOOD

The Merlin Novels

THE CRYSTAL CAVE

THE HOLLOW HILLS

THE LAST ENCHANTMENT

THE WICKED DAY

The Moon-Spinners

BY MARY STEWART

FAWCETT CREST • NEW YORK

A Fawcett Crest Book
Published by Ballantine Books

Copyright © 1962 by Mary Stewart

Published in Great Britain in 1962

ISBN 0-449-20609-2

This edition published by arrangement with
M. S. Mill Company, Inc.

The author is indebted to Mr. A. E. Gunther for permission to quote from his father's edition of *The Greek Herbal of Dioscorides*.

Manufactured in the United States of America

First Fawcett Crest Edition: May 1964
First Ballantine Books: October 1984
Thirty-ninth Printing: February 1991

For
Kitty and Gerald
Rainbow

CHAPTER : ONE

Lightly this little herald flew aloft . . .
Onward it flies. . . .
Until it reach'd a splashing fountain's side
That, near a cavern's mouth, for ever pour'd
Unto the temperate air. . . .

> Keats: *Endymion*.

IT WAS THE EGRET, flying out of the lemon grove, that started it. I won't pretend I saw it straight away as the conventional herald of adventure, the white stag of the fairytale, which, bounding from the enchanted thicket, entices the prince away from his followers, and loses him in the forest where danger threatens with the dusk. But, when the big white bird flew suddenly up among the glossy leaves and the lemon flowers, and wheeled into the mountain, I followed it. What else is there to do, when such a thing happens on a brilliant April noonday at the foot of the White Mountains of Crete; when the road is hot and dusty, but the gorge is green, and full of the sound of water, and the white wings, flying ahead, flicker in and out of deep shadow, and the air is full of the scent of lemon blossom?

The car from Heraklion had set me down where the track for Agios Georgios leaves the road. I got out, adjusted on my shoulder the big bag of embroidered canvas that did duty as a haversack, then turned to thank the American couple for the lift.

"It was a pleasure, honey." Mrs. Studebaker peered, rather anxiously, out of the car window. "But are you sure you're all right? I don't like putting you down like this, in the middle of nowhere. You're sure this is the right place? What does that sign post say?"

The sign post, when consulted, said, helpfully, ΑΓ ΓΕΟΡΓΙΟΣ. "Well, what do you know?" said Mrs. Studebaker. "Now, look, honey—"

"It's all right," I said, laughing. "That *is* 'Agios Georgios,' and, according to your driver—and the map—the village is

7

about three-quarters of a mile away, down this track. Once round that bit of cliff down there, I'll probably be able to see it."

"I surely hope so." Mr. Studebaker had got out of the car when I did, and was now supervising the driver as he lifted my one small case from the boot, and set it beside me at the edge of the road. Mr. Studebaker was large and pink and sweet-tempered, and wore an orange shirt outside his pearl-grey drill trousers, and a wide, floppy linen hat. He thought Mrs. Studebaker the cleverest and most beautiful woman in the world, and said so; in consequence she, too, was sweet-tempered, besides being extremely smart. They were both lavish with that warm, extroverted, and slightly overwhelming kindliness which seems a specifically American virtue. I had made their acquaintance at my hotel only the evening before, and, as soon as they heard that I was making for the southern coast of Crete, nothing would content them but that I should join them for part of their hired tour of the island. Now, it seemed, nothing would please them better than for me to abandon my foolish project of visiting this village in the middle of nowhere, and go with them for the rest of their trip.

"I don't like it." Mr. Studebaker was anxiously regarding the stony little track which wound gently downhill from the road, between rocky slopes studded with scrub and dwarf juniper. "I don't like leaving you here alone. Why—" he turned earnest, kindly blue eyes on me—"I read a book about Crete, just before Mother and I came over, and believe me, Miss Ferris, they have some customs here, still, that you just wouldn't credit. In some ways, according to this book, Greece is still a very, very primitive country."

I laughed. "Maybe. But one of the primitive customs is that the stranger's sacred. Even in Crete, nobody's going to murder a visitor! Don't worry about me, really. It's sweet of you, but I'll be quite all right. I told you, I've lived in Greece for more than a year now, and I get along quite well in Greek —and I've been to Crete before. So you can leave me quite safely. This is certainly the right place, and I'll be down in the village in twenty minutes. The hotel's not expecting me till tomorrow, but I know they've nobody else there, so I'll get a bed."

"And this cousin of yours that should have come with you? You're sure she'll show up?"

"Of course." He was looking so anxious that I explained again. "She was delayed, and missed the flight, but she told

8

me not to wait for her, and I left a message. Even if she misses tomorrow's bus, she'll get a car or something. She's very capable." I smiled. "She was anxious for me not to waste any of my holiday hanging around waiting for her, so she'll be as grateful to you as I am, for giving me an extra day."

"Well, if you're sure . . ."

"I'm quite sure. Now, don't let me keep you any more. It was wonderful to get a lift this far. If I'd waited for the bus tomorrow, it would have taken the whole day to get here." I smiled, and held out my hand. "And still I'd have been dumped right here! So you see, you *have* given me a whole extra day's holiday, besides the run, which was marvellous. Thank you again."

Eventually, reassured, they drove off. The car gathered way slowly up the cement-hard mud of the hill road, bumping and swaying over the ruts which marked the course of winter's overspills of mountain rain. It churned its way up round a steep bend, and bore away inland. The dust of its wake hung thickly, till the breeze slowly dispersed it.

I stood there beside my suitcase, and looked about me.

The White Mountains are a range of great peaks, the backbone of the westerly end of the mountainous island of Crete. To the southwest of the island, the foothills of the range run right down to the shore, which, here, is wild and craggy. Here and there along the coast, where some mountain stream, running down to the sea, has cut a fresh-water inlet in the ramparts of the cliff, are villages, little handfuls of houses each clinging to its crescent of shingle and its runnel of fresh water, backed by the wild mountains where the sheep and goats scratch a precarious living. Some of these villages are approached only by steep tracks through the maze of the foothills, or by caique from the sea. It was in one of them, Agios Georgios, the village of St. George, that I had elected to spend the week of my Easter holiday.

As I had told the Studebakers, I had been in Athens since January of the previous year, working in a very junior capacity as a secretary at the British Embassy. I had counted myself lucky, at twenty-one, to land even a fairly humble job in a country which, as far back as I could remember, I had longed to visit. I had settled happily in Athens, worked hard at the language (being rewarded with a fair fluency), and had used my holidays and week ends in exploration of all the famous places within reach.

A month before this Easter holiday was due, I had been

delighted to hear from my cousin, Frances Scorby, that she planned to visit Greece on a cruise she was making with friends that spring. Frances is a good deal older than I am, being my parents' contemporary rather than my own. When my mother's death, three years before, had orphaned me (I had never known my father, who was killed in the war), I went to live with Frances in Berkshire, where she is part-owner of a rather famous rock-plant nursery. She also writes and lectures on plants, and takes beautiful color-photographs which illustrate her books and talks. My ecstatic letters to her about the Greek wild flowers had borne fruit. It seemed that friends of hers were taking a small hired yacht from Brindisi to Piraeus, where they intended to stay for a few days while they explored Athens and its environs, after which they planned a leisurely sail through the islands. Their arrival in Piraeus was to coincide with my own Easter holiday, but (as I had written at some length to Frances) not even for her would I spend my precious few days' holiday among the Easter crowds, and the milling throng of tourists who had been pouring into the city for weeks. I had suggested that she abandon her party for a few days, join me in Crete, where she could see the countryside—and the legendary flowers of the White Mountains—in peace. We could rejoin the yacht together when it called at Heraklion the following week, on its way to Rhodes and the Sporades; then later, on the way home, she could stay over in Athens with me, and see the "sights" unencumbered by the Easter crowds.

Frances was enthusiastic, her hosts were agreeable, and it was left to me to discover, if possible, some quiet place in southwest Crete, which combined the simple peace and beauty of "the real Greece," with some of the standards of comfort and cleanliness which the new tourist age is forcing on it. An almost impossible mixture of virtues—but I believed I had found it. A café acquaintance in Athens—a Danish writer of travel books, who had spent some weeks exploring the less frequented parts of the Greek archipelago—had told me of a small, isolated village on the southern coast of Crete at the foot of the White Mountains.

"If it's the real thing you want, an unspoiled village without even a road leading to it—just a couple of dozen houses, a tiny church, and the sea—Agios Georgios is your place," he said. "You'll want to swim, I suppose? Well, I found a perfect place for that, rocks to dive off, sandy bottom, the lot. And if you want the flowers, and the views—well, you can walk in any direction you please, it's all glorious, and as wild as anyone could wish. Oh, and Nicola, if you're interested, there's a tiny, deserted church about five miles eastward along the coast; the weeds are right up to the door, but you can still see the ghost of a rather quaint Byzantine mosaic on the ceiling, and I'll swear one of the doorjambs is a genuine Doric column."

"Too good to be true," I had said. "All right, I'll buy it; what are the snags? Where do we have to sleep? Over the taverna, with the genuine Doric bugs?"

But no. This, it appeared, was the whole point. All the other attractions of Agios Georgios could be found in a score of similar villages, in Crete or elsewhere. But Agios Georgios had a hotel.

This had, in fact, been the village *kafenéion,* or coffee shop, with a couple of rooms over the bar. But this, with the adjoining cottage, had been recently bought by a new owner, who was making them the nucleus of what promised to be a comfortable little hotel.

"He's only just started; in fact, I was their first guest," said my informant. "I understand that the authorities are planning to build a road down to the village some time soon, and meanwhile Alexiakis, the chap who bought the taverna, is going ahead with his plans. The accommodation's very simple, but it's perfectly clean, and—wait for it—the food is excellent."

I looked at him in some awe. Outside the better hotels and the more expensive restaurants, food in Greece—even the voice of love has to confess it—is seldom "excellent." It tends to a certain monotony, and it knows no variation of hot and cold; all is luke-warm. Yet here was a Dane, a well-rounded epicure of a Dane (and the Danes have possibly the best food in Europe), recommending the food in a Greek village taverna.

He laughed at my look, and explained the mystery. "It's quite simple. The man's a Soho Greek, originally a native of Agios Georgios, who emigrated to London twenty years ago, made his pile as a restaurateur, and has now come back, as these folk do, and wants to settle at home. But he's determined to put Agios Georgios on the map, so he's started by buying up the taverna, and he's imported a friend of his from his London restaurant, to help him. They've not seriously started up yet, beyond tidying up the two existing bedrooms, turning a third into a bathroom, and cooking for their own satisfaction. But they'll take you, Nicola, I'm sure of that. Why not try? They've even got a telephone."

11

I had telephoned next day. The proprietor had been surprised, but pleased. The hotel was not yet officially opened, he told me; they were still building and painting, I must understand, and there were no other guests there; it was very simple and quiet. . . . But, once assured that this was exactly what we wanted, he had seemed pleased to welcome us.

Our plans, however, had not worked out quite smoothly. Frances and I were to have taken Monday evening's flight to Crete, staying the night in Heraklion, and gone to Agios Georgios next day, by the bi-weekly bus. But on Sunday she had telephoned from Patras, where her friends' boat had been delayed, and had begged me not to waste any of my precious week's holiday waiting for her, but to set off myself for Crete, leaving her to find her own way there as soon as possible. Since Frances was more than capable of finding her way anywhere, with the least possible help from me, I had agreed, swallowed my disappointment, and managed to get onto Sunday evening's flight, intending to have an extra day in Heraklion, and take Tuesday's bus as planned. But chance, in the shape of the Studebakers, had offered me a lift on Monday morning, straight to the southwest corner of Crete. So here I was, with a day in hand, set down in the middle of a landscape as savage and deserted as the most determined solitary could have wished for.

Behind me, inland, the land rose sharply, the rocky foothills soaring silver-green, silver-tawny, silver-violet, gashed by ravines, and moving with the scudding shadows of high cirrus which seemed to smoke down from the ghostly ridges beyond. Below the road, towards the sea, the land was greener. The track to Agios Georgios wound its way between high banks of maquis, the scented maquis of Greece. I could smell verbena, and lavender, and a kind of sage. Over the hot white rock and the deep green of the maquis, the Judas trees lifted their clouds of scented flowers the color of purple daphne, their branches reaching landwards, away from the African winds. In a distant cleft of the land, seemingly far below me, I saw the quick, bright gleam that meant the sea.

Silence. No sound of bird; no bell of sheep. Only the drone of a bee over the blue sage at the roadside. No sign of man's hand anywhere in the world, except the road where I stood, the track before me, and a white vapor-trail, high in the brilliant sky.

I picked my case up from among the dusty salvias, and started down the track.

A breeze was blowing off the sea, and the track led downhill, so I went at a fair speed; nevertheless it was fully fifteen minutes before I reached the bluff which hid the lower part of the track from the road, and saw, a couple of hundred yards further on, the first evidence of man's presence here.

This was a bridge, a small affair with a rough stone parapet, which led the track over a narrow river—the water supply, I supposed, on which Agios Georgios lived. From here the village was still invisible, though I guessed it could not be far, as the sides of the valley had opened out to show a wide segment of sea, which flashed and glittered beyond the next curve of the track.

I paused on the bridge, set down my case and shoulder-bag, then sat down on the parapet in the shade of a sycamore tree, swinging my legs, and staring thoughtfully down the track towards the village. The sea was—as far as I could judge—still about half a mile away. Below the bridge the river ran smoothly down, pool to pool dropping through glittering shallows, between shrubby banks lit by the Judas trees. Apart from these the valley was treeless, its rocky slopes seeming to trap the heat of the day.

Midday. Not a leaf stirring. No sound, except the cool noise of the water, and the sudden *plop* of a frog diving into the pool under the bridge.

I looked the other way, up-stream, where a path wound along the waterside under willows. Then I slid to my feet, carried my case down below the bridge, and pushed it carefully out of sight into a thicket of brambles and rock-roses. My canvas bag, containing my lunch, fruit, and a flask of coffee, I swung back on to my shoulder. The hotel was not expecting me; very well, there was no reason why I should not, in fact, take the whole day "out"; I would find a cool place by the water, eat my meal, and have my fill of the mountain silence and solitude before going down later to the village.

I started up the shady path along the river.

The path soon began to rise, gently at first, and then fairly steeply, with the river beside it rockier, and full of rapids which grew louder as the valley narrowed into a small gorge, and the path to a roughly-trodden way above a green rush of water, where no sun came. Trees closed in overhead; ferns dripped; my steps echoed on the rock. But for all its apparent seclusion, the little gorge must be a highway for

13

men and beasts: the path was beaten flat with footprints, and there was ample evidence that mules, donkeys, and sheep came this way daily.

In a few moments I saw why. I came up a steepish ramp through thinning pines, and emerged at once from the shade of the gorge onto an open plateau perhaps half a mile in width, and two or three hundred yards deep, like a wide ledge on the mountainside.

Here were the fields belonging to the people of Agios Georgios. The plateau was sheltered on three sides by the trees: southwards, towards the sea, the land fell away in shelving rock, and slopes of huge, tumbled boulders. Behind the fertile ground, to the north, soared the mountainside, silver-tawny in the brilliant light, clouded here and there with olives, and gashed by ravines where trees grew. From the biggest of these ravines flowed the river, to push its way forward across the plateau in a wide meander. Not an inch of the flat land but was dug, hoed and harrowed. Between the vegetable fields were rows of fruit trees: I saw locust trees, and apricots, as well as the ubiquitous olives, and the lemon trees. The fields were separated from one another by narrow ditches, or by shallow, stony banks where, haphazard, grew poppies, fennel, parsley, and a hundred herbs which would all be gathered, I knew, for use. Here and there, at the outlying edges of the plateau, the gay little Cretan windmills whirled their white canvas sails, spilling the water into the ditches that threaded the dry soil.

There was nobody about. I passed the last windmill, climbed through the vine-rows that terraced the rising ground, and paused in the shade of a lemon tree.

Here I hesitated, half-inclined to stop. There was a cool breeze from the sea, the lemon blossom smelt wonderful, the view was glorious—but at my feet flies buzzed over mule droppings in the dust, and a scarlet cigarette packet, soggy and disintegrating, lay caught in weeds at the water's edge. Even the fact that the legend on it was ΕΘΝΟΣ, and not the homely Woodbine or Player's Weights, didn't make it anything but a nasty piece of wreckage capable of spoiling a square mile of countryside.

I looked the other way, towards the mountains.

The White Mountains of Crete really are white. Even when, in high summer, the snow is gone, their upper ridges are still silver—bare, grey rock, glinting in the sun, showing paler, less substantial, than the deep-blue sky behind them, so that one can well believe that among those remote and floating peaks the king of the gods was born. For Zeus, they said, was born in Dicte, a cave of the White Mountains. They showed you the very place. . . .

At that moment, on the thought, the big white bird flew with slow, unstartled beat of wings, out of the glossy leaves beside me and sailed over my head. It was a bird I had never seen before, like a small heron, milk-white, with a long black bill. It flew as a heron does, neck tucked back and legs trailing, with a down-curved, powerful wing-beat. An egret? I shaded my eyes to watch it. It soared up into the sun, then turned and flew back over the lemon grove, and on up the ravine, to be lost to view among the trees.

I am still not quite sure what happened at that moment. For some reason that I cannot analyze, the sight of the big white bird, strange to me; the smell of the lemon flowers; the clicking of the mill-sails and the sound of spilling water; the sunlight dappling through the leaves on the white anemones with their lamp-black centres; and, above all, my first real sight of the legendary White Mountains . . . all this seemed to rush together into a point of powerful magic, happiness striking like an arrow, with one of those sudden shocks of joy that are so physical, so precisely marked, that one knows the exact moment at which the world changed. I remembered what I had said to the Americans, that they, by bringing me here, had given me a day. Now I saw that, literally, they had. And it seemed no longer to be chance. Inevitably, here I was, alone under the lemon trees, with a path ahead of me, food in my bag, a day dropped out of time for me, and a white bird flying ahead.

I gave a last look behind me at the wedge of shimmering sea, then turned my face to the northeast, and walked rapidly through the trees, towards the ravine that twisted up into the flank of the mountain.

CHAPTER : TWO

When as *she* gazed into the watery glass
    And through *her* brown hair's curly tangles scanned
Her own wan face, a shadow seemed to pass
    Across the mirror. . . .

                    Oscar Wilde: *Charmides.*

IT WAS HUNGER, in the end, that stopped me. Whatever the impulse that had compelled me to this lonely walk, it had driven me up the track at a fair speed, and I had gone some distance before, once again, I began to think about a meal.

The way grew steeper as the gorge widened, the trees thinned, and sunlight came in. Now the path was a ribbon along the face of a cliff, with the water below. The other side of the ravine lay back from it, a slope of rock and scrub studded here and there with trees, but open to the sun. The path was climbing steeply, now, towards the lip of the cliff. It did not seem to be much used; here and there bushes hung across it, and once I stopped to gather a trail of lilac orchids which lay, unbruised, right at my feet. But on the whole I managed to resist the flowers, which grew in every cranny of the rock. I was hungry, and wanted nothing more than to find a level place in the sun, beside water, where I could stop and eat my belated meal.

Ahead of me, now, from the rocks on the right, I could hear water, a rush of it, nearer and louder than the river below. It sounded like a side-stream tumbling from the upper rocks, to join the main watercourse beneath.

I came to a corner, and saw it. Here the wall of the gorge was broken, as a small stream came in from above. It fell in an arrowy rush right across the path, where it swirled round the single stepping-stone, to tumble once again, headlong, towards the river. I didn't cross it. I left the path, and clambered, not without difficulty, up the boulders that edged the tributary stream, towards the sunlight of the open ground at the edge of the ravine.

In a few minutes I had found what I was looking for. I climbed a tumble of white stones where poppies grew, and came out on a small, stony alp, a level field of asphodel, all but surrounded by towering rocks. Southwards, it was open, with a dizzying view down towards the now distant sea.

For the rest, I saw only the asphodel, the green of ferns by the water, a tree or so near the cliffs, and, in a cleft of a tall rock, the spring itself, where water splashed out among the green, to lie in a quiet pool open to the sun, before pouring away through the poppies at the lip of the gorge.

I swung the bag off my shoulder, and dropped it among the flowers. I knelt at the edge of the pool, and put my hands and wrists into the water. The sun was hot on my back. The moment of joy had slackened, blurred, and spread itself into a vast physical contentment.

I stooped to drink. The water was ice-cold, pure and hard: the wine of Greece, so precious that, time out of mind, each spring has been guarded by its own deity, the naiad of the stream. No doubt she watched it still, from behind the hanging ferns. . . . The odd thing was—I found myself giving a half-glance over my shoulder at these same ferns—that one actually did feel as if one were being watched. Numinous country indeed, where, stooping over a pool, one could feel the eyes on one's back. . . .

I smiled at the myth-bred fancies, and bent to drink again.

Deep in the pool, deeper than my own reflection, something pale wavered among the green. A face.

It was so much a part of my thoughts that, for one dreaming moment, I took no notice. Then, with that classic afterthought that is known as the "double-take," reality caught up with the myth: I stiffened, and looked again.

I had been right. Behind my mirrored shoulder a face swam, watching me from the green depths. But it wasn't the guardian of the spring. It was human, and male, and it was the reflection of someone's head, watching me from above. Someone, a man, was peering down at me from the edge of the rocks high above the spring.

After the first startled moment, I wasn't particularly alarmed. The solitary stranger has, in Greece, no need to fear the chance-met prowler. This was some shepherd lad, doubtless, curious at the sight of what must obviously be a foreigner. He would probably, unless he was shy, come down to talk to me.

I drank again, then rinsed my hands and wrists. As I dried them on a handkerchief, I saw the face there still, quivering in the disturbed water.

I turned and looked up. Nothing. The head had vanished.

I waited, amused, watching the top of the rock. The head appeared again, stealthily . . . so stealthily that, in spite of my common sense, in spite of what I knew about Greece and the Greeks, a tiny tingle of uneasiness crept up my spine. This was more than shyness: there was something furtive about the way the head inched up from behind the rock. And something more than furtive in the way, when he saw that I was watching, the man ducked back again.

For it was a man, no shepherd boy. A Greek, certainly; it was a dark face, mahogany-tanned, square and tough-looking, with dark eyes, and that black pelt of hair, thick and close as a ram's fleece, which is one of the chief beauties of the Greek men.

Only a glimpse I had, then he was gone. I stared at the place where the head had vanished, troubled now. Then, as if he could still be watching me, which was unlikely, I got to my feet with somewhat elaborate unconcern, picked up the bag, and turned to go. I no longer wanted to settle here, to be spied on, and perhaps approached, by this dubious stranger.

Then I saw the shepherds' hut.

There was a path which I hadn't noticed before, a narrow sheep-track which had beaten a way through the asphodel towards a corner under the rocks, where a hut stood, backed against the cliff.

It was a small, un-windowed penthouse, of the kind that are commonly built in Greece, in remote places, to house the boys and men whose job it is to herd the goats and sheep on the bare hillsides. Sometimes they are used as milking places for the sheep, and cheeses are made there, on the spot. Sometimes, in stormy weather, they serve to house the beasts themselves.

The hut was small and low, roughly built of unshaped stones, the spaces packed with clay. It was roofed with brushwood and dried scrub, and would hardly be seen at all from any sort of distance, among the stones and scrub that surrounded it.

This, then, was the explanation of the watcher of the spring. The man would be a shepherd, his flock, doubtless, feeding on some other mountain meadow above the rocks where he lay. He had heard me, and, naturally, had come down to see who it was.

My momentary uneasiness subsided. Feeling a fool, I paused there among the asphodel, half-minded, after all, to stay.

It was well after noon now, and the sun was turning over

18

to the southwest, full on the little alp. The first warning I had was when a shadow dropped across the flowers, as sudden as a black cloth falling to stifle me.

I looked up, with a gasp of fright. From the rocks beside the spring came a rattle of pebbles, the scrape of a foot, and the Greek dropped neatly into my path.

There was one startled moment, in which everything seemed very clear and still. I thought, but not believing it: the impossible really has happened; this is danger. I saw his dark eyes, angry and wary at the same time. His hand—more incredible still—grasped a naked knife.

Impossible to remember my Greek, to cry, "Who are you? What do you want?" Impossible to run from him, down the break-neck mountain. Impossible to summon help from the vast, empty silence.

But of course, I tried it. I screamed, and turned to run.

It was probably the silliest thing I could have done. He jumped at me. He caught me, pulled me against him, and held me. His free hand covered my mouth. He was saying something half under his breath, curses or threats that, in my panic, I didn't understand. I struggled and fought, as if in a nightmare. I believe I kicked him, and my nails drew blood on his wrists. There was a clatter of kicked stones, and a jingling as he dropped the knife. I got my mouth free for a moment, and screamed again. It was little more than a shrill gasp this time, barely audible. But in any case, there was nobody to help. . . .

Impossibly, help came.

From behind me, from the empty mountainside, a man's voice called out, sharply, in Greek. I didn't hear what it said, but the effect on my attacker was immediate. He froze where he stood. But he still held me, and his hand clamped tightly again over my mouth.

He turned his head and called, in a low, urgent voice: "It's a girl, a foreigner. Spying around. I think she is English."

I could hear no movement behind me, of anyone approaching. I strained round against the Greek's hand to see who had saved me, but he held me tightly, with a low, "Keep still, and hold your noise."

The voice came again, apparently from someway off. "A girl? English?" A curious pause. "For pity's sake, leave her alone, and bring her here. Are you mad?"

The Greek hesitated, then said sullenly to me, in strongly accented but reasonably good English: "Come with me. And do not squeak again. If you make one other sound, I will kill you. Be sure of that. I do not like women, me."

I managed to nod. He took his hand from my mouth then, and relaxed his hold. But he didn't let me go. He merely shifted his grip, keeping hold of my wrist.

He stooped to pick up his knife, and motioned towards the rocks behind us. I turned. There was no one to be seen.

"Inside," said the Greek, and jerked his head towards the shepherds' hut.

The hut was filthy. As the Greek pushed me in front of him across the trodden dust, the flies rose, buzzing, round our feet. The doorway gaped black and uninviting.

At first I could see nothing. By contrast with the bright light at my back, the interior of the hut seemed quite dark, but then the Greek pushed me further in, and in the flood of light from the doorway, I could see quite clearly even into the furthest corners of the hut.

A man was lying in the far corner, away from the door. He lay on a rough bed of some vegetation, that could have been ferns or dried shrubs. Apart from this, the hut was empty; there was no furniture at all, except some crude-looking lengths of wood in another corner that may have been parts of a primitive cheese-press. The floor was of beaten earth, so thin in places that the rock showed through. What dung the sheep had left was dried, and inoffensive enough, but the place smelt of sickness.

As the Greek pushed me inside, the man on the bed raised his head, his eyes narrowed against the light.

The movement, slight as it was, seemed an effort. He was ill; very ill; it didn't need the roughly swathed cloths, stiff with dried blood, on his left arm and shoulder, to tell me that. His face, under the two-days' growth of beard, was pale, and hollowed under the cheekbones, while the skin round his eyes, with their suspiciously bright glitter, looked bruised with pain and fever. There was a nasty-looking mark on his forehead, where the skin had been scraped raw, and had bled. The hair above it was still matted with the blood, and filthy with dust from the stuff he was lying on.

For the rest, he was young; dark-haired and blue-eyed like a great many Cretans, and would, when washed, shaved, and healthy, be a reasonably personable man, with an aggressive-looking nose and mouth, square, capable hands, and (as I guessed) a fair amount of physical strength. He had on dark-grey trousers, and a shirt that had once been white, both

20

garments now filthy and torn. The only bed-covering was an equally battered windcheater jacket, an ancient khaki affair which, presumably, belonged to the man who had attacked me. This, the sick man clutched to him as though he were cold.

He narrowed those bright eyes at me, and seemed, with some sort of an effort, to collect his wits.

"I hope Lambis didn't hurt you? You . . . screamed?"

I realized then why he had seemed to be speaking from some distance away. His voice, though steady enough, was held so by a palpable effort, and it was weak. He gave the impression of holding on, precariously, to every ounce of strength he had, and, in so doing, spending it. He spoke in English, and such was my own shaken condition, that I thought at first, merely, what good English he speaks; and only afterwards, with a kind of shock, he *is* English.

Of course that was the first thing I said. I was still only just taking in the details of his appearance; the bloody evidence of a wound, the sunken cheeks, the filthy bed. "You're —you're English!" I said, stupidly, staring. I was hardly conscious that the Greek, Lambis, had dropped his hand from my arm. Automatically, I began to rub the place where he had gripped me. Later, there would be a bruise.

I faltered, "But you're hurt! Has there been an accident? What happened?"

Lambis pushed past to me, to stand over the bed, rather like a dog defending a bone. He still had that wary look; no longer dangerous, perhaps, but he was fingering his knife. Before the sick man could speak, he said, quickly and defensively, "It is nothing. An accident in climbing. When he has rested I shall help him down to the village. There is no need—"

"Shut up, will you?" The sick man snapped it, in Greek. "And put that knife away. You've scared her silly as it is, poor kid. Can't you see she's nothing to do with this business? You should have kept out of sight, and let her go past."

"She'd seen me. And she was coming this way. She'd have come in here, as likely as not, and seen you. . . . She'll blab all over the village."

"Well, you've made sure of that, haven't you? Now keep quiet, and leave this to me."

Lambis shot him a look, half-defiant, half-shamefaced. He dropped his hand from the knife, but he stayed beside the bed.

The exchange between the two men, which had been in

21

Greek, had the effect of reassuring me completely, even if the discovery of the sick man's nationality hadn't already (absurdly enough) begun to do so. But I didn't show it. At some purely instinctive level, it seemed, I had made a decision for my own protection—which was that there was no positive need for me to betray my own knowledge of Greek. . . . Whatever I had stumbled into, I would prefer to stumble out of again as quickly as possible, and it seemed that the less I knew about "this business," whatever it was, the more likely they were to let me go peaceably on my way.

"I'm sorry." The Englishman's eyes turned back to me. "Lambis shouldn't have frightened you like that. I—we've had an accident, as he told you, and he's a bit shaken up. Your arm . . . did he hurt you?"

"Not really, it's all right. . . . But what about you? Are you badly hurt?" It would be a very odd sort of accident, I thought, that would lead a man to attack a stranger as Lambis had attacked me, but it seemed only natural to show some sort of curiosity and concern. "What happened?"

"I was caught by a fall of stone. Lambis thought it was someone further up the hill who set it away, in carelessness. He swore he heard women's voices. We shouted, but nobody came."

"I see." I had also seen Lambis' quick glance of surprise, before the sullen brown eyes went back to the ground. It wasn't a bad lie on the spur of the moment, from a man who plainly wasn't as clear in the head as he would have liked to be. "Well," I said, "it wasn't me. I've only just arrived at Agios Georgios today, and I haven't—"

"Agios Georgios?" The glitter this time wasn't only put there by the fever. "You've walked up from there?"

"From the bridge, yes."

"Is there a track all the way?"

"Not really, I suppose. I followed it up the ravine, but left it where this spring comes in. I—"

"The track comes straight here? To the hut?" This was Lambis, his voice sharp.

"No," I said. "I told you I left the path. But in any case the place is seamed with paths—sheep-tracks. Once you get some way up the ravine, they branch all over the place. I stayed by the water."

"Then it is not the only way down to the village?"

"I don't know; I'd say almost certainly not. Though it may be the easiest, if you're thinking of going down. I wasn't taking much notice." I opened my hand, where I still held

22

some crushed shreds of the lilac orchids. "I was looking at the flowers."

"Did you . . . ?" It was the Englishman this time. He stopped, and waited a moment. I saw he was shivering; he waited with clenched teeth for the fit to pass. He was clutching the khaki jacket to him as if he was cold, but I saw sweat on his face. "Did you meet anyone, on your . . . walk?"

"No."

"No one at all?"

"Not a soul."

A pause. He shut his eyes, but almost immediately opened them again. "Is it far?"

"To the village? Quite a long way, I suppose. It's hard to tell how far, when you're climbing. Which way did you come yourself?"

"Not that way." The phrase was a full stop. But even through his fever he seemed to feel its rudeness, for he added: "We came from the road. Further east."

"But—" I began, then paused. This was perhaps not the moment to tell them that I was quite well aware that there was no road from the east. The only road came in from the west, and then turned northwards over a pass which led it back inland. This spur of the White Mountains was served only by its tracks.

I saw the Greek watching me, and added, quickly: "I started at about midday, but it wouldn't take so long going back, of course, downhill."

The man on the bed shifted irritably, as if his arm hurt him. "The village. . . . Where are you staying?"

"The hotel. There's only one; the village is very small. But I haven't been there yet. I only arrived at noon; I got a lift out from Heraklion, and I'm not expected, so I—I came up here for a walk, just on impulse. It was so lovely—"

I stopped. He had shut his eyes. The gesture excluded me, but it wasn't this that stopped me in mid-sentence. It was the sharp impression that he had not so much shut me out, as shut himself in, with something that went intolerably far beyond whatever pain he was feeling.

I got my second impulse of the day. Frances had often told me that one day my impulses would land me in serious trouble. Well, people like to be proved right sometimes.

I turned sharply, threw the crushed and wilted orchids out into the sunlight, and went across to the bed. Lambis moved as swiftly, thrusting out an arm to stop me, but when I

23

pushed it aside he gave way. I dropped on one knee beside the wounded man.

"Look—" I spoke crisply—"you've been hurt, and you're ill. That's plain enough. Now, I've no desire to push my way into what doesn't concern me; it's obvious you don't want questions asked, and you needn't tell me a single thing; I don't want to know. But you're sick, and if you ask me, Lambis is making a rotten job of looking after you, and if you don't watch your step, you're going to be very seriously ill indeed, if not downright dead. For one thing, that bandage is dirty, and for another—"

"It's all right." He was speaking, still with closed eyes, to the wall. "Don't worry about me. I've just got a touch of fever . . . be all right soon. You just . . . keep out of it, that's all. Lambis should never have . . . oh well, never mind. But don't worry about me. Get down now to your hotel and forget this . . . please." He turned then, and peered at me as if painfully, against the light. "For your own sake. I mean it." His good hand moved, and I put mine down to meet it. His fingers closed over mine: the skin felt dry and hot, and curiously dead. "But if you do see anyone on your way down . . . or in the village, who—"

Lambis said roughly, in Greek, "She says she has not been to the village yet; she has seen no one. What's the use of asking? Let her go, and pray she does keep quiet. Women all have tongues like magpies. Say no more."

The Englishman hardly seemed to hear him. I thought that the Greek words hadn't penetrated. His eyes never left me, but his mouth had slackened, and he breathed as if he were all at once exhausted beyond control. But the hot fingers held on to mine. "They may have gone towards the village—" the thick mutter was still in English—"and if you're going that way—"

"Mark!" Lambis moved forward, crowding me aside. "You're losing your mind! Hold your tongue and tell her to go! You want sleep." He added in Greek, "I'll go and look for him myself, as soon as I can, I promise you. He's probably back at the caique; you torture yourself for nothing." Then to me, angrily: "Can't you see he's fainting?"

"All right," I said. "But don't shout at me like that. I'm not the one that's killing him." I tucked the now unresponsive hand back under the coat, and stood up to face the Greek. "I told you I'm asking no questions, but I am not going away from here and leaving him like this. When did this happen?"

24

"The day before last," sullenly.

"He's been here two nights?" I asked, horrified.

"Not in here. The first night, he was out on the mountain."
He added, as if defying me to go further, "Before I find him
and bring him here."

"I see. And you've not tried to get help? All right, don't
look like that, I've managed to gather that you're in some
sort of trouble. Well, I'll keep quiet about it, I promise you.
Do you think I *want* to get mixed up in whatever skulduggery you're up to?"

"Oriste?"

"Whatever trouble you're in," I translated impatiently.
"It's nothing to me. But I told you, I don't intend to walk
away and leave him like that. Unless you do something about
him—what was his name? Mark?"

"Yes."

"Well, unless something's done about your Mark, here and
now, he will die, and that will be something more to worry
about. Have you any food?"

"A little. I had bread, and some cheese—"

"And fine stuff it looks, too." There was a polythene mug
lying in the dirt beside the bed. It had held wine, and there
were flies on the rim. I picked it up.

"Go and wash this. Bring my bag, and my cardigan.
They're where I dropped them when you jumped on me with
your beastly knife. There's food there. It's not sickroom stuff,
but there's plenty of it, and it's clean. Oh, look, wait a moment, there's a cooking pot of a sort over there—I suppose
the shepherds use it. We ought to have hot water. If you fill
it, I can get some wood and stuff together, and we'll get a
fire going—"

"No!" Both men spoke together. Mark's eyes had flown
open on the word, and I saw a look flash between them
which was, for all Mark's weakness, as electric as a spark
jumping across points.

I looked from one to the other in silence. "As bad as that?"
I said at length. "Skulduggery was the word, then. Fallen
stones, what nonsense!" I turned to Lambis. "What was it, a
knife?"

"A bullet," he said, not without a certain relish.

"A *bullet?*"

"Yes."

"Oh."

"So you see," said Lambis, his surliness giving way to a
purely human satisfaction, "you should have kept away. And

25

when you go, you will say nothing. There is danger, great danger. Where there has been one bullet, there can be another. And if you speak a word in the village of what you have seen today, I shall kill you myself."

"Yes, all right." I spoke impatiently; I was scarcely listening. The look in Mark's face was frightening me to death. "But get my bag first, will you? And here, wash this, *and* make sure it's clean."

I thrust the mug at him, and he took it, like a man in a dream.

"And hurry up!" I added. He looked from me to the mug, to Mark, to the mug again, then left the hut without a word.

"Greek," said Mark faintly from his corner, "meets Greek." There was the faintest definable gleam of amusement in his face, under the pain and exhaustion. "You're quite a girl, aren't you? What's your name?"

"Nicola Ferris. I thought you'd fainted again."

"No. I'm pretty tough, you don't have to worry. Have you really got some food?"

"Yes. Look, is the bullet out? Because if it's not—"

"It is. It's only a flesh wound. And clean. Really."

"If you're sure—" I said doubtfully. "Not that I'd know a darned thing about bullet wounds, so if we can't have hot water, I'd better take your word for it, and leave it alone. But you've a temperature, any fool could see that."

"Out all night, that's why. Lost a bit of blood . . . and it rained. Be all right soon . . . in a day or two." Suddenly he moved his head, a movement of the most violent and helpless impatience. I saw the muscles of his face twist, but not—I thought—with pain.

I said feebly, "Try not to worry, whatever it is. If you can eat something now, you'll be out of here all the sooner, and believe it or not, I've got a flask of hot coffee. Here's Lambis coming now."

Lambis had brought all my things, and the newly-rinsed mug. I took the cardigan from him, and knelt by the bed again.

"Put this round you." Mark made no protest when I took the rough jacket away, and tucked the warm, soft folds of wool round his shoulders. I spread the jacket over his legs. "Lambis, there's a flask in the bag. Pour him some coffee, will you? Thanks. Now, can you lift up a bit? Drink this down."

His teeth chattered against the edge of the mug, and I had to watch to make sure he didn't scald his mouth, so

26

eagerly did he gulp at the hot stuff. I could almost imagine I felt it running, warming and vital, into his body. When he had drunk half of it he stopped, gasping a little, and the shivering seemed to be less.

"Now, try to eat. That's too thick, Lambis; can you shred the meat up a bit? Break the crust off. Come on, now, can you manage this—?"

Bit by bit he got the food down. He seemed at once ravenously hungry, and reluctant to make the effort to eat. From the former fact I deduced thankfully that he was not yet seriously ill, but that, if he could be got to care and help, he would recover fairly quickly. Lambis stood over us, as if to make sure I didn't slip poison into the coffee.

When Mark had eaten all that could be forced into him, and drunk two mugs of coffee, I helped him lower himself back into the bedding, and tucked the inadequate covers round him once more.

"Now, go to sleep. Try to relax. If you could sleep, you'd be better in no time."

He seemed drowsy, but I could see him summoning the effort to speak. "Nicola."

"What is it?"

"Lambis told you the truth. It's dangerous. I can't explain. But keep out of it . . . don't want you thinking there's anything you can do. Sweet of you, but . . . there's nothing. Nothing at all. You're not to get mixed up with us. . . . Can't allow it."

"If I only understood—"

"I don't understand myself. But . . . my affair. Don't add to it. Please."

"All right. I'll keep out. If there's really nothing I can do—"

"Nothing. You've done plenty." An attempt at a smile. "That coffee saved my life, I'm sure of that. Now go down to the village, and forget us, will you? Not a word to anyone. I mean that. It's vital. I have to trust you."

"You can."

"Good girl." Suddenly I realized what his dishevelment and sickness had disguised before; he was very young, not much older, I thought, than myself. Twenty-two? Twenty-three? The drawn look and painfully tightened mouth had hidden the fact of his youth. It was, oddly enough, as he tried to speak with crisp authority that his youth showed through, like flesh through a gap in armor.

He lay back. "You'd . . . better be on your way. Thanks

27

again. I'm sorry you got such a fright . . . Lambis, see her down the hill . . . as far as you can. . . ."

As far as you dare. . . . Nobody had said it, but he might just as well have shouted it aloud. Suddenly, out of nowhere, fear jumped at me again, like the shadow dropping across the flowers. I said breathlessly, "I don't need a guide. I'll follow the water. Good-bye."

"Lambis will see you down." The edged whisper was still surprisingly authoritative, and Lambis picked up my bag and moved towards me, saying flatly, "I will go with you. We go now."

Mark said "Good-bye," in a voice whose dying fall made it utterly final. I looked back from the doorway, to see that he had shut his eyes and turned away, pulling my cardigan close with a small nestling movement. Either he had forgotten about it, or he valued its comfort too highly to have any intention of returning it.

Something about the movement, about the way he turned his cheek into the white softness, caught at me. He seemed all at once younger even than his years; younger by far than I.

I turned abruptly and left the hut, with Lambis close behind me.

CHAPTER : THREE

When the sun sets, shadows, that showed at noon
But small, appear most long and terrible.

Nathaniel Lee: Oedipus.

"I WILL GO FIRST," said Lambis.

He shouldered past me without ceremony, then led the way through the flowers towards the spring. I noticed how his head turned from side to side as he walked; he went warily, like a nocturnal beast forced to move in daylight. It was not a comforting impression.

Here was the naiad's pool, and, not far from it, the trail of orchids I had dropped. A few steps further, and we were out of sight of the hut.

"Lambis," I said, "one moment."

He turned, reluctantly.

"I want to talk to you." I spoke softly, though we could certainly not be heard from the hut. "Also—" this hurriedly, at his movement of protest—"I'm hungry, and if I don't eat *something* before I set off for Agios Georgios, I shall die in my tracks. You could probably do with a sandwich yourself, if it comes to that?"

"I am okay."

"Well, I'm not," I said firmly. "Let me see that bag. There's tons of stuff here, he's eaten very little. I left the coffee for him, and you'd better keep the oranges and the chocolate, and some of the meat. There: we'll leave those. Surely you can help me eat the rest?"

I thought he hesitated, eyeing the food. I added, "I'm going to, anyway. You really needn't see me any further, you know. I'll be quite all right on my own."

He jerked his head sideways. "We cannot stay here, it is too open. There is a place above, where we can see, and not be seen. You can see the hut from there, and the way up to it. This way."

He slung my bag over his shoulder, turned aside from the pool, and began to clamber up through the rocks, towards the place where I had first caught sight of him. I saw him pause once, glancing about him with that tense, wary look, and his free hand crept, in the gesture I was beginning to know, towards the hilt of his knife. He was coatless, and the wooden hilt, worn smooth with much handling, stuck piratically up from the leather sheath in his trouser belt.

He jerked his head again. "Come."

I hesitated, then looked determinedly away from that polished knife hilt, and followed him up the dizzy goat track that led past the spring.

The place he chose was a wide ledge, some way above the little alp where the hut stood. As a hiding place and watch-tower combined, it could hardly have been bettered. The ledge was about ten feet wide, sloping a little upwards, out from the cliff face, so that from below we were invisible. An overhang hid us from above, and gave shelter from the weather. Behind, in the cliff, a vertical cleft offered deeper shelter, and a possible hiding place. A juniper grew half across this cleft, and the ledge itself was deep with the sweet aromatic shrubs that clothed the hillside. The way up to it was concealed by a tangling bank of honeysuckle, and the spread silver boughs of a wild fig tree.

I found myself a place at the back of the ledge, and sat down. Lambis stretched himself full-length near the edge, his eyes watchful on the rocky stretches below us. From this height I could see a wide reach of the sea. Its bright leagues of water hurt the eyes. It seemed a long way off.

We shared what food there was. Lambis abandoned all pretence, and ate ravenously. He didn't look at me, but lay, propped on one elbow, never taking his eyes off the mountainside below us. I kept silent, watching him, and when at length I saw him give a sigh, and reach into a pocket for a cigarette, I spoke, gently.

"Lambis. Who shot Mark?"

He jumped, and turned his head sharply. The ready scowl came down.

"Not that I care," I added, mildly, "but you've made it obvious that you expect them, whoever they are, to have another bash at him, so you're both in hiding. That's all very well, but you can't stay that way indefinitely . . . I mean, forever. And you ought to have the sense to see it."

"Do you think I do not know this?"

"Well, when do you plan to go—if not for help, then for supplies?"

"Is it not obvious that I cannot leave him—?"

"It's obvious he can't be moved, and he ought not to be left, but the way things look now, if someone doesn't get help very soon, he'll get worse. Let's face it, he may even die. If not of the wound, then of exposure. You told me he'd had a night in the open. People die of that—shock, pneumonia, goodness knows what, didn't you know?"

No answer. He was lighting his cigarette, and he didn't look at me, but at least he was making no move to leave me, or hurry me on my way.

I said abruptly, "You came here by boat, didn't you? Was it your own?"

His head jerked up at that, and the match went fizzing down among the dry juniper needles. Absently, he put the heel of his hand down on the tiny gyre of blue smoke to crush it out. If it burnt him, he gave no sign. His eyes were on me, unwinking.

"By—boat?"

"Yes, by boat. I heard you say something about 'the caique,' to Mark." I smiled. "Good heavens, everybody knows that much Greek. And then, Mark lied about how you got here. There's no road from the east; in fact, there's only one road through this corner of Crete, and if you'd come by that you'd not have needed to ask me all those questions about the route down to the village. If Mark hadn't been

30

feverish, he'd have known I'd see through such a silly lie. Well? You can't have come by the supply-boat from Chania, because that'd tie up in Agios Georgios, and—again—you'd know the way. *Was* it your own boat?"

A pause. "Yes, it is mine."

"And where is it now?"

A longer pause. Then a reluctant gesture towards a part of the coast out of our sight, some way to the east. "Down there."

"Ah. Then I assume you'll have supplies on board—food, blankets, medical things?"

"And if I have?"

"Then they'll have to be fetched," I said calmly.

"How?" He said it angrily; but at least, I thought, he was listening. His initial mistrust gone, he might even be halfway to accepting me as a possible ally. "You might not find the boat. The way is not easy. Besides, it is not safe."

So he had accepted me. I waited for a moment, then said, slowly, "You know, Lambis, I think you had better tell me about this—affair. No, listen to me. I know you don't really trust me, why should you? But you've had to trust me this far, and you'll have to, again, when I finally do go down to the village. So why not trust me a bit further? Why not take advantage of the fact that I came along? There may not be much I can do, but there may be something, and I promise to be very careful. I won't interfere where I'm not needed, but obviously I'm less likely to make mistakes, if I know what's involved."

The dark eyes were fixed on my face. They were quite unreadable, but the stony sullenness had gone from his mouth. He seemed to be hesitating.

I said, "I have understood one thing, I think. It was a man from Agios Georgios who shot Mark?"

"We do not know. We do not know who did it."

I said sharply, "If you don't intend to tell me the truth even now—"

"This is the truth. Can you not see? If we knew from where the danger comes, or why, then we would know what to do. But we do not know. This is why I am afraid to go into the village, or to ask there for help from anyone—even the headman. I do not know if this is some affair of family, or who may be concerned in it. You are from England: perhaps you have stayed in Athens, or even in the *Peloponnisos*—" I nodded—"but still you do not know what it is like in these mountain villages of Crete. It is a wild country, still, and the

31

law does not always reach here. Here, in Crete, they still kill sometimes for affairs of family, you understand? They still have the—I do not know the word, family killings and revenge—"

"Vendettas. Blood-feuds."

"Yes, 'vendetta' I know; killing for blood. Blood will always have blood."

He pronounced this involuntarily Shakespearean line in a matter-of-fact voice that chilled me. I stared. "Are you trying to tell me that Mark has injured someone—by mistake, I presume? And was shot at in revenge, or something, by someone he doesn't know? Why, it's absurd! I suppose it *could* have happened, in a country like Crete, but surely they must realize by now—"

"He injured nobody. That was not his mistake. His mistake was that he saw a murder done."

I heard my breath go out between my teeth. "I—see. And the *murderer's* mistake was, that Mark is still alive to talk about it?"

"That is so. And we do not know even who the people were . . . the murderers, and the man they killed; and so we do not know in what direction we can go for help. We only know that they still search for Mark, to kill him." He nodded at my look. "Yes, these are wild parts, *thespoinís*—miss. If a man is injured, his whole family, perhaps his whole village, will support him, even in the case of murder and death. Not always, of course, but sometimes, in some places. Often here, in these mountains."

"Yes, I'd read it, but somehow one doesn't—" I paused, and drew in my breath. "Are you a Cretan, Lambis?"

"I was born in Crete, yes. But my mother was from Aegina, and when my father was killed, in the war, she returned to her mother's house. I lived in Agia Marina, in Aegina."

"I know it. Then you don't belong to this part of the world? It couldn't have been anything to do with you, this horrible affair?"

"No, I was not even here. I found him next morning. I told you."

"Oh yes, so you did. But I still can't think that it literally isn't safe to go down for supplies, and even to see the headman in Agios Georgios. Why, he'd be—"

"No!" He spoke sharply, as if in sudden fear. "You do not know it all. It is not so simple."

I said, gently, "Then supposing you tell me."

32

"I will do that." But he waited for a moment, letting his eyes move slowly over the empty reaches of the mountainside below us. When he was satisfied that there was no movement anywhere, he settled himself more comfortably on his elbow, and took a deep drag at his cigarette.

"I told you I have a caique. I live now in Piraeus. Mark hired me there, to take a voyage to some of the islands. We have been to different places, during two weeks, but no matter of that, two days ago we come round to the south of Crete. We mean to come in to Agios Georgios, perhaps, later that night. I speak of Saturday. Well, Mark he know of an old church, in a hollow of the mountains, not far from the coast, to the east of Agios Georgios. This church is very ancient—" he pronounced it "aunchient"—"perhaps classical, who knows, and I think it is in the old books."

"I've heard of it. There was a classical shrine, I think, then later a church was built on the site. Byzantine."

"So? Well, in the aunchient times there was a harbor nearby. Still, in calm weather, you can see the old wall under the water, and a small caique can get right in where the old landing place was. Mark, he tells me to stop there. We had been sailing for two days, and now they were wanting to go on land, to walk—"

"They?"

"Mark and his brother."

"Oh!" I stared at him, with the beginnings of frightened comprehension. I was remembering the look of agonized helplessness on Mark's face, and something Lambis had said, to quiet him: *I'll go and look for him myself, as soon as I can.*

"I begin to see," I said, rather hoarsely. "Go on."

"Well, Mark and Colin leave the caique, and go up through the hills. This is Saturday, did I say? They are to be gone all the day. They have food and wine with them. I stay with the caique. There is a small thing wrong with the engine, so I am to go along to Agios Georgios for what I need, then return in the evening to meet Mark and Colin. But I find the engine goes right quite easily, so I just stay and fish, and sleep, and swim, until it is evening, and they have not come. I wait and wait, but not knowing when they will come, or if perhaps I should go and look . . . you know how this is—"

"I know."

"Then it is night, and they are not coming, and now I am very anxious. These are wild hills. I do not think they can be lost, but I think of accidents. At last, when I can wait no more, I lock the cabin on the caique, and put the key where they will know to find it, then I take a torch, and go up to find the little church. But you will understand that, even with the torch, it is not possible to find a way."

"I can well believe that."

"I shout, of course, and I go as far as I can, but I do not even find the church. I do not wish myself to be lost, so I go back where I can hear the sea, and I wait for the moon."

"It's rising late, isn't it?"

He nodded. He was talking easily now. "It was a long time to wait. When it rose, it was not a big moon, but I could see the way well enough. I go slowly, very slowly. I find the church, but they are not there. I do not know where to go from there, but then there is cloud, and sharp rain, and it is dark again, very dark. I have to take shelter till first light. I shout, but there is nothing. I do not think they have passed me, back to the boat, so when it is light, I go on. I am lucky. I find a path—not just a goat path, but a wide one, of stones worn flat, as if men went that way. Perhaps in the old days it was the road from Agios Georgios to the church and the auncient harbor. I do not know. But it was a path. I go along it. Then, on it, I see blood."

The bare simplicity of Lambis' style, together with the matter-of-fact tone he used, had an absurdly sensational impact. As he paused, with totally unconscious effect, to grind his cigarette out on a stone, I found myself watching him so tensely that when a shadow scudded across the ledge between us, I flinched from it as if it had been a flying knife. It was only a kestrel, sailing in to feed its young in a nest on the rock above us. The air shrilled with the ecstatic hissing with which they greeted the food.

Lambis never even glanced up, his nerves being that much better than mine. "Now," he said, "I am sure there is an accident. This has happened before the rain, because the rain has washed most of it away, but I see the blood between the stones. I am afraid. I call, but there is no answer." He hesitated, and glanced up at me. "Then—I cannot explain you why—but I do not call any more."

"You don't have to explain. I understand."

I did understand, very well. I could picture it as he had told it me: the man alone on the mountainside; the blood on the stones; the eerie silence, and the echoing rocks; the creeping fear. I had been to Aegina, the idyllic little island in the Saronic Gulf where Lambis had been brought up. There, one solitary hill, sea-girdled, is crowned with a temple which stands among its sunlit pines. From between the pillars, on every side, you can see woods and fields, edged with the calm, blue sea. The road winds through gentle valleys, past slopes where little Christian shrines perch, it seems, every fifty yards or so, among the ferns and wild blue iris. . . . But here, in Crete, it is a different world. These cloud-bound crags, with their eagles and ibexes and wheeling vultures, have, time out of mind—it is said—been the haunt of outlawed and violent men. So, Lambis had hunted in silence. And, finally, he had found Mark.

Mark was lying some three hundred yards further on, full in the path. "He had crawled that way, from where the blood was spilt. How, I do not know. I think at first that he is dead. I see then that he is fainting, and that he has been shot. I do what I can, quickly, then I look for the boy."

"The boy? You mean that the brother—Colin—is *younger?*"

"He is fifteen."

"Oh, God. Go on."

"I do not find him. But now it is light, and I am afraid they—whoever it is who has done this—will come back to look for Mark. I cannot take him back to the boat, it is too far. I carry him away, off the path, up through the rocks and along under the ridge, and then I find this place. It is easy to see that there has been nobody here for many weeks. I look after Mark, and make him warm, then I go back to the place where I find him, to cover the marks with dust, so that they will think he recovered and went away. I will tell you of that later. Now I will tell you what Mark told me, when he could speak."

"Just a minute. You've not found Colin yet?"

"No. There was no sign."

"Then—he's probably alive?"

"We do not know."

The whistling in the cliff had stopped. The kestrel flew out again, rocked in a lovely curve below eye level, then tore away to the right, and vanished.

"What did Mark tell you?"

Lambis had taken out another cigarette. He had rolled over on his stomach, and gazed out over the hot hillside as he talked. Still briefly, unemotionally, he told me Mark's story.

Mark and Colin had walked to the little church (he said), and had their meal there. After they had explored it, they had walked on, up into the hills, intending to spend the whole day out before returning to the caique. Though the day had been fine, clouds had begun to pile up during the latter part of the afternoon, so that twilight came early. The two brothers had gone perhaps a little further than they had intended, and when at length they regained the path with the "worn stones" that led down towards the church, the dusk was already gathering. They were walking fast, not talking, their rope-soled shoes making very little sound on the path, when suddenly, just ahead of them round a bend in the track, they heard voices speaking Greek, raised as if in some sort of quarrel. Thinking nothing of this, they held on their way, but, just as they came round the bluff of rock that masked the speakers from them, they heard shouts, a scream from a woman, and then a shot. They stopped short by the corner, with a very eloquent little tableau laid out just ahead of them at the edge of a wooded gully.

Three men and a woman stood there. The fourth man lay on his face at the gully's edge, and it didn't need a closer look to know that he was dead. Of the three living men, one stood back, aloof from the rest of the group, smoking—apparently unmoved. He seemed, by the very calmness of his gestures, no less than by his position, to be demonstrating his detachment from what was going on. The other two men both had rifles. It was obvious which one had fired the recent shot; this was a dark man in Cretan costume, whose weapon was still leveled. The woman was clinging to his arm, and screaming something. He shook her off roughly, cursing her for a fool, and struck her aside with his fist. At this the second man shouted at him, and started forward, threatening him with his clubbed rifle. Apart from the woman, whose distress was obvious, none of them seemed very concerned with the fate of the dead man.

As for Mark, his first concern was Colin. Whatever the rights and wrongs of what had happened, this was not a moment to interfere. He dropped an arm across the boy's shoulders to pull him back out of sight, with a muttered, "Let's get out of this."

But the third man—he of the unconcerned cigarette—turned, at that unlucky moment, and saw them. He said something, and the faces of the group turned, staring, pale in the dusk. In the moment of startled stillness before any of them moved, Mark thrust Colin behind him. He had opened his mouth to shout—he was never afterwards quite sure what he had been going to say—when the man in Cretan costume threw his rifle to his shoulder, and fired again.

Mark, as the man moved, had flinched back, half-turning to dodge out of sight. It was this movement that had saved him. He was near the gully's edge, and, as he fell, the momentum of his turn, helped by the swing of the haversack on his shoulder, pitched him over it.

The next few minutes were a confusion of pain and distorted memory. Dimly, he knew that he was falling, bumping and sprawling down among rocks and bushes, to lodge in a thicket of scrub (as he found later) some way below the path.

He heard, as from a long way off, the woman screaming again, and a man's voice cursing her, and then Colin's voice, reckless with terror: "You've killed him, you stupid swine! Mark! Let me get down to him! Mark! Let me go, damn you! *Mark!*"

Then the sound of a brief, fierce scuffle at the gully's edge, a cry from Colin, bitten off short, and after that, no further sound from him. Only the woman sobbing, and calling in thick Greek upon her gods; and the voices of the two Cretans, furiously arguing about something; and then, incongruously —so incongruously that Mark, swimming away now on seas of black pain, could not even be sure it was not a dream—a man's voice saying, in precise and unconcerned English: "At least take time to think it over, won't you? Three corpses is a lot to get rid of, even here. . . ."

And that, said Lambis, was all that Mark remembered. When he awoke to consciousness, it was almost daylight. The thought of Colin got him, somehow, up out of the gully and onto the path. There he lay awhile, exhausted and bleeding, before he could summon the strength to look about him. The dead man had gone, and there was no sign of Colin. Mark had retained the dim impression that the murderers had gone inland, so he started to crawl along the path after them. He fainted several times in his passage of three hundred yards. Twice, the rain revived him. The last time, Lambis found him lying there.

Lambis' voice had stopped. I sat for a few minutes—for ages it seemed—in silence, with my hands pressed to my cheeks, staring, without seeing it, at the bright, far-off sea. I had imagined nothing like this. No wonder Lambis had been afraid. No wonder Mark had tried to keep me out of it. . . .

I said hoarsely, "I suppose they'd left Mark for dead?"

"Yes. It was dark, you see, and they may not have wanted to go down the gully after him. It was a very steep place. If he was not then dead, he would be dead by morning."

"Then—when the Englishman told them to 'think it over,' he must have been meaning Colin? The other two 'corpses' being Mark, and the dead man?"

"It seems so."

"So Colin *must* have been alive?"

"The last Mark heard of it, yes," said Lambis.

A pause. I said, uncertainly, "They would come back, by daylight, for Mark."

"Yes." A glance from those dark eyes. "This I guessed, even before I heard his story. When I went back to cover our tracks, I brushed the dust over them, and went down for the haversack, then I hid above, among the rocks, and waited. One came."

Again the breathless impact of that sparse style. "You saw him?"

"Yes. It was a man of perhaps forty, in Cretan dress. You have seen this dress?"

"Oh, yes."

"He had a blue jacket, and dark-blue breeches, the loose kind. The jacket had some—what is the word for little balls of colour along the edge?"

"What? Oh—I suppose I'd call them bobbles, if you mean that fancy braided trimming with sort of tufts on, like a Victorian fringed tablecloth."

"Bobbles." Lambis, I could see, had filed my thoughtless definition away for future reference. I hadn't the heart to dissuade him. "He had red bobbles, and a soft black cap with a red scarf tied round, and hanging, the way the Cretans wear it. He was very dark of face, with a moustache, like most Cretans; but I shall know him again."

"Do you think it was the murderer?"

"Yes. It was very nearly dark when the shooting happened, and Mark did not see faces, but he is certain that the man who did the shooting was in Cretan dress. Not the others."

"What did he do when you saw him?"

"He looked about him, and went down into the gully, looking for Mark. He took a long time, as if he could not believe that he had gone. When he could find no body, he looked puzzled, and then anxious, and searched further, to see if perhaps Mark had crawled away, and died. He searched all the time below, in the gully, you understand. He did not think that Mark could have climbed up to the path. But when he looked for a long time without finding, then he came back to the path. He was very worried, I could see. He searched the path, then, but I think he saw nothing. After a time he went off, but not towards Agios Georgios. He went up there—" a gesture vaguely north—"where I think is another village, high up. So we still do not know from where the murderers come."

"No. I suppose you couldn't—" I hesitated, picking my words. "I mean, if he was alone . . ."

For the first time, Lambis smiled, a sour enough smile. "You think I should have attacked him? Of course. I do not have to tell you that I wait for the chance to force him to tell me the truth, and what they have done to Colin. But there is no chance. He is too far from me, and between us is the slope of open hillside. And he has his rifle, which he carries, so." A gesture, indicating a gun held at the ready. "He is too quick with his gun, that one. I have to let him go. If I take a risk, me, then Mark dies also."

"Of course."

"And because of Mark, who looks to be dying, I cannot follow this Cretan, to see where he goes . . ." Suddenly he sat up, turning briskly towards me. "So now you understand? You see why I speak of danger, and why I do not dare to leave Mark, even to find where Colin is? Mark wishes me to go, but he is too ill, and when he has the fever, he tries to leave the hut, to look himself for his brother."

"Oh, yes, I see that all right. Thank you for telling me all this. And now, surely, you'll let me help?"

"What can you do? You cannot go down now to the village, and buy food or blankets, and then come back here. The whole village would know of it within the hour, and there would be a straight path back here, to Mark. And you cannot go to the boat; it will be dark soon, and I have told you, you could not find the way."

"No, but you could."

He stared.

I said, "Well, it's obvious, isn't it? You go, and I'll stay with him."

You would have thought I had offered to jump straight off the side of the White Mountains. *"You?"*

"What else is there to do? Someone has to stay with him. Someone has to get supplies. I can't get supplies, therefore I stay with him. It's as simple as that."

"But—I shall be gone a long time, perhaps many hours."

I smiled. "That's where the luck comes in. The hotel doesn't expect me until tomorrow. Nobody in Agios Georgios knows I've arrived. Whatever time I get there, nobody's going to ask questions."

He scooped up a handful of the dry juniper needles, and let them run softly through his fingers. He watched them, not looking at me as he spoke. "If they come back, these murderers, to look for Mark, you will be alone here."

I swallowed, and said with what I hoped sounded like resolute calm, "Well, you'll wait till it gets dusk, won't you, before you go? If they haven't been back and found the hut before dark, they're not likely to find it afterwards."

"That is true."

"You know," I said, "this isn't silly heroics, or anything. I don't *want* to stay here, believe me. But I simply don't see what else there is to do."

"You could do what Mark told you, and go down to your hotel and forget us. You will have a comfortable bed, and a safe one."

"And how well do you think I should sleep?"

He lifted his shoulders, with a little twist of the lips. Then he gave a quick glance at the western sky. "Very well. At first dark, I shall go." A look at me. "We shall not tell Mark, until I have gone."

"Better not. He'd only worry about me, wouldn't he?"

He smiled. "He does not like to be helpless, that one. He is the kind that tries to carry the world."

"He must be half out of his mind about Colin. If he could only sleep, then you might even be able to go, and get back again, without his knowing."

"That would be best of all." He got to his feet. "You will stay up here, then, until I give you a signal? I shall see to him before I leave him. There will be nothing for you to do except see that he does not wake with fever, and try to crawl out of the hut, to look for his brother."

"I can manage that," I said.

He stood looking down at me with that unreadable, almost surly expression. "I think," he said slowly, "that you would manage anything." Then suddenly, he smiled, a genuine smile of friendliness and amusement. "Even Mark," he added.

CHAPTER : FOUR

Mark how she wreaths each horn with mist, yon late
and labouring moon.

Wilde: *Panthea.*

LAMBIS LEFT AT DUSK. Soon after the sun had vanished below
the sea, darkness fell. I had been watching from the ledge,
and, in the two long hours before sunset, I had seen no sign
of movement on the mountainside, except for Lambis' short
trips from the hut to get water from the pool.

Now, as the edges of sea and landscape became dim, I saw
him again, small below me, appearing at the door of the hut.
This time he came out a short way, then stopped, looked up
in my direction, and lifted a hand.

I stood up and raised an arm in reply, then made my way
carefully down to meet him.

He said, low-voiced, "He is asleep. I gave him the rest of
the coffee, and I have bathed his arm. It looks better, I
think; he has been a little feverish, talking stupid things, but
no longer fighting to be out. He will be okay with you. I
have filled the flask now with water; you will not need to
come out again."

"Very well."

"I will go now. You are not afraid?"

"I am, a little, but then that's only natural. It doesn't
change anything. You'll take great care?"

"Of course." He hesitated, then there came again that
familiar gesture of hand to hip. "You would like this?"

"This" was his knife. It lay across his palm.

I shook my head. "Keep it. If one of us is going to need it,
I hope it'll be you! In any case, it would be wasted on me—I
wouldn't quite know how to start using it. Oh, and Lambis—"

"Yes?"

"I've been thinking, sitting up there. Isn't it just possible
that Colin may have got away? Or even that they've actually
let him go? They know Mark's got away, and may be still
alive, so they must know it'd only be running into worse
trouble if they kill Colin. I mean, the first murder may be

41

a local affair that they think they can get away with, but it'd be a different matter to involve two British nationals."

"I have thought this myself."

"And if he were free—Colin, I mean—he'd go first of all to look for Mark's body, then, when he didn't find it, he'd go straight to the caique, wouldn't he?"

"I have thought this also. I have been hoping I shall find him there."

I said doubtfully, "As long as *they've* not found the caique . . . I suppose, if they have, they'd be bound to connect it with Mark? Does the path, the 'ancient' path, lead straight to the old harbor? Would they assume that was where Mark and Colin were making for? If so, you'd think they'd have followed it up."

He shook his head. "The path goes on right over the hills, past the church, then it divides towards the hill village to the north, Anoghia, where the Cretan went, and to another village further along the coast to the east. There, there is a road to Phestos, where the antiquities are, and the tourists go. It is certain that the murderers would think that Mark was going that way. Why should they think of a boat? Mark and Colin had a haversack, and it would seem, perhaps, that they were walking, and sleeping out—going, perhaps, to sleep that night in the old church. People do these strange things, especially the English."

"Well, let's hope you're right. Let's hope they never think about a boat. Can it be seen easily, from the shore above?"

"No, but I shall hide it better. There was a cave . . . not quite a cave, but a deep place between rocks, which could not be seen from the shore paths. I shall put her in there; she will be safe enough; there will be no wind tonight."

"But if Colin came back to where you had left her before—"

"He will still find her. If he does go down to the place, and she is not there, you know what he will do, what anyone does. He will think, first, that this is not the same place, and he will search; there are many rocks and little bays, he will search them all, near by. And so he will see her."

"Yes, of course. It's what one does. If you expect to see something in a certain place, you simply don't believe it can't be there." I looked at Lambis with a new respect. "And you? Do you really expect to find him there?"

He gave a quick glance at the door of the hut, as if he were afraid that Mark might hear him. "I know no more than you, *thespoinís*. It may be that they are now afraid because

42

they have shot at Mark, and that they try only to persuade Colin to be silent—and that Colin is even now searching for his brother. I do not know. It may be that there is no danger at all."

"But you don't believe that."

In the pause before he answered, I heard, high overhead in the darkening sky, the call of some late-going gulls. The sound was muted by distance, and very lonely.

"No," he said at length, "I do not believe it. There is danger here. The man I saw, he was dangerous, as a wild beast is dangerous. And the men Mark spoke of . . . yes, there is danger, I can feel it. It is in the air of these mountains."

I smiled, I hope cheerfully. "Perhaps that's only because you're not used to them. You've become a city-bird, like me. High mountains frighten me now."

He said seriously, "The city, the hills, they are all the same, where there are wicked men. When I was a child, in my village, it was the same. We were afraid in our houses, in our own beds . . . only then, for a young boy, the war was also exciting. But this . . . no, not now."

There was a sound from inside the hut, the rustle of dried leaves and a sighing breath, then silence again.

Lambis lowered his voice. "I must go. I will bring everything I can carry. Be careful, *thespoinís*."

"Nicola."

"Nicola, then."

"Good-bye, and good luck." I swallowed. "You be careful, too. We'll see you soon. And for pity's sake don't fall and break a leg in the dark. . . . How long do you think it will take?"

"I shall wait for daylight. Perhaps three hours after that."

"Right," I said, as steadily as I could. "And if you're not back by noon, I'll come and look for *you*."

"Okay."

He was soon invisible down the darkening hillside. His steps faded. I heard the crack of a twig, then, more faintly, the rattle of a displaced stone, and then silence.

The sea birds had gone. To the east, beyond the high towers of rock, the sky looked clouded, but from here to the sea it seemed clear, deepening rapidly towards night. The early stars, king-stars, burned there already, bright and steadfast. I remembered that last night there had been a moon of a kind, a pale quarter, waning, like silver that is polished so thin that it has begun to wear away. . . .

Beside me, the entrance to the hut gaped black, like a cave-mouth. The hut itself crouched back against the rock as if huddling there for protection, as indeed it was. I glanced from it again, up at the night sky. For Lambis' sake, I hoped there would be a moon, any sort of a moon, rising clear of the clouds, and dealing even a little light. But for my own, and Mark's, no night could be dark enough.

I shook the thought away. It did not do to think about the possibility of our being found. We would not be found. And if we were, the whole thing was a mistake, and there was no danger at all. None.

On this reflection—or bit of mental bluster—I turned and groped my way into the darkness of the hut.

"Lambis?"

So he was awake. I went quietly across towards the voice, and sat down at the edge of the brushwood bed.

"Lambis has gone down to the boat, to get supplies, and to see if Colin's there."

"*You?*"

"Yes. Now don't worry, please. Someone had to go down. We couldn't either of us get stuff in the village, and I didn't know the way to the boat. He'll be back by morning. Are you hungry?"

"What? No. A bit thirsty. But look, this is nonsense. I thought you'd have been safe in your hotel by this time. You ought to go, they'll ask questions."

"No, I told you, I'm not expected till tomorrow. My cousin Frances was delayed, and she can't arrive before tomorrow, either, so no one'll be worrying about me, honestly. Now stop thinking about it; I'll get you a drink, there's water in the flask . . . if I can just see to pour it out. . . . Here."

As his hand met mine, gropingly, on the cup, I could feel him searching for words. But he must have been weary, and still fogged with fever, for he accepted my presence without further argument, merely fetching a long sigh when he had drunk, and going back to the first thing I had said. "He's gone to the boat?"

"Yes."

"He's told you all about it? About Colin?"

"Yes. We think it's possible Colin may already have made his way to the boat."

He said nothing. I heard the bedding rustle as he lay back. A dry, sharp scent came from it, not quite strong enough to counteract the smell of dirt and sickness. "How do you feel now?" I asked.

44

"Fine."

I found his pulse. It was light and fast. "I wish to goodness I dared heat some water. How's the arm?"

"It's sore, but it's not throbbing quite so much." He answered patiently, like an obedient child. "It'll be better by morning."

"If we can keep you warm enough," I said, "and you get some sleep. *Are* you warm?"

"Lord, yes, boiled."

I bit my lip. The night, mercifully, was far from cold, and, as yet, the rock surfaces of the mountain breathed warmth. But there were hours to go, and the chill of dawn to come, and the possibility, at that time of year, of low cloud or rain.

Under my fingers the light pulse raced. He lay, slack and silent, in his corner.

He said, suddenly, "I've forgotten your name."

"Nicola."

"Oh, yes. I'm sorry."

"It doesn't matter. You're Mark—Mark what?"

"Langley. When will he get back?"

"He didn't say," I lied. "He's going to move the boat out of sight of the coast paths. He'll need daylight for that."

"But if Colin goes back to the boat—"

"He'll find it. He'll hunt. It'll be quite near, only closer under the cliff. Now stop thinking about it. We can't do anything till daylight, so if you can empty your mind, and rest and sleep, then you might be well enough tomorrow to move down towards the boat."

"I'll try." But he moved restlessly, as if the arm hurt him. "But you? You should have gone. I'd have been all right alone. You really will go tomorrow? You'll get out of this—whatever it is?"

"Yes," I said soothingly, "when Lambis comes back, I'll go. We'll talk about it in the morning. You must be quiet now, and try to sleep."

"Did Lambis say there was an orange somewhere?"

"Of course. Wait a moment till I peel it."

He was silent while I dealt with the orange, and took the piece I handed to him, almost greedily, but when I passed him another, he suddenly seemed to lose all interest, pushed my hand aside, and began to shiver.

"Lie down," I said. "Come on, pull this up round you."

"You're cold yourself. You've got no coat." He sat up, seeming to come to himself. "Heavens, girl, I've got your woolly thing here. Put it on."

"No. I'm fine. *No*, Mark, damn it, you've got a temperature. Don't make me fight you every inch of the way."

"Do as you're told."

"I'm the nurse, you're only the patient. Put the beastly thing on and shut up and lie down."

"I'm dashed if I do. With you sitting there with nothing on but that cotton thing—"

"I'm all right."

"Maybe. But you can't sit there all night."

"Look," I said, in some alarm, for his teeth were beginning to chatter, "lie down, for pity's sake. We'll share the wretched thing. I'm coming in with you, then we'll both be warm. *Lie down.*"

He shivered his way down into the bedding, and I slid down beside him, at his uninjured side. I slipped an arm under his head, and, quite simply, he half-turned away from me and curled his back into the curve of my body. Avoiding the bandaged shoulder, I put my arms round him, and held him closely. We lay like this for some time. I felt him slowly begin to relax into warmth.

"There are probably fleas," he said drowsily.

"Almost certainly, I should think."

"And the bed smells. I wouldn't be surprised if I smelt a bit myself."

"I shall wash you tomorrow, cold water or not."

"You certainly won't."

"You try stopping me. That Greek of yours'll kill you with his notions of super-hygiene. I'd like to see what you look like, anyway."

He gave what might even have been called a chuckle. "It's not worth it. My sisters tell me I'm nice, but plain."

"Sisters?"

"Charlotte, Ann, and Julia."

"Good heavens, three?"

"Yes, indeed. And then Colin."

A little pause. "You're the oldest?"

"Yes."

"I suppose that's why you're not used to doing as you're told?"

"My father's away a lot, and I suppose I've rather got into the habit of looking after things. At present he's in Brazil— he's Resident Engineer on Harbour Construction at Manaos, on the Amazon, and he'll be there two years, off and on. Before that he was in Cuba. It's lucky, really, that I've been able to be at home most of the time . . . though of course

46

they're all away now, mostly—Charlotte's at Drama School, and Ann's in her first year at Oxford. Julia and Colin are still at school."

"And you?"

"Oh, I followed in Father's footsteps—I'm a civil engineer . . . just. I did a couple of years in a drawing office straight after school, then took a degree at Oxford. Passed last year. This trip's a reward, in a way. . . . Father stood us three weeks in the Islands, and of course we waited till now, for the best weather. . . ."

He talked on, half drowsily, and I let him, hoping that he would talk himself to sleep before he thought again, too closely, about Colin.

"What's the time?" He sounded thoroughly drowsy now.

"I can't quite see. You're lying on it. There."

My arm was under his head. I turned my wrist, and felt him peering at it. The luminous dial was worn, but distinct enough. " 'Bout midnight."

"Is that all? Are you sleepy now?"

"Mm. Nice and warm. You?"

"Yes," I lied. "Shoulder comfortable?"

"Marv'llous. Nicola, you're marv'llous girl. Feel quite at home. Feel as if I'd been sleeping with you for years. Nice." I felt him hear what he had said, then his voice came, sharply, shaken into wakefulness. "I'm awfully sorry. I can't think what made me say that. I must have been dreaming."

I laughed. "Think nothing of it. I feel the same. Shockingly at home, just as if it was a habit. *Go to sleep.*"

"U-huh. Is there a moon?"

"A sort of a one, just up. Waning quarter, all fuzzy at the edges, like wool. There must be a bit of cloud still, but there's enough light; just enough to help Lambis, without floodlighting everything he does."

He was silent after that, for so long that I hoped he had gone to sleep, but then he moved his head restlessly, stirring up the dust in the bedding.

"If Colin *isn't* at the boat—"

"You can bet your boots he is. He'll come up with Lambis in a few hours' time. Now stop that, it gets us nowhere. Stop thinking, and go to sleep. Did you ever hear the legend of the moon-spinners?"

"The what?"

"Moon-spinners. They're naiads—you know, water nymphs. Sometimes, when you're deep in the countryside, you meet three girls, walking along the hill tracks in the dusk,

47

spinning. They each have a spindle, and on to these they are spinning their wool, milk-white, like the moonlight. In fact, it *is* the moonlight, the moon itself, which is why they don't carry a distaff. They're not Fates, or anything terrible; they don't affect the lives of men; all they have to do is to see that the world gets its hours of darkness, and they do this by spinning the moon down out of the sky. Night after night, you can see the moon getting less and less, the ball of light waning, while it grows on the spindles of the maidens. Then, at length, the moon is gone, and the world has darkness, and rest, and the creatures of the hillsides are safe from the hunter, and the tides are still. . . ."

Mark's body had slackened against me, and his breathing came more deeply. I made my voice as soft and monotonous as I could. "Then, on the darkest night, the maidens take their spindles down to the sea, to wash their wool. And the wool slips from the spindles into the water, and unravels in long ripples of light from the shore to the horizon, and there is the moon again, rising above the sea, just a thin curved thread, re-appearing in the sky. Only when all the wool is washed, and wound again into a white ball in the sky, can the moon-spinners start their work once more, to make the night safe for hunted things. . . ."

Beyond the entrance of the hut, the moonlight was faint, a mere greyness, a lifting of the dark. Enough to save Lambis a fall or a sprain; enough to steer his boat into hiding without waiting for daylight; but not enough for prying eyes to see the place where Mark and I lay, close together, in the dark little hut. The moon-spinners were there, out on the track, walking the mountains of Crete, making the night safe, spinning the light away.

He was asleep. I turned my cheek on the tickling shrubs. It met his hair, rough, and dusty, but smelling sweetly of the dried verbena in our bed.

"Mark?" It was barely a breath.

No answer. I slipped a hand down under the khaki jacket, and found his wrist. It was clammy, and warm. The pulse was still fast, but regular, and stronger. I tucked the coat round him again.

For no reason, except that it seemed the thing to do, I kissed his hair, very lightly, and settled myself down to sleep.

CHAPTER : FIVE

There bathed his honourable wounds, and dressed
His manly members in the immortal vest.

> Pope: *The Iliad of Homer.*

I GOT SOME SLEEP—enough—though I was stiff when I finally woke. Mark was still sound asleep, curled back against me. His breathing sounded easy and normal, and his skin, where I cautiously felt it, was cool. The fever had gone.

It was still early. The light which came through the doorway was pearled, but without sun. My wrist was somewhere under Mark's cheek, and I dared not move it again to try to see my watch. I wondered whether the cool light were only that of early morning, or if, today, those cirrus clouds were lying lower, across the sun. In some ways, it would be better for us if they were; but they would be cold and damp; and, until we had blankets ...

The thought brought me fully awake. Lambis. Surely Lambis should have been back by now?

I raised my head cautiously, and tried to turn my wrist where it lay under Mark's head. He stirred, gave a little grunting snore, and woke. He put a hand up to rub his eyes, and then stretched. The movement pushed him against me, and the discovery brought him round with a jerk that must have hurt his arm.

"Why, hullo! Good heavens, I'd forgotten you were there! I must have been half-seas-under last night."

"That's the sweetest thing a man's ever said to me after a long night together," I said. I sat up, and began to extricate myself from the bedding, brushing it off me. "If I could have got out without waking you, I'd have done it, but you were so touchingly curled up—"

He grinned, and I realized it was the first time I had really seen him smile. Even with the two-days' beard and the strained pallor of his face, the effect was to make him look very young. "Bless you," he said, as if he meant it. "I got a good sleep and I feel wonderful. I even feel as if I might be able to make a move today. Heaven knows, I'd better. But you—did you get any sleep at all?"

"Some," I said, truthfully. "Enough, anyway. I feel wide awake."

"What's the time?"

"Just after five."

I saw the creases of worry settle back between his brows. He shifted the arm as if it had suddenly begun to hurt.

"Lambis isn't back?"

"No."

"I hope to heaven nothing's happened to him. If I've got *him* into this mess as well—"

"Look," I said, "don't for pity's sake take Lambis onto your shoulders, too. He wouldn't thank you, and it's my guess he can look after himself." I got up, still brushing bits off. "Now, I've been thinking, while you lay snoring. I think we should get you out of this hut. And the sooner the better."

He rubbed a hand over his face, as if chasing the last mists of sleep. His eyes still looked blurred with the clogging weariness and worry of the night. "Yes?"

"If anyone does come looking for you again, and gets up here—and mind you, if they've any sense they'll go hunting where the water is—they're bound to look in the hut first thing. Lambis was right to bring you here in the first place, for shelter. But now that you're a bit better, I think you should find a place in the open, in the warmth and air, a shady place, where we can see around us. You're much better to be hidden out on the mountainside, than in the only obvious shelter on the hill."

"That's true. And I can't say I'll be sorry to get out of this. . . . For a start, could you help me outside now?"

"Sure."

He was heavier than he looked, and also a good deal less able to help himself than he had hoped. It took quite a time before he was at last upright, half-propped against the wall of the hut, half-leaning on me. I saw now that he was not tall, but compactly and toughly built, with broad shoulders and a strong-looking neck.

"Okay." He was panting as if he had run a race, and there was sweat on his face. "Keep near the wall. I can make it."

Slowly, we made it. As we reached the doorway, the sun came up, brilliance streaming from the left between the tall asphodels. Long shadows from the flowers ran along the turf. The corner where the hut stood was still in shadow, and the air was chilly.

I left Mark sitting on the trunk of a fallen olive tree, and went across to the spring.

The pool, too, was still in shadow, and the water was icy. When I had washed, I went back to the hut for the metal pot that I had noticed there. This was a sort of kettle, or small cauldron, which must have been used by the shepherds. Though the outside of the pot was smoked black, the inside was clean enough, with no speck of rust. I scoured it out as best I could, with coarse sand from the stream, then filled it, and went back to Mark.

He was sitting on the ground, now, beside the fallen tree trunk, slumped back against it, looking exhausted, and so ill, in the cold daylight, that I had to control an exclamation of panic. If only Lambis would come; Lambis, blankets, hot soup . . .

I scooped a mugful of the icy water out of the pot.

"Here's a drink. And if you want a wash of a sort, I've a clean hankie. . . . No, on second thoughts, I think you'd better let me. Keep still."

He made no objection this time, but allowed me to wash his face for him, and then his hands. I let it go at that. Cleanliness might be next to godliness, but the water was ice-cold. He looked like a rather badly-off tramp. I had a feeling that I probably looked a pretty suitable mate for him. Today, I hadn't had the hardihood to look into the naiad's pool.

Breakfast was rather horrible. The bread was as hard as pumice, and had to be soaked in the icy water before he could eat it. The chocolate was better, but was cloying and unsatisfying. The orange had gone soft, like limp suede, and tasted of nothing in particular.

The effort of will with which he chewed and choked down the unappetizing stuff was palpable. I watched him with anxiety, and a dawning respect. Stubborn and autocratic he might be, but here was a kind of courage as definite as any gun-blazing heroics, this grim private battle with his own weakness, this forcing himself to remain a lay figure for long enough to gather effective strength, when every nerve must have been screaming the necessity of action. To me, it was a new slant on courage.

When the beastly little meal was finished, I looked at him uncertainly. "There was a place where Lambis took me yesterday; it's a sort of ledge, and there's plenty cover, and you can see for miles. The only thing is, it's a bit higher up. Round that bluff and then up, quite a clamber. There, do you see? If you can't manage it, I can scout round now, and find something else."

"I'll manage it."

How he did, I shall never quite know. It took us the best part of an hour. By the time he was lying, white-faced and sweating, on the ledge, I felt as if I had run from Marathon to Athens myself, and with bad news to tell at the end of it.

After a while I sat up, and looked down at him. His eyes were shut, and he looked terrible, but the sun was on the ledge, and he was lying with his face turned almost greedily towards its growing warmth.

I got to my knees. "I'm going back for the haversack now, and to cover our tracks at the hut. And when I get back, I don't care what you say, I'm going to light a fire."

His eyelids flickered. "Don't be silly."

"I'm not. But first things first, and the essential thing for you is warmth. You must have something hot to drink, and if I'm to do your arm, I must have hot water." I nodded towards the cleft-like cave behind us. "If I lit a small one, deep in there, with very dry stuff that didn't make much smoke, we could get something heated. Better to do it now, before anyone's likely to be about."

He had shut his eyes again. "As you like," indifferently.

It didn't take long to cover our traces in the hut. Any shepherd might have left the bedding, and, while it might still look suspicious, I felt reluctant to remove it, in case Mark should need it again that night. I merely ruffled it over, until it showed no signs of having been recently lain on, then, with a broom of twigs, scattered dust over our recent footprints.

A quick look round, and then I was climbing back to the ledge, a fresh potful of water held carefully in my hands, and the bag and haversack over my shoulder, filled with as much dry kindling as they would hold.

Mark lay exactly where I had left him, eyes shut. I carried my load quietly into the cleft. As I had hoped, this ran back fairly deeply into the cliff, and, some way in, under a smoothed-off overhang for all the world like a chimney breast, I built the fire. When it was ready, I made a swift but cautious survey from the ledge. Nothing, nobody, no movement, except of the kestrel hunting along the edge of the ravine. I went back and set a match to the fire.

I am not much good at making fires, but with the dry cones, and the verbena scrub I had collected, anyone could have done it. The single match caught hold, fingered the strands of dead stuff with bright threads, then went streaming up in a lovely blaze of ribbon flames. The sudden heat was wonderful, living and intense. The pot crackled as it heated, tilting dangerously as a twig charred and broke under it, and the water hissed at the edges against the burning metal.

I glanced upwards anxiously. What smoke there was, was almost invisible, a transparent sheet of vapor no thicker than pale-grey nylon, sliding up the curved cliff face, to vanish, before it reached the upper air, in a mere quivering of heat-vapor. Ten minutes of this could do no harm.

The pot hissed and bubbled. I broke the last of the chocolate into the mug, poured boiling water over it, and stirred it with a bone-white twig which was as clean as the weather could scour it. The fire was dying rapidly down in a glow of red ash. I replaced the pot in its still hot bed, then carried the steaming mug out to Mark.

"Can you drink this?"

He turned his head reluctantly, and opened his eyes. "What is it?" His voice sounded blurred, and I wondered, with a pang of real fear, if I had done wrongly in allowing the dreadful effort of the climb. "Good lord, it's hot. How did you do it?"

"I told you. I lit a fire."

I saw the sudden flicker of alarm in his eyes, and realized that he had been too exhausted to take in what had been said earlier. I smiled quickly, and knelt beside him.

"Don't worry, the fire's out. Drink this now, all of it. I've saved some hot water, and I'm going to do your arm when you've had this."

He took the mug, and sipped the scalding liquid. "What is it?"

"My own recipe; healing herbs gathered under a waning moon in the White Mountains."

"It tastes to me like weak cocoa. Where in the world did you get it?" His head jerked up as a thought struck him, and some cocoa spilled. "Have they—has Lambis come?"

"No, not yet. It's only the chocolate, melted up."

"There wasn't much left, I saw it. Have you had yours?"

"Not yet. There's only one mug. I'll have mine if you'll get that drunk up. Hurry up."

He obeyed me, then lay back. "That was marvelous. I feel better already. You're a good cook, Nicolette."

"Nicola."

"I'm sorry."

"So you should be. Now grit your teeth, hero, I'm going to take a look at your arm."

I went back to my fire, which had died down to white ash. I drank a mugful of hot water—which tasted surprisingly good—then went back to Mark, with the steaming pot, and my courage, held carefully in both hands.

I am not sure which of us showed the more resolution during the ensuing process, Mark or myself. I knew very little about wounds and nursing—how should I?—and I had a strong feeling that the sight of anything unpleasant or bloody would upset me shamefully. Besides, I might have to hurt him, and the idea was horrifying. But it had to be done. I tightened my stomach muscles, steadied my hands, and—with what I hoped was an air of calm but sympathetic efficiency—set myself to undo the distinctly nasty wrappings that Lambis had last night put back on Mark's arm.

"Don't look so scared," said the patient comfortingly. "It stopped bleeding hours ago."

"Scared? Me? For pity's sake, where did Lambis *get* this stuff?"

"Part of his shirt, I think."

"Good heavens. Yes, it looks like it. And what in the world's this? It looks like *leaves!*"

"Oh, it is. More of your healing herbs gathered under a waning moon. It's something Lambis found, I can't remember what he called it, but he swore his grandmother used it for practically everything, from abortions to snake bite, so you'd think—" He stopped on a sharp intake of breath.

"I'm sorry, but it's stuck a bit. Hang on, this will hurt."

Mark didn't answer, but lay there with his head turned away, examining the rock above the ledge with apparent interest. I gave him a doubtful look, bit my lips together, and started to sponge the stuff loose from the wound. Eventually, it came.

The first sight of the exposed wound shocked me inexpressibly. It was the first time I had seen any such thing, and the long, jagged scoring where the bullet had ploughed through the flesh looked sickening. Mark had been lucky, of course, several times lucky. Not only had the murderer, aiming at his heart, scored a near miss, hitting nothing that would matter, but the bullet had gone cleanly through, ploughing its way upwards for about four inches through the flesh of the upper arm. To me, on that first shrinking glance, it looked awful enough. The edges were not lying cleanly to-

54

gether, and the jagged scar looked inexpressibly raw and painful.

I blinked hard, braced myself, and looked again. This time, to my surprise, I was able to see the wound without that slight lurching of the stomach. I put the dirty wrappings aside, out of sight, and concentrated.

Find out if the wound was clean; that was the main thing, surely? These dried smears and crusts of blood would have to be washed away, so that I could see. . . .

I started gingerly to do this. Once, Mark moved, uncontrollably, and I faltered, cloth in hand, but he said nothing. His eyes seemed to be following the flight of the kestrel as it swept up to the nest above us. I went doggedly on with the job.

The wound was washed at last, and I thought it was clean. The flesh surrounding it looked a normal enough color, and there was no sign of swelling anywhere. I pressed gentle fingers here and there, watching Mark's face. But there was no reaction, except that almost fierce concentration on the kestrel's nest over our heads. I hesitated, then, with a hazy memory of some adventure novel I had read, bent down and sniffed at the wound. It smelt faintly of Mark's skin, and the sweat of his recent climb. I straightened up, to see him smiling.

"What, no gangrene?"

"Well," I said cautiously, "hope on, hope ever, it takes some days to set in. . . . Oh, Mark, I don't know a darned thing about it, but it honestly does look clean to me, and I *suppose* it's healing."

He twisted his head to look down at it. "It looks all right. Keep it dry now, and it'll do."

"All *right!* It looks just *awful!* Does it hurt terribly?"

"That's not the thing to say at all, didn't you know? You should be bright and bracing. 'Well, my lad, this looks wonderful. On your feet now, and use it all you can.' No, really, it does look fair enough, and it is clean, though heaven knows how. Maybe those herbs did do the trick; queerer things have happened. Though if I'd been in a fit state to know that it was Lambis' old shirt, that he'd worn at least since we left Piraeus—"

"These tough types. It just shows what you can do when you leave it all to Nature. Who'd want silly little modern things like antiseptics? Lie still, will you? I'm going to tie it up again."

"What with? What's that?"

55

"Nicola's old petticoat, that she's been wearing ever since Athens."

"But look here——"

"Lie *still*. Don't worry, I washed it this morning. It's been drying like a flag of truce over that bush just inside the cleft."

"I didn't mean that, don't be silly. But you can't shed any more clothes, my goodness. I've got your sweater, and now your petticoat——"

"Don't worry. I won't give you anything else. If it comes to that, I've nothing else to spare. There, that looks better, and it'll keep it dry. How does it feel?"

"Wonderful. No, honestly, it does feel better. No more throbbing, just beastly sore, and hurts like blazes if I jar it."

"Well, there's no need for you to move any more. You stay where you are, and keep a lookout on the hill. I'm going to bury these rags, and then I'll bring up a fresh supply of water, so that we can stay up here if we have to."

By the time I had got back with the water and fresh kindling, and relaid my fire in readiness, it was a few minutes short of eight o'clock. I lay down beside Mark, and propped my chin on my hands.

"I'll watch now. Lie down."

Without a word, he did as he was told, closing his eyes with that same air of fierce and concentrated patience.

I looked down the long, bare wings of the mountain. Nothing. Eight o'clock of a fine, bright morning.

It was going to be a long day.

CHAPTER : SIX

Push off. . . .

        Tennyson: *Ulysses.*

IT WAS, IN FACT, barely twenty minutes before the man appeared.

I saw the movement, far down the hillside, southeast of where we lay. My first thought was, naturally, that this might be Lambis returning, but then, as the tiny figure toiled nearer, it struck me that he was making remarkably little effort to conceal himself.

I narrowed my eyes against the sun. At that distance I could make out very little, except that the man was wearing something dark, which could have been Lambis' brown trousers and navy-blue jersey; but he did not seem to be carrying anything except a stick, and not only did he walk openly across the barest stretches of the hillside, but he seemed to be in no hurry, pausing frequently, and turning to stare about him, with his hand up to his eyes as if to shield them from the glare of the sun.

When he had stopped for the fourth time in as many minutes, I had decided—still more in curiosity than apprehension—that it could not be Lambis. Then, as his hand lifted, I caught the flash of the sun on something he held to his eyes. Binoculars. And then, as he moved on, another gleam, this time on the "stick" that he carried under one arm. A rifle.

I lay flattened against the juniper needles that strewed the ledge, watching him, now, as I would have watched a rattlesnake. My heart, after the first painful kick of fear, settled down to an erratic, frightened pumping. I took deep breaths, to help control myself, and glanced down at Mark beside me.

He lay motionless, with shut eyes, and that awful look of exhaustion still on his face. I put a hand out, tentatively, then drew it back. Time enough to disturb him when the murderer came closer.

That it was the murderer, there could be no possible doubt. As the small figure, dwarfed by distance, moved nearer across an open stretch of the mountainside, I caught a glimpse of red—the red head-band of which Lambis had spoken—and the impression of the baggy outline of Cretan dress. Besides, the man was patently hunting for something. Every minute or so he paused to rake some part of the hillside with his glasses, and once, when he turned aside to beat through a stand of young cypresses, he did so with his rifle at the ready. . . .

He came out from the shadow of the grove, and paused again. Now the glasses were directed upwards . . . they were swinging towards the ledge . . . the shepherds' hut . . . the way Lambis would come. . . .

The glasses moved past us, back eastwards, without a pause, and were directed for a long look at the tree-thicketed rocks above the cypress grove where he stood. Finally he lowered them, gave a hitch to his rifle, and began to make his way slowly uphill, until a jutting crag hid him from view.

I touched Mark gently. "Are you awake?"

His eyes opened immediately at the whisper, and their expression, as he turned his head, showed that the significance of my stealthy movement and dropped voice hadn't escaped him. "What is it?"

"There's someone out there, some way below us, and I think he may be your man. He seems to be looking for something, and he's got a gun."

"In sight of the ledge now?"

"Not at the moment."

Mark turned awkwardly onto his stomach, and cautiously peered down through the junipers. I put my mouth to his ear. "Do you see those cypresses away down there? The grove beyond the stunted tree with a dead branch like a stag's horn? He's been making his way uphill from there. You can't see from here, but there are trees above there, away beyond that cliff, and the top of a gorge like this one, only smaller. I think I saw a little waterfall running down to it." I swallowed, painfully. "I—I said he'd hunt where the water was."

Mark was craning his neck to study the rocks above and below our own ledge. "I wasn't fit to notice, when we were on our way up here. This place really can't be seen from below?"

"No, at least no one would think there was a ledge. All you can see is these shrubs, and they look as if they were in a crack in the face of the cliff."

"And the way up?"

"That's hidden, too, among those bushes at the bottom, by the fig tree."

"Mm. Well, we'll have to chance it. Can you crawl back into that cave without showing yourself or making a single sound?"

"I—I think so."

"Then get back in there, now, while he's out of sight."

"But if he comes up here at all, he'll look in there, and there's nowhere we can hide. It's quite bare." I shifted my shoulders. "Anyway, I—I'd rather stay out here. If there was a fight, we'd stand a better chance out here—"

"A fight!" Mark's breath was sucked in with sudden, furious exasperation. "What sort of a fight do you think we could put up against a rifle? Penknives at thirty yards?"

"Yes, I know, but I could surely—"

"Look, there isn't time to argue, just get in there out of sight, for pity's sake! I can't make you do as I say, but will you please, for once, *just do as you're told?*"

I have never seen anyone's jaw drop, but I'm sure mine did, then. I felt it. I just sat there gaping at him.

"He's looking for me," said Mark, with a kind of angry patience. *"For me.* Only. He doesn't even know you exist—or Lambis either, for that matter. You'll be quite safe in the cave. Now, have you got that, dimwit?"

"But . . . he'll kill you," I stammered, stupidly.

"And just how," said Mark savagely, "do you propose to stop him? Get killed yourself as well, and add that to my account? Now get in there and shut up. I haven't the strength to argue."

I turned, without a word.

But it was too late. Even as I began to slither backwards from my hide between the junipers, Mark's good hand shot out, and gripped and held me still.

For a moment I couldn't see why; then, just a glimpse, nearer through the green, I saw the red head-dress. Immediately afterwards—so close was he now—I heard plainly the grate of his boot soles in the dust, and the flick of a kicked pebble.

Mark lay like an image. He looked, despite the bandaged arm and the shocking pallor, surprisingly dangerous. Surprisingly, when you saw that all the weapon he had was a clasp-knife, and a pile of stones.

The Cretan came on steadily, along the path by which Lambis had gone. It would lead him past the little field of asphodel, below the shepherds' hut, past the spring which marked the beginning of the climb to our ledge. . . .

I could see him clearly now. He was a strongly-built man, not tall, but tough-looking, with mahogany-dark skin. While I could not at that distance make out his features, I could see the squared cheekbones, and full lips under a thick moustache. The sleeves of his dark-blue shirt were pushed up, showing brown knotty forearms. I could even see the scarlet trimming of the sleeveless jacket, and the swathed sash with the knife stuck into it, that completed the Cretan "heroic" dress.

He lifted the field glasses again. We lay as still as stones. A long, heart-shaking minute passed. The sun poured onto the rock; the scents of verbena and thyme and sage winnowed up around us in the heat. Encouraged by our stillness, a small brown snake crept out from the rock a few feet away, lay for a moment watching us, his little eyes catching the light like dewdrops; then he poured himself away down a hole. I hardly noticed; there was room for no more fear; this was hardly the moment to worry about a small brown snake, while a murderer stood down there at the edge of the alpine meadow, with his glasses to his eyes. . . .

The swing of the glasses checked. The man froze like a pointer. He had seen the shepherds' hut.

If he was a local man, he must already have known of its existence, but it was obvious, I thought, that until this moment he had forgotten it. He dropped the glasses on their cord round his neck, and shifted his rifle forward once more; then, with his eyes fixed unwaveringly on the door of the hut, he moved forward, warily, through the asphodel.

I turned my head, to meet a question in Mark's eyes. I knew what it was. Was I certain I had removed all traces? Feverishly, I cast my mind back: the bedding; the floor; my bag and its contents; Mark's haversack; the traces of our meal; the dressings from Mark's shoulder; the orange peel. Yes, I was certain. I gave Mark a jerky little nod of reassurance.

He sketched the ghost of a thumbs-up sign, which meant congratulation, then gestured with his head towards the cleft behind us. This time there was a smile in his eyes. I returned it, after a fashion, then obediently slithered back, rather in the style of the small brown snake, into the shadow of the narrow cave.

The cleft ran back at an angle to the ledge, so that from where I settled myself, well towards the back, I could see only a crack of daylight, with a narrow section of the ledge, and one of Mark's legs, from the knee down.

For all its illusion of shelter, the cave was worse than the ledge, for there, at least, I had been able to see. I sat close, listening to my own heart-beats.

Presently, I heard him. He was walking carefully, but in the tranced stillness of the morning his steps sounded loud. They came nearer, moved from grass to stone, from stone to dust, were lost behind a barrier of rock where the trickle of the spring drowned them. . . .

Silence. So long a silence that I could have sworn, watching that narrow section of light, that the sun wheeled, and the shadows moved. . . .

Then suddenly, he was here, just below the ledge. The soft steps trod through the stony dust. The bushes by the fig tree rustled as he parted them. I saw the muscles of Mark's leg tense themselves.

The rustling stopped. The footsteps felt their way through dust again, moved away a little, paused. . . .

In my mind's eye I could see him standing, as before, with

the glasses to his eyes, raking the crannies and clefts above him for a possible hiding place. Perhaps even now he was discovering the cave where I crouched, and wondering how to get up to it. . . .

A shadow swept across the sector of light. The kestrel. I heard, in that deadly stillness, the small sound it made as it met the edge of the nest: I could swear, to this day, that I heard the whiffling of air in its feathers as it braked, flaps down, for the final approach. The hissing, mewing delight of the young ones shrilled as piercingly in the stillness as a double-sized pipe band on the dead air of a Scottish Sunday.

The flake of shadow swept out again. The young ones fell abruptly silent. A twig cracked under the fig tree.

Then all at once, it seemed, the watcher had moved away. It was possible that the fearless approach of the bird had convinced him that there was nothing on that section of the cliff; whatever the case, he had certainly gone. The sounds retreated, faded, ceased. As my pulses slowly steadied, I found that I had shut my eyes, the better to hear that reassuring diminuendo.

Once more, at last, silence. I opened my eyes on the wedge of light at the mouth of the cleft, to see that Mark's leg had vanished.

If I had been in a fit state to think at all, I suppose I would have assumed that he had merely inched further along the ledge, the better to watch the Cretan out of sight. But as it was, I stared at the empty gap of light with horror, for two eternal minutes, with my common sense in fragments, and my imagination racing madly through a series of nightmare pictures that would have done credit to a triple-X film. . . . Perhaps, after all, the murderer hadn't gone; perhaps, even now, Mark was lying, throat cut, staring at the sky, while the murderer waited for me at the mouth of the cleft, with dripping knife. . . .

But here, at last, some sort of courage and common sense asserted itself. For one thing, the man had had a rifle, and for another, disabled though Mark was, the Cretan could hardly have shot, stabbed, or clubbed him to death in perfect silence. . . .

I craned forward to see. Nothing but a tuft of salvia, purple-blue, with scented gray leaves, flattened where Mark had lain. Nothing to be heard, either, but a faint rustling. . . .

The snake. That was it. He had been bitten by the snake. With hideous promptitude, the new picture presented itself:

Mark, dead in (silent) agony, lying with blackened face staring at the sky. . . .

If I didn't stare at the sky pretty soon myself, I should go mad. I crawled forward to the mouth of the cleft, lay flat, then peered out.

Mark wasn't lying dead, and his face wasn't black. It was, on the contrary, very white indeed, and he was on his feet, looking as if he had every intention of climbing down from the ledge in pursuit of the murderer. Of the latter there was no sign. Mark was pulling aside the trails of honeysuckle that masked the entrance to the ledge.

"Mark!"

He turned, as sharply as if I had thrown something.

I was across the ledge like an arrow, and had hold of his sound arm. I said furiously, "And just were do you think you're going?"

He answered with a sort of desperation, "He's gone back along the hillside. I want to see where he goes. If I could follow, he might lead straight to Colin."

I had just been very badly frightened, and was still ashamed of my reactions to that fear. It made it difficult, for the moment, to think straight. "Do you mean to tell me that you were just *going,* and leaving me *alone in there?*"

He looked bewildered, as if the question were irrelevant; as I suppose it was. "You'd have been quite safe."

"And you think *that's* all that matters? You think I don't even care whether you—" I stopped short. Things were coming straight now, rather too straight for speech. In any case, he wasn't listening. I said, still angrily, because I was annoyed with myself, "And just how far do you think you'd get? Have a bit of sense, will you? You wouldn't get a hundred yards!"

"I've got to try."

"You can't!" I swallowed, conscious of the greatest reluctance to say anything more at all. I never wanted to leave the shelter of that ledge as long as I lived. But one must save a rag of pride to dress in. "I'll go," I said huskily, "I can keep out of sight—"

"Are you mad?" It was his turn to be furious; more, I could see, with his own helplessness than with me. That the conversation was conducted in hissed whispers did nothing to detract from its forcefulness. We glared at one another. "You don't even begin to—" he began, then stopped, and I saw his face change. The relief that swept into it was so vivid that for the moment all exhaustion and worry seemed wiped away, and his smile was almost gay. I swung round, to look where he was looking.

A man had dropped lightly from the tumble of rocks above the little alp, and was making a cautious way between the clumps of asphodel. Brown trousers, dark-blue jersey, bare head: Lambis. Lambis, watching the watcher, following him down to Colin. . . .

In a few moments more he, too, skirted the base of the cliff, and vanished.

"He got away," said Lambis, breathlessly, in Greek. "There's another gorge further along the hill, where a stream runs down. It's full of trees—plenty of cover. I lost him there."

It was perhaps an hour later. Mark and I had waited, watching the hillside, until we saw Lambis returning. He approached slowly and wearily, pausing at length at the edge of the flowery plateau to look up towards the rocks where we lay. It was obvious from his bearing that he was alone, so Mark had waved some sort of signal to show him where we were, while I had made a hurried way down, to meet him on the narrow path above the spring. He was empty-handed still. I guessed that he had cached whatever he had been carrying, in order to follow the Cretan.

"Was he heading downhill—down the gorge?" I asked quickly. "That's probably another way down to Agios Georgios; in fact, I don't see where else it can go. Did you see?"

The Greek shook his head, then rubbed the back of his hand over his forehead. He looked tired, and was sweating profusely. He had spoken in his own language as if too exhausted to attempt English, and I had answered in the same tongue, but he gave no sign that he had noticed this. "No, I couldn't get too close to him, you understand, so it was not easy to follow him. I lost him among the rocks and bushes. He could have climbed out of the gorge and gone further east, or he may have been making for the village. Look, I must tell Mark. He got up there?"

"Yes. I helped him up. He's much better. What about Colin?"

"Eh? No. Nothing. He wasn't there. He had not been to the boat." He spoke, I thought, as if his mind was not quite on what he was saying. He had hardly looked at me, but kept his eyes on the upper rocks where Mark lay. He rubbed a hand again across his damp face, and made as if to push past me without further speech.

I caught at his sleeve in a sudden flash of apprehension. "Lambis! Are you telling me the truth?"

He paused and turned. It seemed to take two or three seconds before his eyes focused on me. "The truth?"

"About Colin. Have you got bad news for Mark?"

"No, of course I haven't! Of course I'm telling you the truth, why not? I went to the boat last night; he was not there. There was no sign, no sign of him at all. Why should I lie to you?"

"I—it's all right. I just thought. . . . Sorry."

"It is because I have nothing to tell him that I am angry now. If I had found out something from this man—" a quick exasperated shrug—"but I did not. I have failed, and this is what I have to tell Mark. Now let me go, he will be wondering what's happened."

"Wait just a moment, he knows you haven't got Colin, we were watching you from the ledge. But the food—did you get the food and stuff?"

"Oh. Yes, of course I did. I brought all I could carry. I should have been here a long time ago, but I had to stop and hide, because of that one." He jerked his head downhill, a curiously dismissive gesture. "When I saw him come this way, I hid the things, and came, quickly. It was a good thing you'd left the hut."

"He saw it, did you know?"

"Yes. I guessed that he had. When I came here, he was just coming along under this ledge, and I knew he must have seen the hut. But he was still hunting . . . and I had heard no shot . . . so I knew that you had gone. I guessed you would be here."

"Where did you put the food? We ought—never mind, Mark'll want to hear your news first. Come along, then, let's hurry."

This time it was Lambis who hung back. "Listen, why don't you go for the food straight away, yourself? Just the food, leave the other things; I can carry them later."

"Well, all right. If you think I can find the place."

"It's near the top of the gorge where I lost him. Follow round where you saw me go—see? There's a goat track of a kind; it takes you along the foot of the ridge to where the stream runs down into the gorge. It's rocky at the top, but there are trees, lower down. You can see their tops."

"Yes."

"At the head of the gorge, where the spring leaves the rocks, there is an olive tree. It is in shelter, and has grown big, and very old, with a hollow body. You must see it, there are no others near. I left the things inside it. I shall come when I have seen Mark."

Almost before he had finished speaking, he had turned away. I got the sharp impression of preoccupation, almost as if I had been dismissed, and with relief. But the nagging little thought that this brought to me didn't last long. Even if Lambis (having presumably fed on board the caique) could so lightly dismiss the thought of food and drink, I could not. The very thought of what the hollow tree contained, drove me towards it at the speed with which a pin approaches a magnet.

I found it easily enough. It was the only olive tree in sight, but even without that, I felt sure that I should have flown straight to the food by instinct, like a vulture to its kill, even had that been buried in the very middle of Minos' labyrinth.

I rummaged eagerly in the hollow trunk. There were two blankets, wrapped round what appeared to be a sizable collection of stuff. I untied the blankets, and foraged for what he had brought.

There were medical supplies, bandages, antiseptic, soap, a razor. . . . But for the moment I pushed these aside, to concentrate on the food.

The thermos flask, full. Some tins, among them one of Nescafé, and some sweetened milk. Tins of corned beef. Biscuits. A small bottle of whisky. And, final miracle, a tin-opener.

I threw these happily into one blanket, tied the corners up into a bundle, and set off back again.

Lambis met me halfway. He didn't speak, just nodded at me as he made way for me on the path. I was glad of this, as it is not easy to speak politely with one's mouth full of Abernethy biscuit, and to speak Greek—which contains gutturals—would have been less elegant still.

All the same, I would have been the happier for something to lighten the look he gave me. It wasn't that the distrust had come back; it was something far less positive than that, and slightly more disconcerting. Say, rather, that confidence had been withdrawn. I was back on the outside.

I wondered what he and Mark had been saying.

I found Mark sitting at the back of the ledge, leaning

65

against the rock, staring out over the open hillside. He turned with a start when I spoke.

"Here's the thermos," I said. "Lambis says there's soup in it. There, have the mug, I'll use the top of the thermos. Get yours straight away, will you? I'm going to light the fire again, for coffee."

I waited for his protest, but it didn't come. He took the flask from me without speaking. I added, hesitatingly: "I—I'm sorry Lambis didn't have better news."

The thermos top seemed to have stuck. He gave it a wrench with his good hand, and it came. "Well, it's what I expected." He glanced up then, but I had the impression that I wasn't fully in focus. "Don't worry any more, Nicola." A smile, that looked like something taken out to wear, that one wasn't used to. "Sufficient unto the day. Let's eat first, shall we?"

I left him carefully pouring soup, and hurried into the cleft to get the fire going.

It was a wonderful meal. We had the soup first, then corned beef, sandwiched between the thick Abernethy biscuits; some cake stiff with fruit; chocolate; and then the coffee, scalding hot, and sweetened with the tinned milk. I ate ravenously; Lambis, who had fed himself on the boat, took very little; Mark, making, after the first few mouthfuls, an obvious effort, did very well. When, at last, he sat, cradling his half-empty cup of coffee between his hands, as if treasuring the last of its warmth, I thought he looked very much better.

When I said so, he seemed to come with a jerk out of his thoughts. "Well, yes, I'm fine now, thanks to you and Lambis. And now, it's time we thought about what happens next."

Lambis said nothing. I waited.

Mark blew a cloud of smoke, and watched it feather to nothing in the bright air. "Lambis says this man was almost certainly making for Agios Georgios, and—since it's the nearest—it does seem only reasonable to suppose that, whoever these blighters are, they come from there. That makes it at once easier, and more complicated. I mean, we know where to start looking, but it's certain, now, that we can't go down there for official help." He shot a quick glance at me, as if prepared for a protest, but I said nothing. He went on: "All the same, obviously, the first step is to get down there—somehow—and find out about my brother. I'm not such a fool as to think—" this with a touch of weary hopelessness— "that I could do very much myself yet, but even if I can't make it, Lambis will go."

Lambis made no reply; indeed, he hardly seemed to be listening. I realized, suddenly, that between the two men, everything that had to be said had already been said. The council of war had been held already—while I had been sent to get the food—and its first conclusions reached. I thought I knew what they were.

"And so," Mark was saying smoothly, without looking at me, like someone trying out a delicate tape-recorder set somewhere in the middle distance, "will Nicola, of course."

I had been right. First order in council: *Women and camp-followers, out of the way; the campaign's about to start.*

He was addressing me directly now. "Your cousin's coming today, isn't she? You'll have to be there, or there'll be questions asked. You could be down at the hotel, and checked in—" a glance at his wrist—"good heavens, by lunchtime, probably. Then you can—well, forget all this, and get on with that holiday of yours, that Lambis interrupted."

I regarded him. Here we were again, I thought: the smile, friendly, but worn as a vizard to anxiety; the obstinate mouth; the general wariness of manner which meant "thank you very much, and now, please go away—and stay away."

"Of course," I said. I pulled my canvas bag towards me over the juniper needles, and began putting my things into it, rather at random. He was perfectly right, I knew that; and anyway, there was nothing more I could do. With Frances coming today, I would have to get out, and keep out. Moreover—I was rather sharply honest with myself here—I wasn't exactly eager to run into any more situations such as I had met last night and today, with their tensions, discomforts, and moments of extreme fear. Nor was I prepared to be regarded—as Mark, once on his feet, would obviously regard me—as a responsibility, even a liability.

So I smiled rather tightly at him, and pushed things into my bag.

"Bless you." The smile he gave me now was one of swift and genuine relief. "You've been wonderful, I don't have to tell you how wonderful, and I won't want to seem filthily ungrateful now, after all you've done, but—well, you've seen something of what's going on, and it's obvious that if I can keep you out of it, I must."

"It's all right, you don't have to bother. I'm the world's crawlingest coward anyway, and I've had enough excitement to last me a lifetime. I shan't cramp your style. You won't see me for dust once I get within sight of the hotel."

"I hope to heaven your luggage is still where you left it. If it's not, you'll have to be thinking up some story to account for it. Let me see. . . ."

"I'll dream up something, something they can't disprove till I've left. Good heavens, you don't have to start worrying about that! That's *my* affair."

If he noticed that one, he let it pass. He was crushing out his cigarette, frowning down at it, withdrawing into those dark thoughts again.

"There's one more thing, and it's desperately important, Nicola. If you do see Lambis—or even me—around in the village, or anywhere else for that matter, you don't know us."

"Well, of course not."

"I had to mention it, you understand. Will the British Embassy in Athens find you?"

"The British Embassy?" Lambis had looked up sharply.

"Yes." Mark's eyes met his, in that now-familiar, excluding look. "It's where she works." Then, to me, "I can get you there?"

"Yes."

"I'll write to you. Another thing . . ."

"What?"

He wasn't looking at me, he was fingering the stones beside him. "You'll have to promise me something, for the sake of my peace of mind."

"What is it?"

"You won't go near the police."

"If I'm getting out of your affairs, I'm not likely to complicate them by doing that. But I still can't see why you don't go at least to the headman in Agios Georgios. Personally, I'm all for doing the simplest thing, and going straight to the authorities, wherever I am. But it's your affair." I looked from one man to the other. They sat in uncompromising silence. I went on, slowly, feeling more than ever an intruder: "Mark, you know, you haven't done anything wrong. Surely, now they realize you're just an English tourist—"

"That won't hold water." He spoke drily. "If they didn't realize on Saturday night, they did on Sunday, and this morning. And still our friend's looking for me with a gun."

Lambis said, "You're forgetting Colin. He is the reason for this." His gesture took in the ledge, the scraps of food, all the evidence of our rough-and-ready camp. "Until we know where Colin is, how can we do anything? If he is still alive, he is their—I do not know the word—*ó ómeros.*"

"Hostage," said Mark.

"Yes, of course. I—I'm sorry. Well . . ." My voice faded feebly, as I looked from one to the other; Mark wooden, Lambis sullen and withdrawn once more. Suddenly I was conscious of nothing but a longing to escape, to be away down the mountainside, back to yesterday—the lemon grove in the sunshine, the egret, the point where I came in. . . .

I got up, and Lambis rose with me.

I said, "Are you coming too?"

"I will see you part of the way."

I didn't demur this time; didn't want to. Besides, I supposed he would want to make his own way into the village, once he had seen me, so to speak, off his pitch. I turned to Mark. "Don't get up, don't be silly." I smiled, and put down a hand, which he took. "Well, I'll say good-bye. And good luck, of course."

"You got your cardigan?"

"Yes."

"I'm sorry I couldn't return your petticoat."

"That's all right. I hope your arm will soon be better. And of course I hope . . . well, that things will turn out right." I lifted my bag and slung it over my shoulder. "I'll be going. I expect in a couple of days' time I'll think all this has been a dream."

He smiled. "Pretend it has."

"All right." But I still hesitated. "You can trust me not to do anything silly; for one thing, I'd be too scared. But you can't expect me to shut my eyes and ears. You see, if Agios Georgios *is* the guilty village, then I'm bound to see that man with the rifle, and find out who he is, and all about him. And I'm bound to find out who speaks English. I certainly won't bother you, unless I hear something terribly important. But if I do, I—I think I ought to know where to find you. Where's the boat?"

Lambis looked swiftly at Mark. Mark hesitated, then said, across me, in Greek, "We'd better tell her. It can do no harm. She knows nothing, and—"

"She understands Greek," said Lambis sharply.

"Eh?" Mark threw a startled, incredulous look at me.

"She speaks it almost as well as you do."

"*Does* she?" I saw his eyes flicker, as he did a bit of rapid back-thinking, and, for the first time, a trace of color came up under his skin.

"It's all right," I said blandly, in Greek. "You haven't given much away."

"Oh well," said Mark, "it serves me right for being rude. I'm sorry."

"That's all right. Are you going to tell me about the boat? After all, you never know, *I* might need help. I'd feel better if I knew where to find you."

"Well," said Mark, "of course," and he began to give me instructions as to how to reach the caique from the ruined Byzantine church. "And you could ask anyone the way over to the church itself, that would be quite a normal trip for an English visitor to want to make. I think that's clear enough? Yes? But I hope it won't be necessary for you to come."

"That," I said, "has been made awfully clear. Well, good-bye again. All the best."

Lambis went first. My last glimpse of Mark was of him sitting stiffly, as if braced against the warm rock, with the empty mug beside him, and that gray look of worry still draining the youth from his face.

CHAPTER : SEVEN

Oh mistress, by the gods, do nothing rash!
                              Matthew Arnold: *Merope.*

LAMBIS SPOKE VERY LITTLE on the way down through the ravine. He kept a short way ahead of me, reconnoitring with some caution at the corners, but most of the time we walked as fast as the roughness of the path would allow. We met nobody, and came in good time through the tangle of young oaks above the lemon groves. Already, through the boughs, I could see the white flanks of a windmill, and the gleam of sunlight on the open water of the stream.

Lambis stopped in a patch of sunlight, and waited for me to catch up with him.

Beside the path where he stood was a little wayside shrine. This was merely a wooden box, wedged somehow back among a pile of rocks, with primitive little oil-lamps burning in front of a brightly colored plaque of the Panaghia, the Virgin who is at once Mother of God, and the Mother herself, the ancient Goddess of the earth. A beer bottle, standing to one side, held oil for the lamps. Verbena grew near, and violets.

Lambis gestured towards the lit lamps, and the small bunch of flowers that stood there in a rusty tin.

"I will leave you here. People come this way, and I must not be seen."

I said good-bye, wished him luck again, and leaving him there, went down through the lemon groves towards the open sunlight with, it must be confessed, a definite lightening of the spirits.

It was about noon, and the heat of the day. The breeze had dropped, and even the silky poppy heads and the quaker grass that bordered the path hung motionless. The white sails of the windmills rested still and slack. A donkey browsed beside a tumbledown wall, in the shade of an ilex. Flies buzzed over the dust.

There was nobody about. People would be at home for the midday meal, or eating it in the fields, somewhere in the shade. I could see no one except a boy, sprawled sleepily in the sun while his goats cropped the vetches, and one man, working a field away, beyond a thick barrier of sugar cane. Neither looked up as I passed.

I stopped for a moment, gratefully, as I reached the spare shade of the pines at the edge of the lower valley. I looked back.

There it all lay, the hot fields, the lemon trees, the wooded gorge leading up into the silver wilderness of rock.

From here, there could be seen no sign of life in that empty landscape. Lambis had long since disappeared; the lemon trees hung without a quiver; above them the mountainside was dead, empty of all motion. But this time yesterday . . .

There was the movement of wings over the gorge. For a split second I stared, incredulous. But this time the wings weren't white: what had caught my eye was the slow wheel of enormous brown feathers climbing the sky. An eagle? More likely a vulture, I thought; perhaps the lammergeier itself. At any other time I would have watched with excitement. Now, because the big bird had reminded me of the white egret, and of yesterday, I felt the tears rising in my throat.

I turned my back on it, and made my way down to the bridge.

When I reached it, I thought for a moment that my luck had deserted me. Two children were leaning over the parapet, spitting orange-pips into the water; a boy and a girl, thin and dark and burned brown, with huge dark eyes and black hair, and the shy manners of the country children. They were spitting very close to my suitcase.

"How do you do?" I said formally.

They stared in silence, backing a little, like calves. I regarded them. I knew quite well that now they would never let me out of their sight until I reached the hotel, and probably not even then. I, the stranger, was their capture. I was news. Whatever I said or did, as from now, would be all over the village within the hour.

I crooked a finger at the boy. "What's your name?"

He began to grin, probably at the humor of my speaking Greek. "Georgi."

It always was. "And yours?" I asked the little girl.

"Ariadne." I could hardly hear the whisper.

"Hullo, then, Georgi and Ariadne. I'm a foreigner, English. I've come from Chania this morning, to stay at the hotel in Agios Georgios."

Silence. There was no answer to this, so they didn't make one. They stood and stared, the boy with the beginnings of that urchin grin, the girl Ariadne taking in every detail of my frock, sandals, bag, wrist watch, hair-do. . . . Even from a child of eight it was not a comfortable scrutiny: I had done my best, with comb and lipstick, before I finally left the ledge, but I would hardly, I thought, look as if I had just recently left the portals of Chania's best hotel.

"Georgi," I said, "do you think you could carry a case down to the hotel for me?"

He nodded, looking round him, then reached for my canvas bag. "This?"

"No, no, a proper case. It's in the bushes, hidden." I added, carefully, "I came with a car from Chania, and carried my case down from the road. I left it here, because I wanted to eat my—have my coffee, that is, in the shade. . . ." I glanced upstream: the goat-herd or the workman might just have seen me pass . . . "in the shade further up the river. So I hid my case and left it here. Can you see it? Down there, under the bridge?"

The little girl ran to the parapet and peered over. The boy went more slowly after her. "You can't see it? I hid it very well," I said, laughing.

72

A shriek from Ariadne. "There, there, Georgi! See!"

Georgi scrambled over the parapet, hung by his hands, and dropped some ten feet into the bushes. He could easily have gone round by the bank, but, being a boy, and a Cretan at that, he no doubt felt obliged to do it the hard way. His sister and I watched him with suitable expressions of admiration, while he dusted his hands on his seat, dived intrepidly (and quite unnecessarily) through some brambles, and finally dragged my case from its hiding place. He carried it up to the road—this time by the orthodox route—and the three of us set off for the village.

Ariadne, her shyness gone, skipped along beside me, chattering all the time, in a dialect that was too fast and in places too thick for me to follow. Georgi trudged along more slowly, concerned, I could see, to carry my case with apparent ease. Both children answered my questions readily, supplying a lively commentary of their own which I made no attempt to check.

Yes, the hotel was just at this end of the village. Yes, it faced the sea; the back of it, you understand, looked right on the bay. There was a garden, a beautiful garden, right on the shore, with tables and chairs, where you could eat wonderful food, "real English food," promised Ariadne, wide-eyed, while Georgi hurried to explain this magnificence. It was due to the new owner—I had heard of Stratos Alexiakis, of course, since I came from England, and so did he? He was very rich, and he came from London, which was in England, and he spoke English so that you could not tell he was a Cretan. Indeed, he—

"How can you tell?" I asked, laughing.

"Tony says so."

"Tony? Who's he?"

"The barman," said Georgi.

"No, the cook," amended Ariadne, "*and* he waits at table, and sits at the desk, and—oh, he does everything! Mr. Alexiakis is not always there, you see."

"A sort of manager?" I said. I remembered what my Danish informant had told me about the new owner's "friend from London." "This Tony—" I hesitated. Somehow I didn't really want to ask the next question. "Did he come from England, too?"

"He is English," said Georgi.

A short silence. "*Is* he?" I said.

"Yes, oh yes!" This was Ariadne. "Mr. Alexiakis had a taverna there, a *huge* taverna, very splendid, and so—"

73

"Are there any other English people in Agios Georgios just now?" It would have been a natural question to ask, anyway; and the context made it doubly so. I hoped my voice sounded normal.

"No." Georgi's replies were getting shorter. His face had reddened, and there were beads of sweat on it, but I knew better than to offer to relieve him of the case. His pride as a *pallikári*—a man's man—was involved. "No," he said, shifting the case from one hand to the other, "only Tony, and the English ladies. That is you." He looked doubtfully at me, and finished on a question, "They said there would be two ladies?"

"My cousin's coming later today." I didn't feel like attempting to explain further, and luckily, being children, they took the statement for granted, as they had taken my apparent eccentricity over the suitcase. I was thinking furiously, and not very pleasantly. I had told Mark—had known quite well—that if the *dramatis personae* of his murder-play were in fact from Agios Georgios, I would be bound, in such a tiny place, to come across traces of them almost straight away. But to do so as soon as this, and in the hotel itself . . .

I wetted my lips. I might be wrong. After all, people could come and go. I tried again. "Do you get many visitors here?"

"You are the first at the new hotel. The first this year." This was Ariadne, still intent on offering me what honor she could.

"No," Georgi contradicted her, stolidly. "There was another, a foreigner."

"English?" I asked.

"I don't know. I don't think so."

"He *was* English!" cried Ariadne.

"The fat one who went all the way to see the old church on the mountain? And took the picture that was in the *Athens News*? I'm sure he wasn't!"

"Oh, *that* one! No, I don't know what he was. I wasn't counting him, he wasn't a proper visitor." By "visitor," I gathered that Ariadne meant "tourist." I had already recognized my Danish friend. "No, I meant the one who came here the other day. Don't you remember? Tony met him at the harbor, and we heard them talking as they went to the hotel, and you said it was English they spoke."

"He wasn't a proper visitor either," said Georgi obstinately. "He came by caique one afternoon, and stayed

74

only one night, and went away again next morning early. I think he must have gone by the road. There was no boat."

I said, "When did he come?"

"Three days ago," said Ariadne.

"Saturday, it was," said Georgi.

"What do you come here for, to Agios Georgios?" asked Ariadne.

I must have gazed at her blankly for a moment, before, with an effort as great as any Georgi was making, I heaved myself back out of deep waters into the safe shallows of small-talk.

"Oh, just for a holiday. It's—it's so very pretty here." I gestured, rather lamely, towards the flower-strewn rocks, and the glittering sea. The children looked at me blankly. It had not occurred to them that scenery could be pretty. I tried another harmless lead. "The vines are good this year?"

"Yes, they are good. They are the best vines in Crete."

Stock response; of course they were. "Really? We don't have vines in England. Or olives, either."

They looked at me, shocked. "Then what do you eat?"

"Bread, meat, fish." I realized too late that bread and meat were a rich man's diet, but the admiration in their eyes showed no trace of envy. If there is one thing a Greek respects above intelligence, it is riches. "And drink?" asked Ariadne.

"Tea, mostly."

This time the look in their faces made me laugh. "Yes, but not Greek tea. It's made differently, and it's *nice*. We make our coffee differently, too."

This didn't interest them. "No vines!" said Ariadne. "Tony at the hotel says that in England everybody has electricity and a wireless and you can have it on all day and all night as loud as you like. But also, he says, it is very cold and full of fog, and the people are silent, and London is not a healthy place to live in. He says it is better here."

"Does he? Well, you do get the sun, don't you? We do see it sometimes in England, but not like this. That's why we come here for holidays, to sit in the sun, and swim, and walk in your hills, and look at the flowers."

"The flowers? You like flowers?" Ariadne, darting like a humming-bird, was already pulling up the anemones in handfuls. I had to restrain myself. To me, they were exotics as gorgeous as any I had seen at Kew; to the child, weeds. But I ate meat every day. Riches? Perhaps.

Georgi wasn't interested in flowers. The case changed

hands again, as he stumped heroically forward. "You like swimming?"

"Very much. Do you?"

"Of course. No one bathes here yet; it's still too cold, but later it's very good."

I laughed. "It's quite warm enough for me. Where's the best place to swim?"

"Oh, that way is best." He waved his free hand vaguely towards the west. "There are bays, with rocks, where you can dive."

"Oh yes, I remember, a friend told me that was the best way. Does one have to go far?"

"To the Dolphins' Bay? No, not very."

"It's miles and *miles!*" cried Ariadne.

"You are only small," said her brother contemptuously, "and your legs are short. For me, or for the *thespoinís*, it is not far."

"My legs are not much shorter than yours!" Ariadne bristled, with every intention, I saw, of doing instant battle. I intervened hastily, wondering, with some pity, at what age the Cretan girls are actually taught their place in the masculine scheme of things, "Why do you call it Dolphins' Bay? Do you really see dolphins there?"

"Oh, yes," said Georgi.

"Sometimes they come amongst the swimmers!" cried Ariadne, happily diverted. "There was a boy once, who used to ride on them!"

"Was there?" What ancient story was this, still surviving here among the children? Pliny's boy from Baiae? Arion on the dolphin's back? Telemachus, the son of Odysseus? I smiled down at her. "Well, I've never even seen a dolphin. Do you suppose they'd come and play with me?"

Truth struggled in her face with the Greek's desire to please the stranger at all costs. "Perhaps . . . but it is a long time since they did this. . . . I am eight years old, but it was before I was born, *thespoinís*. People tell stories. . . ."

"But you'll *see* them," promised Georgi, confidently, "if the weather stays warm. It's best if you go out in a caique, into deeper water. Sometimes, when I have been out fishing, we have seen them, swimming near the boat, sometimes with their young ones. . . ."

And, my earlier questions forgotten, he embarked happily on the Cretan version of the fisherman's yarn, until he was interrupted by his sister, who pushed into my arms an enormous bunch of slim, purple-red gladioli, the sort that are called "Byzantine" in our seedsmen's catalogues, where the corms retail at about fivepence each. In Crete, they grow wild in the wheat. The bundle was shaggy with lilac anemones, dragged up anyhow, and scarlet tulips with pointed petals—a variety that rates at least sevenpence apiece in Frances' nurseries.

"For you, *thespoinís!*"

My delighted thanks took us round the last bend in the track, and there was the hotel.

This was, at first sight, hardly deserving of the name.

Originally, there had been two houses, square-built and two-storeyed, joined to make one long, lowish building. The one on the right had been an ordinary dwelling-house—large, as village standards went—of perhaps five rooms in all. The other had been the village *kafenéion* or coffee-shop: its big ground-floor room, with shutters pulled back, was open to the street, and played, now, the dual role of village *kafenéion* and hotel dining room. Across one corner of this room was a curved counter, stacked with crockery and glasses, and with shelves of bottles behind it. Between the coffee-making apparatus, and the stove for *loukoumáthes,* were some sophisticated-looking pyramids of fruit. A door at the back of the room led, presumably, to the kitchen premises. The restaurant still had the scrubbed board floor and whitewashed walls of the village coffee-shop, but the white cloths on the tables were of starched linen, and on some of them were flowers.

At the end of the building, against the outer wall of the restaurant, was an outside stairway, built of stone, leading to the rooms above. This was still in use, it appeared; each worn step was whitened at the edge; and on every one stood a flowering plant, blue convolvulus with long belled strands looping down the wall below; scarlet geraniums; and carnations of every shade from deep flame to the mother-of-pearl flush of a Pacific shell. The walls of the building were newly whitewashed, and the paint-work blue.

The effect was simple, fresh, and—with the flowers, and the tamarisk trees at the back, and the glimpse of the sea beyond—delightful.

Georgi dumped my case with a flourish that effectively hid his relief, and was persuaded, without much difficulty, to accept five drachmae. His *pallikarás* dignity concealing his delight, he went staidly off, with Ariadne scampering beside him. But just before he was out of sight past the first cottage wall, I saw him break into a run. The news was on the wing already.

Georgi had abandoned me at the edge of a covered terrace which had been built right along the front of the hotel. In the shade of its trellised roof were set a few little metal tables, where the elders of the village sat. This morning three of them were there, two playing backgammon, the third watching in motionless appraisal. A youth sat on a table near them, swinging his legs and smoking; he looked up, and watched me with some interest, but the old men never even gave me a glance.

As I turned towards the main door—it had been that of the house on the right—the youth turned his head, and called something, and a man who had been busying himself somewhere at the back of the dining room came hurrying out past the backgammon players.

"You must be Miss Ferris?"

The voice was unmistakably English. This, then, was "Tony." I looked at him with sharp interest.

He was young, somewhere under thirty, it was difficult to guess where; of middle height, slightly-built, but moving with the kind of tough grace that one associates with ballet. His hair was fairish, fine and straight, rather too long, but impeccably brushed. His face was narrow-featured, and clever, with light-blue eyes. He wore close-fitting and very well tailored jeans, and a spotlessly white shirt. He was smiling, a rather charming smile; his teeth were small and even, like milk-teeth.

"Yes," I said. "How do you do? You're expecting me for tonight, aren't you? I know I'm a little early, but I was hoping for lunch."

"Early?" He laughed. "We were just going to put the police on your trail. You've no idea. Miss Scorby thought—"

"Police?" I must have sounded startled beyond all reason, and I thought I saw the flicker of surprise in his eyes. My heart jumped painfully, then ground jaggedly into top gear. "Miss Scorby? What are you talking about? Is my cousin here already?"

"No, no. She rang up last night. She said the boat was still held up in Patras, but that she'd gone by train to Athens, and managed to catch the flight after all."

"Oh, good for her! Then she'll get today's bus? She'll be here for dinner?"

"For tea. She said she wasn't going to wait for the bus; she thought the vegetable caique might be more fun, and would get her here sooner." The small teeth showed. "An enterprising lady. She should be here any time now. The boat's overdue as it is."

I laughed. "I might have known Frances would make it! And *before* she was due, at that! That's marvellous!"

"Yes, she did think she'd been rather clever. She thought she'd be catching you up in Heraklion—you were both to have got the bus today, weren't you?—but you'd gone. They told her you'd left yesterday, with a message saying you were coming straight here."

He finished on a note of perfectly normal inquiry. I managed to say, I hoped naturally, "I did. I did leave Heraklion yesterday, and I fully intended to come on here, if I could. But I was offered a lift by some sweet Americans, and they decided to stay overnight in Chania, to look at the Turkish quarter. They'd offered to bring me on here today, and there was no hurry, as I didn't think you were expecting me."

"Ah, well, that explains it. We weren't really worried, you know, dear, we thought you'd have let us know if you were coming sooner, and, to tell you the truth, I doubt if we could have taken you before today."

"Full up?"

"No, no, nothing like that. But busy, you know, busy. We're still only half in order here. Did you walk down from the road?"

"Yes. I had some coffee near the bridge, and then Georgi carried my case the rest of the way."

"Well, come and sign the Golden Book, then I'll show you your room."

The lobby was merely a wide passage running straight through the house. Halfway along it stood an old-fashioned table with a chair behind it, and a rack holding four keys. This was the reception desk. A door beside it was marked "Private."

"Not just the Ritz, you know," remarked Tony cheerfully, "but all in good time, we're expanding like mad. We've got four whole bedrooms now. Not bad, for Agios Georgios."

"It's delightful. But how do you come to be here—you're English, aren't you?" The visitors' book was brand new, its blank pages as informative as a shut eye.

"Yes, indeed. My name's Gamble, but you can call me Tony, everybody does. Gamble by name, and gamble by nature, to coin a phrase. There's money to be made over here, you know, with this tourist boom, and hotels going up everywhere like mushrooms; not so much just yet, perhaps, but when they build the road this way—real money. We want to be ready for that. And the climate's nice, too, for some-one like me, with a chest." He paused, perhaps feeling that he had been a shade overeager with his explanations. Then he smiled, and an eyelid flickered. *"La dame aux camélias,* and all that, you know. That's really what persuaded me to settle so far from the dear old Vicarage."

"Oh?" I said. "Bad luck. Ariadne did tell me that you'd found London unhealthy. That must have been what she meant. Well, this seems a lovely place, so I wish you luck. Is this where I write, at the top?"

"Yes, just there." A beautifully-kept finger indicated the first line of the virgin page. "Our very first guest, dear, did you know? One thing, you can be certain the sheets are clean."

"I wouldn't have dreamed of doubting them. But what about my Danish friend, the man who sent me here? You should have collected his signature—it's famous, in a mild way." I gave his name.

"Oh, yes, but he doesn't count. We weren't officially 'open,' and Stratos only put him up for the publicity, and because there was nowhere else. We were still painting."

I wrote my name with what I hoped was a casual flourish. "And the Englishman?"

"Englishman?" His stare was blank.

"Yes." I picked up the blotting-paper and smoothed it over my signature. "I thought those children said you'd had an Englishman here last week?"

"Oh, him." There was the tiniest pause. "I know who they mean." He smiled. "He wasn't English; he was a Greek, a friend of Stratos'. I suppose those brats heard him talking to me?"

"Probably, I hardly remember. There." I pushed the book across to him.

He picked it up. "Nicola Ferris. A very pretty start to the page. Thanks. No, dear, he didn't count either; he didn't even stay here, just called on business, and left the same night. Well, come and see your room." He flicked a key off its hook, picked up my case, and led the way back towards the front door.

"You said the boat was due now?"

"Any minute, but you know how it is. She'll certainly be here by teatime." He grinned over his shoulder. "And that's one of your worries away, let me tell you. I make the tea myself."

"Oh? Good. She loves her tea. Not me; I've had time to get acclimatized."

"Acclimatized? You mean you've been over here for a bit?" He sounded genuinely interested.

"Over a year. I work at the British Embassy in Athens."

I thought his glance was appraising. He swung my case as it if weighed no more than an ounce. "Then you'll talk the lingo, I suppose? This way, dear. We go up the outside steps; rather primitive, I'm afraid, but it's all part of our simple, unstudied charm."

I followed him up the flower-bordered steps. The smell of carnations was thick as smoke in the sun.

"I've picked up a bit of Greek." I had had to decide on this admission when I met the children, and he would certainly find out—in fact, I had already implied—that I had talked to them. I added, apologetically, "But it's terribly difficult, and of course there's the alphabet. I can ask simple questions, and so on, but as for *talking*—" I laughed. "In my job, we tend to mix, most of the time, with our own people, and I room with an English girl. But one day I really mean to get down to learning the language. What about you?"

"Oh my dear, a little, only a little, and ghastly Greek at that, I do assure you. I mean, one gathers it *works,* but I never speak it unless I have to. Luckily, Stratos' English is quite shatteringly good. . . . Here we are. Primitive, but rather nice, don't you think? The décor was my own idea."

Originally, the room had been plain and square, with roughly plastered walls, a scrubbed wooden floor, and a small window cut in the thick wall facing the sea. Now the rough walls were washed blue-white, some fresh straw matting covered the floor, and the bed, which looked comfortable, was covered with a dazzling white counterpane. The sun, reaching round towards afternoon, already poured a slanting shaft through the window embrasure; the shutters were open, and there were no curtains, but outside there was a vine sifting the sunlight, so that the walls of the room were patterned most beautifully with the moving shadows of leaf and tendril.

"A shame to shut it out, don't you think?" said Tony.

"It's lovely. Is *this* your 'décor'? I thought you meant you'd designed it."

"Oh well, you could say I did in a way, I stopped them spoiling it. Stratos was all for Venetian blinds, and two colours of wallpaper, just like home sweet home."

"Oh? Well, I'm sure you were right. Is, er, 'Stratos' your name for Mr. Alexiakis?"

"Yes, he's the owner, you knew that? Did your Danish friend tell you about him? Quite the romantic local-boy-makes-good story, isn't it? That's what all the emigrants from these poverty-stricken rabbit hutches dream of doing—coming home after twenty years, buying up the place, and showering money on the family."

"Oh, he has a family?"

"Well, there's only a sister, Sofia, and between you and me, dear, there's a little bit of difficulty about showering money on her." Tony dumped my case on a chair, and turned confidingly, with very much the air of one who has been missing the pleasures of a nice, cozy gossip. "It would mean showering it on her husband, too, and dear Stratos doesn't, but *doesn't*, get on with her brother-in-law. But then, who does? I can't say I just fell madly for him myself, and I'm fearfully easy to please, far too easy-going, really. I remember—"

"What's wrong with him?"

"Josef? Oh, first of all, he's a Turk. Not that I mind *that*, but some of these village types think it's just the *last* thing, next to a Bulgarian or a German. And the poor girl was left well-off, respected papa and all that, just the job for a nice local Cretan boy, but she had to go and marry this Turkish foreigner from Chania, who's frittered and drunk most of it away—won't lift a finger, *and* rather pushes her around. Oh, the usual, you know, *such* a dreary tale. What's more, he won't let her go to church, and *that*, of course is the last straw. Quaint, isn't it?"

"Can't the priest help?"

"We haven't one, dear, he only visits."

"Oh. Poor Sofia."

"Yes, well, things have looked up for her since brother Stratos got home."

"He must have done well for himself; he had a restaurant, didn't he? Where was it, Soho somewhere?"

"Oh, you wouldn't know it, it wasn't big—though of course the locals think it was the Dorchester, no less, and give Stratos an income to match. Far be it from him to disillusion them. It was a nice little place, though, I was there myself for six years. That's where I picked up my bit of Greek; most of the boys were Greeks, made Stratos feel at home, he said. Ah well," he twitched the peach-coloured table cloth straight, "it's quite amusing here, tarting the place up a bit, though I don't know that little Tony'd just want to settle here for life. We're going to build, you know, onto the other end. Get a nice long, low block, facing the sea. Take a look at that view."

"It's wonderful."

The window faced southwest, over one end of the land-locked bay. To the left, I caught a glimpse of the edge of a roof; that was all; the rest of the village was out of sight. Directly below me, through the masking vine, I could see a flat space of gravel where a few tables and chairs were set—this, no doubt, would be Ariadne's "beautiful garden." What flowers there were, grew in pots, enormous earthenware *pithoi*, like the old wine-jars from the Cretan palaces. A clump of tamarisk trees stood where the gravel gave way to the flat rock of the foreshore; this, smoothed and fissured by water, burned white in the sun. In every cranny of rock blazed the brilliant pink and crimson sunbursts of ice-daisies, and, just beside them, the sea moved lazily, silky and dark, its faint bars of light and shadow gently lifting and falling against the hot rock. Beyond the stretch of sea, at the outer curve of the bay, tall cliffs towered jaggedly, their feet in the calm summer water, and along their bases curled the narrow golden line of shingle that rings the islands of the tideless Aegean. Even this, if the wind stiffened from the south, would be covered. A small boat, painted orange and cobalt, rocked, empty, at anchor a little way out from the shore.

"Next stop, Africa," said Tony, behind me.

"It's lovely, oh, it's lovely! I'm glad I came before you've built your new wing, you know."

"Well, I do see what you mean, not that we're exactly plan-ning to compete with the Riviera," said Tony cheerfully. "If it's peace and quiet you want, dear, we've bags of that."

I laughed. "Well, that's what we came for. Is it warm enough to swim yet? I asked Georgi, but he has a different sort of built-in thermostat from me, and I don't know if I can take his word for it."

"Well, heavens, don't take mine, I've not tried it, and I don't suppose I ever shall, not being just a child of Nature. I wouldn't risk the harbour, it's dirty, but there are bound to be plenty places where it's safe. You'd better ask Stratos; he'll know if there are currents and things. Your cousin'll go with you, I suppose?"

"Oh, she'll probably sit on the shore and watch—though it wasn't safety I was thinking about; there won't be any currents here that could matter. No, Frances isn't a swimmer, she's mainly interested in the flowers. She's a rock-garden expert, and works in a big nursery, and she always takes a busman's holiday somewhere where she can see the plants in their natural homes. She's tired of Switzerland and the Tyrol, so, when I told her what I'd seen last spring over here, she just had to come." I turned away from the window, adding casually: "Once she sees the place, I probably shan't be allowed time off for swimming. I'll have to spend the whole time tramping the mountainside with her, hunting for flowers to photograph."

"Flowers?" said Tony, almost as if it were a foreign word he had never heard before. "Ah, well, I'm sure there are plenty nice ones around. Now, I'll have to be getting down to the kitchen. Your cousin's room is next door—that one, there. There's only the two in this end of the place, so you'll be lovely and private. That's a bathroom there, no less, and that door goes through to the other side of the house. Now, if there's anything you want, just ask. We don't rise to bells yet, but you don't need to come down; just hang out of the door and yell. I'm never far away. I hear most that goes on."

"Thanks," I said, a little hollowly.

"Cheerio for now," said Tony amiably. His slight figure skated gracefully away down the stairway.

I shut my door, and sat down on the bed. The shadows of the vine moved and curtseyed on the wall. As if they were my own confused and drifting thoughts, I found that I had pressed my hands to my eyes, to shut them out.

Already, from the fragments I had gleaned, one thing showed whole and clear. If the murder which Mark had witnessed had had any connection with Agios Georgios, and if his impression of the Englishness of the fourth man had been correct, then either Tony, or the mysterious "Englishman" from the sea—whom Tony had denied—must have been present. There were no other candidates. And, in either case, Tony was involved. The thing could be, in fact, centred on this hotel.

I found a wry humour in wondering just what Mark would have said, had he known that he was packing me off, with prudent haste, from the perimeter of the affair into its very centre. He had wanted me safely out of it, and had made this abundantly clear, even to the point of rudeness; and I— who had taken my own responsibilities for long enough—had resented bitterly a rejection that had seemed to imply a sexual superiority. If I had been a man, would Mark have acted in the same way? I thought not.

But at least emotion no longer clouded my judgment. Sitting here quietly, now, seeing things from the outside, I could appreciate his point of view. He wanted to see me safe —and he wanted his own feet clear. Well, fair enough. In the last few minutes, I had realized (even at the risk of conceding him a little of that sexual superiority) that I wanted both those things, quite fervently, myself.

I took my hands from my eyes, and there were the patterned shadows again, quiet now, beautiful, fixed.

Well, it was possible. It was perfectly possible to do as Mark had wished; clear out, forget, pretend it had never happened. It was obvious that no suspicion of any sort could attach itself to me. I had arrived as expected, having successfully dropped the dangerous twenty-four hours out of my life. All I had to do was forget such information as came my way, ask no more questions, and—how had it gone?—"get on with that holiday of yours, that Lambis interrupted."

And meanwhile, Colin Langley, aged fifteen?

I bit my lip, and snapped back the lid of the suitcase.

CHAPTER : EIGHT

She shall guess, and ask in vain. . . .
> Thomas Lovell Beddoes: *Song of the Stygian Naiades.*

THERE WAS A WOMAN in the bathroom, just finishing with a cloth and pail. When I appeared, towel on arm, she seemed flustered, and began picking up her tools with nervous haste.

"It's all right," I said, "I'm not in a hurry. I can wait till you've finished."

But she had already risen, stiffly, to her feet. I saw then that she was not old, as her movements had led me to imagine. She was of medium height, a little shorter than I, and should have been broadly built, but she was shockingly thin, and her body seemed flattened and angular under the thick, concealing peasant clothing. Her face, too, was meant to be full and round, but you could see the skull under the skin—the temporal bone jutting above deep eye-sockets, the sharp cheekbones, and the squared corners of the jaw. She was shabbily dressed, in the inevitable black, with her dress kilted up over the hips to show the black underskirt below, and she wore a black head-covering, wrapped round to hide neck and shoulders. Under this her hair seemed thick, but the few wisps which had escaped the covering were grey. Her hands were square, and must have been stronger than they looked; they seemed to be mere bones held together by sinews and thick, blue veins.

"You speak Greek?" Her voice was soft, but full and rich, and still young. And her eyes were beautiful, with straight black lashes as thick as thatch-eaves. The lids were reddened, as if with recent weeping, but the dark eyes lit straight away with the pleased interest that every Greek takes in a stranger. "You are the English lady?"

"One of them. My cousin will arrive later. This is a lovely place, *kyria*."

She smiled. Her mouth was thinned almost to liplessness, but not unpleasantly. In repose it did not seem set, but merely showed a kind of interminable and painful patience, a striving for mindlessness. "As for that, it is a small village, and a poor one; but my brother says that you know this, and that many people will come, only to be tranquil."

"Your—brother?"

"He is the patron." She said this with a kind of pride. "Stratos Alexiakis is my brother. He was in England, in London, for many years, but last November he came home, and bought the hotel."

"Yes, I heard about it from Tony. It's certainly very nice, and I hope he does well."

I hoped the conventional words had concealed my surprise. So this was Sofia. She had the appearance of the poorest peasant in a poor country—but then, I thought, if she was helping her brother start up his hotel, no doubt she would wear her oldest clothes for the rough work. It occurred to me that if she had fallen heir to Tony's cooking it hadn't—as yet—done her much good.

"Do you live in the hotel?" I asked.

"Oh, no," hastily, "I have a house, down the road a little, on the other side of the street. The first one."

"The one with the fig tree? I saw it. And the oven outside." I smiled. "Your garden was so lovely; you must be very proud of it. Your husband's a fisherman, is he?"

"No. He—we have a little land up the river. We have vines and lemons and tomatoes. It is hard work."

I remembered the cottage, spotlessly clean, with its ranked

86

flowers beside the fig tree. I thought of the hotel floors, which she had been scrubbing. Then of the fields, which no doubt she would till. No wonder she moved as if her body hurt her. "Have you many children?"

Her face seemed to shut. "No. Alas, no. God has not seen fit." A gesture to her breast, where a tiny silver ornament—a Greek cross, I thought—had swung loose on its chain while she was scrubbing. Encountering this, her hand closed over it quickly, an oddly protective movement, with something of fear in it. She thrust the cross quickly back into the breast of her frock, and began to gather her things together.

"I must go. My husband will be home soon, and there is a meal to get."

My own meal was a good one: lamb, which the Cretans call *amnós*—many of the classical terms still survive in the dialect—and green beans, and potatoes.

"*Sautées*, my dear, in olive oil," said Tony, who served me. "Butter's too scarce here, but I do assure you I made them go steady on the oil. Like them?"

"Fine. But I like olive oil. And here, where it's fresh from the cow, it's terrific. You were right about the wine, *King Minos, sec.* I must remember that. It's dryish for a Greek wine, isn't it?—and the name is wonderfully Cretan!"

"Bottled in Athens, dear, see?"

"Oh, no, you shouldn't have showed me that!" I glanced up. "I met Mr. Alexiakis' sister upstairs."

"Sofia? Oh, yes. She helps around," he said vaguely. "Now, will you have fruit for afters, or *fromage*, or what my dear friend Stratos calls 'compost'?"

"It depends rather on what that is."

"Between you and me, tinned fruit salad, dear. But don't worry, we'll really let ourselves go at dinner. The caique gets in today—oh, of course, you know all about that."

"I'm not worrying, why should I? That was excellent. No, *not* an orange, thank you. May I have cheese?"

"Sure. Here. The white one's goat and the yellow one with holes is sheep, so take your pick. . . . Excuse me one moment. Speak of angels."

He twitched the coffee percolator aside from its flame, and went out of the dining room, across the terrace into the sunlight of the street. A woman was waiting there, not beckoning to him, or making any sign, just waiting, with the patience of the poor. I recognized her; it was Stratos' sister, Sofia.

If only one could stop doing those uncomfortable little addition-sums in one's head. . . . If only there was some way to switch off the mechanism. . . . But the computer ticked on, unwanted, adding it all up, fraction by fraction. Tony and the "Englishman." And now, Tony and Sofia. There had been a woman there, Mark had said. Sofia and her brother . . .

I ate my cheese doggedly, trying to ignore the unwanted answers that the computer kept shoving in front of me. Much better concentrate on the cheese, and there was some wine left and the coffee, which was to follow, smelt delicious; *café français*, no doubt Tony would call it. . . . Here, the computer ticked up a fleeting memory of Mark, dirty, unshaven, hag-ridden, swallowing indifferent thermos coffee, and choking down dry biscuits. I stamped fiercely on the switch, expunged the memory, and turned my attention back to Tony, graceful and immaculate, standing easily in the sun, listening to Sofia.

She had put one of those flattened claws on his arm, almost as if in pleading. Her coif was drawn up now, shadowing half her face, and at that distance I could not see her expression, but her attitude was one of urgency and distress. Tony seemed to be reassuring her, and he patted the hand on his arm before he withdrew it. Then he said something cheerfully dismissive, and turned away.

As he turned, I dropped my gaze to the table, pushing my cheese plate aside. I had seen the look on Sofia's face as Tony turned and left her. It was distress, and she was weeping; but there was also, unmistakably, fear.

"*Café français*, dear?" said Tony.

Not even the computer—aided by two cups of coffee— could have kept me awake after lunch. I carried my second cup out to the garden, and there, alone with the drowsy sound of bees, and the tranquil lapping of the sea, I slept.

It was no more than a cat-nap, a doze of half an hour or so, but it must have been deep and relaxing, for, on waking, I found that I had none of the hungover feeling that one sometimes gets from sleeping in the afternoon. I felt fresh and wide-awake, and full of a sense of pleasant anticipation which resolved itself into the knowledge that Frances would soon be here. Frances, who would know just what to do . . .

I didn't pursue this thought; didn't even acknowledge it. I sat up, drank the glassful of water—tepid now—that had been served with my coffee, and dutifully set about writing a postcard to Jane, my Athens roommate. That Jane would be very surprised to get it, was another of the things I didn't acknowledge; I merely told myself that I wanted a walk, and that the card would be a good excuse for a quiet little stroll down as far as the village post office. I certainly did not stop to consider why I should need the excuse, or why, indeed, I should want a walk, after the amount of exercise I had already had that day. Jane (I said to myself, writing busily) would be delighted to hear from me.

The message that was to arouse all this astonished delight ran as follows: *Arrived here today; lovely and peaceful. Frances due here this afternoon. She'll be thrilled when she sees the flowers, and will spend pounds on film. Hotel seems good. Am hoping it will be warm enough to swim. Love, Nicola.*

I wrote this artless missive very clearly, then took it into the lobby. Tony was there, sitting behind the table, with his feet up, reading *Lady Chatterley's Lover.*

"Don't get up," I said hastily. "I just wondered if you had stamps. Just one, for a local post card; one drach."

He swung his feet down, and fished below the table to pull open a cluttered drawer.

"Sure. One at one drach, did you say?" The long fingers leafed through three or four sad-looking sheets of postage stamps. "Here we are. Only two left, you're lucky."

"Thanks. Oh, are there any at five? I might as well get them now, for air mail to England."

"I'll see. Five. . . . How nice that one's very first tourist knows all the ropes. I can never remember that sort of thing —I'd make the lousiest information clerk ever. Railway time-tables simply *panic* me, you've no idea."

"Then you've come to the right place. D'you mean," I asked innocently, "that you've never written home once, since you came to Greece?"

"My dear, I couldn't shake the dust of the dear old vicarage off my feet fast enough. No, I'm sorry, we've no fives, only twos and fours. Are you in a hurry, because I can easily get some for you?"

"Don't trouble, thanks, I'd like to go out anyway, to explore. Oh look, I'm sorry, I can't even pay you for this one now, I've left my purse upstairs. I'll be down in a minute."

"Don't worry about that. We'll put it on the bill. Double for the trouble, and don't mention it, just like the Ritz."

"No, I'll need it anyway, to get the stamps in the village. And I must get my dark specs."

I left the post card lying on the desk, and went upstairs to my room. When I got back, I could swear the card had not been moved, not even a millimetre.

I smiled at Tony.

"I suppose this town does have a post office?"

"It does indeed, but I won't insult you by directing you, dear. Agios Georgios isn't exactly complicated. Once down the main street and straight into the sea. Have a lovely walk." And he subsided into *Lady Chatterley's Lover*.

I picked up my post card and went out into the street.

"Street," of course, is a misleading word for the dusty gap between Agios Georgios' straggling houses. Outside the hotel was a wide space of trodden, stony dust where hens scratched, and small, brown, half-naked children played under a pistachio tree. The two cottages nearest the hotel were pretty in their fresh whitewash, each with a vine for shade, and with a low white wall fencing the tiny yard where the vine grew. Sofia's house stood by itself at the other side of the street. This was a little bigger than the others, and meticulously kept. A fig tree—that most shapely of trees—grew near the door, its shadow throwing a vivid pattern against the brilliant white wall. The little garden was crammed with flowers: snapdragons, lilies, carnations, mallows—all the spired and scented profusion of the English summer, growing here, as rank as wild flowers, in the Cretan April. Against the outer wall of the house was a primitive fireplace whose blackened pots stood on trivets of a design so old that it was as familiar as the skin of one's hands. A vine-covered wall at the back did its best to hide a cluttered yard where I saw the beehive-shape of a baking oven.

I walked slowly downhill. All seemed innocent and quiet in the afternoon heat. Here was the church, very small, snow-white, with a Reckitt's-blue dome, perched on a little knoll with its back to the cliffs. In front of it some loving hand had made a pavement of sea-pebbles, blue and terracotta and slate-grey, hammered down on patterns into the iron ground. Beyond it, the street sloped more steeply towards the sea, and here, though every house had a pot or two of flowers outside, the place looked barer, and there had been very little use of paint or whitewash. It was as if the richness of the flowery hills had faded and died, dwindling down to starve in the sea-bare poverty of the harbour.

And here was the post office. It was, also, the only shop

the village boasted; a dark cave of a place, with double doors open to the street, beaten earth floor, and sacks of produce standing everywhere—beans, maize, and pasta, along with huge square tins swimming with oily-looking pilchards. On the counter were earthenware bowls of black olives, a stack of cheese, and a big, old-fashioned pair of scales. Beside the door, casually supporting a stack of brushes, was the letter-box, painted the dark post-office blue. And, on the wall opposite the doorway, the telephone, in the very middle of the shop. You threaded your way between the sacks to get to it.

The shop was, obviously, the meeting place of the village women. Four of them were there now, talking over the weighing of some flour. As I entered, a little hesitantly, conversation stopped abruptly, and they stared; then good manners reasserted themselves, and they looked away, talking more quietly, but not, I noticed, about the foreigner; their conversation—about some sick child—was taken up where it had ceased. But all made way for me, and the shop keeper put down the flour scoop and said inquiringly: "Miss?"

"These ladies—" I said, with a gesture meaning that I could not take their turn.

But I had to in the end, defeated by their inflexible courtesy. "I only came for some stamps, please. Six at five drachs, if you will be so good."

Behind me I heard the stir and whisper: "She speaks Greek! Listen, did you hear? English, and she speaks Greek. . . . Hush, you ill-mannered one! Silence!"

I smiled at them, and made some remark about their village, and was, on the instant, the centre of a delighted group. Why did I come to such a place? It was so small, so poor, why did I not stay in Heraklion, where there were big hotels, like in Athens or London? Did I live in London? Was I married? Ah, but there was a man? No? Ah, well, one could not always be fortunate, but soon, soon, if God willed. . . .

I laughed, and answered as best I could, and asked, in my turn, as many questions as I dared. Did they not get many strangers, then, in Agios Georgios? Many English? Oh, yes, Tony, of course, but I meant visitors like myself, foreigners. . . . The Danish gentleman, yes, I had heard of him, but nobody else? No? Ah, well, now that the hotel was getting under way, and so efficiently, no doubt there would soon be many visitors, Americans too, and Agios Georgios would prosper. Mr. Alexiakis was making a good job of it, wasn't he? And his sister was helping him? Yes Sofia, I had met her; I believed she lived in the pretty house at the top of the village, opposite the hotel. . . .

But on Sofia, we stuck. Beyond swiftly-exchanged glances —kind enough, I thought—and murmurs of "Ah, yes, poor Sofia, it was lucky for her that such a brother had come home to look after her," the women said nothing more, and the conversation died, to be ignited again by one of them, young and pretty, with a child clinging to her hand, and an air of assurance, inviting me to her house. The others, who seemed only to have waited for her lead, pressed eagerly forward with similar invitations. How long was I to be in Agios Georgios? I would come and see them, yes, and bring my cousin, too. Which house? The one by the harbour wall —the one above the bakery—behind the church . . . it was no matter (this with laughter), I had only to walk in, there was no house in Agios Georgios where I would not be welcome, so young and pretty, and speaking such good Greek. . . .

Laughingly promising, but temporarily parrying all the charming invitations, I finally escaped, not much the wiser about Georgi's phantom Englishman, but having learned what I had come for, and more as well.

First, the telephone was out. Even without my promise to Mark, there was no chance, whatever happened, of getting in touch with authority, either the Embassy, or even Heraklion, by telephone. The one in the hotel, impossible. The one in the post office, open to the day in what amounted to the Ladies' Clubroom—in English or in Greek, it couldn't even be tried. We were on our own.

I found that, without conscious direction, I had reached the tiny harbour. A sea wall, and a little curved pier, held the water clear and still as a tear in the flower-cup. Someone had scrawled CYPRUS FOR GREECE along the harbour wall, and someone else had tried to scratch it out. A man was beating an octopus; some family would eat well tonight. Two boats lay at anchor, one white, with vermilion canvas furled along her beautiful spars, the other blue, with the name *Eros* along her bows. On *Eros* a youth was working, coiling down a rope. He was wiry and quick-moving, and wore a green sweat-shirt and blue denim trousers tucked into short gumboots. It was the lad who had been watching the backgammon players. He eyed me curiously, but did not interrupt his work.

I stood there a moment or two longer, conscious of eyes

watching me from the dark doorway of every house, where the women sat. I thought: if only Lambis' boat would come in now, sailing quietly in from the east, with them all on board; Lambis at the engine, and Mark steering, and Colin in the bows, with a fishing line, laughing. . . .

I turned sharply away from the shining stretch of the empty sea, and, the terms of my self-deceit forgotten, brought my mind back with a jerk to my problem, the other thing that I had discovered in the village shop—that there was, in fact, no house in Agios Georgios which could have anything to hide. Colin Langley was not here. Nothing could be served by my prying further in a village where every woman must know all her neighbours' affairs. Any answer to the mystery was only to be found at the hotel.

Or—and here I started to walk slowly back up the street, conscious of the eyes that watched me from the dark doorways—or at Sofia's cottage.

There might, in fact, be one house in Agios Georgios at which I was not welcome.

Well, there was nothing like trying. And if the husband was still at home, over his meal, then I should be quite interested to meet him, too.

I wondered if he favoured Cretan dress.

CHAPTER : NINE

She seem'd an ancient maid, well-skill'd to cull
The snowy fleece, and wind the twisted wool.
Pope: *The Iliad of Homer*.

SHE WAS SITTING just inside the door of her cottage, spinning.

In all my months in Greece, I had never quite got used to the pleasure of watching the peasant women at this primitive task. The soft, furry mass of white wool on the distaff, the brown fingers pulling it out like candy-floss to loop across the front of the black dress, the whirling ball of woollen thread on the spindle—these made a pattern that it would have been hard not to appreciate.

She had not looked up at my approach; the trunk of the

fig tree must have hidden the movement from her. I paused for a moment, just beyond its shade, to watch her. In the deep shadow where she sat, the lines of trouble could no longer be seen; her face showed the smooth planes of youth, while even the ugly hands, caught in the fluid movements of her task, had taken on a kind of beauty.

I thought, then, of the legend I had told Mark, the story of the moon-spinners that had been intended to send him to sleep, and to bring me comfort. I looked again at Sofia, a black-clad Cretan woman, spinning in the hot afternoon. An alien, a suspect, an incomprehensible native of this hard, hot country, whose rules I didn't know. Somebody to be questioned.

I walked forward and put my hand on the gate, and she looked up and saw me.

The first reaction was pleasure, of that I was sure. Her face split into a smile, and the dark eyes lighted. Then, though she did not move her head, I got the impression that she had cast a quick glance into the cottage behind her.

I pushed open the gate. "May I come in and talk to you?" I knew that such a direct query, though perhaps not good manners, could not, by the rules of island hospitality, be refused.

"Of course." But I thought she looked uneasy.

"Your husband has gone?"

She watched me with what could have been nervousness, though the deft, accustomed movements helped her to an appearance of ease, as a cigarette will sometimes help in a more sophisticated situation. Her glance went to the small fire of twigs outside, where a pot still simmered. "He did not come." Then, making as if to rise, "Be pleased to sit down."

"Thank you—oh, please don't stop your spinning, I love to watch it." I entered the tiny yard, and, obedient to her gesture, sat on the bench near the door, under the fig tree. I began to praise her spinning, admiring the smoothness of the wool, and fingering the piece of woven cloth she showed me, until soon she had forgotten her shyness, and put down her work to fetch more of her weaving and embroidery to show me. Without being asked, I left my seat, and followed her indoors.

The cottage had two rooms, with no door between them, merely an oblong gap in the wall. The living-room, opening straight off the yard, was scrupulously neat, and very poor. The floor was of earth, beaten as hard as a stone, with a drab, balding rug covering half of it. There was a small fireplace in one corner, unused at this time of year, and across the back of the room ran a wide ledge, three feet from the floor, which served apparently as a bed-place, and was covered with a single blanket patterned in red and green. The walls had not yet been freshly whitewashed, and were still grimed with winter's smoke. Here and there, high up in the plastered walls, were niches which held ornaments, cheap and bright, and faded photographs. There was one in a place of honour, a child—a boy—of perhaps six; behind this was a fuzzy print, much enlarged, of a young man in what looked like irregular battle dress. He was handsome in a rather glossy and assured way. The boy was very like him, but stood shyly. The husband, I supposed, and a lost child? I looked for the family ikon, but could see none, and remembered what Tony had told me.

"My little boy," said Sofia, behind me. She had come out of the inner room with an armful of cloths. She betrayed neither resentment nor surprise that I should have followed her into the house. She was looking sadly at the picture, with—you would have sworn—no other thought in mind. "He died, *thespoinís*, at seven years old. One day he was well, and at school, and playing. The next—pff—dead. And it was the will of God that there should be no more."

"I'm sorry. And this is your husband?"

"Yes, that is my husband. See, this cushion that I have made last year . . ."

She began to lay the things out in the sunlight near the door. I bent over them, but turning, so that I could see into the inner room.

This was darkened, with shutters drawn against the sun. It was merely a small oblong box of a room, with a double bed, a wooden chair, and a table by the window covered with a pink cloth with bobbles on. Every corner of the house seemed open to the view. . . .

She was putting up her work again.

"And now, if you will sit in here, where it is cool, I will get you a glass of the peppermint drink which I make myself."

I hesitated, feeling ashamed. I had not wanted to take her meagre hospitality, but, since I had asked myself into her house, I had forced her to offer it. There was nothing to do but thank her, and sit down.

She reached to a shelf near the door where, behind a faded curtain of that same red and green, stood a stock (how pitifully scanty a stock) of food. She took down a small bottle and glass.

"Sofia?"

It was a man's voice calling from outside. I had heard—but without attending—the footsteps coming rapidly down the track from the bridge. They had paused at the gate.

Sofia, near the door, turned quickly, glass in hand. The man was still beyond my range of vision, and he could not have seen me.

"All is well," he said shortly. "And as for Josef—what is the matter?"

This, as Sofia made some little hushing gesture, indicating that she was not alone. "Someone is with you?" he asked sharply.

"It is the English lady from the hotel, and—"

"The English lady?" The swiftly spoken Greek was almost explosive. "Have you no more sense than to invite her in to show off your work, when at—"

"It is all right to speak Greek in front of her," said Sofia. "She understands it perfectly."

I heard his breath go in, as if he had shut his mouth hard on whatever he had been going to say. The latch clicked.

I stepped forward. The newcomer had swung open the gate, and we met in the sunlit doorway.

He was a powerful-looking man in the late forties, broadly built and swarthy, with the gloss of good living on his skin. His face was square, going to fat a little, with high cheekbones and the inevitable moustache; a typically Greek face, which could have been the one I had last seen under the red head-dress, but I didn't think it was. In any case, he was not wearing Cretan dress. He had obviously been working, and wore shabby grey trousers covered with dust, and a khaki shirt, with a scarlet kerchief knotted at the neck. A brown linen jacket hung from his shoulders. This last garment looked expensive, and bore, almost visibly, the label of a Knightsbridge "sports" department. My interest focussed and sharpened. This must be my host, Stratos Alexiakis.

"This is my brother," said Sofia.

I was already giving him my nicest smile, and my hand. "How do you do? I'm sorry, I know I shouldn't have taken Kyria Sofia's time, when her husband is expected home for his meal. But I was walking through the village, and your sister was the only person I knew, so I invited myself in. I'll go now."

96

"No, no, indeed!" He had retained my hand, and now led me, almost forcibly, to the seat under the fig tree. "I am sorry, I would never have spoken so, if I had realized you understood me! But my sister's husband is not a man for company, and I thought if he came home to find her gossiping—" a grin and a shrug—"well, you know how it is if a man is hungry, and a meal not ready. No, no, please sit down! What would my sister think of me if I drive her guest away? You must taste her peppermint drink; it is the best in the village."

Sofia, her face expressionless, handed me the glass. There was nothing to show that either of them were relieved at the way I had interpreted his remarks. I tasted the drink, and praised it lavishly, while Stratos leaned one powerful shoulder against the doorjamb, and watched me benignly. Sofia, standing stiffly in the doorway, watched him.

"He is late," she said. The statement sounded tentative, like a question, as if Stratos might have known the reason why.

He shrugged, and grinned. "Perhaps, for once, he is working."

"He did not—help you in the field?"

"No."

He turned back to me, speaking in English.

"You're comfortable at my hotel?" His English was excellent, but still, after twenty years, hadn't lost the accent.

"Very, thank you, and I love my room. You've got a good place here, Mr. Alexiakis."

"It is very quiet. But you told me on the telephone that this is what you want."

"Oh, yes. I live in Athens, you see, and it gets a bit crowded and noisy towards summer. I was longing to get away somewhere, where the tourist crowds didn't go. . . ."

I talked easily on, explaining yet again about my own and Frances' reasons for choosing Agio's Georgios. I didn't even try to conceal from myself, now, that I wanted to establish a very good reason for the time I intended to spend exploring the mountain and shore round about. A movie camera, I thought, as I talked on and on about film (of which I know nothing), is an excellent excuse for a lot of unholy curiosity. . . .

"And the boat," I finished, "will pick us up on Monday, if all goes well. The party's going on to Rhodes from here, and I'll join them for a couple of days, then I must go back to

Athens. They'll go on to the Dodecanese, then my cousin'll come to stay with me in Athens, on her way home."

"It sounds very nice." I could see him chalking up the score; a party, a boat, a private tour; money. "So you work in Athens? That accounts for your excellent Greek. You make mistakes, of course, but you are very fluent, and it is easy to understand what you mean. Do you find that you follow all you hear, as well?"

"Oh, no, not really." I wondered, as I spoke, how often tact and truth go hand in hand. "I mean, I couldn't translate word for word, though I get the gist of speech pretty well, except when people talk fast, or with too much of a regional accent. Oh, thank you," to Sofia, who had taken my empty glass. "No, no more. It was lovely."

Stratos was smiling. "You've done very well, all the same. You'd be surprised how many English people stay over here for quite some time, and never trouble to learn more than a word or two. What is your work in Athens?"

"I'm a rather unimportant junior secretary at the British Embassy."

This was chalked up, too, and with a shock: I saw it.

"What does she say?" This, almost in a whisper, from Sofia.

He turned his head, translating carelessly: "She works at the British Embassy."

"Oh!" It was a tiny exclamation as the glass slipped to the ground, and broke.

"Oh dear!" I exclaimed. "What a shame! Let me help!"

I knelt down, in spite of her protests, and began to pick up the fragments. Luckily the glass was thick and coarse, and the pieces were large.

Stratos said, without stirring, "Don't worry, Sofia, I'll give you another." Then, with a touch of impatience, "No, no, throw the pieces away, girl, it'll never mend. I'll send Tony across with a new glass for you, a better one than this rubbish."

I handed Sofia the pieces I had collected, and stood up. "Well, I've enjoyed myself very much, but, in case your husband does come home soon, *kyria*, and doesn't appreciate a crowd, I think I'll go. In any case, my cousin should be arriving any minute now."

I repeated my thanks for the drink, and Sofia smiled and nodded and bobbed, while giving the impression that she hardly heard what I was saying, then I went out of the gate, with Stratos beside me.

He walked with his hands dug deep into his pockets, and

his shoulders hunched under the expensive jacket. He was scowling at the ground so ferociously that I began to wonder uneasily what he might say. His first words showed, disarmingly enough, that he was deeply chagrined that I had seen the threadbare poverty of his sister's home.

"She won't let me help her." He spoke abruptly, as if I should have known what he was talking about. "I've come home with money, enough to buy all she needs, but all she will take is a little payment for work in the hotel. Scrubbing work. My sister!"

"People are proud sometimes."

"Proud! Yes, I suppose it's that. It's all she has had for twenty years, after all, her pride. Would you believe it, when we were children, my father had his own caique, and when his uncle died, we inherited land, the land up at the head of the plateau, where it is sheltered, the best in Agios Georgios! Then my mother died, and my father had ill-health, and the land was all there was for my sister's dowry. I went to England, and I worked. Oh, yes, I worked!" His teeth showed. "But I have something to show for those years, while she— every drach she has, she makes herself. Why, even the fields—"

He broke off, and straightened his shoulders. "Forgive me, I should not throw my family troubles at you like that! Perhaps I needed a European ear to pour them into—did you know that a great many Greeks regard themselves as living East of Europe?"

"That's absurd, when you think what Europe owes them."

"I dare say." He laughed. "Perhaps I should have said an urban and civilized ear. We're a long way from London, are we not—even from Athens? Here, life is simple, and hard, especially for women. I had forgotten, in the time I have been away. One forgets that these women accept it. . . . And if one of them is fool enough to marry a Mussulman, who uses his religion as an excuse for . . ." his shoulders lifted, and he laughed again. "Well, Miss Ferris, and so you're going to hunt flowers and take movies while you're here?"

"Frances will, and I dare say I'll tag along. Does the *Eros* belong to you, Mr. Alexiakis?"

"The *Eros?* Yes, did you see her, then? How did you guess?"

"There was a boy working on her, that I'd seen up at the hotel. Not that that meant anything, but I just wondered. I rather wanted to ask . . ." I hesitated.

"You would like to go out, is that it?"

"I'd love it. I'd always wanted to see this coast from the sea. Some children told me there was a good chance of seeing dolphins; there's a bay a short distance to the west, they said, with rocks running out deep, and sometimes dolphins even come in among the swimmers."

His laugh was hearty, even a little too hearty. "I know the place. So that old legend still goes on! There hasn't been a dolphin seen there since the time of Pliny! I ought to know, I fish that way quite often. Not that I go out much with the caique, that's Alkis' job; I'm not used to hard work of that kind any more. But the caique was going cheap, so I bought her; I like a lot of irons in the fire, and some day, when business gets keen, I shall make money with visitors. Meanwhile, I get my fish cheap, and soon, I think, we shall be able to bring our own supplies from Chania."

We were in front of the hotel now. He stopped.

"But of course you may go out with Alkis, any time. You must go eastwards, the coast is better, and some way along there is a ruin of an old harbour, and, if you walk a little way, there is an old church, if these things interest you?"

"Oh, yes. Yes, of course they do."

"Tomorrow, then?"

"I—well, no, that is, perhaps my cousin'll have some ideas . . . I mean, she's just been cruising, after all, and I expect she'll want a day or so ashore. Later, I—I'd love it. You . . . don't use the caique yourself, you said?"

"Not often. I have little time at present. I only fish for sport, and for that I have a small boat."

"Oh, yes, that little boat beside the hotel? The orange one? You mean you go light-fishing, with those huge lamps?"

"That's right, with a spear." Again that grin, friendly, slightly deprecating, claiming—but not offensively—a common bond of knowledge unshared by the villagers. "Nice and primitive, eh? But terrific sport—like all primitive pastimes. I used to be very good at it when I was a young man, but one gets a little out of practice in twenty years."

"I watched the light-fishers once, in the bay at Paros. It was fascinating, but one couldn't see much from the shore. Just the lights bobbing, and the man lying with the glass, peering down, and sometimes you could see the one with the spear, striking."

"Do you want to come out with me?"

"I'd love to!" The words were out, genuinely, thoughtlessly, before it came back to me, with a kick of recollection, that—until I knew a great deal more about him—I quite definitely was not prepared to spend a night with Stratos Alexiakis in a small boat, or anywhere else.

"Well," he was beginning, while my mind spun uselessly, like a gramophone with a broken spring, when Tony came running down the steps to meet us, as lightly as something out of the chorus of *The Sleeping Beauty*.

"*There* you are, my dears, you've met. Stratos, that wretched get from Chania wants twelve drachs each for the wine, he says he won't send it else. Dire, isn't it? He's on the blower now, could you cope? Did you have a nice walk, dear? Find the post office? Marvellous, isn't it? But you must be *flaked*. Let me bring you a lemon *pressé*, eh? Guaranteed straight off our very own tree. Oh, look, isn't that the caique, just come in? And someone coming up from the harbour as ever was, with Georgi carrying her case. How that child always manages to be in the way of making a couple of drachs. . . . Just like our Stratos here, madly lucky. It is your cousin? Now, isn't that just ducky? By the time Miss Scorby's unpacked it'll be just nice time for tea."

CHAPTER : TEN

And, swiftly as a bright Phoebean dart
Strike for the Cretan isle: and here thou art!

Keats: *Lamia.*

"WELL," said Frances, "it's very nice to be here. And the tea is excellent. I suppose Little Lord Fauntleroy makes it himself?"

"Hush, for goodness' sake, he'll hear you! He says if you want him, you only have to yell, he's always around. What's more, he's rather sweet. I've fallen for him."

"I never yet met the male you didn't fall for," said Frances. "I'd begin to think you were ill, if you weren't somewhere along the course of a love affair. I've even learned to know the stages. Well, well, this is really very pleasant, isn't it?"

We were sitting in the hotel "garden," in the shade of the vine. There was nobody about. Behind us, an open door gave on the empty lobby. Tony was back in the bar: faintly, round the end of the house, came the sound of talk from the café tables on the street.

The sun was slanting rapidly westward. There was a little ripple now, running across the pale silk of the sea, and the breeze stirred the sleepy scent from the carnations in the wine-jars. In full sunlight, at the edge of the gravel, stood a big pot of lilies.

Frances stretched her long legs in front of her, and reached for a cigarette. "Yes, this was a ve-ery good idea of yours. Athens at Easter could be a bit much, I can see that. I'd forgotten, till you wrote, that the Greek Easter would be later than ours. We had it last week end when we were in Rome. I imagine the Greek country Easter'll be a bit of a contrast, and I must say I'm looking forward to it. Oh, thanks, I'd love another cup. Now, how long since I saw you? Good heavens, nearly eighteen months! Tell me all about yourself."

I regarded her with affection.

Frances, though a first cousin, is very much older than I. She was at this time something over forty, and though I know it is a sign of immaturity to think of this as being a vast age, I know that it seemed so to me. From the earliest days I remember, Frances has been there. When I was very small I called her "Aunt Frances," but she put a stop to that three years ago—at the time when, after my mother's death, I went to live with her. Some people, I know, find her formidable; she is tall, dark, rather angular, with a decisive sort of voice and manner, and a charm which she despises, and rarely troubles to use. Her outdoor job has given her the kind of complexion which is called "healthy"; she is as strong as a horse, and an excellent business woman. She dresses well, if severely. But her formidable exterior is deceiving, for she is the most genuinely tolerant person I know, and sometimes carries "live and let live" to alarming lengths. The only things she cannot stand are cruelty and pretentiousness. I adore her.

Which is why, on her command to "tell her all about myself," I did just that—at least, I plunged into a haphazard and pretty truthful account of my job, and my Athens friends. I didn't trouble to edit, though I knew that some of the latter would have fitted a bit oddly into Frances' staid Berkshire home.

She heard me out in amused silence, drinking her third cup of tea, and tapping ash into the nearest *píthos*.

"Well, you seem to be getting a lot of fun out of life, and

after all that's what you came for. How's John? You don't mention him."

"John?"

"Or was it David? I forget their names, though heaven knows why I should, as your letters are spotted with them like a currant-cake, while the fit's on. Wasn't it John, the reporter from the *Athens News?*"

"Oh, him. That was ages ago. Christmas, anyway."

"So it was. Come to think of it, your last two letters were remarkably blank. Heart-whole and fancy-free?"

"Entirely." I pulled a pink carnation near to me on its swaying stalk, and sniffed it.

"Well, it makes a change," said Frances mildly. "Of course, it's all very well having a heart like warm putty, but one of these days your impulses are going to land you in something you won't easily get out of. Now what are you laughing at?"

"Nothing. Is the *Paolo* calling for us on Monday?"

"Yes, all being well. You are coming with us to Rhodes, then? Good. Though just at the moment I feel I never want to move again. This is what the travel guides call 'simple,' but it's nice, and terribly restful. . . . Listen."

A bee in the lilies, the soft murmur of the sea on the shingle, the subdued Greek voices . . .

"I told Tony I wished they could keep it like this," I said. "It's heaven just as it is."

"Mmm. And you were right, my love. The flowers I've seen so far, even just along the roadside, are enough to drive a woman to drink."

"But you came by boat!"

"Oh, yes, but when we were stuck that Sunday night, in Patras, three of us hired a car and went exploring. We didn't have time to go far before dark, but I made the driver stop so often, while I rushed off into the fields, that he thought I was mad—or else that my bladder was permanently diseased. But as soon as he gathered that it was just the flowers I was looking at, do you know what he did?"

I laughed. "Picked some for you?"

"Yes! I came back to the car, and there he was, six foot two of what *you* would recognize as magnificent Hellenic manhood, waiting for me with a bunch of orchids and anemones, and a kind of violet that sent my temperature up by several degrees. Aren't they sweet?"

"Well, I don't know which violet—"

"Not the violets, ass, the Greeks." She stretched again, luxuriously. "My goodness, I'm glad I came! I'm going to

103

enjoy every minute, I can see that. Why, oh *why* do we live in England, when we could live here? And incidentally, why does Tony? Live here, I mean, when he could live in England?"

"He said there was money to be made here when they build the new wing, which is a polite way of saying when they build a hotel that *is* a hotel. I wondered if he had money in it himself. He *says* he's got a weak chest."

"Hm. He looks a pretty urban type to settle here, even for a short spell . . . unless the *beaux yeux* of the owner have got something to do with it. He came with him from London, didn't he? What's *he* like?"

"Stratos Alexiakis? How did you—oh, of course, I told you the set-up in my letter, I forgot. He seems very nice. I say, Frances."

"Mmm?"

"Would you care for a walk along the shore? It gets dark here fairly soon. I—I'd quite like a stroll, myself."

This was not true, but what I had to say could hardly be said under the listening windows.

"All right," she said amiably, "when I've finished this cup of tea. What did you do with yourself in Chania, if that's how you pronounce it?"

"You don't say the "ch" like ours; it's a *chi*, a sort of breathed 'k,' like in 'loch' . . . Chania."

"Well, what was it like?"

"Oh, it—it was very interesting. There are Turkish mosques."

Another thing I should have mentioned about Frances: you can't fool her. At least, I can't. She's had too much practice, I suppose, in detecting the little off-white lies of my childhood. She glanced at me, as she shook another cigarette loose from the pack. "Was it, now? Where did you stay?"

"Oh, it's the biggish hotel in the middle of the town, I forget the name. You're chain-smoking, you'll get cancer."

"No doubt." Her voice came muffled through the lighting of the cigarette. She looked at me across the flame, then she got to her feet.

"Come along, then. Why the shore?"

"Because it's lonely."

She made no comment. We picked our way through the vivid clumps of ice-daisies, to find that a rough path of a sort led along the low, dry rocks that backed the shingle. Further along there was a ridge of hard sand, where we could walk side by side.

I said, "I've got something I want to talk to you about."

"Last night's stay in Chania?"

"Clever, aren't you? Yes, more or less."

"Is that why you laughed when I said that your impulses'd land you in trouble one day?" As I was silent, she glanced at e sideways, quizzically. "Not that I'm any judge, but Chania seems an odd place to choose to misbehave in."

"I wasn't even *in* Chania last night! And I haven't—!" I proke off, and suddenly giggled. "As a matter of fact, I *did* spend the night with a man, now that I come to think about it, I'd forgotten that."

"He seems," said Frances tranquilly, "to have made a great impression. Well, go on."

"Oh, Frances, darling, I do love you! No, it's not some foully embarrassing love-tangle—when did I ever? It's— I've run into trouble—not my trouble, someone else's, and I wanted to tell you about it, and ask you if there's anything in the world I can do."

"If it's not your trouble, do you have to do anything?"

"Yes."

"A heart like warm putty," said Frances resignedly, "and sense to match. All right, what's his name?"

"How d'you know it's a he?"

"It always is. Besides, I assume it's the one you spent the night with."

"Oh. Yes."

"Who is he?"

"He's a civil engineer. His name's Mark Langley."

"Ah."

"It isn't 'ah' at all! As a matter of fact," I said, very clearly, "I rather detest him."

"Oh, God," said Frances, "I knew this would happen one day. No, don't glare at me, I'm only teasing. Well, go on. You've spent the night with a detestable engineer called Mark. It makes a rousing start. Tell all."

Her advice, when I had at length told all, was concise and to the point.

"He told you to get out and stay out, and he's got this man Lambis to look after him. They sound a pretty capable pair, and your Mark's probably fairly well all right by now. The two of them will be back on their boat, you may be sure, with everything under control. I should stay out."

"Y—yes, I suppose so."

"Besides, what could you do?"

105

"Well, obviously, I could tell him what I've found out. I mean, I'm absolutely certain it must be Tony and Stratos Alexiakis and Sofia."

"Quite probably. Granted that your Mark remembers accurately what he saw and heard, and that there was an Englishman there on the scene of the murder, along with a man in Cretan dress and another Greek, and a woman. . . ." She paused a moment. "Yes, once you've accepted Tony's involvement, the others follow as the night the day. It's a little closed circle, Tony, Stratos, Sofia, Josef—and the stranger, whether English or Greek, whom Tony certainly knew and talked to."

I stopped in my tracks, staring at her. "Him? But how? He wasn't there. There was only the Greek, and the Cretan, and—"

"My dear," she said gently, "you've got yourself so involved with Mark's side of this that you've forgotten how it started."

"How it started?"

"There was a murdered man," she said.

Silence, broken only by the crisping of the shingle at the sea's edge. I stooped, picked up a flat pebble, and skimmed it at the surface of the water. It sank immediately. I straightened up, dusting my hands.

"I've been awfully stupid," I said humbly.

"You've been right in the thick of it, honey, and you've been frightened. It's easy for me, walking calmly in at half-time. I can see things more clearly. Besides, I'm not emotionally involved."

"Who said I was?"

"Aren't you?"

I was still watching the place where my pebble had struck. "Frances, Colin Langley's only fifteen."

She said gently: "Darling, that's the point. That's why I'm telling you to keep away from it unless you actually do find out what's happened to him. Otherwise you might only do harm. Look, don't you think we'd better go back now? The sun's nearly gone, and the going's getting beastly rough."

This was true. As I had told my story, we had been making our way round the bay, and had reached the foot of the big cliffs at the far side. What had looked from the distance like a line of shingle round their feet, proved to be a narrow storm-beach of big boulders piled there by the south wind and the sea. Above this, between the topmost boulders and the living cliff, ran a narrow path, steep and awkward. It

106

skirted the headland, then dived steeply down towards the crescent beach of a small, sandy bay.

"It looks nice along there," said Frances. "I wonder if that's your Bay of the Dolphins?"

"I think that's further along; the water's too shallow here at the edge, and Georgi said you could get right out along the rocks above deep water, and even dive. Look, that must be it, beyond the next headland, I think you can see the rock-stacks running out. With the sun going down behind them, they look just like shadows."

We stood for a few minutes in silence, shading our eyes against the glitter of the brilliant sea. Then Frances turned away.

"Come along, you're tired. And you could do with a good stiff drink before dinner, by the look of you."

"It's an idea." But my voice sounded dreary, even to myself. I turned to follow her back the way we had come.

"Don't think I don't know how you feel." Her tone was matter-of-fact and curiously soothing. "It isn't just to keep you out of trouble that I'm telling you to keep away from Mark. I can give you good reasons. If you went trailing up there looking for him, you might be seen, followed, anything: you might lead them to him. Or, if you made them suspicious, you might—and this is more important—frighten them into killing Colin . . . if, that is, Colin is still alive."

"Oh, God, I suppose you're right. I—I've not been thinking very straight." I put a hand to my head. "If you'd seen Sofia. That's what really frightened me . . . when Josef didn't come home. You should have seen her face."

Incoherent as I was, she understood me. "You mean that she's not worrying in case he's broken his neck out there on the mountainside, but because she's afraid of what he may be doing?"

"Yes. And there are only two things I can think of that he might be doing."

She was blunt. "Meaning that if Josef is your Cretan murderer—and I'd risk a bet on it myself—he's either still out hunting for Mark, to kill him, or he's mounting guard over Colin somewhere?"

"And she's terrified." I swallowed. "If he's with Colin, and she knows it, and she's afraid of what he may be doing . . . Well, there it is."

My voice trailed off, miserably. She didn't answer, and we trudged along for some minutes in silence. The sun had gone now, dipping swiftly into the sea, and the shadow of the cliffs had reached after us. The breeze had dropped. At the other side of the bay there was a light in the hotel. It seemed a long way away.

I said at length, "You're right, of course. Mark told me to keep out, and he meant it. Unless I actually found Colin—"

"That's it, you see. That's why he wouldn't go to the authorities, he told you that. If any question were asked, or if Mark and Lambis came here openly, or if anyone shoved the affair to the point where accusations were made—I wouldn't give you twopence for the boy's chances of surviving to tell his part of the story. He's the hostage."

"I see that. Mark told me himself, after all. All right, I—I'll stay put, Frances, don't worry. But all the same—"

"Well?"

"There's nothing to stop me *looking* for him, is there? If I'm terribly careful? I—I can't just put him out of my head, can I?"

"No, love. You go ahead. I don't see how you could stop looking, even if you wanted to. It isn't just a thing one forgets overnight, like losing a pencil. All you can do, for the sake of your own peace of mind, is to assume he's still alive, and keep your eyes open. One thing, for a start: if he's alive, he's got to be fed."

"Of course! And not too far away, at that. If one kept a tight eye on Sofia—I'll bet it's she who feeds him . . . though it could be Tony, I suppose."

She smiled. "My bet's on Sofia. Whoever does it probably has to get up at crack of dawn to avoid being seen, and I don't just see Little Lord Fauntleroy frisking around in the dew."

"Well, I shall, and tomorrow as ever was. I'll go for an early-morning swim near the hotel, and keep my eyes skinned."

"You do that," said Frances. "Look, there's someone out there now. That's the little boat putting out, isn't it? The man in it—is that Stratos Alexiakis?"

A man, a dim figure in the fast-falling dusk, had been stooping over the small boat, which was now moored beside the rocks by the hotel. He climbed in, and cast her off. He busied himself over something in the stern, and presently we heard the splutter of an engine. The boat started towards us, keeping well inshore.

"I think so," I said. "He must have taken an out-board motor down. . . . I wonder where he's going?"

We had both stopped to watch him. He was standing well forward, and, as he drew nearer, we could see that the rudder had a long lever attached, to enable him to steer while peering over the shoulders of the boat into the lighted water. The huge lamps were in their places in the bows, but were as yet unlit.

She was drawing level with us, and he had seen us. It was Stratos. He grinned and waved, then he moved aft for a minute, and the engine slowed to a soft *put-put*, so that the boat seemed to be just drifting by. I could make out the white letters on her bows: ΨΥΧΗ.

His voice came cheerfully over the water. "Hullo there! Would you like to come?"

"Another time!" We both grinned and waved in what we hoped was a cordial refusal. "Thanks all the same! Good fishing!"

He raised a hand, stooped again to the engine, and *Psyche* veered away in a long, lovely curve for the tip of the headland. Her wash lapped the shore beside us, and the small shingle hissed and grated.

"Hm," said Frances, "very matey."

"I asked him about light-fishing before."

"Well, there's something for us, anyway. Detection without tears. Colin's not along that way, or Stratos would hardly welcome visitors." She turned to go, then said quickly, "What's the matter?"

I was standing still, like a dummy, with the back of my hand to my mouth.

"Frances! The *Eros!*"

"The what?"

"He's got a boat, a big one, lying in the harbour! *That's* where he'll be!"

She said nothing for a moment, regarding me with a frowning look I couldn't quite read. Then she nodded. "Yes, that's something we could try. If we're allowed near the *Eros*, we may be sure she's innocent; if not, then I think you can certainly go straight up to look for Mark tomorrow. It would be the easiest thing in the world for those two to bring their caique in after dark, and board the *Eros*, and search her. They could be clear away in no time. We could do something about keeping Stratos and Co., away from the harbour—burn down the hotel, or something like that."

I laughed, then looked curiously at her. "Do you know, I believe you meant that?"

"If it was the only thing that would do the trick," said

109

Frances crisply, "why not? There's a boy being frightened and hurt by a bunch of thugs, and what's more, he probably believes, all this time, that his brother's dead. Oh, yes, if a little arson would help, I don't mind in the least burning Mr. Alexiakis' hotel, with him inside it. Meanwhile, we can certainly take a look at the *Eros*. We'll go straight down to-night, if only to put your mind at rest."

"We?"

"Why not? It'd look more natural. Look, is that Tony on the terrace, waiting for us?"

"Yes."

"Then for heaven's sake let's start looking natural straight away. I'm supposed to be a botanist, and you seem to have given me a build-up that would have flattered Linnaeus. Now, would you like to pause one moment, and peer passionately at this plant here—no, *here*, you owl, the one in the rock!"

"Is it rare?"

"Darling, it grows in every wall in the South of England. It's pellitory-of-the-wall, but you can bet your boots Tony won't know that! Go on, pick a bit, or one of those mesembryanthemums or something. Show willing."

"The ice-daisies?" I stooped obediently. Tony was waiting under the tamarisks, not fifty yards away. "Look," I said, holding it out to her, "they've shut. Don't they look like tiny plastic parasols?"

"Dear heaven," said Frances devoutly, "and to think I once hoped to make a naturalist of you! And another thing, that egret you mentioned; according to the books, there are no egrets in Greece."

"I know that." Without looking his way, I knew that Tony had come out from under the tamarisks, and was standing at the edge of the gravel. My voice must be carrying clearly to him. "Just as there aren't any golden orioles, either—officially. But I've seen them at Epidaurus, and honestly, Frances, I saw a pair today between Chania and Kastelli, and I couldn't be wrong about a golden oriole; what else could they have been? I admit I might be wrong about the egret, but I can't think what else that was, either!"

"A squacco heron? They look white in flight. Oh, no, you said black legs and yellow feet. . . . Why, hullo, Tony, something smells good."

I said cheerfully, "I hope it's not the octopus I saw down at the harbour today?"

"No, my dears, it's a *fricassée*, my very own *fricassée* of

110

veal . . . done with wine, and mushrooms, and tiny, tiny peas. I call it *veau à jouer*."

"Why on earth?"

"Well, veal by Gamble," explained Tony. "Now, ladies, dinner's almost ready. I'll have your drinks waiting for you when you come down. What's it to be?"

CHAPTER : ELEVEN

What bird so sings, yet so does wail?
O 'tis the ravish'd nightingale.
   Jug, jug, jug, jug, tereu, she cries,
   And still her woes at midnight rise.

Lyly: Campaspe.

THE CAIQUE was still where she had been, lying without movement in the still waters of the harbour. There was a riding-light on the mast; its reflection glimmered, stilly, feet below the level of her keel. Another light, bigger, glowed in its iron tripod at the end of the pier. Apart from these, all was darkness, and the dank, salt smell of the harbour water.

The youth, Alkis, must have left the caique for the night, for the dinghy no longer nuzzled her sides. It lay alongside the pier, at our feet.

We regarded it in silence.

Then a voice spoke suddenly from somewhere beside my elbow, nearly startling me straight into the harbour.

"You want to row out?" asked Georgi. "I'll take you!"

I glanced at the caique again, lying so quietly in the darkness. Stratos was away fishing, Tony was in the bar, Alkis had presumably gone home. On the face of it, it looked like the sort of chance that shouldn't be missed. . . . But . . . with Georgi? If Alkis had made the offer, well and good. That would have been proof enough, and we could have refused him, with another possibility safely eliminated. But to row across now, and, perhaps, actually find Colin there . . . in the village . . . at this time of night . . .

"What's he saying?" asked Frances.

I told her of Georgi's offer, and my own conclusions.

"I'm afraid you're right. We'll have to wait till morning

to find out. If we did find him on board—" a little laugh—
"the only solution would be to up anchor, and sail full speed
away, *Eros* and all, to meet the other caique. No doubt
that's exactly what your capable friend would do, but let's
face it, this is one of the occasions where being a woman has
its limitations. I suppose you *can't* drive one of those things,
can you?"

"Well, no."

"That's that, then."

"There is the rowing boat." I offered the suggestion with
a marked lack of conviction, and she made a derisive sound.

"I can just see us rowing along the coast of southern Crete
in the pitch darkness, looking for a caique that's been hidden
in a creek somewhere. I'm sorry, but we'll have to accept
our female limitations and wait till morning."

"As usual, you're so right." I sighed. "Well, I'll tell Georgi
that we'll ask Stratos properly, in the morning." I looked
down at the boy, who had been following this incomprehensible exchange wide-eyed. "Thanks a lot, Georgi, but not
tonight. We'll ask Mr. Alexiakis tomorrow."

"We can ask him now," said Frances drily. "Here he comes
. . . and how nice it would have been, wouldn't it, if we'd
both been on the *Eros,* struggling madly with the gears and
the starting-handle? I think, Nicola, my pet, that you and I
must definitely keep to the less strenuous paths of crime."

The soft *put-put* of the light-boat's engine sounded clearly,
now, as she rounded the pier.

"Here he is!" announced Georgi buoyantly, skipping to
the extreme edge of the concrete, where he stood on tiptoe.
"He's been spear-fishing! *Now* you will see the big fish, the
sea bass! He must have got one, or he wouldn't have come
back so soon!"

I found myself watching the boat's approach with, ironi-
cally, relief: at least now there was no question of heroics.
Moreover, they were unnecessary. We could find what we
wanted to find, the easy way. We didn't have to wait till
morning.

We didn't even have to ask; Georgi did it for us. The boat,
with its engine cut, glided alongside, and Stratos threw
Georgi a rope, sending us a cheerful greeting.

"What did you get?" demanded Georgi.

"I wasn't spear-fishing. I've been to the pots. Well, ladies,
out for another walk? It's Miss Scorby, is it not? How do
you do? I see you lose no time in exploring our big city. It's a
pity you didn't take the trip with me, it's a lovely night."

"The ladies were wanting to go to the *Eros*," said Georgi. "Shall I carry those up for you?"

"No, I'm taking the boat round again to the hotel. I came to put some gear on the *Eros*." He stood easily in the rocking boat, looking up at us. "Do you really want to have a look at her? She's not much of a boat, but if you're interested—" a gesture of invitation completed the sentence.

I laughed. "As a matter of fact, it was Georgi's idea, he wanted to row us out. I would like to see her, of course, but let's wait till daylight, when we take that trip. What have you caught?"

"*Schàros*. You'll have it tomorrow; it's very good."

"I've heard of it, but I've never had it. Is that it? How do you catch them?"

"You set pots, rather like lobster pots, and bait them with greenstuff. I assure you, they're better than lobster, and handsome too, aren't they? Here, Georgi, you can take this to your mother. . . . How that boy guessed I'd be coming in this way. . . ." This with a grin and a grimace, as Georgi ran happily off, clutching the fish.

"Was that what he was waiting for?"

"Sure. He knows everything, that child; he'd be a godsend at Scotland Yard. You ladies don't want a lift back to the hotel, then?"

"Oh, no, thank you, we're doing a tour of the town."

Stratos laughed. "'Agios Georgios by Night?' Well, you'll hardly need a guide, or a body guard, or I'd offer to come with you. Good night."

He thrust with an oar against the pier, and the boat drifted away towards the silent bulk of the *Eros*.

We walked back towards the houses.

"Well, I suppose that's something," I said at length. "The caique's innocent, and our tour of the village doesn't worry him, either. *Or* the fact that our nosy little Georgi's sculling around the place night and day, and nattering Greek to me nineteen to the dozen. In fact, I'd have said Stratos hadn't a care in the world. Wherever Colin is, Stratos isn't worrying about his being found."

"No," was all Frances said, but not quite guardedly enough. We were passing a lighted doorway, and I saw her expression. My heart seemed to go small, painfully, as flesh shrinks from the touch of ice.

I said it at last. "You've been sure all along that Colin's dead, haven't you?"

"Well, my dear," said Frances, "what possible reason can they have for keeping him alive?"

The night was very dark. Though it would soon be midnight, the moon was not yet up, and the stars were veiled by cloud. I had borrowed Frances' dark-blue poplin coat, and, hugging this round me, waited at the head of the stone steps outside my room.

There was still a light in Sofia's cottage. Though I had forced myself to admit that Frances might be right about Colin, I wasn't prepared to accept it without an effort, and I was ready to ride herd on Sofia all night if need be, and, if she left the cottage, to follow her. But midnight came, and the next slow half-hour, and still the lamplight burned, though every other house in the village was darkened.

It was twelve-thirty before a move was made, and then it was a harmless one; the crack of light round the cottage door vanished, and a small light flowered behind the thick curtains of the bedroom window. She had sat up late, perhaps to wait for Josef, and now she was going to bed. But I stayed where I was: if Sofia had not stirred from her cottage and the yard behind it, it might be for a good reason. I would give her a few minutes longer, and then, Frances or no Frances, I was going to take a look at that yard myself.

I went like a ghost down the steps, and skirted the open ground like a stealthy cat, hugging the shelter of the pistachio trees. The dust underfoot made silent walking and I slipped soundlessly past Sofia's garden wall, and round the end of her house into the narrow lane that twisted up from the end of the village towards the meagre vineyards under the cliff.

Here was the yard gate, in the wall behind the cottage. Beyond it, visible only as dimly looming shapes, were the huge cone of the baking-oven, the great spiky pile of wood in a corner, and the shed backed against the rough wall that edged the lane.

I wondered if the gate would creak, and put a cautious hand down to it, but the hand met nothing. The gate stood wide already.

I paused for a moment, listening. The night was very still. I could hear no sound from the cottage, and no window faced this way. My heart was beating light and fast, and my mouth felt dry.

Something moved beside my feet, almost startling me into a cry, until I realized it was only a cat, on some errand as secret as my own, but apparently quite ready to welcome a partner in crime. It purred softly, and began to strop itself on my ankles, but when I stooped it slid away from my touch, and vanished.

It seemed I was on my own. I took a long breath to steady those heart beats, then went in through the gate.

The door of the shed must lie to the right. I felt my way towards it, treading cautiously among the debris underfoot.

Somewhere beyond the cottage, across the square, a door opened suddenly, spilling light, and throwing the squat shape of the cottage into relief. As I shrank back towards the shadow of the wood-pile, the light was lopped off again as the door shut, and I heard rapid steps cross a strip of board flooring, then tread quickly across the square through the dust, coming this way.

Stratos, coming over from the hotel to see his sister. If Colin were here—if Stratos came into the yard . . .

He didn't. He pushed open the garden gate and went quietly to the cottage door. It wasn't locked. I heard the latch click, then the soft sound of voices, question and answer. Sofia must have brought the lamp out of the bedroom again, to meet him at the door, for again I could see the faint glow of light from beyond the dark bulk of the cottage.

His visit was certainly not secret, and his purpose, therefore, not likely to be sinister, but while through my confusion I realized this, I wasn't taking any chance of being found by him in Sofia's yard at nearly one in the morning. If I had to be found, much better be found in the lane. . . .

From what I had seen of this in daylight, it was a dirty and unrewarding little cul-de-sac that led up between clumps of cypress, to peter out in a small vineyard under the cliff. What excuse I could give for being there I didn't know, but since Stratos had no earthly reason for suspecting me, no doubt I could get away with the age-old excuse of sleeplessness, and a walk in the night air. And anything was better than being caught lurking here. I melted quickly out of the gate and into the lane.

There I hesitated. One glance towards the hotel was enough to tell me I couldn't get that way without being seen; the light from the cottage door fell clear to the garden wall, and I could even see the moving edge of Stratos' shadow. It would have to be the lane.

I trod softly, hurrying away from the gateway, and almost immediately stepped on a loose stone that nearly brought me down. Before I had recovered, I heard the cottage door shut, and Stratos' quick steps to the gate.

I stood still, face turned away. I could only hope that, coming fresh from the lamplight, his eyes would not yet be adjusted to the dark. Otherwise, if he looked this way as he passed the corner of the wall, he would be bound to see me.

My fists were pressed down hard into the pockets of Frances' blue coat, while my mind spiralled like a feather in a current of air. What could I say to him? What plausible reason could I give for a midnight stroll up this unappetizing dead-end of a lane?

The answer came, piercingly sweet and loud, from a clump of cypresses beyond the wall, a nightingale's song, pouring into the silence from the crowded spires of the grove, and straight away it seemed as if the whole of that still night had been waiting, just for this. I know I held my breath. The trills and whistles and long, haunting clarinet-notes poured and bubbled from the black cypress. The bird must have sung for two full minutes while I stood there, blessing it, and waiting, with one ear still tuned for Stratos' retreating steps.

The nightingale stopped singing. Clearly, ten yards away, I heard the rattle of loose change in a pocket, then the scrape of a match. Stratos had stopped at the corner, and was leisurely lighting a cigarette.

The flaring match seemed unnaturally bright. If he looked up now. . . .

He was lifting his head to inhale the first breath of smoke. My hand, thrust down in the pocket of Frances' coat, met the shape of a packet of cigarettes.

I turned. "Mr. Alexiakis?"

His head jerked round, and the match dropped into the dust, and fizzled out. I moved towards him, with one of Frances' cigarettes in my hand. "Do you mind? Have you a light, please? I came out without one."

"Why, Miss Ferris! Of course." He came to meet me, and struck and held a match for me. "You're out very late, aren't you? Still exploring?"

I laughed. " 'Agios Georgios by Night?' Not really. I did go up to bed, but then I heard a nightingale, and I had to come out to track it down."

"Ah, yes, Tony told me you were keen on that sort of thing." He sounded unworried to the point of indifference. He leaned a shoulder back against the wall behind him, gesturing with his cigarette in the direction of the cypresses. "Up there, was it? They always sing there, ever since I was

116

a boy I remember them. I don't notice them now. Was there one tonight? It's a little early for them."

"Just one, and he seems to have stopped." I smothered a yawn. "I think I'll go to bed now. It's been such a long day, but such a lovely one. Perhaps tomorrow——"

I stopped short, because he had moved with a sharp, shushing gesture, as if some sound had startled him. I had heard it, too, but it had not registered with me as quickly as it had with Stratos; for all that relaxed, indifferent air, the man must be as alert as a fox.

We had been standing close against the wall of the shed that I had come to search. This was built of big, rough stones, crudely plastered, and with many gaps between. The sound had come apparently through some gap just beside us—a small, scraping sound, then a soft rustle as of spilled dust. Something moving, inside Sofia's shed.

Stratos had stiffened, head cocked. I could see the sideways gleam of his eyes in the tiny glow of his cigarette.

I said quickly, "What is it?"

"I thought I heard something. Wait."

Colin, I thought wildly, *it's Colin* . . . but then I saw that fear was making me stupid. If it were indeed Colin, then Stratos would know it, and would certainly not have informed me of the boy's presence in the shed. But if there was someone in that shed, I knew who it would be. . . . I didn't even think of Lambis, who might very well have hung around till dusk to start a close search of the village; my mind jumped straight to Mark. There was no reason why I should have been so sure, but, as clearly as if I had heard him speak, I knew he was there, just on the other side of the wall, waiting and listening, and trying, after that one betraying movement, not even to breathe. . . .

I moved away quickly, scraping my feet carelessly among the stones. "I didn't hear a thing. Are you going back now? It may just have been——"

But he was already moving, and, close to him as I was I could see that his hand had dropped, quite casually, to his hip. As he went through the yard gate I was on his heels.

I had to stop him somehow, somehow give warning. I cried out, "Good heavens, is that a gun?" and put a detaining hand on his arm, holding him back, trying to sound merely nervous and feminine, and, with the genuine tremor in my voice, probably succeeding. "For goodness sake!" I quavered. "You don't need that! It'll be a dog or something, and you really can't just shoot it! Please, Mr. Alexiakis——"

"If it is a dog, Miss Ferris, I shall not shoot it. Now, please, you must let me—ah!"

From the shed had come a whole series of sounds, now quite unmistakable. A scrape and a clatter, a curious clucking noise, and the thud of a small, soft body landing from a height. Then from the half-open door shot a vague, slim shape which slid mewing between our feet, and was gone into the shadowed lane.

Stratos stopped, and his hand dropped from his hip. He laughed. "A cat! This is the criminal on my sister's property! You may calm yourself, Miss Ferris, I shall certainly not shoot *that!*"

"I'm sorry," I said shamefacedly. "That was silly of me, but guns and things do panic me. Besides, you might have got hurt or something. Well, thank goodness that's all it was! I was talking to that cat in the lane a while ago; he must have been ratting."

"Nothing so useful," said Stratos cheerfully. "My brother-in-law keeps a decoy quail in there. The cats can't get at it, but they keep trying. Well, we'll shut the door, shall we?"

He pulled it shut, and turned out of the yard. We walked back to the hotel together.

Sofia's yard seemed darker than ever. The shed door was still shut. The cat had gone, and the nightingale was silent in the cypresses. A cracked bell from somewhere near the harbour told three.

The door opened with only the slightest creak. I slipped through it into the shed, and pulled it shut behind me.

"Mark?" It was only a breath.

No reply. I stood still, listening for his breathing, and hearing only my own. There was brushwood stacked somewhere; I could smell rosemary, and dried verbena, and all the sweet sharp scents of the bed he and I had shared last night.

"Mark?" I began to feel my way cautiously over to the wall that skirted the lane. A small sound behind me brought me round sharply, with eyes straining wide against the dark, but it was only the scrabbling of claws, and a small rustling movement from a corner where the quail's cage must be. No other sound.

I groped my way over to the wall. As my hands met the stone the nightingale, outside in the grove, began to sing again. The sound filled the darkness, full and near. I felt along the wall. Stone, rough stone, cold stone. Nothing else;

and no sound but the rich music from the cypress grove. I had been wrong; Mark hadn't been here after all; the strong sense I had had of his presence had only been something evoked by the verbena-scents of the piled brushwood. It had been the cat, and only the cat, that we had heard.

My hand met something that wasn't stone, something smooth and sticky, and still faintly warm, that made the hair rise up the back of my neck, and my stomach muscles tighten sharply. I pulled the hand away and stood there, holding it stiffly before me, fingers splayed.

So instinct had been right, after all. Mark had been there, leaning against the wall within inches of Stratos and me, perhaps betrayed by exhaustion into some revealing movement, while his shoulder bled against the stone. In sudden fear I stooped to feel if he had fallen there, at the foot of the wall. Nothing. The shed was empty. There was only his blood.

Outside, the nightingale still sang in the cypresses.

I don't remember getting back to the hotel. I know I took no care. But I met no one, and no one saw me running back across the square, with one hand closed tightly over its smeared palm.

CHAPTER : TWELVE

.... One clear day when brighter sea-wind blew
And louder sea-shine lightened, for the waves
Were full of god-head and the light that saves. ...
Swinburne: Thalassius.

THE WATER was smooth and gentle, but with an early-morning sting to it, and a small breeze blew the salt foam splashing against my lips. The headland glowed in the early sunlight, golden above the dark-blue sea that creamed against the storm-beach at its feet.

Here, where I swam, the water was emerald over a shallow bar, the sunlight striking right down through it to illumine the rock below. It threw the shadow of the boat fully two fathoms down through the clear, green water.

Psyche rocked softly at her old moorings, orange and

119

blue. I swam up to her, and threw an arm over the side. She tilted and swung, but held solid, squatly-built and fat-bellied, heavier than she looked. I waited a moment to get my breath, then gripped and swung myself in.

The boat rocked madly, bucked round on her rope, then accepted me. I thudded down on the bottom-boards, and sat there, dripping and panting, and rubbing the salt drops from my eyes.

I had had no reason for coming out to Stratos' boat, except that a boat anchored in a bay is a natural challenge to an idle swimmer. I sat on the broad stern-seat, resting in the sun, and reflecting that this was as good a place as any from which to watch the hotel.

If I had had any doubts about the innocence of Stratos' fishing trip last night, one look at the boat would have dispelled them. There was no hiding place for anything larger than a puppy, and nothing to be seen except the small-boat clutter that one might expect; oars, carefully laid along the sides, a baling-tin, a rope basket for fish, a kind of lobster pot—the *schăros* pot, I supposed—made of cane, a coil of rope, some hollow gourds for use as floats, and a folded tarpaulin. The only things strange to me were the fish-spear —a wicked double trident, with five or six barbed prongs set in a circle—and the glass. This was a sort of sea-telescope, a long metal tube with a glass the size of a dinner plate set in the end. The fisherman lies in the bows, pushes this thing under water as far as it will go, and watches the depths.

I fingered it curiously, then lifted it, and lay down on the flat boarding behind the big brackets that hold the lights. I carefully lowered the glass into the sea, and peered down through it.

You might, in a simpler world, have said it was magic. There was the illuminated rock of the sea bed, every pebble clear, a living surface shifting with shadows as the ripples of the upper sea passed over it. Seaweeds, scarlet and green and cinnamon, moved and swayed in drowsy patterns so beautiful that they drugged the eye. A school of small fish, torpedo-shaped, and barred like zebras, hung motionless, then turned as one, and flashed out of sight. Another, rose-coloured, and whiskered like a cat, came nosing out of a bed of grey coralline weed. There were shells everywhere.

I lay and gazed, with the sun on my back, and the hot boards rocking gently under me. I had forgotten what I had come out for; this was all there was in the world; the sea, the sun hot on my skin, the taste of salt, and the south wind. . . .

Two shadows fled across the glimmering underworld. I looked up, startled.

Only two birds, shearwaters, flying low, their wings skimming the tops of the ripples; but they had brought me back to the surface. Reluctantly, I put the glass back where it had been, and turned to look at the hotel.

People were beginning to move now. A shutter was thrown back, and presently a wisp of smoke curled from the chimney. In the village a black-clad woman carried a jar to the well, and a couple of men were making for the harbour.

I sat there for a little longer, prolonging the moment, basking in the sheer physical joy brought by the salt water and the sun. Then I slid over the boat's side, and swam back to the hotel.

I picked up my towel from under the tamarisks, and padded up the steps to my room. Sofia's cottage door was open, and I caught a glimpse of her moving inside. She was sweeping. Below me, in the restaurant, Tony was singing *"Love me tender"* in a passionate counter-tenor. Stratos, in his shirt-sleeves, was outside in the square, talking to a couple of half-naked workmen with buckets and trowels. In the other cottages, people were moving about.

I went in to dress.

"Not a move out of place," I reported to Frances. "Everything as innocent as the day. I'm beginning to think the whole thing was a mirage." I stretched, still feeling the luxurious physical pleasure of the salt water, and the mood it had inspired. "And, oh my goodness, how I wish it was! I wish we had nothing in the world to think about except tramping off into the hills and looking at the flowers!"

"Well," said Frances, reasonably, setting down her coffee cup—she was finishing her breakfast in bed, while I sat on the edge of the table, swinging my legs—"what else *is* there? We can hardly plan anything. We've done all that lies ready to hand, and it does look now as if Lambis and your Mark have given the village a good going-over between them."

"That's at least the fourth time you've called him my Mark."

"Well, isn't he?"

"No."

Frances grinned. "I'll try to remember. As I was saying, all we can do now is behave as we normally would, and keep our eyes open. In other words, we go out for the day and take the camera."

I remember that I felt a kind of shame-faced relief. "Okay. Where d'you want to go?"

"Well, since we've seen the shore and the village, the mountain seems the obvious choice, so we can extend our search there quite nicely. Anyway, nothing will keep me away from those irises you told me about last night."

"So thick on the ground that you had to tread on them," I said cheerfully, "and cyclamens, all over the rock. And wild gladioli and tulips. And three colours of anemone. A yellow oxalis as big as a penny. Rock-roses the size of breakfast cups and the colour of Devonshire cream. And, of course, if you go really high, those purple orchids that I told you about—"

Frances gave a moan, and pushed her tray aside. "Get out of this, you little beast, and let me get up. Yes, yes, yes, we'll go as high as you like, and I only hope my aged limbs will stand it. You're not pulling my leg about the orchids?"

"No, honestly. Lady's-slippers, or something, as big as field mice, and trailing things, like the ones in shops that you can never afford."

"I'll be with you in half an hour. Get Ceddie to have some lunch put together. We may as well take the whole day."

"Ceddie?"

"Little Lord Fauntleroy. I forgot, your generation never reads," said Frances, getting out of bed. "A thumping good lunch, tell him, *and* some wine."

The on-shore breeze had found its way well inland, and it was deliciously cool by the river-bridge. We went along the river, up the path that I had taken yesterday.

Our progress was slow. Frances, as I had known she would be, was enraptured by everything she saw. The sugar canes, standing deep along the ditches, rustling. A pair of turtle doves, flying up out of a patch of melon flowers. A jay, vivid and chattering. A nest of rock-nuthatches that I found on a broken wall. And the flowers . . . Soon she stopped exclaiming, and in a short while managed to overcome the feeling that one ought not to touch—let alone pick —the pale lilac anemones with indigo hearts, the miniature marigolds, the daisies, purple, yellow and white. Between her delight, and my own delight in her pleasure (for Greece was, I liked to think, my country, and I was showing her round it), we reached the upper plateau with its fields and windmills before I even had time to remember my preoccupations of yesterday.

There were a few people at work among the fields. We saw a man and his wife working with primitive long-handled hoes, one on either side of a furrow of beans. In another field a donkey stood patiently beside the ditch, waiting for its owner. Further on, a child sat on a bank beside a patch of crude pasture where vetches and camomile grew, watching over his little flock of four goats, two pigs, and a ewe with her lamb.

We left the main track and picked our way along the narrow beaten paths between the fields, pausing frequently for Frances to use her camera. Everything made a picture —the child, the beasts, the men bent over their work; even the long views of the plateau and the upper mountain were brought alive by the whirling sails of the windmills. These were everywhere on the plateau, dozens of them, skeleton structures of iron like small pylons, ugly in themselves, but now, with their white canvas sails spread and spinning in the morning's breeze, they looked enchantingly pretty, like enormous daisies spinning in the wind, filling the hot morning with the sigh of cool air and the sound of spilling water.

Then Frances found the irises.

These were the same as I had seen further up the hillside, tiny irises three inches high, lilac and bronze and gold, springing out of ground baked as hard and—you would have sworn—as barren as fireclay. They grew on the stony banks, on the trodden pathway, in the dry verges of the bean field, and swarmed as thick as butterflies right up to the walls of a windmill.

This, as luck would have it, was no ugly iron pylon, but a real mill, one of the two wheat-mills that served the plateau. It was a solidly built, conical structure, much like the windmills we know, with a thatched roof, and ten canvas sails. The sails, unlike those of the water-mills, were furled along their spokes, but this idle mill, with its arched doorway and dazzling whitewash, was beautiful. The irises—in places crushed and trodden—were thick around it, and just beside the doorstep stood a clump of scarlet gladioli. Behind the white mill crowded the lemon groves that edged the plateau, and beyond these rose the silver slopes of Dicte.

Muttering strange oaths, Frances reached for her camera yet again. "My God, I wish I'd brought five miles of film, instead of five hundred miserable feet! Why didn't you tell me that the very *dust* of this country was so damned photo-

123

genic? If only there was some movement! Why aren't the sails going?"

"It's a wheat-mill. The owners only run it when somebody hires them to grind the wheat. Each settlement has two or three, to serve everyone."

"Oh, I see. Well, look, would *you* go into the picture, and—ah, that's lucky, there's a peasant woman . . . just what it needs, the very job. . . ."

The door of the mill had been standing half-open. Now it gaped wider, and a Greek woman, clothed in the inevitable black, and carrying a cheap rexine shopping bag, came out. She turned, as if to pull the door shut, then she saw us, and stopped short in the act, with her hand still out to the big old-fashioned key that jutted from the lock.

Frances' camera whirred on, unconcernedly; but my heart had started to beat in erratic, painful thuds, and the palms of my hands were wet.

I thought, If I tell Frances that's Sofia, that'll be two of us acting our heads off, instead of only one. Frances, at least, must be left to behave naturally. . . .

The camera stopped. Frances lowered it, and waved and smiled at Sofia, who stood like stone, staring at us, with her hand still out to the door.

"Nicola, go and tell her it's a movie, will you? There's no need to pose, I want her moving. Ask her if she minds. And get in the picture yourself, please; I want that turquoise frock beside the gladioli. Just walk up to her and say something. Anything."

Just walk up to her and say something. Dead easy, that was. *"Have you got Colin Langley hidden in the mill, Sofia?"* The sixty-four-thousand-dollar question.

I swallowed. I was scrubbing my hands surreptitiously on my handkerchief. "I'll ask her," I said, steadily enough, "to show me into the mill. You'll get a good picture as we go into that dark archway."

I walked across the irises to greet Sofia.

Frances still has the film. It is the only one, of many which she has of me, in which I walk and behave as if quite oblivious of the camera. As a rule, in front of a camera, I am stiff and shy. But on this occasion I wasn't thinking about Frances and her film, only about the woman who stood unmoving in the bright sunlight, with that half-shut door beside her, and her hand on the big key. It is a very effective piece of film, but I have never liked watching it. This was not a day that I care, now, to remember.

I trod through the irises, and smiled.

"Good morning, *kyria*, I hope you don't mind being photographed? This is my cousin, who's very keen, and she'd like a picture of you and the mill. This is your mill?"

"Yes," said Sofia. I saw her tongue wet her lips. She bobbed her half-curtsey at Frances, who made some gesture of greeting, and called out "How do you do?" I hoped that both would assume that an introduction had been made.

"It's a moving picture." My voice sounded strained, and I cleared my throat. "She just wants us to stand and talk here for a moment . . . there, you can hear the camera going again . . . and then, perhaps, walk into the mill."

"Walk—into the mill?"

"Why, yes, if you don't mind? It makes a bit of action, you see, for the film. May we?"

For one long, heart-stopping minute I thought she was going to refuse, then she put a hand flat against the door, and pushed it wide. With an inclination of the head, and a gesture, she invited me in. It was a movement of great dignity, and I heard Frances give a little grunt of satisfaction as the camera got it.

I mounted the single step, and went into the mill.

Just inside the door a stone stairway, built against the wall, spiralled upwards. Within its curve, on the ground, stood sacks of grain, and a pile of brushwood for repairing the thatch. Against the wall was a stack of tools; a rough hoe, a spade, something that was probably a harrow, and a coil of light rope. A sieve hung from a nail.

I couldn't hear if the camera was still going. Sofia was just behind me. I looked up the curling stairway.

"May I go up?" Already, while I was speaking, I had mounted two steps, and my foot was on a third before I paused to glance back at her. "I've always wanted to see inside a mill, but the only other one I've been to was derelict. That was on Paros. . . ."

Sofia had her back to the light, and I couldn't see her face. Again I sensed that hesitation, and again my pulses thudded, while I gripped the narrow handrail. But she could hardly, without a boorishness comparable to my own, have refused.

"Please do." Her voice was colourless. She put her bag down on the floor, and followed me closely up the stairs.

The chamber on the first floor was where the flour was weighed. Here were the old-fashioned scales, a contraption of chains and bar and burnished bowls, which would be slung from a hook on the massive wooden beam. All about the floor stood the big square tins which caught the milled flour as it came down the chute from the grindstones. Some of the tins were full of a coarse, meal-coloured flour. Here, too, were sacks of grain.

But no Colin Langley. And no place to hide him.

So much I took in while I was still climbing out of the stair well. The place was as innocent as Stratos' boat had been. There was no hiding place for anything much bigger than a mouse. As I stepped out on to the boarded floor, a mouse did indeed whisk out of the way between two tins, carrying some titbit in its mouth.

But there was another stairway, and another floor. . . .

Beside me Sofia said, still in that colourless voice that was so unlike her: "Since you are interested, *thespoinís*. . . . That is the chute down which the flour comes. You see? These are the scales for weighing it. You hang them up, so. . . ."

I watched her in the light from the single window. Was it imagination, or was she more waxen-pale than ever in the bright glare of morning? Certainly she was acting with a reserve which might have been construed as uneasiness, or even anxiety, but her stolid peasant dignity had come to her aid, and I could see nothing in her face that I could put a name to; except that, today, my intrusion and interest in her doings was less than welcome.

She had finished whatever she was explaining to me, and began to dismantle the scales with an air of finality.

"And now, if the *thespoinís* will excuse me—"

"Oh, don't put them away yet!" I cried. "I know my cousin'll want to see this—it's terribly interesting! Frances!"

I ran to the stairs and called down, adding warmly, as poor Sofia hesitated, scales in hand, "It's awfully good of you; I'm afraid we're being a lot of trouble, but it really is marvellous to see all this, and I know my cousin will love it all! Here she comes. Now I must just go up *quickly*, and see the rest—"

"*Thespoinís*—" Something had touched that colourless voice at last. It was sharp. "*Thespoinís*, there is nothing up there except the millstones, nothing at all! Do not go up; the floor is rotten!"

This was true. From below I had seen the holes in the boards.

I said cheerfully, not even pausing: "It's all right, I'm

not afraid. After all, I suppose it holds you when you have to come up here to work, doesn't it? I'll be careful. Heavens, are these the grindstones? It's a marvel there's ever wind enough to move them at all!"

I hadn't yet paused to think what I would do if Colin were there, but the small, circular room was empty—if one could apply that word to a space almost filled by the giant millstones, and crowded with primitive machinery.

The ceiling was conical, and was the actual roof of the mill. From the apex of this wigwamlike thatch down the centre of the chamber, like a tent-pole, ran the huge axle on which the millstones turned. These, some eight to ten feet across, looked as if no power short of a steam-turbine could ever move them. Jutting out from the wall was a metal lever by which the whole roof could be swung round on its central pivot, to catch any wind that blew; and a vast, pegged wheel, set at right angles to the millstones, no doubt transferred the drive to them from the sails. This driving wheel was of wood, hand-hewn and worm-eaten, like the floor. But everything was clean, and the room was fresh and very light, for there were two windows cut in the thick walls, one on either side, at floor level. One of these was shuttered, and fastened with a wooden peg; and, beside it, pushed back into a rough pile against the wall, was a jumble of brushwood left over—as was apparent—from a recent job of thatching.

I stepped over the hole in the aged flooring, and looked thoughtfully down at the brushwood. A clay jar hung from a nail nearby, and a short-handled broom stood underneath it. The brushwood looked as if it had just been bundled back against the wall, and the floor had been newly swept. . . .

I wondered how recently the jar had been used, and whether, if I tilted it, I would find a few drops of water still in the bottom. . . .

I had no chance to try, for now Sofia was at the head of the stairs, and I could hear Frances coming up.

I turned quickly. "Frances! This is wonderful, it's like the Bible or Homer or something. Bring the camera up, there's plenty of light!" Then, brightly, to Sofia, "I'm so glad we've seen this! We have nothing like this, you know, in England —at least, I believe there still are some windmills, but I've never seen inside one. May my cousin take a picture? Would it be all right to open the other window?"

I chattered on at her, as disarmingly as I could. After all, she could only be annoyed; I had shown myself yesterday to be a busybody without manners, and if an extension of this character today would get me what I wanted, then my reputation was gone in a good cause.

Frances came quickly up, exclaiming with pleasure. Sofia, unbending perhaps at her palpably innocent interest, moved willingly enough to unlatch the window, and began to explain the action of the millstones. I translated what she said, asking a few more harmless questions, and then, when Frances had started work with the camera, and was persuading Sofia to mime some of the movements with lever and grain-chute, I left them casually—oh, so casually!—and started down the stairs again.

I had seen what I was looking for. Of that I was sure. Sofia had cleaned up efficiently, but not quite efficiently enough. After all, I myself had just done the self-same job in the shepherds' hut, and my eye was fresh to the signs. Nobody who was not looking for it would have guessed that, until recently, a prisoner had been kept in the mill. But I had been looking, and I knew what to look for.

I was sure I was right. The brushwood on the top floor had been ruffled up again, and pushed back, but someone had lain there. And Sofia had swept the floor, but had overlooked the fact of the rotten boards beside the bedding. Some of her sweepings must have fallen through onto the floor below. . . .

I ran lightly down the steps, and paused on the landing. Yes: again I had been right. On the boards beneath the hole were a few fragments of broken brushwood and dusty fronds. This, in itself, would have meant nothing, but among them there were crumbs. It had been a crumb of bread that I had seen the mouse carrying. And here were more, as yet unsalvaged, tiny traces of food which, without the mouse, and the sharpened eyes of suspicion, I would never have seen.

I never thought I should live to be grateful for the time that one has to wait about while Frances takes her films. I could hear her now, conversing with Sofia with—presumably —some success, and much laughter. Sofia, no doubt feeling herself safe, appeared to be relaxing. The whirr of the camera sounded loud in the confined space. I ran on down the stairs.

I had remembered the coil of rope that lay beside the grain sacks. If you had a prisoner, presumably you tied him. I wanted to see that rope.

I reached the ground floor, and paused for a moment throwing a swift glance round me. I could hear them still busy with the camera, and, even if they came down, I should have plenty of warning: they could not see me until they were halfway down the stairs. I bent over the rope.

The first thing I saw was the blood.

It sounds simple when I write it like that, and I suppose I had even been expecting it. But what one expects with the reasoning mind, and one's reactions to it as a fact, are two very different things. I think it was the driving need for haste, and secrecy, that saved me. Somehow, I managed to stay cool enough, and, after the first moment or so, to look more closely.

There was very little blood; only (I told myself) the sort of stain one might get from bound wrists scraped raw with struggling. The slight staining came at intervals along one of the ropes, as it might if it were coiled round someone's wrists.

Somehow, I fumbled among the coils to find the ends of the rope. They were unfrayed, still bound.

As I let them fall back where they had lain, Sofia's shopping bag caught my eye, standing near. Without a second's compunction I pulled the mouth wide, and looked inside.

There wasn't much; a bundle of the faded, red-and-green patterned cloth that I had seen in her house, a crumpled newspaper stained with grease, and another strip of the cloth, much-creased, and stained as if with damp.

I opened the bundle of cloth; there was nothing in it but a few crumbs. The newspaper too; the marks on it could have been made by fat, or butter. She must have brought the boy's food wrapped in paper, then bundled up in a cloth. Then there was the other cloth, the creased strip, that looked as if it had been chewed. . . .

Just that, of course. The boy could hardly have been left here, lying bound. They would have had to gag him.

I dropped it back into the bag, with hands that shook, then pushed the other things back after it, and straightened up.

It was true, then. Colin had been here; and Colin had gone. The unfrayed rope told its own tale; there had been no escape, no bonds sawn through. The rope had been untied, then neatly coiled away, presumably by Sofia when she had cleared away the gag, the bedding, and the traces of food.

But if Colin was still alive—my brain was missing like a faulty engine, but it hammered on, painfully—if they still had Colin, alive, then surely he would still be bound? If the rope was here, discarded, then might it not mean that Colin had been set free deliberately, and that he might now, in his turn, be looking for Mark?

I had been standing, staring blindly down at the clutter of stuff beside the wall. Now, my eyes registered, with a jerk that was almost physically painful, the thing at which they had been staring, unseeingly; the thing that stood there beside the rope, gleaming in its obviousness.

The spade. Once I had seen it, I could see nothing else.

It was an old spade, with a well-worn handle, but the blade shone with recent use, as if it were new. There was still earth clinging to it. Some of this had dried and crumbled, and lay in little piles on the floor. The spade had been used very recently, and for deep digging: not just the dry, dusty topsoil, but the deep, damp earth that would cling. . . .

I shut my eyes on it then, trying to push aside the image that was forming. Someone had been digging; all right, that was what a spade was for, wasn't it? The fields had to be tilled, hadn't they? It needn't mean a thing. Anybody could have been using it, for a variety of reasons. Sofia could have been digging vegetables, or Josef, or Stratos. . . .

And now the picture, unimportant, unremembered until this moment, showed complete—yesterday's picture of these tranquil fields: the sleeping boy; the man, alone, digging behind that patch of sugar cane, beyond the mill. He had been a broad-shouldered man, with a red kerchief round his neck. He had not noticed me, nor I him. But now, in my mind's eye, I could see him again, clearly.

As I had seen him later, when he had finished his work and had come down to Sofia's cottage to tell her what he had done, and that she could come up to the mill to clear away.

Somehow, I got outside. The sun was brilliant on the irises, and a sulphur butterfly quested among the purple petals.

The back of my hand was pressed so hard to my mouth that my teeth hurt it.

"I'll have to tell Mark," I said, against the bitten flesh. "Dear God, I'll have to tell Mark."

CHAPTER : THIRTEEN

Ah! if you see the purple shoon,
The hazel crook, the lad's brown hair,
   The goat-skin wrapped about his arm,
Tell him that I am waiting. . . .

                Wilde: *Endymion.*

"NICOLA—Nicky, honey—what is it?"

"It's all right. Give me a minute, that's all."

"I knew there was something. Look, we can sit down here. Take your time."

We had reached the wayside shrine above the lemon grove. The fields were out of sight; the windmill no more than a gleam of white through the trees. I could not remember getting here: somehow, I must have taken a civil leave of Sofia: somehow waited, while she and Frances exchanged farewell compliments; somehow steered a blind way up through the trees, to stop by the shrine, staring wordlessly at Frances.

"Here," she said, "have a cigarette."

The sharp smell of the match mingled, too evocatively, with the scents of verbena and lavender that grew beside the stones where we sat. I ran my fingers up a purple spike of flowers, shredding them brutally from the stem, then let the bruised heads fall; but the scent of lavender was still stronger on the flesh of my hand. I rubbed it down my skirt, and spoke to the ground.

"They've killed Colin. You were right. And they've buried him down there . . . just near the mill."

There was a silence. I was watching some ants scurrying to examine the fallen flower-heads.

"But—" her voice was blank—"how do you know? Do you mean you saw something?"

I nodded.

"I see. The mill. Yes, why not? Well, tell me."

When I had finished, she sat a little longer in silence, smoking rather hard. Then I saw her shake her head sharply, like someone ridding themselves of a stinging in-

131

sect. "That nice woman? I can't believe it. The thing's fantastic."

"You didn't see Mark, lying up there in the dirt, with a bullet hole in him. It's true enough, he's dead. And now I'll have to tell Mark. We can get the police on it, now that it's too late." I swung round on her, anxiously. "You said you guessed something was wrong. You mean I showed it? Would Sofia guess I knew something?"

"I'm sure she wouldn't. I wasn't sure myself, and I know you pretty well. What could she have guessed, anyway? She's not to know you knew anything about it; and there was nothing to see, not unless someone was deliberately looking for traces."

"It was the mouse. If I hadn't seen the mouse with that bit of bread, I'd never have found anything. I'd have wondered about the brushwood, but it would never have entered my head to hunt for crumbs, or to look at that rope."

"Well, she didn't see the mouse, so it wouldn't occur to her, either. I should stop worrying about that side of it. She'll have gone off quite satisfied with the result of her tidying-up, and you and I are still well in the clear."

The ants were scurrying about aimlessly among the lavender flowers.

"Frances, I'll have to tell Mark."

"Yes, I know."

"You agree I should, now?"

"I'm afraid you'll have to, darling."

"Then—you think I'm right? You think that's what's happened?"

"That Colin's dead? I'm afraid it looks like it. In any case, Mark ought to hear the evidence. It's got well beyond the stage at which he can deal with things himself. Are you going now?"

"The sooner I get it over, the better. What about you?"

"You'll be better on your own, and in any case, I ought to be here to cover up for you if you're late back. I'll stay around, taking film and so on, and then go back for tea, as arranged. I'll tell them that you've gone further than I cared to, but that you'll keep to the paths, and be back by dark." She gave me an anxious smile. "So take care of yourself, and see that you are. I'm not at all sure that I could be convincing if you chose to spend another night up there!"

"You needn't worry about that, I'll be even less welcome than I was last time." I hadn't meant to speak quite so bitterly. I got quickly to my feet, adding prosaically: "Well, the sooner the better. How about dividing the lunch packet?"

My plan, if it could be called a plan—was relatively simple.

It was possible that Mark and Lambis, after last night's foray, had gone back for the night to the shepherds' hut, sooner than undertake the long trek over to their caique. But, if the blood in Sofia's shed was evidence, Mark might not have been able to face the stiff climb to the hut. He and Lambis could have holed up for the night somewhere nearer the village, and it might even be that Mark (if his wound had broken open badly) would have to stay hidden there today.

Whatever the case, it seemed to me that my best plan was to find the track which led across to the ruined church—the track on which the first murder had been committed—and follow that along the lower reaches of the mountainside. It was a reasonable way for a tourist to go, it would lead me in the same general direction that Mark and Lambis would have to take, and it was, as I knew, visible for long stretches, not only from the alp and the ledge, but from a wide range of rocks above.

I remembered how clearly the man had stood out, yesterday, against the stand of cypresses behind the track. If I stopped there, and if Mark and Lambis were anywhere above me, they would surely see me, and I could in some way make it apparent that I had news for them. No doubt—since I had promised that I would only interfere again if I had vital news —they would show some sign, to let me know where they were, and after that I could make my way up to them as cautiously as I could. If no signal showed from above, then I would have to decide whether to go up and look at the ledge and the hut, or whether to push on along the track, and try to find the caique. It was all very vague and unsatisfactory, but for want of more exact knowledge, it was the best I could do.

As for the murderer, whom I was determined, now, to identify with Josef, I had coldly considered him, and was confident that there I ran very little risk. If I should meet him on the track, I had every excuse (including Stratos' own advice to visit the Byzantine church) for being there. It was only after I had exchanged signals with Mark that I should need caution, and then no doubt Mark and Lambis would make it their business to protect me. It was odd that this

133

idea didn't irk me, as it would have done yesterday. Today, I could think of nothing beyond the moment when I should have discharged my dreadful burden of news, and with it the responsibility for future action.

From the shrine, where I had left Frances, a narrow path led up through the last of the lemon trees, onto the open ground above the plateau. Like the track from the bridge, it looked as if it was much used by the village flocks, so it occurred to me that it might eventually join the old mountain road which led towards the church and the "ancient harbour."

This proved to be the case. Very soon my narrow path took me upwards over bare, fissured rock where someone had tried to build a dry wall, to join a broader, but by no means smoother, track along the mountainside.

It was already hot. On this stretch of the hill there were no trees, other than an occasional thin poplar with bone-white boughs. Thistles grew in the cracks of the rock, and everywhere over the dry dust danced tiny yellow flowers, on thread-like stalks that let them flicker in the breeze two inches above the ground. They were lovely little things, a million motes of gold dancing in a dusty beam, but I trudged over them almost without seeing them. The joy had gone: there was nothing in my world now but the stony track, and the job it was taking me to do. I plodded on in the heat, weary already. There is no one so leaden-footed as the reluctant bringer of bad news.

The track did not bear steadily uphill. Sometimes it would twist suddenly upwards, so that I had to clamber up what was little more than a dry water-course. Then, out of this, I would emerge on to a stretch of bare, hot rock that led with flat and comparative ease along some reach of the mountain's flank. At other times I was led—with an infuriating lack of logic—steeply downhill, through drifts of dust and small stones where thistles grew, and wild fig trees flattened by the south wind. Now and again, as the way crossed an open ridge, or skirted the top of a thorn thicket, it lay in full view of the high rocks that hid the shepherds' hut: but whether I could have seen Mark's ledge, or whether he, if he was still there, could have seen me, I did not know.

I kept my eyes on the nearer landscape, and plodded steadily on. It would be time enough to expose myself to the gaze of the mountainside when I had reached the grove of cypresses.

It was with curiously conflicting feelings of relief and

dread that, following the track round a jutting shoulder, I saw at length, dark against the long open wing of the mountain, the block of cypresses.

They were still a fair distance off. About halfway to them I could see the jagged scar, fringed with the green of treetops, which was the narrow gully running roughly parallel to the big ravine up which I had first adventured. It was at the head of this gully, in the hollow olive tree, that Lambis had hidden the provisions yesterday.

It was downhill all the way to the gully. I paused at the edge at last, where the track took a sudden sharp run down to the water. At this point the stream widened into a shallow pool, where someone had placed stepping-stones. Downstream from this, the stream-bed broadened soon into a shallow trough where the water tumbled from pool to pool among the bushy scrub, but upstream, the way I might have to go, was a deep, twisting gorge crowded with the trees whose tops I had glimpsed from the distance. It was the thickest cover I had seen since I had left Frances in the lemon grove, and now, though reason told me that I had no need of cover, instinct sent me scrambling thankfully down towards the shady pool with the thought that, if I must rest anywhere, I would do so here.

Where the track met the pool it widened, on both banks, into a flattened area of dried mud, beaten down by the feet of the flocks which, year in and year out, probably since the time of Minos, had crowded down here to drink, on their journey to the high pastures. There had been a flock this way recently. On the far side the bank, sloping gently up from the water, was still muddy where the sheep had crowded across, splashing the water up over the flattened clay. Superimposed on the swarming slots in the mud I could see the blurred print of the shepherd's sandal. He had slipped in the clay, so that the print was blurred at the toe and heel, but the convoluted pattern of the rope sole was as clear as a photograph.

A rope sole. I was balanced on the last stepping-stone, looking for a dry place to step on, when the significance of this struck me, and—after a horrible moment of teetering there on one leg like a bad imitation of Eros in Piccadilly—I stepped straight into the water. But I was too startled even to care. I merely squelched out of the stream, carefully avoiding that beautiful police-court print, and stood there shaking my soaking foot, and thinking hard.

It was very possible that, as I had first thought, this was the print of the shepherd's foot. But if that was so, he had the same kind of shoes as Mark.

This, again, was possible, but seemed unlikely. Most of the Greek country folk appeared to wear either canvas slippers with rubber soles, or else a kind of cheap laced plimsoll; and many of the men (and some of the women) wore boots, as in summer the dry fields were full of snakes. But rope soles were rare; I knew this, because I like them, and had been trying both in Athens and Heraklion to buy some for this very holiday, but with no success.

So, though it was possible that a Cretan shepherd was wearing these rope soles, it was far more likely that Mark had been this way.

The thought brought me up all standing, trying to revise my plans.

The print was this morning's, that much was obvious. Whatever had happened last night, this meant that Mark was fit enough to be on his feet, and heading away from the village—not for the hut, but back towards the caique.

I bit my lip, considering. Could he—*could* he have already found out what I was on my way to tell him? Had he somehow found his way into the mill, before Sofia had been able to remove traces of its occupant?

But there I checked myself. I couldn't get out of it that way. I still had to try to find him . . . But it did look as if the job might be simplified, for there were other prints . . . A second, much more lightly defined than the first, showed clearly enough; then another, dusty and blurred; and another . . . then I had lost him on the dry, stony earth of the bank.

I paused there, at fault, staring round me at the baked earth and baking stone, where even the myriad prints of the tiny, cloven hoofs were lost in the churned dust. The heat, unalloyed in the gorge by any breeze, drove down from the fierce sky as from a burning-glass.

I realized, suddenly, how hot and thirsty I was. I turned back into the shade, set down my bag, and stooped to drink. . . .

The fourth print was a beauty, set slap down in a damp patch under a bush, right under my eyes.

But not on the track. He had left it here, and headed away from it, up the gully-bottom, through the tangle of trees beside the water. He wasn't making for the caique. He was heading—under cover—up in the direction of the shep-herds' hut.

I gave a heave to the bag over my shoulder, and stooped to push after him under a swag of old-man's-beard.

If it had been shelter I wanted, there was certainly plenty of it here. The cat-walk of trodden ground that twisted up under the trees could hardly have been called a path; nothing larger than rats seemed to have used it, except for the occasional blurred prints of those rope-soled feet. The trees were spindly, thin-stemmed and light-leaved, aspens, and white poplars, and something unknown to me, with round, thin leaves like wafers, that let the sun through in a dapple of flickering green. Between the stems was a riot of bushes, but luckily these were mostly of light varieties like honeysuckle and wild clematis. Where I had to push my way through, I was gratified to notice various signs that Mark had pushed his way through, too. Old Argus-Eyes, I thought, momentarily triumphant. Girl Crusoe in person. Not such a slouch at this sort of thing after all. Mark would have to admit. . . . And there the mood faded, abruptly, back to its dreary grey. I plodded doggedly on.

The stream grew steeper, the way more tangled. There were no more signs now, and if there were footmarks I never saw them. The air in the bottom of the gully was still, and the shade was light, letting a good deal of sunshine through. I stopped, at length, to have another drink, then, instead of drinking, turned from the water with sudden resolution, sat down on a dry piece of fallen tree trunk in the shade, and opened my bag.

I was hot, tired, and exhausted by depression. It was going to help no one if I foundered here. If the news I was bearing (I thought crudely to myself) had knocked the guts out of me, better have a shot at putting them back in working order.

I uncorked the bottle of *King Minos, sec,* and, with a silent blessing on Frances, who had insisted on my taking it, took a swig that would have done credit to Mrs. Gamp and her teapot. After that I felt so much better that—in homage to the gods of the place—I poured a few drops on the ground for a libation, then tackled lunch with something like an appetite.

Frances had also given me at least two-thirds of Tony's generous lunch packet. With a little more help from King Minos, I ate a couple of the fresh rolls crammed with roast mutton, some olives from a poke of grease-proof paper, and then a rather tasteless apple. The orange I would not face, but dropped it back into the bag.

A little stir of the breeze lifted the treetops above me, so that the sun-motes spilled dazzlingly through on to the water, and shadows slid over the stones. A couple of butter-flies, which had been drinking at the water's edge, floated off like blown leaves, and a goldfinch, with a flash of bril-liant wings, flirted its way up past me into some high bushes in an overhanging piece of cliff.

I watched it, idly. Another slight movement caught my eye, a stir of light colour among some piled boulders below the overhang, as if a stone had moved. Then I saw that there was a lamb, or a ewe, lying up there, under a tangle of honeysuckle. The breeze must have lifted the fleece, so that the ruffling wool had shown momentarily above the boulders.

I watched, attentive now. There it was again, the stroking finger of the breeze running along the wool, and lifting it, so that the light caught its edge and it shone softly for a moment, like bloom along the stone.

I had been wrong, then. The footprint had not been Mark's. The sheep were somewhere nearby, and with them, no doubt, would be the shepherd.

I began quickly to pack the remnants of lunch away, thinking, more confusedly than ever, that now I had better revert to my first haphazard plan, and make for the cypress grove.

I got to my feet warily, then stood, listening.

No sound except the chatter of the water, and the faint hushing of the wind in the leaves, and the high liquid twit-tering of the goldfinches somewhere out of sight. . . .

I had turned back downstream, to find a place where I could clamber more easily out of the gully, when it occurred to me that the sheep had been oddly still and quiet, all through the time that I had been eating. I glanced back. It lay on the other side of the stream, some way above me, half-under the overhang. It could have slipped from above, I thought, unnoticed by the shepherd, and it might well be dead; but if it was merely trapped on its back, or held down by thorns, it would only take me a few moments to free it. I must, at least, take time to look.

I stepped across the stream, and clambered up towards the boulders.

The sheep were certainly dead; had been dead some time. Its fleece was being worn as a cloak by the boy who lay curled under a bush, in the shelter of the boulders, fast asleep. He wore torn blue jeans and a dirty blue shirt, and the sheepskin was pulled over one shoulder, as the Greek shepherds wear it, and tied into place with a length of frayed string. This, not Mark, was the quarry I had been stalking. The mud on his rope-soled shoes was hardly dry.

The noise of my approach had not disturbed him. He slept with a sort of concentration, deep in sleep, lost in it. A fly landed on his cheek, and crawled across his eye; he never stirred. His breathing was deep and even. It would have been quite easy to creep quietly away, and never rouse him.

But I made no such attempt. I stood there, with my heart beating in my throat till I thought it would nearly choke me. I had seen that kind of sleep before, and recently—that almost fierce concentration of rest. I thought I had seen those eyelashes before, too; I remembered the way they lay on the brown cheeks in sleep. And the way the dark hair grew.

The thick lashes lifted, and he looked straight at me. His eyes were blue. There was the quick flash of alarm shown by any sleeper who is startled awake to find himself being stood over by a stranger; then a second look, half-relieved, half-wary, as he registered my harmlessness.

I cleared my throat, and managed a hoarse *"Cháirete."* It is the country greeting, and means, literally, "Rejoice."

He stared for a moment, blinking, then gave me the conventional "Good day."

"Kalí méra." His voice sounded stupid and slurred. Then he thrust his knuckles into his eyes, and pushed himself into a sitting posture. He moved, I thought, a little stiffly.

I wetted my lips, and hesitated. "You're from Agios Georgios?" I still spoke in Greek.

He was eyeing me warily, like a shy animal. *"Óchi."* The denial was hardly audible, a thick mutter as he got quickly to one knee, and turned to grope under the bush, where he had put down his shepherd's stick.

This was the genuine article, gnarled fig-wood, polished by years of use. Shaken by a momentary doubt, I said sharply: "Please—don't go. I'd like to talk to you . . . please. . . ."

I saw his body go tense, just for a second; then he had dragged the stick out from where it lay, and was getting to his feet. He turned on me that look of complete and baffling stupidity that one sometimes sees in peasants—usually when one is arguing the price of some commodity for which they are overcharging by about a hundred per cent. *"Then katal-*

avéno (I don't understand)," he said, *"adío,"* and jumped past me, down the bank towards the stream. Round the wrist of the hand that held the stick was tied a rough bandage of cloth in a pattern of red and green.

"Colin—" I said, shakily.

He stopped as if I had struck him. Then, slowly, as if to face a blow, he turned back to me. His face frightened me. It still looked stupid, and I saw now that this was real; it was the blank look of someone who is beyond feeling punishment, and who has long since stopped even asking the reason for it.

I went straight to the root of the matter, in English. "Mark's alive, you know, and he was quite all right, last time I saw him. It was only a flesh wound. That was yesterday. I'm on my way to find him now. I—I'm a friend of his, and I think I know where he'll be, if you'd care to come along?"

He didn't even need to speak. His face told me all I wanted to know. I sat down abruptly on a boulder, looked away, and groped for a handkerchief to blow my nose.

CHAPTER : FOURTEEN

"Wonder of time," quoth she, "this is my spite,
That, thou being dead, the day should yet be light."
                    Shakespeare: *Venus and Adonis.*

"Do you feel better now?" I asked.

It was a little time later. I had made him sit down then and there, by the stream, and drink some of the wine, and eat the rest of the food I had brought. I hadn't asked him any questions yet, but while he ate and drank I told him all I could about Mark's end of the story, and my own.

He said very little, but ate like a young wolf. They had fed him, I gathered, but he "hadn't been able to eat much." This was all he had said so far about his experiences, but the change in him—since the news about Mark—was remarkable. Already he looked quite different; the bruised look was gone from his eyes, and, by the time the *Minos, sec* was half down in the bottle, there was even a sparkle in them, and a flush in his cheeks.

"Now," I said, as he gave the neck of the bottle a final wipe, corked it, and set it down among the wreck of papers that was all he had left of my lunch, "you can tell me all your side of it. Just let me get all this rubbish stowed away, and you can tell me as we go. *Were* you in the windmill?"

"I'll say I was, tied up like a chicken and dumped on a bundle of rubbish," said Colin warmly. "Mind you, I hadn't a clue where I was, when they first took me there; it was dark. In fact, I didn't know till today, when I left, except that I'd got the impression I was in a sort of round tower. They kept the shutters up all the time—in case I saw them, I suppose. What are you doing?"

"Leaving the crumbs for the mice."

"Crumbs for the *mice?*"

I laughed. "You'd be surprised how much the mice have done for us today. Never mind, skip it. How did you get away? No, wait, let's get on our way. You can tell me while we go; and start at the very beginning, when Mark was shot at, and the gang jumped on you."

"Okay." He got to his feet eagerly. He was very like his brother to look at; slighter, of course, and with a frame at once softer and more angular, but promising the same kind of compact strength. The hair and eyes, and the slant of the brows were Mark's, and so—I was to discover—were one or two other things.

"Which way are we going?" he asked briskly.

"For the moment, back down the gully for a bit. There's a place quite near, a clump of cypresses, which you can see from anywhere higher up. I'm going over to that. If he and Lambis are somewhere about, they'll be keeping a lookout, and they'll surely show some sort of signal, then we can go straight up to them, via the gully. If not, then we'll aim for the caique."

"If it's still there."

This thought had been worrying me, too, but I wasn't going to admit it. "It will be. They knew, if you were free, that you'd make straight for it; where else could you go? Even if they've moved it again, you can bet your life they're keeping a good lookout for you."

"I suppose so. If you're going up into the open to signal them, had I better stay down here?"

"Oh, yes. And whichever way we go, we'll stay in cover. Thank goodness, anyway, one of my problems is gone—

141

you'll know the way from the old church to the caique. Come on."

"How did you find me, anyway?" asked Colin, scrambling after me across the stream, and down the narrow gully-path.

"Followed your tracks."

"What?"

"You heard. That's one of the things we'll have to put right before we go. You left some smashing prints down by the stepping-stones. You can sweep them out while I go up to the cypress grove."

"Well, but how did you know they were mine?"

"Oh, I didn't, I thought they were Mark's. You've the same sort of shoes."

"Have a heart, Nicola, he takes nines!"

"Well, I wasn't really thinking. Anyway, you'd slipped in the mud, and the toe and heel were blurred, so the prints looked longer. If it hadn't been for recognizing Mark's shoes, I'd never have noticed them. He was—a bit on my mind, at the time. All the same, you'd better wipe them out."

"Gosh—" Colin sounded thoroughly put out at this evidence of his inefficiency—"I never thought of prints. I suppose, with its being dark, and then I was pretty well bushed—"

"You had other things to think about. Here we are. There, see them? Now, I'll go up, and if there's no one to be seen, then I'll give the all-clear, and you can come out and deal with the evidence, while I show myself up yonder and wait for the green light." I paused, and looked at him uncertainly. In the shadow of the trees he looked disconcertingly like his brother. "You—you will still be here, won't you, when I come back?"

"You bet your sweet life I will," said Colin. "But look here—"

"What?"

He was looking uneasy. "Look, I don't like you going out there, it mightn't be safe. Can't we think of some other way?"

"I'm quite safe, even if I bump head-on into Josef, as long as *you* keep out of sight," I said firmly. "You're very like your brother, aren't you?"

"For my sins," said Colin, and grinned.

He waited there in the dappled shade while I climbed to the rim of the gully. I looked about me. The landscape was as bare of life as on the first four days of Creation. I gave Colin a thumbs-up sign, then set off briskly for the cypress grove.

The track was smooth, the sun brilliant, the sky a glorious, shining blue. The tiny yellow flowers danced underfoot, like jewels in the dust. The goldfinches flashed and twittered over the lavender bushes, and the freckled snake slipping across the path was as beautiful as they. . . .

Everything, in fact, was exactly the same as it had been an hour before, except that now I was happy. My feet were as light as my heart, as I almost ran across the rocks towards the dark, standing shadow of the grove.

I had been wondering how to attract the men's attention quickly. It now occurred to me, for the first time, that there was no reason why I should not simply make a noise. I felt like singing. Well, why not sing?

I sang. The sound echoed cheerfully round the rocks, and then was caught and deadened by the cypresses. Remembering how sound had carried on this same hillside yesterday, I was certain that I would be heard clearly by anyone in the reaches immediately above.

I took my stance, deliberately, in front of the thickest backdrop of cypress, then paused, as if to look at the view. At last I was able to tilt my head, shade my eyes, and stare towards the head of the main ravine.

Even knowing the place as well as I did, it took some time to get my bearings. I had to start from the ravine, and let my eye travel to the rock where the naiad's spring was . . . yes, there was a recess—looking absurdly small—where the flower-covered alp must lie. The shepherds' hut would be back in that corner, out of sight. And the ledge . . .

The ledge defeated me. It might have been in any one of half a dozen places; but I had the general direction right, and I watched patiently and carefully, for something like six minutes.

Nothing stirred. No movement, no flicker of white, no sudden flash of glass or metal. Nothing.

The test was far from satisfactory, but it would have to do. I gave it another minute or two, then turned to hurry back. Overriding even my desire to find Mark quickly was the fear—irrational, perhaps, but nevertheless strong—that Colin, in some mysterious manner, would have vanished again while I was away from him. But no, he was there, sitting under a bush. He rose to greet me, his face eager.

I shook my head. "Not a sign. I honestly didn't expect it.

143

They'll have gone to the caique. So we'll go after them, and we'd better hurry, because I've got to get back."

"Look, you don't have to fag yourself going all that way. I can manage on my own," said Mark's brother.

"I dare say, but I'm coming with you. For one thing, I've got a lot that Mark ought to know; for another, even Josef might think twice before shooting you in front of me."

"Well," said Colin, "let me go in front. I can clear the way a bit with this stick. And give me that bag; I oughtn't to be letting you carry it."

"Thank you." I surrendered the bag meekly, and followed him up the path through the trees.

He went at a fair speed. Every moment he seemed more himself again, and obviously all he wanted now was to find his brother with the least possible delay, and shake the Cretan dust off his rope soles. I didn't blame him.

"What did you sing that for?" he asked, over his shoulder.

"Sing what? I can't even remember what I *was* singing."

"Love me tender."

"Was it? Oh, yes, I believe it was."

"No wonder Mark didn't come out!" he said, laughing.

It was a crudity I wouldn't have expected of him, young as he was. I felt the blood sting my cheeks. "What *do* you mean?"

"Oh, he's a complete long-hair. Nothing more tuneful than *Wozzeck* will do for Mark, or somebody-or-other's concerto for three beer glasses and a bassoon. Charlie's the same, but with her it's show-off; too too drama school for words, Charlie is. Charlie's my sister Charlotte. Julia and I like pop—she's the next youngest to me. Ann's tone-deaf."

"Oh, I see."

"You're a bit out of date, though, aren't you?"

"I suppose so. But look, I'm dying to hear what happened to you. Suppose you tell me, and we might be able to get some sort of a story pieced together before we find Mark."

So he told me, in snatches, breathlessly, as we toiled up the gully.

When Mark had fallen, wounded, from the track, Colin had run to him, only to be dragged back by Stratos and Josef. In the resulting struggle Colin had been knocked on the temple, and had fainted, but only for a few minutes. When he came to, they had secured him with some sort of rough bonds, stuffed a rag in his mouth, and were carrying him downhill, he could not tell in which direction. He kept as limp and still as he could, in the hazy hope that they

144

might leave him for dead, or even relax sufficiently to give him a chance to get away.

It was a long way, and rough, and by now it was fairly dark, so his captors used most of their energy for the trek, and a good deal of their talk was in Greek, but he gathered that they were disagreeing violently about something.

"I can't be absolutely sure I remember properly," he said, "because of course I was muzzy in the head, and scared because I thought they'd murder me any minute—and besides, I was half-crackers about Mark . . . I thought he was either dead, or lying bleeding to death somewhere. But some of the argument was in English—when the ones that called themselves Stratos and Tony got going—and I do remember quite a bit of what was said."

"Try, anyway. It could be important."

"Oh, I've tried. I had nothing else to do for three days except think what it was all in aid of; but it's more *impressions,* than actual *memory,* if you see what I mean. I do know that Tony was blazing mad at them for shooting Mark and taking me along. We'd never have traced them, he said, we hadn't seen them properly; and in any case they could give each other alibis, 'but taking the boy like this—it's stupid!' "

"Well," I said, "so it was. I still don't know why they did it."

"Sofia," said Colin, simply. "I'd had this cut on the head, and I was bleeding like a pig. She thought if they left me, I'd bleed to death, and she made such a fuss and she was so cut up about the whole thing, I gathered, that they gave in, and just hustled me away. It was partly Tony, too. In the end he said that they might get away with Mark's shooting as an accident, but if we were both found dead, or badly hurt, there'd be a fuss that might take in the whole district, and uncover 'Alexandros' murder,' and that would get back to them, and 'the London affair.' "

" 'The London affair'?" I asked sharply.

"I think that's what he said, I can't be sure."

"It could be. And the man who was murdered was 'Alexandros,' was he? It certainly sounds as if he might be someone catching up on Stratos and Tony from their London life, doesn't it? I wonder if he was Greek or English? He talked English to Tony, but then Tony's Greek isn't good."

"He'd be Greek, surely, if his name was—oh, I see, you mean they may just have been, what's the word? giving his name the Greek form?"

"Hellenizing, yes. But it doesn't matter; if you heard right, then he was killed for something that happened in London. I remember now, Tony did say something about London 'not being healthy'—not to me, he was only joking, to some children, but it struck me at the time. Well, to get back to Saturday night, what on earth did they intend to do with you?"

"Quite honestly, I think they were in such a general flap about what had happened, that they were just getting away from it as quickly as they could. I gathered that Stratos and Tony were livid with Josef for losing his head and shooting Mark, and that Josef was all for cutting their losses and killing me as well, then and there, but Stratos was swithering a bit, and Tony and Sofia were dead against it. In the end they sort of gave up, and bundled me off—clear out first and think later; you know. In fact, Tony was all for bolting— really bolting, I mean, getting right away. He wanted to get straight out. I remember all that bit clearly, because I was praying he wouldn't go; with him being English, I thought I might stand a better chance talking to him than the others. And he *hadn't* a part in it, really."

"You mean Tony wanted to clear out on his own?"

"Yes. I remember exactly what he said. 'Well, once you shot that tourist, you landed yourselves, whatever you do with the boy. I had nothing to do with it, or with Alex, and you know that's true. I'm getting out. I'll take my cut here and now, and don't pretend you'll not be glad to see the last of me, Stratos, dear.' That was the way he talked, in a kind of silly voice; I can't quite describe it."

"Don't bother, I've heard it. What did Stratos say?"

"He said, 'They're no use to you, they're still hot. You can't get rid of them yet.' Tony said, 'I know that. You can trust me to be careful,' and Stratos gave a beastly sort of laugh and said, 'I'd as soon trust you as I'd—'" Colin stopped abruptly.

"Yes?"

"Oh, just an expression," said Colin. "A—a slang expression, I can't quite remember what. Meaning that he wouldn't trust him, you know."

"Oh, yes. Well, go on."

The gorge had widened out as we climbed higher. There was room now to walk two abreast.

"Then Stratos said where could he go, he had no money, and Tony said, 'For a start, you can give me some,' and Stratos said, 'Blackmail?' and Tony said, 'Well, I could talk quite a lot, couldn't I? And *I've* done nothing that matters. There's such a thing as Queen's Evidence.' "

"He's got a nerve," I said, half-admiringly. "Fancy coming out with that one, to old Stratos, with two men left for dead, and a bleeding boy on your hands. I—er, I meant that literally."

Colin grinned. "I was, too, buckets of it, and it wasn't much of a cut, when all came to all. Well, I thought Stratos would blow his lid at that, but he must have known Tony didn't mean it, because he didn't answer, and then Tony laughed in that silly way and said, 'Dear boy, we were going to split anyway, so come through with the stuff now, and we'll call it a day. Where is it?' Stratos said, 'When I think it's time to come through, I'll tell you. And not so much of the holier-than-thou stuff, either. What about Alex?' Tony said, 'You mean the other time? I only helped afterwards; it was nothing to do with me,' and Stratos gave that laugh again and said, 'Nothing ever is. You'd like to stand by looking like the Queen of Hearts and keeping your lily hands clean, wouldn't you? Well, you'll get them dirty soon enough. We've got to get the pair of them buried yet. So save your breath.' "

"And that was all?"

"Tony just laughed and said, 'You poor sweets, I'll have some coffee and sandwiches ready for you when you get back from the graveyard.' Then," said Colin, "we got to the mill. I just knew it was a building of some sort, because I heard a door creak open, and then they humped me up the stairs. It was foully bumpy."

"It can't be exactly easy to carry a body up a narrow spiral staircase."

"It's beastly for the body," said Colin cheerfully. "They got a rope from somewhere, and one of them tied me up properly. By that time, Tony had gone. I heard him say, 'I said you could count me out. I had nothing to do with it, and I'll have nothing to do with this, either. If you touch him, you're bigger fools than I thought you were.' And he went."

"The Levite," I said.

"What? Oh, passing by on the other side, you mean? I suppose so, but he may have been some use, because after he'd gone there was another really terrific argument, and the woman started sort of screaming at the men, till it sounded to me as if someone had put a hand over her mouth. It was dark, of course; they used their torch in flashes, and kept well back where I couldn't see them. When Sofia insisted on doing my head, she had her veil pulled right up so's I could only see her eyes. She cleaned my face and put something over the cut. It had stopped bleeding. Then she took that horrible gag out of my mouth and gave me a drink, and made them put a more comfortable one on. She was crying all the time, and I think she was trying to be kind. The men were arguing in whispers, in Greek. In the end Stratos said to me, in English, 'You will be left here, and we will not hurt you. You cannot escape, even if you get the ropes off. The door will be watched, and you will be shot.' I had a feeling that it might be bluff, but I wasn't wild keen to call it, not just then, anyway. And later, when I did try to get free, I couldn't." He paused. "That was all. In the end, they went."

"If I'd only known. I passed your mill twice when you were in it."

"Did you? I suppose," said Colin wisely, "that if there'd been only the one, you'd have thought of it straight away, but with those dozens, all with their sails going, and so conspicuous, you wouldn't even notice them. If you see what I mean."

"Oh, yes. *The Purloined Letter.*"

"The what?"

"A story by Poe. A classic about how to hide something. Go on. What happened next day?"

"Sofia came very early and gave me food. She had to loose my hands and take the gag off for that, so I tried to ask her about Mark, and begged her to let me go. Of course she would know I'd be asking about Mark, but all she would do was shake her head and dab her eyes on her veil, and point up the mountain. In the end, I latched onto it somehow that the men had gone up to look for him by daylight."

"Josef had, anyway."

"Yes, and found him gone. But I wasn't to know that, more's the pity. Mind you, I'd a pretty good idea that once they'd made sure Mark was dead, I'd be for the high jump myself, but I couldn't get any more out of Sofia, when she came again. That night, when she brought my food, she wouldn't talk at all. Her eyes just looked scared, and sort of dumb. Then yesterday morning I knew they'd decided to kill me. I'm sure they had. That's what made me sure Mark was dead."

He might have been discussing the weather. Already the past had slipped away from him in the moment of happiness and present hope. In spite of that tough independence he was, I thought, still very much a child.

He went on: "I didn't think it all out at the time, but, looking back, I think I can see what had happened. They'd been worrying themselves sick about where Mark had got to; Josef must have spent the whole two days out raking the countryside, and found no trace. You said he'd been up to the hill villages too, and he'd have drawn blank there; and of course nothing had happened in Agios Georgios. So they'd reckoned they could count Mark dead. I don't think Josef would ever have thought twice about murdering me, but I expect Sofia made trouble with Stratos, and Tony may have been against it, too—if he ever bothered to mention it again, that is. He may just have shut his eyes and let them get on with it."

"Perhaps. I think you're right, though; I don't see how they could ever have let you go—I know Frances just assumed they'd have murdered you. What happened?"

"It was Josef, not Sofia, who brought the food yesterday. I'd heard a man's boots coming up the stairs and I managed to roll over and peek down through those holes in the floor. He was in that Cretan rig, with a knife in his belt, and the rifle in one hand and my food in the other. He stopped on the floor below, stood the rifle against the wall, and—you remember those square tins?"

"Yes."

"He pulled an automatic out of his pocket, and hid it down behind one of them."

"An automatic? You mean a pistol?"

"Well, I think they're the same. This, anyway."

His hand reached under the sheepskin cloak, to produce a deadly-looking gun. He paused, weighing it on his hand, and grinning at me with the expression of a small boy caught with some forbidden firework.

"Colin!"

"I suppose it's Alex's. Pity he didn't get time to use it first. Heavy, isn't it?" He held it out obligingly.

"I wouldn't touch it if you paid me! Is it loaded?"

"No, I took them out, but I brought them along. See?"

"You seem to know how to handle the thing," I said, reassured.

"Not really, but we mess around with rifles in the Cadets, and one can guess. Not much use against a rifle, of course, but it makes you feel sort of better to have it, doesn't it?"

"For heaven's sake!" I stared at this capable child with—it

149

must be confessed—a touch of exasperation. The rescue was going all wrong. Colin, it now seemed, was escorting me to Mark. No doubt Lambis would be detailed to see me home. . . .

"As a matter of fact," said Colin frankly, "I'm terrified of it." He put it away. "I say, haven't we climbed far enough? It's getting pretty open here."

We were approaching the head of the gorge. Some way further up I could see where the stream sprang out of the welter of rocks and trees under the upper ridge. I thought I recognized the old, arthritic olive tree where Lambis had hidden the food.

"Yes, this is where we leave cover. For a start, you can let me show myself first again, in case anyone's about."

"Okay. But d'you mind if we have a rest first—just for a minute? Here's a decent place to sit."

He clambered a little way up the south side of the gully, where there was some flattish ground, and lay down in the sun, while I sat beside him.

"Finish your story," I said.

"Where was I? Oh, Josef hiding the gun. Well, he picked up his rifle and came on upstairs. While I was trying to eat, he just sat there, with the rifle across his knees, watching me. It put me off my food."

"I can imagine."

"I'd been trying to think up some Greek, but I don't really know any." He grinned. "You just about heard my full repertoire when you woke me up."

"You did wonders. If I hadn't known, I'd just have thought you were dim, and a bit sulky. Where'd you get the fancy dress? Sofia?"

"Yes. Anyway, in the end I managed to think up a bit of classical Greek, and tried that. I remembered the word for 'brother'—*adelphós*—and tried that on him. Apparently it's still the same word. I'd never have thought," said Colin ingenuously, "that Thucydides and all that jazz would ever have come in useful."

"It worked, then?"

His mouth thinned, no longer young-looking. "I'll say it did. He said, *'Nekrós,'* and even if it hadn't been obvious what that means, he drew his hand across his throat, like this, as if he was cutting it. Then he grinned, the stinking little sod. I'm sorry."

"What? Oh—it's all right."

"Mark always goes down my throat with his boots on if I swear."

"*Mark* does? Why?"

"Oh, well—" he rolled over, staring down the gully—"I mean, naturally one swears at school, but at home, in front of the girls, it's different."

"If Charlotte's at Drama School," I said drily, "I'd have thought she'd have caught up with you by now."

He laughed. "Oh, well, I told you he wasn't exactly with it. But he's all right, old Mark, as brothers go." He returned briskly to his narrative. "After that, Josef just shut me up when I tried to speak. It was after he'd gone that I realized he'd let me see him. He'd sat there in full view, with daylight coming through the shutters. The only reason for that I could think of was that they were going to kill me anyway. I tried pretty hard to get away, that day, but I only hurt my wrists. But it wasn't Josef, that evening, after all, it was Sofia. She came very late—it had been dark for hours—and she untied me. I didn't realize at first that she'd done it—I couldn't move. She rubbed my legs, and put oil on my wrists, and bandaged them, then she gave me some soup. She'd brought it all the way in a jug, and it was only just warm, but it was awfully good. And some wine. I ate a bit, wondering how soon my legs would work, and if I could get away from her, then I realized she was signing me to go with her. Mind you, I was scared to, at first. I thought this might be—well, the pay-off. But there wasn't any future in staying where I was, so I followed her downstairs. She went first, and I managed to sneak the pistol from behind the tin, then went down after her. It was pretty dark, just breaking dawn. It was then I saw I'd been in a windmill. The other mills were all standing quiet, like ghosts. It was beastly cold. Oh, I forgot, she'd brought this sheepskin thing, and the stick, and I was jolly glad of them both, I may tell you; I was as shaky as a jelly for the first few minutes. She took me quite a long way, I had no idea where, through some trees and past a little cairn affair—"

"The shrine. There's a Madonna in it."

"Oh, is there? It was too dark to see that. We went quite a way, and then it was light enough to see, more or less, and we'd got to that wide track, so she stopped. She pointed the way to me, and said something I couldn't make out. Perhaps she was telling me it was the track to the church, where they'd first found us; she'd think I'd know the way from there. Anyway, she sort of pushed me on my way and then

151

hurried back. The sun came up with a bang, and it was light, and you know the rest."

"So I missed her, after all. If only I'd pulled myself together, and stayed on watch! Well, then, I suppose you just decided it was safer to lie up in the gully and hide during daylight?"

"Yes. As a matter of fact, I was too tired and stiff to get far, so I thought I'd hole up out of sight and rest for a bit. I had the gun, after all; it made me feel a lot safer." He laughed. "I certainly never meant to go 'out' like that! It must have been hours!"

"You were dead to the world. Are you all right now? Shall we go on?"

"Sure. Man, oh man, *get* those birds! What are they?"

The shadows had moved across the uneven ground below us, swinging smoothly in wide, easy circles. I looked up.

"Oh, Colin, they *are* lammergeiers! Bearded vultures! I thought I saw one yesterday! Aren't they rather gorgeous?"

I could find time, today, to be moved and excited by this rare, huge bird, as I had been moved by the beauty of the speckled snake. I had seen the lammergeier before, at Delphi, and again yesterday, but never so close, never so low, never the two of them together.

As I stood up, they swung higher.

"It's the biggest bird of prey in the 'old world,' " I said. "I believe the wing span's nearly ten feet. And they're rather handsome, too, not like the other vultures, because they haven't got that beastly bare neck, and—Colin? Is anything the matter? Aren't you well?"

He had made no move to rise when I did, and he wasn't watching the birds. He was staring, fixed, at something near the foot of the gully.

I looked. At first, I saw nothing. Then I wondered why I hadn't seen it straight away.

Near a little clump of bushes, not very far from where we sat, someone had recently been digging. The earth lay now in a shallow, barrow-shaped heap, and someone had thrown stones and dry thorns over it to obliterate the marks of recent work. But it had been a hasty job, done perhaps without the right tools, and, at the end nearest to us, the crumbling stuff had already fallen in a bit, exposing an earthy shape that could have been a foot.

The shadows of the vultures crawled across it; and again, across it.

Before I could speak, Colin was on his feet, and slithering down the slope.

"Colin!" I was stumbling after him. "Colin, don't go over there! Come back, *please!*"

He took no notice. I doubt if he heard me. He was standing over the grave. It was a foot, no doubt of that. I grabbed him by the arm.

"Colin, please come away; it's beastly, and there's no point in poking around here. It'll be that man they killed, that poor Greek, Alexandros. . . . I suppose they had to bring him across here, where there was enough soil—"

"He was buried in the field by the mill."

"What?" I said it blankly, my hand falling from his arm.

"He was buried in the field by the mill." Colin had turned to stare at me, with that stranger's face. You'd have thought he'd never seen me before. "I heard them digging. All the first night, I heard them digging. And then again yesterday, someone was there, tidying up. I heard him."

"Yes. Stratos. I saw him." I looked at him stupidly. "Well, who can it be? It's so—so recent . . . You'd think—"

"You were lying to me, weren't you?"

"I? Lying to you? What do you mean?" Then the look in his face shocked me into understanding. I said sharply, "It's not *Mark,* don't be so silly! I wasn't lying, it was only a flesh-wound, and he was better—*better,* do you hear? And last night, even if the wound *was* bleeding again, it—couldn't have been as bad as *that!*" I found I had hold of his arm again, and was shaking it. He stood like stone. I dropped the arm, and said, more quietly, "He'd be all right. Lambis wouldn't be far off, and he'd look after him. It *was* healing cleanly, Colin, I'll swear it was."

"Well, then, who's this?"

"How do I know? It *must* be the man they killed."

"I tell you, he was buried in the field. I heard them."

"All right, you heard them. That still doesn't make it Mark. Why should it?"

"Josef shot him. That was why Josef didn't get back for me last night, when I'll swear he meant to. He was up here, burying Mark. Or else Stratos . . . What time was Stratos at that shed with you last night?"

"One o'clock, twenty past, I hardly know."

"Stratos went back to kill him later. He knew it hadn't just been the cat. He only wanted to put you off and get you back to the hotel, so he could—"

"Mark might have had something to say about that!" I

153

was still trying to sound no more than reasonable. "Give him a little credit!"

"He was hurt. And if he'd been raking round the village for hours, he'd be flaked out, you know he would. If it comes to that, the blood mayn't have been from his shoulder at all. Perhaps that was where Stratos—"

"Colin! Shut up and don't be silly!" I could hear the nerves shrilling through my voice like wires. I swallowed, and managed to add, more or less evenly, "Stratos didn't leave the hotel again before I went back to the shed and found Mark gone. Do you think I wasn't watching? Give me some credit, too! And they'd hardly have killed him in the village and carried him up here to bury him . . . Anyway, what about Lambis? Where's he in all this?"

"Perhaps they killed him, too. Or he got away."

"He wouldn't run away."

"Why not? If Mark was dead, and he thought I was, too, why should he stay? If he'd any sense at all, he'd go . . . with the caique."

His stony insistence was carrying through to me. I found I was shaking. I said, more angrily than I had meant to, "This is all bilge! You haven't a thing to go on! It isn't Mark, I tell you it isn't! It . . . this could be anyone. Why, it mightn't even *be* anyone. Just because a bit of soil looks like a—Colin, what are you doing?"

"I have to know. Surely you see that? I've got to know." And, with a stiff, abrupt little movement, that somehow had whole chapters of horrors in it, he reached out a foot, and dislodged a little of that dry dirt.

A small cascade of it trickled down with a whispering sound. It was the foot that was exposed, and the ankle, in a sock that had been grey. There was no shoe. A bit of trouser leg was showing. Dark grey flannel. There was a triangular tear in it that I remembered well.

There was a moment's complete stillness, then Colin made a sound, a small, animal noise, and flung himself to his knees at the other end of the mound, where the head should be. Before I had quite realized what he was about, he was tearing at the bushes and stones with his hands, flinging them aside, careless of cuts and scratches, digging like a dog into the pile of dirt. I don't know what I was doing; I believe I tried to pull him back, but neither words nor frantic hands made any impression at all. I might as well not have been there. The dust rose in a smoking cloud, and Colin

154

coughed and scrabbled, and then, as he dug lower, the dust was caked. . . .

He was lying on his face. Under the dirt now was the outline of his shoulders. Colin scooped a drift of stony earth away, and there was the head . . . Hiding it, half-buried, was a branch of withered scrub. I stooped to pull this aside, but gently, as if it could have scratched the dead flesh. Its leaves crumpled in my hands, with the smell of dried verbena. And then, sticking up in obscene tufts from the red dust, I saw the dark hair, with the dirt horribly matted over a sticky blackness. . . .

I'm not clear about what happened next. I must have flinched violently back, because the branch I was grasping came dragging out of the piled earth, dislodging as it did so a fresh heap of stuff which came avalanching down from above over the half-exposed head and shoulders. My own cry, and Colin's exclamation as his wrists and hands were buried deep in the falling debris, were followed, sharply, by another sound that split the still air with its own kind of terror. A shot.

I think I simply stood there, stupid and sick, with the branch in my hand, and Colin, startled into a moment's immobility, kneeling at my feet. Then he moved. Vaguely I remember him dragging his hands out of the earth, and more stuff tumbling with its choking cloud of dust, and the branch being torn from my hands and flung down where it had been . . . then I was crouching in the shelter of a thicket a little way off, with my head in my hands, sweating and sick and cold, till Colin came pelting after me, to seize me by the shoulder and shake me, not gently.

"Did you hear the shot?"

"I—yes."

He jerked his head seawards. "It came from over there. It'll be them. They may be after Lambis."

I merely stared. Nothing that he said seemed to mean very much. "Lambis?"

"I'll have to go and see. I—can come back for him later." Another jerk of the head, this time towards the grave. "You'd better stay out of sight. I'll be okay, I've got this." His face still had that stunned, sleepwalker's look, but the gun in his hand was real enough.

It brought me stumbling to my feet. "Wait. You're not going alone."

"Look, I've got to go that way anyway, I've got to find the

155

caique, it's all I can do. But for you—well, it's different now. You don't have to come."

"I do. I'm not leaving you. Go on. Keep right up under the cliffs where the bushes are."

He didn't argue further. He was already scrambling up the side of the gully, where the cover was thickest. I followed. I only asked one more question, and then I didn't quite dare make it a direct one. "Was he—was he covered right up again?"

"Do you think I'd leave him for those stinking birds?" said Colin curtly, and swung himself up among the trees at the gully's edge.

CHAPTER : FIFTEEN

No spectre greets me,—no vain Shadow this:
Come, blooming Hero. . . .

Wordsworth: *Laodamia.*

THE RUINED CHURCH WAS TINY. It stood in a green hollow full of flowering weeds. It was just an empty shell, cruciform, the central cupola supporting four half-cups that clung against it like a family of limpets clinging to the parent, and waiting for the rising tide of green to swamp them. This, it threatened soon to do: a sea of weeds—mallow and vetch, spurge and thistle—had washed already half up the crumbling walls. Even the roof was splashed with green, where the broken tiles had let fern-seeds in to mantle their faded red. A wooden cross, bleached by the sea winds, pricked bravely up from the central dome.

We paused at the lip of the hollow, peering down through the bushes. Nothing moved: the air hung still. Below us now we could see the track running past the door of the church, and then lifting its dusty length through the maquis towards the sea.

"Is that the way to the caique?" I whispered. Colin nodded. He opened his lips as if to say something, then stopped abruptly, staring past me. As I turned to look, his hand shot out to grip my arm. "Over there, see? I saw someone, a man. I'm sure I did. Do you see where that streak of white runs

156

down, above the knot of pines? To the right of that . . . no, he's gone. Keep down, and watch."

I flattened myself beside him, narrowing my eyes against the bright afternoon glare.

His hand came past me, pointing. "There!"

"Yes, I can see him now. He's coming this way. Do you think—"

Colin said sharply, "It's Lambis!"

He had half-risen to one knee, but I shot out a hand and pulled him down. "You can't be sure at this distance. If it was Lambis, he'd be keeping under cover. Hang on!"

Colin subsided. The small figure came rapidly on; there must have been a path there; he made good speed along the hillside, towards where the main track must lie and he was certainly making no attempt at concealment. But now I saw him more clearly; brown trousers, dark-blue seaman's jersey and khaki jacket, the way he moved . . . Colin was right. It was Lambis.

I was just going to say as much, when I saw, a little way beyond Lambis and above the path he was following, another man emerging from a tangle of rocks and scrub where he must have been concealed. He began to make his way more slowly along, above Lambis' path, converging downhill upon it. He was still hidden from the advancing Lambis, but he was plain enough to me . . . the loose breeches and bloused jacket, the red Cretan cap, and the rifle.

I said hoarsely, "Colin . . . behind Lambis . . . that's Josef."

For a seven or eight paralyzed seconds we watched them: Lambis, unaware of his danger, coming steadily and rapidly on; Josef, moving slowly and carefully, and, as far as I could make out, already within easy range. . . .

The gun nosed forward beside me, light trembling on the barrel, which was not quite steady.

"Shall I fire a shot to warn him?" breathed Colin. "Or would Josef—"

"Wait!" My hand closed on his wrist again. I said, unbelievingly, "Look!"

Lambis had paused, turned, and was looking around him as if expecting someone. His attitude was easy and unafraid. Then he saw Josef. He lifted a hand, and waited. The Cretan responded with a gesture, then made his way unhurriedly down to where Lambis awaited him.

The two men stood talking for a few minutes, then I saw Lambis' arm go out, as if he were indicating some path, and Josef lifted the field glasses to his eyes, and turned them eastwards. They swept past the church, the hollow, the bushes where we lay, and passed on. He dropped them, and presently, after a little more talk, moved off again, alone, at a slant which would by-pass the hollow, and take him straight down towards the coastal cliffs.

Lambis stood watching him for a moment, then turned towards us, and came rapidly on his way. His course would lead him straight to the church. And—I saw it, as he came nearer—he now had Josef's rifle.

Colin and I looked at one another.

Lambis?

Neither of us said it, but the question was there, hanging between us, in the blank, frightened bewilderment of our faces. Vaguely, I remembered Lambis' evasive replies when I asked him about his birthplace. It had been Crete; was it here, perhaps? Agios Georgios? And had he used Mark and Colin as the cover for bringing his caique here, for some purpose connected with Stratos and his affairs?

But there was not time to think now. Lambis was approaching fast. I could hear his footsteps already on the rock beyond the hollow.

Beside me, Colin drew in his breath like a diver who has just surfaced, and I saw his hand close round the butt of the gun. He levelled it carefully across his wrist, aiming at the point where Lambis would appear on the track beside the church.

It never occurred to me to try to stop him. I simply found myself wondering what the range of an automatic was, and if Colin was a good enough shot to get Lambis at the foreshortened angle he would present.

Then I came to myself. I put my lips to Colin's ear. "For heaven's sake, hang on! We've got to talk to him! We've got to know what's happened! And if you fire that thing, you'll bring Josef back."

He hesitated, then, to my relief, he nodded. Lambis came out into the clearing below us. He was walking easily, without even a hand on his knife—as well he might, I thought bitterly. I remembered the way he had followed Josef out of sight yesterday—to have a conference, no doubt. Another thought struck me: if Josef had been to the village, then he would have told Stratos and Sofia that I was involved. But they had not known . . . or they surely could not have behaved the way they did. So he hadn't yet been back to the village . . . and now we would do our best to see that he never got back there again.

The rights and wrongs of it never entered my head. Mark was dead, and that thought overrode all else. If Colin and I could manage it, Josef and the treacherous Lambis would die, too. But first, we had to know just what had happened.

Lambis paused at the door of the church to light a cigarette. I saw Colin fingering the gun. There was sweat on his face, and his body was rigid. But he waited.

Lambis turned, and went into the church.

There was the sound, magnified by the shell of the building, of stone against stone, as if Lambis were shifting pieces of loose masonry. He must have used this place as a cache, and he had come this way to collect something he had hidden there.

Colin was getting up. As I made to follow, he whispered fiercely, "Stay where you are!"

"But look—"

"I'll manage this on my own. You keep hidden. You might get hurt."

"Colin, listen, put the gun out of sight. He doesn't know we saw him with Josef—we can go down there openly, and tell him you're found. If he thinks we don't suspect him, we can get the rifle from him. *Then* we can make him talk."

As clearly as if the boy's face were a screen, and a different picture had flashed on to it, I saw the blind rage of grief give way to a kind of reason. It was like watching a stone mask come alive.

He pushed the gun back out of sight under his cloak, and made no objection when I stood up with him. "Pretend you're a bit shaky on your pins," I said, and slipped a hand under his elbow. We went down into the hollow.

As we reached level ground, Lambis must have heard us, for the slight sounds inside the church stopped abruptly. I could smell his cigarette.

I squeezed Colin's elbow. He called out, in a voice whose breathlessness (I thought) wasn't entirely faked:

"Mark? Lambis? Is that you?"

Lambis appeared in the doorway, his eyes screwed up against the sun.

He started forward, "*Colin!* How on earth—? My dear boy —you're safe! Nicola—*you* found him?"

I said, "Have you anything to drink, Lambis? He's just about done."

"Is Mark there?" asked Colin faintly.

"No. Come inside out of the sun!" Lambis had Colin's other arm, and between us we steered him into the church's airy shade. "I was just on my way down to the caique. There's water in the flask. Sit the boy down, Nicola . . . I'll get him a drink."

Mark's haversack lay in one corner, where Lambis had dragged it from its hiding place in a tumble of masonry. Apart from this, the place was empty as a blown egg, the stone-flagged floor swept clean by the weather, and the clustered domes full of cross-lights and shadows, where the ghost of a Christos Pantokrator stared down from a single eye. The rifle stood where Lambis had set it, against the wall by the door.

He was stooping over the haversack, rummaging for the flask. His back was towards us. As Colin straightened, I let his arm go, and moved to stand over the rifle. I didn't touch it, I'd as soon have touched a snake, but I was going to see that Lambis had no chance to grab it before Colin got control. The automatic was levelled at Lambis' back.

He had found the thermos. He straightened and turned, with this in his hand.

Then he saw the gun. His face changed, almost ludicrously. "What's this? Colin, are you mad?"

"Keep your voice down," said Colin curtly. "We want to hear about Mark." He waved the gun. "Go on. Start talking."

Lambis stood like a stone, then his eyes turned to me. He was looking scared, and I didn't blame him. Colin's hand wasn't all that steady, and the gun looked as if it might go off at any moment. And Lambis' question hadn't been quite idle: Colin did indeed look more than a little unhinged.

"Nicola," said the Greek sharply, "what is this? Have they turned his brain? Is that thing loaded?"

"Nicola," said Colin, just as sharply, "search him. Don't get between him and the gun—Lambis, stand still, or I promise I'll shoot you here and now!" This as Lambis' eyes flicked towards his rifle. "Hurry up," added Colin, to me. "He hasn't a gun, but he carries a knife."

"I know," I said feebly, and edged round behind Lambis.

Needless to say, I had never searched anyone before, and had only the vaguest recollection, from films and so on, how it was done. If it hadn't been for the grim relics buried in the gully, and for the look in Colin's face, the scene would have been pure farce. Lambis' English had deserted him, and he was pouring forth a flood of questions and invective which Colin neither heeded nor understood, and to which I didn't even listen. I found the knife straight away, in his pocket, and dropped it into my own, feeling stupid, like a child playing pirates. I stood back.

Lambis said furiously, in Greek: "Tell him to put that thing down, Nicola! What the hell are you playing at, the pair of you? He'll shoot someone! Has he gone crazy with what they did to him? Are you mad, too? Get hold of that bloody gun, and we'll get him down to—"

"We found the grave," I said, in English.

He stopped in mid-tirade. "Did you?" The anger seemed to drop from him, and his face looked strained all at once, the dark sunburn looking almost sickly in the queer cross-lights of the church. He seemed momentarily to have forgotten Colin and the gun. He said hoarsely: "It was an accident. I would have you to understand that. You know I would not mean to kill him."

I was standing back against the doorjamb—the unheeded Doric column—fingering in my pocket the knife I had taken from him. Under my hand I could feel the chasing of the handle, and remembered suddenly, vividly, the pattern of the blue enamelling on the copper shaft. I remembered his using this very knife to slice the corned beef for Mark. . . .

"*You* did it?" I said.

"I did not want him dead." He was repeating himself in a kind of entreaty. "When you get back to your people in Athens, perhaps you will help me . . . if you tell them that this was an accident . . ."

Something broke inside me. Where I found the Greek words I do not know. Looking back, what I spoke was probably mainly English, with bits of Greek and French thrown in. But Lambis understood, and so—he told me later—did Colin.

"*Accident?*" I forgot the need for quiet, and my voice rose sharply. "Accident? Then I suppose it's an accident that you're running round now on the hillside with that swine who shot at Mark and wanted them to murder Colin? And don't think I don't know all about you and your precious friends, because I do! You can take it from me, I know every move your filthy gang have been making—Stratos, and Tony, and Sofia, and Josef . . . and now you! And don't try to pretend you're not in it up to your neck, because we *saw* you— no, hold your damned mouth, and let me finish! Help you? You want shooting out of hand, and I shan't raise a finger to stop Colin doing it, but first of all we want to know just what you're doing in all this. Who pays you, and why? Why did you have to bring him here? And why did you kill him? Why did you have to pretend to save his life, you filthy Judas? Was it because I happened along? If I'd stayed—he was such a marvellous person—if only I'd known—I'd have murdered you myself before I'd have let you hurt him! If only I'd stayed. . . ."

The tears came, then, uncontrollably, but the blurring of my vision didn't prevent me from seeing, over the speechless, half-comprehending stupefaction of Lambis' face, the flash of a different expression, as his eyes flickered from my face to something just beyond me. Behind me, and beyond, outside the door . . .

A shadow moved in the doorway. Baggy breeches and a Cretan cap. A man coming in fast, with a knife in his hand.

I shrieked, "Colin! Look out!"

Colin whirled, and fired. Lambis shouted something at the same moment, and jumped for him. The shot thudded into the doorjamb, midway between the newcomer and me, and the noise slammed, deafeningly, round and round the walls. Then Lambis had Colin's gun-hand; his other arm was tight round the boy's body; the gun went flying to the floor. I never moved. In the same moment that I cried out, I had seen the newcomer's face.

Now I said, "Mark!" in a high, silly voice that made no sound at all.

The shot had stopped him just inside the doorway. Lambis let Colin go, and stooped to pick up the gun. Colin stood blinking against the light, looking dazed and stupid, as if a touch would have knocked him over.

"Colin," Mark said.

Then Colin was in his arms, not saying a word, not making a sound, you'd have sworn not even breathing. "What have they done to you? Hurt you?" I hadn't heard that voice from Mark before. The boy shook his head. "You're really all right?" The boy nodded. "That's the truth? Yes? Then we'll go. This is the end, thank God. We'll go straight to the caique."

I didn't hear if there were any more. I turned and walked past them, and out of the church. Lambis said something, but I took no notice. Regardless now of who could see me, I started up the slope of the hollow, back towards Agios Georgios.

The tears still blurred my eyes, and twice made me stumble; stupid tears, that need never have been shed. I dashed them away. I had cried more over this affair than I remembered having done for years. It was time I got out of it. It was over.

Besides, it was getting late, and Frances would be wondering what had happened to me.

CHAPTER : SIXTEEN

This done, he march'd away with warlike sound,
And to his Athens turn'd.

> Dryden: *Palamon and Arcite.*

BEFORE I had gone thirty yards, I heard him behind me.

"Nicola!"

I took no notice.

"Nicola . . . please wait! I can't go at this speed."

I faltered, then looked back. He was coming down the track with no noticeable difficulty. The only sign of his recent injury was the sling, made from the hanging fold of the Cretan head-dress, that cradled his left arm. He looked very different from the unkempt, half-bearded invalid of yesterday; he had shaved, and washed his hair, but—as with Colin —it was the relief and happiness of the moment that altered his appearance so completely. My first thought was a vague surprise that I should have recognized him so quickly; my second, that the "heroic" costume suited him disturbingly well.

"Nicola—" he sounded breathless—"don't hurry off, please; I've got to thank you—"

"You shouldn't have bothered. It's all right." I thrust my damp handkerchief out of sight into a pocket, gave him a smile of a sort, and turned away again. "You and Colin had better get down to the caique, and away. You're all right now? You look a whole lot better."

"Lord, yes, I'm fine."

"I'm glad. Well, all the best, Mark. Good-bye."

"Wait, please. I—"

"Look, I've got to get back. Frances will be sending out search parties, and it'll take me all of three hours to get home."

"Nonsense!" He was standing in front of me now, squarely

in the middle of the path. "Two hours downhill, if that. Why did you run away like that? You must know—"

"Because it's all over and done with, and you don't want me mixed up in it any more. You and Lambis and Colin can go to your b-boat and sail away, and that is that."

"But, my dear, for goodness' sake give us time to thank you! It's you who've done everything, while I was laid up there, about as useful as a pint of milk! And now everything's wonderful—mainly thanks to you. Look, don't be so upset—"

"I'm not upset at all. Don't be absurd." I sniffed, and looked away from him at the level brilliance of the sun. To my fury, I was beginning to cry again. I rounded on him. "We thought he'd murdered you. We found that grave, and . . . *it* . . . had your clothes on. It was quite horrible, and I was sick. If that isn't enough to upset me—"

"I know. I'm desperately sorry that you should have come across that. It's the man Colin calls Josef; you'll have guessed that. Lambis killed him, yesterday morning, when he followed him down the hill, remember? He didn't mean to; naturally what we wanted out of Josef was information about Colin, but it happened accidentally. Lambis had been stalking him, not daring to get too close, because of the rifle, when he came suddenly round a bend of that gully, and there was Josef having a drink, with the gun laid to one side. I suppose the noise of the stream had prevented his hearing Lambis coming. Well, catching him like that, Lambis jumped him. Josef hadn't time to reach the rifle, and pulled his knife, but Lambis was on top of him, so he didn't get a chance to use it. He went down, hard, with his head against the rock, and that was that."

"I . . . see. Yesterday? When Lambis came back, and sent me away, for the food . . . he told you then?"

"Yes. He'd hidden the body behind some bushes, and come back to report."

"You never said a word to me."

"Of course not. But you see why we didn't dare to go down and stir up the local police? We didn't even know who the man was, or where he was from. And Lambis was worried sick, naturally. I thought it best to let ill alone, until we knew where we were."

"If I'd known . . ." I was thinking about the spectre of Josef, which had stalked so frighteningly behind my shoulder this last twenty-four hours. "You could have trusted me."

"Good God, you know it wasn't that! I just thought the
164

less you knew about that, the better. I didn't want you involved."

That did it. I said furiously: "Involved? Heaven give me strength, *involved*? I suppose I hadn't been involved enough already? I'd been scared to death by Lambis, I'd spent a perfectly beastly night with you, and I'd ruined a very expensive petticoat. I'd also dressed your horrible shoulder, and cooked and slaved and—and *worried* myself silly! About Colin, I mean. And all you could think of was to get rid of me because I'm a g-girl, and girls are no use, and you were too damned bossy and stiff-necked to admit I *could* help! Well, Mr. God-almighty Mark Langley, I *did* find Colin, and if he'd still been locked up in that filthy windmill, I'd *still* have found him! I *told* you I could go about on the mountain and in the village safely, and I can, and I have, and I've found out more than you and that horrible Lambis have in *days*. And you needn't think I'm going to tell you *any* of it, because you can just go and find it out for yourselves! *You* didn't tell me anything, so of course I thought he'd murdered you, and Colin and I were going to shoot you both, and you're jolly lucky we didn't!"

"I'll say we are. That bullet was pretty near on target as it was."

"Stop laughing at me!" I cried furiously. "And don't think I'm crying about *you,* or that I meant a *single word* I said about you to Lambis just now! I couldn't have cared less if it *had* been you in the g-grave!"

"I know, I know—"

"And I'm not crying, I never cry, it was only that awful body . . . and . . . and—"

"Oh, Nicola, darling, I'm sorry, truly I am. I'm not laughing. I'd give anything if the pair of you hadn't had that shock, and I'm desperately sorry you had that fright just now, over Lambis and me. But we'd been planning to go down into the village, you remember, and I thought Josef's clothes might just help me to get by, in the dark." He grinned. "In any case, my own were pretty well past it. Those pants were hardly decent as it was."

"I saw the tear in them when Colin pulled the earth off, and the s-socks had a h-hole in."

And I sat down on a stone, and wept bitterly.

He dropped down beside me, and his arm went round my shoulders. "Oh, Nicola. . . . Dear heaven, can't you see, this is just the sort of thing I was trying *not* to let you in for?" He shook me, gently. "And they weren't my socks, darling, I

165

did draw the line at his footgear and underthings! We took everything else he had, and buried the boots. . . . All right, go on, cry, you'll feel better just now."

"I'm not crying. I never cry."

"Of course you don't. You're a wonderful girl, and if you hadn't come along when you did, we'd have been sunk."

"W-would you?"

"Certainly. I might have died of Lambis' poultices, or Josef would have found me in the hut, or Colin might never have got to us safely. . . . What's more, you saved me from getting shot last night, though you didn't know it. I was in that shed, along with the cat, when you stopped to have a smoke with your fierce friend in the lane."

"I know. I went back later. There was blood on the wall."

"You went back?" His arm moved as a muscle tightened, and I heard his voice change. "You *knew?* So—when you tried to stop that chap coming in—?"

"He's Josef's friend." I was crumpling my wet handkerchief into a small, tidy ball. I still hadn't looked at Mark. "He's one of them. I told you I'd found them."

There was a sharp silence. I heard him draw in his breath to speak, and said quickly: "I'll tell you all about them. I—I didn't really mean it when I said I wouldn't; of course I will. But tell me about you first. When I found the blood last night I thought . . . I'm not sure what I thought. Are you really all right?"

"Yes, perfectly. I knocked my shoulder, swanning around there in the dark, and started it bleeding, but it stopped soon enough, and there seems to be no damage."

"What happened yesterday after I'd left you?"

He dropped his arm and sat back on his heels. "Nothing, really. After Lambis had seen you down to the cultivation, he doubled back to meet me, and we buried Josef after a fashion. It took a fair time, and when we'd finished I was so knocked up that I wasn't much use for anything, but I wasn't going to waste any more time before we took a look at the village. I told you Lambis hadn't been sure which way Josef was heading when he killed him, but the odds were it was Agios Georgios. . . . Anyway, we went down as far as we dared, and lay up above the village and watched till dark. I felt better after the rest, so we got down into the place and did the best kind of search we could. I thought the Cretan clothes a good idea—if anyone caught a glimpse of me skulking up a back alley, I wouldn't look so blatantly foreign, and I might just have got by with grunting 'good night' in Greek. Well, we neither of us found a trace of Colin, as you know. You said he was in a windmill?"

"Yes. But go on. What happened when you got out of the shed?"

"Nothing whatever. I met Lambis as arranged, and we got up into the rocks again and holed up till morning. I was very little use to anyone by that time, and getting pretty sure we'd never find Colin. . . ." A pause. "This morning Lambis went down again, but all I could do was get up to the church to cache our stuff, then take the rifle and hide where I could watch the track where the first murder took place. I thought someone might possibly come to look for Josef, or for traces of me. If they had come, in Josef's clothes I could probably have got well within range before they saw it wasn't him. But never mind that now. Nobody came—not even you. You must have by-passed the track. Which way did you come?"

"We stayed under cover, in the little gully where the body was. Didn't you hear me singing? After I'd found Colin I tried to locate you."

He shook his head. "Not a thing. I wish I had. And Lambis drew blank, too. He'd gone to look at the cultivation."

"This morning? We were there, Frances and I."

"I know. He saw you both at one of the windmills. Was that the one?" He smiled. "There's irony for you. He saw you go in, so he didn't bother about that one; he just hung around till you'd gone, and the Greek woman, then broke into the other mill. And found nothing, of course. Then he made his way back to me. That was all. A fine, useless effort."

"I begin to see why this is such good guerilla country. If it hadn't been so awful it would be comic—the whole boiling of us climbing about on the mountain, with never a glimpse of each other. Was it you who fired a shot?"

"Yes, to guide Lambis to me. A shot's safer than shouting; it's a sound one takes for granted in the country. Did that frighten you, too?"

I shook my head, but said nothing. I wasn't going to explain to Mark that the shot had been the least of my worries at the time. I stuffed the handkerchief away into my pocket, rubbed the back of my hand hard over my eyes, and smiled at him.

"All right now?" he said gently.

"Of course."

"That's my girl." His arm came round me again in a

quick, hard hug, then let me go. "Now come back with me, and we'll have our council of war."

Colin and Lambis were sitting by the bushes that edged the hollow. They had chosen a flat little clearing, where the small flowers grew, and baby cypresses like thin dark fingers pointed up through the green. These smelt delicious in the hot sunshine. Below us, the bank was thick with the creamy rock-roses. The track wound down through them, to disappear among the folded ridges that marked the coast. Here and there, a gap showed a blinding wedge of sea.

As we came up, Colin was laughing at something Lambis had said. The haversack was open between them, and Colin was already rootling purposefully through what food was there. He waved my wine bottle at Mark as we approached.

"Hurry up, Marco Polo, if you want any of this. It's nearly all gone."

"Then I suggest you leave some for Nicola. Where'd you get it, anyway?"

"She brought it."

"Then most certainly she ought to drink it. Hand it over. Here, Nicola, have some now."

"It was for you," I said.

" 'My wine is dew of the wild white rose,' " misquoted Mark, "and what could be nastier, come to think of it? No, really, I'm getting almost used to water; drink it yourself."

As I obeyed, I saw Colin grin at Lambis' puzzled look. "Don't listen to Mark. That was just Keats. Go on, Lambis, this one's a classic, say 'What *are* Keats'?"

Lambis grinned. It was obvious that he was used to being Colin's butt, and for the moment the two of them seemed much of an age. Lambis, like the others, looked quite different; much younger, and with the heavy, sullen set gone from his mouth. I realized that it had been put there by worry, and felt more than ever ashamed.

"Well," he was saying placidly, "what are they?"

Colin opened his mouth to whoop with mirth, then quickly shut it again. "So I should think," said his brother. "If you did but know it, Lambis' English is a darn' sight better than yours. The Lord alone knows where you get it, things must have changed a lot since I was at that Borstal of yours myself. A Borstal—" to Lambis— "is an English school. Now, attention all, this is serious, and we haven't a lot of time. Nicola, here's a place to sit."

As the Greek moved aside to make room for me, I smiled

168

at him a little shyly. "Lambis, I ought to have known. I'm sorry, I truly am. It was only because we'd had such a shock, Colin and I . . . and I honestly couldn't imagine who else *could* be buried there. And then there were the clothes. I said some awful things. Can you forgive me?"

"It does not matter. You were a little disturbed with seeing the dead body. Such things are not nice for ladies." And on this masterly piece of understatement Lambis grinned amiably, and dismissed the matter.

"Well," said Mark crisply, taking charge, "we can't keep you very long, so if you could bear to start . . ."

I said, "I've been thinking. I really think you'd better hear Colin's side of it first. One or two things he overheard, when he was actually in the lions' den, seem to provide a clue to the rest."

So Colin told them the story he had told to me, and afterwards Mark—a rather grimmer-faced Mark—detailed him to keep a lookout with the field glasses, while he and Lambis turned back to me.

"I don't know quite where to start—" I felt suddenly shy— "because a lot of it may mean nothing. Shall I just try to tell you more or less all that's happened, and let you draw conclusions?"

"Please. Even if it's irrelevant."

"*Oriste?*" from Lambis.

"Even if it's rot," translated Colin, over his shoulder.

"Even if it doesn't seem to matter," amended his brother. "Don't take any notice of the brat, Lambis, he's above himself."

"And that," said Colin, "is an idiom, meaning—"

"Belt up or I'll do you," said Mark, coming down to Colin's level with a rush. "Nicola?"

I told them then, as briefly as I could, all that had happened since I had left the mountainside on the previous day. When I had finished, there was silence for perhaps a minute.

Then Mark said, slowly, "It makes a picture, of a sort. I'll try to sum up, shall I, from the fragments we've got? I think you were right—the bits that Colin overheard provide the clue to the rest. The main thing is, that something Stratos had, and had promised to divide later, was 'hot.' " He glanced at Lambis. "That's a slang expression—thieves' language, if you like. It means that they had stolen property in their possession, which the police were on the lookout for, and which could be identified if found."

"In the plural," I said. " 'They' were hot."

"Yes, in the plural. Things small enough, in the plural, to be portable; small enough to come through the Customs (we'll look at that later, but we can assume they brought them from London); things small enough to hide, even in Agios Georgios."

"Jewels?" suggested Colin, bright-eyed. I could see that, for him, this was becoming simply an adventure—something with a happy ending already settled by his brother's presence, to be stored up, and talked about next term at school. At least, I thought thankfully, he didn't seem the type to store up nightmares.

Mark saw it too. He gave Colin a fleeting grin. "All the treasures of the East, why not? But I'm afraid it doesn't really matter terribly what it is . . . for the moment, anyway. All *we* need is a coherent story that we can present to the Consul and the police in Athens . . . something that'll tie up Stratos and Co., good and hard with Alexandros' murder. Once that's done, our end of the story'll be accepted, however many alibis are cooked up in Agios Georgios. If we can establish the fact that Josef was a criminal and a murderer, then Lambis will get away with justifiable homicide, or self-defence, or whatever they do get away with here. And that's all I'm bothered with just now. He wouldn't be in this mess, but for us, and all I care about is to see he gets clear out of it."

Lambis glanced up, caught my eye, and grinned. He had his knife out, and was whittling away at a curly piece of wood, carving it to a shape that looked like a lizard. I watched, fascinated, as it began to take shape.

Mark went on, "Now, it's the London end of it that'll give us the connection. . . . Colin heard them say that any investigation would 'get back to the London affair.' This is what's valuable—we can be sure the connection between Stratos and the murdered man is originally a London one, and it sounds to me as if the London police are on the job already—or have been. The stuff was 'hot,' after all." He paused. "Let's see how much we can assume. Stratos and Tony came from London six months ago, and brought with them this 'hot' stolen property. They have arranged to settle here, probably until the hue and cry has died down, then Tony will take his share, and go. They must have intended to leave England anyway, since Stratos apparently wound up his affairs, and what better cover could they have than Stratos' own home, where he'd come naturally, and where

170

Tony might very well come to help him start up his business? You know—" looking up— "it does sound as if the loot, whatever it is, must be pretty considerable."

"You mean because it's worth a long wait."

"Exactly. You can't tell me your friend Tony wants to spend years of his life in Agios Georgios. Do you think for one minute that that tin-pot hotel is worth his while?"

"Oh, it's a change from the dear old vicarage," I said.

" 'The loot,' " said Lambis. "What is that?"

"The swag," said Colin. "The lolly, the pickings, the—"

Lambis put a hand to the side of his head, and pushed him over into a rosemary bush.

"The stolen property," I said, laughing.

"Order, children," said Mark. "Stratos and Tony, then, are concerned in some crime in London, presumably a top-flight robbery. They blind off with the—they leave the country with the stolen property (how good you are for us, Lambis) and settle down here to wait. Stratos must be the leader, or senior partner, since he has the stuff hidden away, and Tony doesn't know where it is. Then we come to Alexandros."

"He came looking for Stratos," I said. "He knew Tony, and talked English to him, and Tony took him along to meet Stratos. I'll bet Alexandros came from London, too."

Colin rolled over eagerly. "He was their partner in the robbery, and they did him down, and he came to claim his share, so they murdered him!"

"Could be," said Mark, "but Stratos did appear quite happy to cut his sister in on the deal—I mean, divide the, er—"

"Loot," said Lambis.

"—the loot with his sister. So it doesn't seem likely that he'd murder a partner just because he claimed his share. Tony doesn't seem to think there's much risk, anyway."

I said, hesitantly, "Couldn't it be quite simple—that it did happen much as Colin says, but that they did quarrel, and Stratos just lost his temper? I'll swear he's that kind of man; one of those big, full-blooded toughies—*pallikaráthes*, Lambis—who can suddenly lose all his self-control, and who's strong enough to do a lot of damage when he does. And in a country where everybody carries guns as a matter of course. . . . Mark, you saw the actual murder. You said they were shouting. Wasn't it done like that?"

"Well, yes, it was. There were arguing violently, then the whole thing seemed to explode . . . but don't ask me who exploded first, or how. The murder does seem likely to have its roots back in something that happened in London; this 'affair,' whatever it is, that they're so afraid is going to catch them up. Apparently that, let alone the Alexandros murder, is serious enough to frighten them into a dashed silly action like taking Colin along. I imagine that Stratos probably—and Tony certainly—hold British passports. It would be interesting to know if we have an extradition treaty with Greece."

"I can tell you that," I said. "We have."

"Ah," said Mark. He glanced at his watch. "Let's cut this short. I think we've got all we need. We can give the police a lead to Stratos and Co., long before they suspect we're even operative. It shouldn't be hard for the London end to identify a couple of Soho Greeks and a—well, Tony; they're probably marked down as 'wanted' anyway, only they've just not traced them. Then, if the police here slap a watch onto them immediately, they may find the stuff . . . and there's your connection, your motive . . . *and* Lambis in the clear for attacking a potential murderer."

"The police'll have to be quick," I said uneasily. "Stratos must know Colin'd go straight for help."

"If he knows he's escaped. But if Colin was right—and I think he was—then they did mean to kill him, and Sofia knew this. She may let Stratos think Colin has been disposed of. We can't count on it, but she might keep her mouth shut for a while, for her own sake. Stratos'll worry about where Josef has got to, but I doubt if—yet—he'll take the desperate step of bolting from Agios Georgios."

"If I were Stratos," I said, "I'd shift the body—Alexandros', I mean—just in case of an inquiry. It was silly to bury it on their own land."

"If you'd tried burying someone up here in four inches of dust," said Mark, "you'd see their point. But I agree. He very well may. The fact that they put him there at all might mean that they didn't intend Colin to get away, after what he'd seen and heard."

"They *were* going to kill me?"

"I don't see how else they'd be safe," said Mark frankly. "They could be fairly sure I was lying dead somewhere. Without Lambis, I would have been. You can be sure they were only waiting for definite news of me. Even if Sofia had persuaded Stratos to let you alone, she must have known she couldn't protect you forever . . . not from the kind of man

Josef appears to have been, anyway . . . so she decided to let you go."

Colin looked anxious. "Will she be all right when they do find out I've gone?"

Mark glanced at me.

I said slowly, "I'm sure Stratos wouldn't harm her, even if he dared. I've been thinking about it, and I don't think you need worry seriously. He might hit her in a temper, but he'd never kill her. And she's used to rough treatment, poor soul. What's more, the fact that she did save you, may save *her* from quite a lot, once the police inquiries get going." I glanced at Lambis. "And you . . . you can be pretty sure she'll be happier and better off as a widow than she ever has been since she married that beastly waster."

"That is good to hear," was all Lambis said, but I thought his expression was lighter as he bent again over the little lizard.

"It's true. Look, I must go."

"Lord, yes, you must," said Mark. "Sister Ann, do you see anyone coming?"

Colin put the glasses to his eyes again.

"Not a sausage."

"Not a what?" Lambis looked up, blade suspended again over the lizard's spine.

"Not a sausage," repeated Colin. "You know quite well what—"

"I know quite well what not a sausage is," reported Lambis. *"Óchi loukánika.* But I do not know that you have an idiom where it walks about in the mountains. I like to learn."

"Get you!" said Colin, admiringly. I reflected that by the time Lambis had spent a month in the company of the brothers Langley, his knowledge of the odder byways of the English language would be remarkable.

Mark was getting to his feet. I noticed all at once that he was looking tired. There were lines from nostrils to mouth, and a shadow round his eyes. He put a hand down to me, and pulled me to my feet. "I wish you hadn't to go down there."

"The way I feel now," I said frankly, "if it weren't for Frances, I'd go down to your caique with you now, luggage or no luggage, and hightail it straight for Athens! But that's only the way I *feel.* Cold reason tells me that none of them will even think of suspecting that I know anything about it!"

"I'm sure they won't." But the look he gave me was doubtful. "The only thing is . . . I don't feel we can just set off

173

now for Athens, without making quite certain that you and your cousin really are safe."

"Well, but why shouldn't we be?"

"No reason at all. But we've no possible way of knowing what's been going on down there since Colin got away, and I—well, I just don't like cutting communications altogether, without knowing what sort of situation we're leaving behind us. You'll be pretty isolated, if anything should happen, and you're right in Stratos' territory."

I realized then why he was watching me so doubtfully; he was waiting for me to assert my independence. For once, I had not the least desire to do so. The thought of leaving these capable males, and walking down alone to Stratos' hotel, was about as attractive as going out unclothed into a hailstorm.

"When are your friends calling for you?" asked Mark.

"On Monday."

He hesitated again. "I'm sorry, but I really think . . . I'd be inclined not to wait until Monday."

I smiled at him. "I'm with you there. All else apart, I quite definitely do *not* want to be around when the police start nosing about. So I think we'll find a good excuse for leaving, tomorrow as ever was. The sooner I see the bright lights of Heraklion, the happier I shall be!"

"That's very wise." He looked immeasurably relieved. "Can you invent a good reason?"

"Easily enough. Don't worry, we'll think up something that won't alarm your birds. They'll be so glad to get rid of us, all things considered, that they won't ask any questions."

"True enough. Can you get in touch with the boat that was going to pick you up?"

"No, but it's calling at Heraklion first for supplies, and to let the party visit Cnossos and Phestos. Frances and I can have a car sent for us tomorrow, and we'll go to the Astir Hotel and wait for them. . . ." I laughed. "And I defy any harm to come to us there!"

"Fine," said Mark. "The Astir? As long as I know where you are. . . . I'll get in touch with you just as soon as I can."

We had begun, as we talked, to walk slowly back down the slope towards the church. "What will you do when you leave?" I said. "Go to Heraklion, or make for Athens straight away?"

"I'd like to get straight to Athens, to the British authority

174

there, and get the London inquiries started, but I don't know. Lambis, how long will it take us to Athens?"

"In this weather, anything from twelve to fifteen hours."

"Fair enough. That's what we'll do. I imagine the Embassy will rally round with flags flying, when they hear one of their ewe lambs is a witness in the middle of a capital crime."

"They'll be furious, more like," I said ruefully.

"Which brings me to the last thing." We had reached the church, and stopped there, by the door.

"Yes?"

"I said before that I don't want to leave the place tonight, without knowing you're all right."

"I know you did, but how can you? Once I'm clear away from here, you can take it for granted."

"I'm not taking anything about your safety for granted."

It was odd, but this time his cool assumption of responsibility never raised a single bristle: not a stir. All I felt was a treacherous glow, somewhere in the region of the stomach. I ran a hand down the genuine Doric column, rubbing an abstracted thumb along the raw edge of the bullet hole. "I don't see how."

"Well, I've been thinking how. Listen, everyone. Lambis is going with Nicola now, to see her safe down to the fields. Colin and I'll wait here for you, Lambis, in the church. I— I'll rest till you get back. Then we three are going down to the caique, and we'll put straight out from shore. It'll be dusk before long, so we'll wait for that, then move along, well out, till we get west of Agios Georgios. After dark, we'll put in nearer, and lie off for a while. The sea's like glass, and looks like staying that way, thank heaven. Lambis, d'you know anything about the coast west of the village?"

"A little only. It is much like this, small bays at the foot of rocks like these. Near the village there are shallow bays, sandy."

"Is there anywhere where a caique could put in, if necessary?"

Lambis frowned, considering. "I do not know. I have noticed a bay, a little way to the west—"

I said, "I think there is. There's a bay the children called the Dolphins' Bay, past the second headland along from the village. There are rocks running right out into deep water: I saw them from a distance, a sort of low ridge running out like a pier. It must be deep alongside, because the children told me you could dive from them."

Lambis nodded. "I think that is the bay I saw. Past the

second headland to the west of the village? Yes, I noticed the place as we come by."

"Could you put in there, if necessary?" asked Mark.

"I can use my lights, once we have the headland between us and the hotel?"

"Surely."

Lambis nodded. "Then in this weather it should be quite easy. Okay."

"Fine." Mark turned to me. "Now, how about this? If, when you get down there this evening, you think there's the least thing wrong—any sort of suspicion, any danger . . . oh, you know what I mean . . . in other words, if you get the feeling that you and Frances ought to get out of there, and fast, without waiting for morning, then we'll be waiting at the mouth of your Dolphins' Bay till, what shall we say?— two in the morning. No, half past: that should give you time. Have you an electric torch? Good. Well, any time between midnight and two-thirty A.M., we'll be watching for it. We'll have to fix a signal . . . say, two long flashes, then two short, then pause half a minute, and repeat. We'll answer. That do?"

I grinned at him. "Corny."

"Oh, sure. Can you think of anything better?"

"No."

"What happens if the bay's full of light-fishers?" asked Colin.

"It won't be," I said. "There are *schăros* pots there, and they're collected before that time. No, it's fine, Mark. I can hardly wait."

"'Man, oh man, it's terrific!" Colin still had that boys'-adventure-story glow about him.

Mark laughed. "It's pretty silly, really, but it's the best we can do, short of putting into Agios Georgios and scaring every bird within miles."

"It won't be necessary, anyway," I said. "It's just a flourish, to go with that pirate's rig of Mark's. Now I'll go. Anybody coming, Sister Ann?" This to Colin, who had mounted some sort of decaying buttress outside the church wall, and was once again raking the hillside beyond the hollow with Josef's glasses.

"*Óchi loukánika.*"

"Then I'll be off. Heavens, if I make the hotel by dinnertime it's all I'll do! *What* excuse can I give for staying out till now? No, don't worry, I'll simply say I came over to see the church—Stratos suggested it to me himself, so he'll probably be pleased. Nothing succeeds like the truth."

"You told me," said Colin, from above us, "that you were supposed to be collecting flowers."

"Oh, lord, yes! Well, I'll grab a handful or two on the way down."

"Have this for a start . . . and this . . . and this . . ." Colin had already yanked half a dozen random weeds from the overgrown stones above his head. "And I'm sure *this* one's as rare as rare. . . ." He stretched to pull down a straggling handful from a high vertical crack.

"Frances is going to be very impressed by that lot," said Mark drily. "And so's Stratos, come to that."

"Why not? All these are probably howlingly rare in England."

"Including the dandelion? Don't forget he's lived twenty years there, and Tony's English."

"Well, Londoners." Colin scrambled down, unabashed. "They won't know any better. You can tell them it's a Cretan variety, only found here at two thousand feet. And look at that purple thing, dash it, I'll bet they haven't even got *that* at Kew! There, Nicola—" he pushed the bunch of exotic weeds at me— "and don't forget this is *dandeliona Langleyensis hirsuta,* and fearfully rare."

"Well, I wouldn't know any better." I accepted them gratefully, refraining from pointing out that *dandeliona Langleyensis* was, in fact, a hawkweed. "Thanks a lot, I'm sure Frances will love them."

"I'll ring you up at the Astir," said Mark, "and let you know what's going on. Then I suppose we meet in Athens?"

"If we don't all foregather in Dolphins' Bay tonight," I said cheerfully. " 'Bye for now. See you both in Athens. Be good, Colin, take care of Mark. And stop worrying about me. I'll be all right."

"Famous last words," said Colin gaily.

"Shut up, you clot," said Mark, quite angrily.

CHAPTER : SEVENTEEN

But having done whate'er she could devise,
And emptied all her Magazine of lies
The time approach'd. . . .

> Dryden: *The Fable of Iphis and Ianthe*

LAMBIS LEFT ME at the stepping-stones, which was just as
well. Tony was waiting for me at the shrine, sitting on the
rocks among the verbena, smoking.

"Hullo, dear. Had a nice day?"

"Lovely, thanks. I suppose my cousin gave up, and went
back for tea?"

"She did. She seemed quite happy about you, but I was
trying to make up my mind to come and look for you. These
aren't the hills to be messing about on by oneself."

"I suppose not." I sat down beside him. "But I stayed
pretty well on the track, and anyway, if one goes high enough,
one can see the sea. I couldn't really have got lost."

"You could have turned an ankle. Cigarette? No? Then
we'd have had to spend all night looking for you. Calamity!"

I laughed. "I suppose so. But one can't spend one's whole
life expecting the worst, and I did so want to get over to see
the church."

"Oh, so that's where you've been?"

"Yes. My Danish friend told me about it, and Mr. Alexiakis said it was easy to find if one kept to the track, so I went
over. It's a long way, but it's well worth the trek, isn't it?"

Tony blew a smoke ring, and tilted his head gracefully to
watch it widen, blur, and wisp off into the sunlight. "Me,
I wouldn't know, dear, I've never been further than this.
Mountains are not, but not, my thing."

"No? They're not Frances' thing either. At least, they
used to be, but she broke her ankle once, and it's a bit
gammy, so she doesn't do much scrambling now." This was
true.

"So she said. Are those for her?"

"Yes." I allowed myself a dubious look at the flowers in
my hand. Lambis and I had added what we could on the

way down, but even the eye of faith could hardly have called it a selection to excite a botanist. I had intended to root out the more obvious undesirables before I got to the hotel; as it was, I could only hope that Tony hadn't noticed that most of the gems of my collection grew right down as far as the village street. "I don't know if she'll want any of these." I looked hopefully at him. "Do you know anything about flowers?"

"I can tell a rose from a lily, and an orchid from either."

"Oh, well, I don't know much about them myself. I just brought what I saw. Birds are more my line, but Frances says I don't know much about them, either." I turned the bunch of flowers over. "These are probably as common as mud, most of them."

"Well, that's a dandelion, for a start. Really, dear—"

"Hawkweed, quite a different thing. Variety *Langleyensis hirsuta,* and only found above two thousand feet. I do know *that* one. Frances told me where to look for it."

"Oh? Well, you seem to have had quite a day. Did you see anyone else up there?"

"Not a soul." I smiled. "You said we'd come to the right place if we wanted peace and quiet. There wasn't a sign of life, unless you count the birds—and all I saw of *them* was a hoodie, and a pair of lesser kestrels, and a mob of goldfinches near the stepping-stones."

Tony, it appeared, did not count the birds. He got up. "Well, are you rested? Shall we go down?"

"Good heavens, did you come right up here just to meet me?"

"I wanted a walk. The lemons smell good, don't they?" We left the lemon grove, and skirted the field where the wheat mill stood. A swift glance showed me that the door was tightly shut, and that no key jutted from the lock. I looked away quickly, my mind racing. Had Tony really come up here to meet me, perhaps to find out where I had been and what I had seen; or had he come up to the mill? Did he know that Colin was no longer there? If so, did he suspect Sofia, or would he assume that Josef had taken the boy up into the hills to silence him? It was even possible that Sofia herself had confided in him; he, like her, had been opposed to the idea of further murder. I stole a glance at him. Nothing in his face or bearing betrayed that he was thinking of anything more serious than how to avoid the mule-droppings in the track. Certainly there was no hint that he was engaged in a kind of verbal chess with me.

Well, so far we had each made the move we wanted. And if I could, I would avoid letting him make another. Quickly, I tried a diversion. I pointed up into an ilex tree. "Look, there's a jay! Aren't they pretty things? They're so shy at home that you hardly ever see them properly."

"Is that what it was?" He had hardly glanced at it. He made his next move; pawn advancing to queen's square: "Don't you think these windmills are just ducky?"

"They're lovely." I hoped the queen's hesitation wasn't showing. But whatever he knew, or didn't know, I must say and do the natural thing. I said it, with a rough-and-ready compromise. "We took some ciné-film up here this morning —there were people working in the fields, and Frances got some lovely shots of that mill."

"Was Sofia up here?"

"Mr. Alexiakis's sister? Yes, she was. She's very nice, isn't she? I'd never have taken her for his sister; she looks so much older."

"That's the difference between the fleshpots of Soho and the empty fish-nets of Agios Georgios, dear. Especially if your husband's a fisherman who won't fish. Josef's idea of bringing home the bacon is to slope off into the hills armed to the teeth like a Cretan brigand. Not that there's anything to shoot in these parts. If he brings home a rock-partridge once a month he thinks he's done his bit towards the happy home."

I laughed. "Have I seen him yet? Does he spend his time playing backgammon at the hotel?"

"Not he. No, he's off somewhere just now on a ploy of his own. I thought you might have seen him up yonder. That's why I asked. Did Sofia let you into the mill?"

Check to the queen. This diversion hadn't worked, either. Then I saw that my trapped feeling came only from myself, from the guilty knowledge of my own involvement. Tony could have no possible reason for suspecting I knew anything at all. The only reason he would be asking me these questions was if he really wanted to know.

Sofia, then, had told him nothing. For one frantic moment I wondered what to say. Then I saw, sharply, that Sofia would have to protect herself. It was my job to look after my own side, and that included me. It would be no help to Tony and Stratos, now, to know that Colin had gone. They couldn't get him. And Sofia would have to face them some day. Meanwhile I must look after myself, and Frances. The truth was the only armor for innocence.

I had stooped to pick an iris, and this had given me the moment I wanted. I straightened up, tucking the flower into the bunch I carried. "Into the mill? Yes, she did. She was awfully kind, because I think she was in a hurry, but she showed us round, and Frances got some lovely shots of the interior. We were awfully lucky to run across her; I'd never have known whose mill it was, and it's usually kept locked, I suppose?"

"Yes," said Tony. The light eyes showed nothing but mild interest. "You saw the whole works, then? How nice. The mill-stones and all that?"

"Oh, yes. She showed Frances how they worked."

"Ah," said Tony. He dropped his cigarette on the dusty path, and ground it out with his heel. He smiled at me: Tony, to whom it didn't matter whether or not Colin had been murdered in the small hours of the morning; Tony, the passer-by on the other side; the chess-expert who was enjoying a game that made my palms sweat with the effort of being natural. "Well, dear," he said lightly, "I'm glad you had a good day. Ah, there's the bridge, not far to go now. You'll just about have time to change before dinner, *and* it's octopus, which you'll adore, if you've a taste for flavoured india-rubber."

So the game was over. Relief made me as gay as he was. "I don't mind it, but it's not the main dish, surely? Oh, Tony, and I'm ravenous!"

"I gave you each enough lunch for two."

"You certainly did. I ate nearly all of it, what's more, and left the rest for the birds. If you'd given me less, I'd have been down a couple of hours ago. I hope you didn't want the bottle back?"

"No. I hope you buried it out of sight? It offends the gods of the place," said Tony, blandly, "if undesirable objects are left unburied hereabouts."

"Don't worry, I buried it under some stones—after pouring the correct libations with the last of the wine."

"Correct libations?"

"One for Zeus—he was born up there, after all. And then my own private one for the moon-spinners."

"The what?"

"The moon-spinners. Three ladies who spin the moon away every month, to bring a good dark night at the end of it. The opposite of the hunters' moon—a night that's on the side of the hunted things . . . like Josef's rock-partridges."

"A night of no moon," said Tony. "Well, isn't that interest-

181

ing? What my dear old father used to call a night for the Earl of Hell."

I raised my eyebrows. "That seems an odd expression for a vicar."

"A what?" For one glorious moment I saw Tony disconcerted. Then the pale eyes danced. "Oh, yes. But then my father was such an *odd* vicar, dear. Ah, well, I dare say your libation will work. There'll be no moon tonight. Black enough," he added cheerfully, "to hide anything. Or anybody."

Frances was sitting in the garden, but the door to the hall was open, and as soon as Tony and I entered the hotel, she saw us, and came hurrying in.

"My dear! Practically a search-party! Tony was sure you'd be lying with a broken leg, surrounded by vultures, but I assured him you'd be all right! Had a good day?"

"Wonderful! I'm sorry if I worried you, but I decided while I was up there that I'd make for that old Byzantine ruin I told you about, and it's positively miles! But I had a marvellous day!"

Tony had lingered to watch our meeting, but now disappeared through the door behind the reception table. He left it ajar. I heard Stratos' voice say something in soft Greek which I couldn't catch.

Frances' eyes were on my face, worried and questioning. I must have looked very different from the depressed messenger she had seen off that morning.

"Are those for me?" She was conscious, as I was, of the open door.

"Yes. . . . If only you'd come a little bit further up, I found the very thing we were looking for! Brought it back, too, alive and undamaged. Here, hawkweed *Langleyensis hirsuta,* as good as new."

I detached the common little hawkweed from the bunch, and handed it to her. I saw a spasm pass across her face, to be followed swiftly by something like understanding. Her eyes came up to mine. I nodded, every muscle of my face wanting to grin with triumph; but I fought them into stillness. I saw her eyes light up. "It should be all right, shouldn't it?" I said, touching the yellow petals. "It's quite fresh and undamaged."

"Darling," said Frances, "it's a treasure. I'll put it straight away. I'll come up with you."

I shook my head at her quickly. It might be better not

182

to look as if we wanted to hurry off together into privacy. "Don't bother, I'll bring the things down for you when I've changed. Here are the rest. I don't suppose there's much that matters, but there wasn't much time. Order a *tsikóuthia* for me, will you, like a lamb? I'll join you out there till dinner, and let's pray it's soon, I'm starving."

I ran upstairs to my room, where the last of the sunlight still lingered as a rosy warmth on the walls. The shadows of the vine were blurred now, ready to fade and spread into the general darkness.

I took off my linen jacket, and dropped it on the bed, then kicked off my dusty shoes. Only now did I begin to realize how tired I was. My feet were aching, and grimed with dust that had seeped through my canvas shoes. The thin straw matting felt gratefully smooth and cool to my bare feet. I pulled off my frock and threw it after the jacket, then went over to the window, pushed it wide, and leaned on the cool stone sill, looking out.

In the distance, above their gold-rimmed bases, the cliffs towered, charcoal-black. Below them, the sea lay in indigo shadow, warmed, where the sun still touched it, to a deep shimmering violet. The flat rocks near the hotel, lying full in the lingering light, were the colour of anemones. The ice-daisies had shut, and the mats of leaves that covered the rocks looked dark, like seaweed. The wind had changed with evening, and a light breeze blew off-shore, ruffling the water. Two gulls sailed across the bay, shadows identifiable only by their long, grieving cry.

I looked out towards the open sea. A caique was setting out for the night's fishing, with its *gri-gri,* the unpronounceable little Indian file of small boats following behind it, like ducklings behind the mother duck; light-fishers being towed out to the good fishing grounds. Presently, away out, the lights would scatter and bob on the water like points of phosphorus. I watched them, wondering if the mother-boat were the *Eros,* and looked beyond her, straining my eyes over the dimming sea for a glimpse of another caique, a stranger, slipping lightless along, far out.

Then I pulled myself up. This wouldn't do. If I was to play the innocent, I must clear my mind of any thoughts of the others. In any case, they were out of my picture. Lambis' caique would slip past in the darkness towards the Bay of Dolphins, with three people on board who had probably forgotten all about me, and had their faces and thoughts thankfully set for Athens, and the end of their adventure. And meanwhile I was tired, hungry, and dusty, and I was wasting time. If Stratos' hotel would run to a hot bath. . . .

It would. I bathed fast, then, back in my room, hurried into a fresh frock, and quickly did my face and hair. The bell sounded just as I was slipping on my sandals. I seized my handbag, and ran out, almost colliding with Sofia on the landing.

I had apologized, smiled, and asked how she did, before it struck me, like a fresh shock, that this very day I had seen her husband's grave. The thought caught at my speech, and made me trail off into some stammered ineptitude, but she seemed to notice nothing wrong. She spoke with her former grave courtesy, though, now that I was looking for them, I could see the strain lines, and the smudges of sleepless terror under her eyes.

She looked past me through the open door of my room.

"I'm sorry, I should have tidied it," I said hurriedly, "but I've only just got in, and the bell went. . . . I did clean the bathroom."

"But you should not trouble. That is for me." She walked into my room and stooped to pick up my shoes. "I will take these down and brush them. They are very dirty. You went far today, after I saw you at the mill?"

"Yes, quite a long way, right across to the old church your brother told me of. Look, don't bother about those old things—"

"Yes. They must be cleaned. It is no trouble. Did you meet anybody . . . up there?"

I wondered if it was Josef she was worrying about, or Colin. I shook my head. "Nobody at all."

She was turning the shoes this way and that in her hands, as if studying them. They were navy canvas, much the same colour as the ones Colin had been wearing. Suddenly, I remembered the way his foot had prodded at that dreadful grave. I said, almost sharply, "Don't bother about those, really."

"I will do them. It is no trouble."

She smiled at me as she said it, a gesture of the facial muscles that accentuated, rather than hid, the strain below. Her face looked like yellowed wax smeared thinly over a skull, all teeth and eye sockets. I remembered Colin's brilliant blaze of happiness, the vivid change in Mark, and the light-hearted way the two of them had fooled with Lambis. This, we owed to Sofia. If only, if only it were true that Josef had been a brute, and could die unmourned. If only it were true that she had hated him. . . . But could one ever really, honestly, hate a man with whom one had shared a bed, and to whom one had borne a child? I thought not, but then one thinks like that at twenty-two. . . .

I lingered for a moment longer, fretted by that feeling of guilt which was surely not mine, then, on an awkward "Thank you," I turned and hurried down the outer stair and round the side of the hotel to where Frances awaited me with a vermouth for herself and a *tsikóuthia* for me.

"How can you drink that stuff? It's quite revolting."

"All true Philhellenes cultivate the taste. Oh, that's *good*." I stretched back in my chair, and let the drink trickle back over my palate and into my throat. I lifted the glass to Frances, and at last allowed the triumph of the day to reach my mouth and eyes. "It's been a lovely day," I said, "a wonderful day. Here's to . . . us, and our absent friends."

We drank. Frances regarded me smilingly. "I'll tell you something else, you ignorant little blighter. Among that first-class bunch of weeds you brought me, you have put, by—I am sure—the merest chance, a thing that is really quite interesting."

"Great Zeus almighty! Good for me! D'you mean Hairy Hawkweed?"

"I do not. It's this." A few plants stood in a glass of water at her elbow. She detached one of them gently, and handed it to me. "It was clever of you to bring the root as well. Careful, now."

The plant had round leaves, furry with white down, and purple, trailing stems, vaguely familiar. "What is it?"

"Origanum dictamnus," said Frances.

"Oh?"

"You may well look blank. Dittany, to you, a kind of marjoram. You may even have seen it in England—not that you'd have noticed, but it's found sometimes in rockgardens."

"Is it rare, or something?"

"No, but it's interesting that you found it here. It's a Cretan plant—hence the name. *Dictamnus* means that it was first found in this very spot, on Dicte."

"Dicte? The birthplace of Zeus! Frances, this is exciting!"

"And *origanum* means 'joy of the mountains.' Not because it's anything much to look at, but because of its properties. The Greeks and Romans used it as a healing herb, and as a dye, and for scent. They also called it 'the herb of happiness' and used it to crown their young lovers. Nice, isn't it?"

"Lovely. Have you just been looking all this up to impress me with?"

"I have, actually." She laughed, and picked up the book that lay on the table beside her. "It's a book on Greek wildflowers, and it quotes some rather nice things. There's a long bit about *Origanum,* quoted from a medical book by a first-century Greek, Disocorides. It's in a rather heavenly seventeenth-century translation. Here it is." She turned a page and pointed to the place:

Dictamnus, which some call Pulegium Sylvestre (but some Embactron, some Beluacos, some Artemidion, some Creticus, some Ephemeron, some Eldian, some Belotocos, some Dorcidium, some Elbunium, ye Romans Ustilago rustica) is a Cretian herb, sharp, smooth, like to Pulegium. But it hath leaves greater, & downy, & a kind of woolly adherence, but it bears neither flower nor seed, but it doeth all things that the Sative Pulegium, but more forcibly by a great deal, for not only being drank but also being applied and suffumigated it expells the dead Embrya. And they say also that ye goats in Crete being shot, & having fed on the herb do cast out ye arrows. . . . Ye root of it doth warm such as taste it: it is also a birth hastener, & likewise ye juice of it being drank with wine helpeth ye bitten of serpents. . . . But ye juice of it, being dropt into a wound, it forthwith cures.

"What are you looking like that for?" asked Frances.

"Nothing. I was just wondering if the Cretans still used it for healing. I mean, a thing that'll do anything, 'from abortion to snake-bite—' "

"Nothing more likely. They'll have lores passed down, time out of mind. Ah, well, so that's 'the joy of the mountain'." She took it from me, and replaced it in water. "Well, it's nothing very great, I suppose, but it would be very interesting to see it actually growing. Do you remember where you got it?"

"Oh, my goodness, I'm not sure." Lambis and I had, so to speak, grazed in motion, like harried deer. "But I could probably pin it down to within a couple of square miles. Very steep," I added kindly, "about one in three . . . and occasionally perpendicular. Would you have liked—I mean, do you really want to go and see it?" Mark's plan for our leaving was humming in my head like a knell. Poor Frances; it seemed hard. And what danger, what possible danger could there be?

"I do, rather." Frances was watching me with a slightly puzzled look.

"I—I'll try to remember where it was," I said.

She watched me a moment longer, then got briskly to her feet. "Well, let's go and eat. You look dog-tired. Tony has promised octopus, which he says is a delicacy unknown even to the better London restaurants."

"Understandably."

"Oh? Oh dear. Well, all experience is an arch where-through," said Frances. "Oh, give me the polythene bags, will you? It doesn't matter about the rest, but I'd like to get *Origanum* safely under hatches. I'll look at it later."

"Oh, lord, I forgot them. I did get them from your room, but I dropped them in my jacket pocket, and then came down without it. I'll get them now."

"Don't bother; you've done enough for one day; it can wait."

"No, really, it'll only take a second." As we traversed the hallway I caught a glimpse of Sofia, with my shoes in her hand, vanishing through Stratos' office door. She must have finished upstairs, so, I thought thankfully, I shouldn't run into her again. Disregarding Frances' protest, I left her at the restaurant door, and ran up to my room.

Sofia had left it very tidy: my jacket hung behind the door, the discarded dress lay neatly over the chair-back, the towels had been folded, and the coverlet taken off the bed. Frances' polythene bags weren't in the first pocket I tried—when was anything, ever?—but I found them in the other, and ran downstairs again.

Dinner was a cheerful meal, and even the octopus passed muster, as we ate it under Tony's apparently anxious surveillance. The lamb which followed it was wonderful, though I had not even now grown reconciled to eating the tender, baby joints from the suckling lambs. "They can't afford to let them graze," I said, when I saw that Frances was distressed. "There just isn't enough pasture to let them grow any bigger. And if you're going to be in Greece over Easter, I'm afraid you'll have to get used to seeing the Paschal lamb going home with the family to be eaten. The children treat it as a pet, and play with it, and love it; then its throat is cut, and the family weeps for it, and finally feasts on it with re-joicing."

"Why, that's horrible! It's like a betrayal!"

"Well, that's what it's symbolizing, after all."

"I suppose so. But couldn't they use our sort of symbols, bread and wine?"

"Oh, they do. But the Easter sacrifice in their own homes—well, think it over. I used to think the same as you, and I still hate to see the lambs and calves going home to their deaths on Good Friday. But isn't it a million times better than the way we do it at home, however 'humane' we try to be? Here, the lamb's petted, unsuspicious, happy—you see it trotting along with the children like a little dog. Till the knife's in its throat, it has no idea it's going to die. Isn't that better than those dreadful lorries at home, packed full of animals, lumbering on Mondays and Thursdays to the slaughterhouses, where, be as humane as you like, they can smell the blood and the fear, and have to wait their turn in a place just reeking of death?"

"Yes. Yes, of course." She sighed. "Well, I don't feel so dreadful for having enjoyed that. The wine's rather good; what did you say it was?"

"King Minos."

"Then here's to the 'herb of happiness.' "

"Here's to it, and to *hawkweed Langleyensis*—oh!"

"Now what?"

"I've just remembered where I found it, your dittany."

"Oh? Good. I hope it's somewhere I can get at."

I said slowly, "I think it is. It was actually growing at the old church; in fact, it was growing *on* it. And I'm sure there was more where that piece came from."

"That's fine; I'd very much like to see it growing. Did you say there was a reasonable track the whole way?"

"There's a track, yes, but I wouldn't call it 'reasonable.' It's beastly rough in places. You'd be all right, though, if you watched your step. All the same—" I smiled at her, my illogical feeling of guilt fading—"it would be much easier, and far more fun, going by boat. Apparently there's an old harbour not too far from the church. We might take a caique along the coast one day, and just walk straight into the hills from there." I was thinking, thankfully, that now I needn't feel so guilty about having to drag Frances away from here in the morning. We could take a car over from Heraklion to Agia Gallini, and hire a caique from there, and I would show her the exact spot where Colin had pulled the dittany off the wall of the little church.

"We'll have to fix it up," said Frances, "but it can wait a day or two; you won't want to go straight to the same place tomorrow. Oh, Tony, may we have coffee on the terrace, please? If you're ready, Nicola . . ."

"I think I'll get my jacket after all," I said, as I rose. "Give *Origanum* to me; I'll put him out of harm's way upstairs."

I laid the polythene bag with its precious plant carefully on my table, and lifted my jacket down from behind the door. As I put it on, something—something hard—in one of the pockets, swung against a corner of the table with a dull little thud. I put my hand in, and touched cold metal: the thin, sharp blade of a knife.

The cold shape met my palm with the tingle of a small electric shock. Then I remembered. I brought the thing out of my pocket, and looked at it. Lambis' knife, of course; the one I had taken from him during that ghastly, serio-comic skirmish up there in the ruined church. I should have remembered to return it. Well, I could still do so, when my gay "see you in Athens" came true.

I was turning to put the thing out of sight in my case, when something occurred to me that brought me up all standing, with a little formless fear slipping over my skin like ice-water. When I had come up to get the polythene bags for Frances, surely I had felt in both pockets of the jacket? Surely I had? I frowned, thinking back. Then certainty came; I had had my hand in both pockets; I could not have missed the knife. It hadn't been there.

Sofia. It was the only explanation. Sofia must have found the knife when she hung my jacket up. She had taken it . . . why? To show to Stratos and Tony? Had she taken it with her, that time I saw her vanishing into Stratos' office, only to return it quietly while I was at dinner? *Why?*

I sat down abruptly on the edge of the bed, furious at the wave of panic which swept over me, trying to think coherently.

Lambis' knife. It didn't matter; I must remember that. It didn't matter. Nobody here would recognize it: nobody here had seen Lambis, or even knew of his existence. The knife could not possibly link me with the affair; not possibly.

Why, then, had Sofia done what she had done? Simply because, I told myself, she and her companions were, like all criminals, touchy at the least thing. It wasn't usual for the ordinary, innocent woman tourist to carry an un-sheathed and very business-like knife. She had thought it worth showing to her brother; but that was, surely, as far as it would go? There was no reason why I should not have bought such a thing as a souvenir; business-like though it was, it was also rather pretty, with the copper hilt worked with blue enamel, and a sort of filigree chasing on the root of the blade. I turned it over in my hand, examining it. Yes, that was the story: if anyone asked me, I would say that I had bought the thing in Chania, partly as a toy, and partly because I knew I should want some sort of tool to dig up plants for Frances. That was why I had taken it with me today. . . . Yes, that would do . . . I had used it today . . . that would account for the used look of the thing, and the couple of chips and notches that showed in the enamel of the handle.

I stood up, relieved, and ready to dismiss my fears. That story would do, and meanwhile I would put it away, and I must certainly remember to return it to Lambis. He would have been missing it.

The thing slipped from my fingers, and fell, to quiver, point down, in the floor-boards. I was sitting on the bed again, my hands to my cheeks, my eyes shut in a vain effort to blot out the picture that my memory had conjured up. . . .

Lambis, relaxed in the sunshine beside Colin, whittling away at the little wooden lizard. After we had left the church; after I had taken this knife from his pocket. He hadn't missed it at all; his own knife, his accustomed knife, had had a wooden handle. . . . I remembered it now, and remembered the sheath of embossed leather that he had worn thrust into his waistband, and which lay beside him as he did his carving. . . .

And this knife? This enamelled copper affair that I had taken from his pocket, and forgotten to return? This pretty, deadly bit of Turkish enamel-work?

"He pulled his knife," Mark had said, *"and then went down hard, with his head on the rock, and that was that. . . . We took everything else he had, and buried the boots."*

Josef. Josef's weapon, marked and notched into unmistakability. Found in my pocket by Josef's wife. Shown to Tony; shown to Stratos. Then quietly slipped back where they had found it.

I didn't stop then to consider what they might make of it, or if I could invent some story of finding it on the hillside. I just sat there, fighting off the waves of senseless panic that bade me get away, myself and Frances, get away, straight away, that very night, to friends and lights and normal places and people and sanity.

To Mark.

After a bit, I put the knife in my suitcase, steadied myself, and went down the stairway.

CHAPTER : EIGHTEEN

Thus far her Courage held, but here forsakes:
Her faint Knees knock at ev'ry Step she makes.

Dryden: *Cinyras and Myrrha.*

"AH, MISS FERRIS," said Stratos.

He was in the hallway, behind the table, not doing anything, just standing there, waiting for me. From behind the closed door of the office came voices, Tony's and Sofia's, the latter lifted on a high, urgent note, which stopped abruptly as Stratos spoke.

"I hope you had a pleasant day," he said.

"Very, thank you." I smiled, hoping he couldn't tell that my lips were stiff, and the nerves tingling in my fingertips. "A pretty long one, but I've enjoyed it thoroughly."

"So you've been across to the old church, Tony tells me?" His tone was quite normal, friendly even, but something in it drove me to respond as if to an accusation.

"Oh, yes, I did." My voice was hoarse, and I cleared my throat. "The track was quite easy to follow and the church was well worth visiting—you were quite right about that. I was only sorry I hadn't a camera with me."

"Ah, yes, it is Miss Scorby who is the photographer, is it not?" Still nothing in the even voice that I could put a name to. The black Greek eyes watched me. I find it hard at the best of times to read in them any but the more normal expressions: Stratos' eyes, now, might as well have been behind smoked glass.

I smiled into those blank eyes, and put another brick of truth on the wall of innocence I was trying to build. "We got some marvellous pictures this morning, up in the fields. I think the one of your sister at the mill should be a winner. Did she tell you she'd been playing film star?"

It was difficult to keep myself from glancing towards the office door. Behind it, Sofia was talking again, on a dreadful wailing note. Stratos' eyelids flickered, and he raised his voice. "Sofia told me about it, yes. She showed you over the mill, I believe." Behind him the sounds sank abruptly to a murmur; then I heard Tony speaking softly and urgently. "I hope you found it interesting," said Stratos politely.

"Oh, very. I only wish I could have seen it working, but I suppose that only happens when someone wants some wheat ground?"

"Perhaps that will happen while you are here." His voice was non-committal, his eyes suddenly alive, intent and wary.

I saw it then. He had not yet had time to think, to assess what had happened. Tony must just have told him that Colin was no longer in the mill, and Sofia—bewildered and no doubt frightened by the discovery of Josef's knife in my pocket—had walked into the conference, to be met with angry accusations, and a startled reassessment of the situation. What I was hearing now from behind the office door must be the tail end of quite a pretty scene. And it was apparent that Stratos himself was considerably shaken; he was confused, alarmed, and very ready to be dangerous, but for the present, wariness held him back. He wasn't prepared, yet, to be bolted into the open. He wanted time to think. And all he needed from me, for the moment, was reassurance on two points: namely, that nothing had happened to make me suspicious and therefore dangerous: and—a corollary to this—that I was prepared to stay placidly in Agios Georgios, under his eye, until my holiday came to its natural end. The one would presuppose the other. I only hoped that the knowledge would content him.

I said, smoothly enough, "If it does, I hope you'll let me know."

I smiled at him again, and turned away, but he made a slight movement as if he would have stopped me. "Tell me this, Miss Ferris—"

He was interrupted. The office door opened, and Tony came out. He didn't come far; just shut the door, very softly, behind him, and stayed there leaning back against the jamb, loose-limbed and graceful as ever. He was smoking, the cigarette hanging from the corner of his mouth. He neither smiled nor greeted me, just stood there, and when he spoke he didn't trouble to remove the cigarette.

"Were you asking Miss Ferris about the fishing?" he said.

"Fishing?" The Greek's head jerked round, and the men's eyes met. _hen Stratos nodded. "I was just going to." He turned back to me. "You were asking me before about the fishing?"

"Fishing?" It was my turn to sound blank.

"You said you would like to go fishing, did you not?"

"Oh. Yes, I did. Of course."

"Would you care to come out tonight?"

"Tonight?" For a moment, both thought and speech were beyond me. My brain felt light and empty as a bubble. Then I saw what to say. Whatever he suspected, whatever he was trying to find out about me, it could do nothing but good to establish those two facts for him here and now.

I said, "Why, I'd love it! Thank you so much! You mean light-fishing?"

"Yes."

"But you've missed the *gri-gri*."

"Oh, you saw them? I do not go with them. I told you I fish for pleasure, not for food. I stay near the shore. Then you will come?"

"I'd love it," I said enthusiastically. "What about Frances?"

"I have spoken to her. She does not wish to go."

"Oh, I see. Then—"

"I'll come with you." Tony had removed the cigarette at last, and was smiling at me, his eyes light and cold.

I smiled back at him. I was sure, now, that they weren't going to mention the knife, and relief made me genuinely gay. "Will you really? That'll be fun! I didn't think boats would have been your thing, somehow."

"Oh, they're not. But this is a trip I wouldn't miss for worlds, dear. I can crew for Stratos."

"There's no need." The Greek spoke roughly. His big hands moved sharply among some papers on the table in front of him, and I saw a vein beating in his temple, up near the hairline. I wondered just what was going on; if Tony was insisting on coming along in order to keep a tight eye on his companion, or merely to help him in whatever plans he might have for me. . . .

"Will you be going tomorrow night?" I asked.

"Tomorrow night?"

I moistened my lips, looking from one to the other in what I hoped was pretty apology. "The thing is . . . if it's all the same to you . . . I think I honestly am a bit tired tonight. I've had a long day, and now that heavenly dinner's made me sleepy. *Would* you be going out tomorrow night?"

A tiny pause. "I might."

"Then would you—yes, I think I *would* rather leave it till then, if it's all the same to you?"

"Of course." Of all the emotions, relief is the hardest to conceal, and I thought there was relief in the gesture with which he dismissed the plan. He was sure of me now. He smiled. "Any time. The boat is at your service."

I lingered, hesitating. There was no harm in making him even surer. "There was one thing I was going to suggest, Mr. Alexiakis. You remember how you said we might make a sea-trip one day in the *Eros?* Well, I did wonder if we might hire it some day soon? I wondered if it would be possible to take a trip along the coast, that way—" I waved vaguely eastwards—"to where the ancient harbour was? The thing is, I found a plant growing on the ruins, today, that's got my cousin all excited. She says it's Cretan dittany, do you know it?"

He shook his head.

"Well, she wants to see it growing, and to photograph it, but I think it would be too far and too rough for her to go the whole way over by the track. I did wonder if it wouldn't be rather fun to take the sea-trip. I thought if we could land at the old harbour, then we could simply walk inland to the church; it can't be far, I could see the sea from just above it. Then she could see the dittany growing, and get her pictures. Come to that, I'd like some pictures of the church myself, *and* of the harbour. Do you think we could do that? There's no hurry," I finished, "any day will do, when you're not wanting the caique."

"Of course," he said heartily, "of course. It is a good idea. I will take you myself. You must just tell me the day before you wish to go. And, for the light-fishing . . . that is settled? Tomorrow night?"

"Yes. Thank you, I'll look forward to it."

"So shall I," said Stratos, smiling, "so shall I."

This time, he made no attempt to detain me when I went out to where Frances sat with the coffee under the tamarisks. Their boughs were ethereal in the diffused electric light, like clouds. Behind them was the black, murmuring sea, and the black, blank sky. The night of no moon. I thought of Stratos, the *pallikarás*, with that vein beating in his temples, and a murder weighing on his mind. And of Tony. And of myself, out in a small boat with them, alone out there somewhere in the blackness. . . .

I didn't really pause to ask myself what he could be planning to do, or whether I really had won for myself a respite until tomorrow. I only knew that somewhere out in that same blackness was a lightless caique, with Mark on board, and that, come hell or high water, Frances and I were getting out of this place tonight.

The stone treads of the stairway were comfortingly silent under our feet. Somewhere, once, a dog barked, and then fell quiet. The sea whispered faintly under the off-shore wind; a wilderness of darkness; a huge, quiet creature breathing in the night.

"Keep to the rocks if you can," I breathed to Frances. "The shingle will make a noise."

We padded, soft-shoed, along the smoothed ridges of the rock, where the mats of ice-daisies muffled our steps. The night was so dark that, even from here, the solid oblong of the hotel was hardly visible—would have been quite hidden if it had not been blocked in with whitewash. No light showed. Further down the village the darkness was thick also; only two pinpricks of light showed where someone was still awake well after midnight. The faintest ghost of a glimmer from the church hinted at lamps left burning in front of the ikons all night.

We felt our way along, each yard an agony of suspense; having to move so slowly, but longing to switch on the torch and hurry, hurry . . .

Now, perforce, we were on shingle. It sounded as loud as an avalanche under our cautious steps. After a dozen slithering paces, I put a hand on Frances' arm, and drew her to a halt.

"Wait. Listen."

We waited, trying to hear beyond the sound of our own breathing. If we had made any noise loud enough to be heard, so, if we were being followed, would our pursuers.

Nothing; only the breathing of the sea.

"You're sure there'll be no moon?" whispered Frances.

"Sure." The sky was black velvet, obscured by the veil of cloud drawing slowly across from the White Mountains. Later, perhaps, it would be thick with stars, but now it was black, black and comforting for the hunted. The moon-spinners had done their work. Somewhere out beyond the black horizon, the drowned moon was waiting to unspin in stranded light towards the shore. But not tonight.

I touched Frances' arm again, and we went on.

It is only when one has been out in the night for some time that one begins to see the different densities, even the colours, of darkness. The sea, a living darkness; the shingle, a whispering, shifting, clogging darkness; the cliffs that rose now on our right, a looming lamp-black mass that altered the sound of our footsteps, and of our very breathing. Our progress here was painfully slow, with the cliffs pressing close on our right, thrusting out jagged roots of rock to trip us, and, on the other side, barely a yard away, the edge of the sea, giving a foot, taking a foot, always moving, only visible as a faintly luminous line of pale foam; the only guide we had.

I have no idea how long this part of the journey took. It seemed like hours. But at last we had traversed the full curve of the bay, and towering in front of us was the high, cathedral-like cliff that stuck out into the sea, right out into deep water that lapped hollowly round its base, creaming up among the fallen boulders of the narrow storm-beach which provided the only way round. We had clambered round the point by daylight; could it be done in the dark?

It had to, of course. But, as a form of exercise, I cannot recommend carrying a suitcase for a mile or so along sand and shingle at dead of night, and then edging one's way along a narrow path where a false step will mean plunging into a couple of fathoms of sea that, however quiet, is toothed like a shark with jagged fangs of rock.

I glanced back as I reached the point. The last pinprick of light from the village had disappeared; the bay we had traversed showed only as a gap of darkness.

Frances, behind me, said breathlessly, "Out to sea . . . lights. All over the place."

I turned to look, disconcerted to see the blackness alive with tiny lights. Then I realized what it was.

"It's the light-fishers," I told her. "They're a long way out. I saw them going. I suppose we were too low to see them from the bay. Can you manage this? We oughtn't to show the torch yet."

"Faint yet pursuing," she said cheerfully. "Actually, I can see fairly well; I've got my night-sight now."

The second bay was small, only an inlet, paved with beautifully firm, pale sand that showed up well in the gloom, and provided safe walking. We made good time, and in ten more minutes we had reached the second headland, where, too, the going was comparatively easy. A fairly obvious path had been beaten along the narrow storm-beach which lay piled against the point like the foam under a moving prow. I made my way cautiously round the cliff, then down

196

to the hard sand of the Bay of Dolphins. I could see Frances, still on the path, as a vaguely moving shadow, feeling her way carefully down to where I waited.

"All right?"

"Yes." She was breathing rather heavily. "Is this the bay?"

"Yes. The spit of rock runs out from the far side of it. We'll have to get out along that, over the deep water. Now we can use the torch, thank heaven. Here," I pressed it into her hand, "you'd better have it. Give me your case."

"No. I can easily—"

"Don't be daft, it isn't far, and my own weighs nothing. The going's tricky here . . . it looks as if there are rock-pools and things . . . so one of us had better be mobile, and light the way. You can take my shoulder-bag; here. I'll follow you."

Reluctantly, she handed me her case, and took the bag and the torch. The beam of light looked brilliant after the unalleviated blackness; it threw the sand and rocks into such vivid relief that for the first few moments the sense of distance and proportion was almost annulled.

At least, that was how it seemed to me, and I must suppose that is what happened to Frances, for she had taken only three or four steps when, suddenly, with a bitten-off exclamation of pain, she seemed to lurch forward, then pitched down onto the sand as if shot. The darkness came down like a blanket as the torch flew from her hand, to be doused on the nearest rock with the ominous, the final sound of breaking glass.

I dropped the cases and was down beside her. "Frances!" What is it? What happened?"

Such had been the havoc wrought on my nervous system during the last three days that I honestly believe that, for a mad moment, I expected to find her dead.

But she was very much alive, and swearing. "It's my blasted ankle. Did you ever *know* such a fool, and I had the torch, too. Is the bloody thing broken?"

"I'm afraid so. But your foot—"

"Oh, it's the same old ankle. It's all right, don't worry, it's only wrenched; the usual. If I sit here a moment and swear hard enough, it'll pass off. Hell, and I'm wet! You were right about the rock-pools; the sand just seemed to shelve straight down into one, or something. I couldn't see. And now, if the torch has gone—" She broke off, aghast. "Nicky, *the torch!*"

"Yes, I know. It can't be helped. He—he'll surely come

close in to look for us, anyway, and we can hail him."

"If we see him."

"We'll hear, surely?"

"My dear girl, he won't use his engine, will he?"

"I don't know. He might; there are those other boats out fishing, it wouldn't be the sort of sound that people would notice. It'll be all right, Frances, don't worry."

"It'll have to be," she said grimly, "because *our* boats are nicely burned. I can't see us trekking all that way back, somehow, not now."

"If the worst comes to the worst," I said, falsely cheerful, "I'll stagger back with the cases and unpack, sharpish, then go and tell them we've been having a midnight swim, and will they please come out and collect you."

"Yes," said Frances, "and then they'll come streaming along in force, and run into Mark and Co."

"Then it'd be over to Mark. He'd like that."

"Maybe. Well, it serves me right for not bringing you up better. If I'd taught you to mind your own business—"

"And pass by on the other side?"

"Yes, well, there it is. If we will be anti-social, and come to the god-forsaken corners of the earth in order to avoid our fellow trippers, I suppose we have to take what comes. You couldn't have done anything else, even to this horror-comic episode tonight. One can't touch murder, and not be terrified. We can't get out fast enough, in my opinion. *Damn* this ankle. No, don't worry, it's beginning to cool down a bit. What's the time?"

"Nearly half-past one. Have you any matches?"

"No, but there's my lighter. That might do it. I *am* sorry about the torch."

"You couldn't help it."

"Give me a hand now, and help me up, will you?"

"There. Manage? Good for you. I'll tell you what, I'll dump the cases here, back against the cliff, and we'll get you along the 'pier' if we can—as far as we can, anyway. Then I can come back for them . . . or maybe we'd better leave them till we see Mark coming in. Sure you can make it?"

"Yes. Don't worry about me. Look, is that the torch?"

A tiny edge of starlight on metal showed where it lay. Eagerly I picked it up and tried it. Useless. When I shook it gently, there was the rattle of broken glass.

"*Kaput?*" asked Frances.

"Very *kaput*. Never mind. The luck couldn't run all the way all the time. Press on regardless."

It was a slow, dreadful progress across the bay, our steps less certain than ever after the brief illumination and the fall. Frances hobbled along nobly, and I tried to seem unhurried, and perfectly confident and at ease; but the night was breathing on the back of my neck, and I was flaying myself mentally for having tried this final escapade at all. Perhaps I had been stupid to panic so, over the discovery of Josef's knife. Perhaps they hadn't even seen it; it had been in my pocket all the time. Perhaps Stratos' manoeuvre to get me to himself out in the light-boat had been no more than the host's anxiety to please, and there had never been any danger except in my own imagination. I need never have subjected Frances to this ghastly trek, this schoolboys' escapade that probably wouldn't even work. If I'd kept my head and waited till tomorrow ... Tomorrow, we could have telephoned for a car, and then walked to it, in sunlight, through the public street.

But here we were in the dark, committed. It must have been all of thirty minutes more before I had got Frances out along the ridge of rock. With my help, she shuffled, half-crawling, along it, until she had found a place to sit, a few feet above deep water. She fetched a long sigh of relief, and I saw her bend, as if to massage her ankle.

"You were marvellous," I told her. "Will you give me the lighter now?"

She felt in her pocket, and passed it to me. I went a little further along the rock-ridge. Its top sharpened presently into a hog's-back, then dropped steeply to deep water, where the ridge had been broken and split by the sea. Ahead of me I could see the fangs of rock which marked the broken ridge, running straight out to sea, their bases outlined with ghostly foam, as the breeze freshened beyond the immediate shelter of the cliffs.

I found a flat place to stand, then, with the lighter ready in my hand, faced out to sea.

They should see the flame quite well. I remembered hearing how, in the blackout during the war, flyers at some considerable height could see the match that lit a cigarette. Even if I couldn't manage the pattern of flashes that we had agreed upon, surely a light, any light, from this bay at this time, would bring Mark in ... ? And once he was near enough, a soft hail would do the rest.

I cupped a hand round the lighter, and flicked it. Flicked it again. And again. ...

When my thumb was sore with trying, I allowed myself to

realize what had happened. I remembered the splash with which Frances had fallen, and the way she had wrung out the skirts of her coat. The lighter had been in the pocket. The wick was wet. We had no light at all.

I stood there, biting my lips, trying to think, straining eyes and ears against the darkness.

The night was full of sound. The sea whispered and hummed like a great shell held to the ear, and the dark air around me was alive with its noise. There were more stars now, and I thought I should even be able to see if any craft bore shorewards. The great space of the sea ahead looked almost light, compared with the thick blackness of the cliffs towering round me.

Then I heard it; or thought I did. The slap of water against a hull; the rattle of metal somewhere on board.

Stupidly, I was on tiptoe, straining forward. Then, some way out, well beyond the encircling arms of the bay, a light came past the point from my right, bearing eastward. A small boat, not using an engine, moving slowly and erratically across the black void, the light making a dancing pool on the water. One of the *gri-gri,* standing in nearer the shore; that was all. I thought I could see a figure outlined against the light, crouching down in the bows. At least, I thought, he wasn't likely to spot Lambis' caique, riding lightless somewhere out in the roads; but, with the light-boat so near, I dared not risk a hail for Mark to hear.

I went back to Frances, and told her.

"Then we'll have to go back?"

"I don't know. He'll have seen the light-boat, too. He may think we daren't flash our signal because of that. He—he may stand in to the bay, just to see." I paused, in a misery of indecision. "I—I don't see how we *can* go back now, Frances. They may have found out—that man—"

"Look!" she said sharply. "There!"

For a moment I thought she was just pointing at the light-boat, which, pursuing its slow course across the mouth of the bay, would soon be cut off from view by the eastern headland.

Then I saw the other boat, low down in the water; a shape, silent and black, thrown momentarily into relief as the light passed beyond it. The unlighted boat lay, apparently motionless, a little way outside the arms of the bay.

"That's it!" My voice was tight in my throat. "That's him. He's not coming in. He's doing just what he said he would;

waiting. There, the light-boat's out of sight; Mark would expect us to signal now, if we were here. . . . And we can't afford to wait any longer to see if he will come in. . . . It's ten past two already. Can't you do it, either?"

"Afraid not." She was working away at the lighter. "It's had a pretty fair soaking, I'm afraid it's no use—what *are* you doing, Nicola?"

I had dropped my coat on the rock beside her, and my shoes went to join it. "I'm going out after him."

"My dear girl! You can't do that! Look, can't we risk shouting? He'd hear us, surely?"

"So would anyone else within miles, the way sound carries over water. I daren't. Anyway, we've no time to try: he'll be away in twenty minutes. Don't worry about me, he's well within range, and the water's like glass in the bay."

"I know, the original mermaid. But don't for pity's sake go beyond the headland. I can see the white-caps from here."

My frock, and the sweater I had been wearing over it, went down on the pile. "All right. Now don't *worry,* I'll be okay. Heaven knows I'll be thankful to be doing something." My petticoat dropped to the rock, then my socks, and I stood up in briefs and bra. "Not just the correct dress for calling on gentlemen, but highly practical. I've always longed to swim naked, and I dare say this is as near as I'll get. Here's my watch. Thanks. See you later, love."

"Nicky, I wish you wouldn't."

"Damn it, we've got to! We can't go back, and we can't stay here. Needs must—which is the only excuse for heroics. Not that these are heroics; if you want the truth, nothing could keep me out. I'm as sticky as all-get-out after that horrible walk. Keep working at that beastly lighter, it may yet function. *Adío, thespoinís.*"

I let myself down into the water without a splash.

The first shock of it was cold to my over-heated body, but then the silky water slid over the flesh with the inevitable shiver of pure pleasure. The filmy nylon I was wearing seemed hardly to be there. I thrust away from the rock into the smooth, deep water, shook the hair back from my eyes, and turned out to sea.

I swam steadily and strongly, making as little splash as I could. From this angle, the cliffs stood up even more massively against the night sky.

I headed straight out to sea, with the ridge of rock to my right as a guide, and soon drew level with the place where

I had stood with the lighter. Beyond this spot, the ridge of rock was split and broken by the weather into a line of stacks and pinnacles. As I left the shelter of the inner bay, I could feel that the breeze had stiffened slightly: I could see foam creaming at the bases of the rock-stacks, and now and again a whitecap slapped salt across my mouth. Where I swam, fairly near the rocks, the lift and fall of the water against them was perceptible.

Another fifty yards or so, and I paused, resting on the water, stilling my breathing as best I could, and trying to see and hear.

Now more than ever I was conscious of the fresh breeze blowing out from the land. It blew steadily across the water, bringing with it, over the salt surface, the tang of verbena, and the thousand sharp, sweet scents of the maquis. I wondered if it would set up any currents that might make it hard for me to get back, if I should have to. . . .

From my position, low down in the water, I could no longer see the outline of the caique—if, indeed, I had ever seen it. It might, I told myself, have drifted in-shore a little, until its black silhouette was merged in the dense blackness of the eastern headland; but this, with the off-shore breeze, was unlikely. Even to keep her from drifting seawards, they would have to use anchor or oars.

I strained across the moving, whispering darkness. As before, it was full of sounds, far fuller than when, on the ridge, I had stood insulated by the air from the subdued and roaring life of the sea. Now, the humming was loud in my ears, drowning all other sounds, except the suck and slap of water against the rock-stacks hard to my right. . . .

Meanwhile, time was running out. And I had been right. Lambis was making no attempt to stand into the bay. Why should he, indeed? If I was to find the caique, I would have to leave the line of the ridge, and swim across the open bay, with the tip of the headland as a guide.

I hesitated there, treading water, strangely reluctant, all at once, to leave even the cold shelter of the stacks for the un-discovered darkness of the open bay. I suppose there is noth-ing quite so lonely as the sea at night. I know I hung there in the black water, suddenly frightened, doubtful, half-in-credulous of the fact that I was there at all; conscious only that behind me was an alien country where I had behaved foolishly, and where folly was not tolerated; and that be-fore me was the limitless, empty, indifferent sea.

But I was committed. I had to go. And, if they weren't there, I had to come back. . . .

I took a breath, and turned away from the rock-ridge, bearing steadily seawards, towards the dim outline of the headland, the point where I thought the caique might be lying. I swam fast. It might take me ten minutes to come within distance of a soft hail. And in about ten minutes he would up anchor, and go. . . .

I had travelled, I suppose, not more than thirty yards, when I was brought up sharply in my course by a new sound, not of the sea; the sound—unmistakable, and near—of metal on wood. A boat's sound. But this came, not from ahead of me, but from the right, further out to sea.

I stopped, treading water again, conscious now of the fast beating of my heart. A line of foam ran past me. The sea hummed. I was inside its great, roaring shell, rocked to and fro in an echoing confusion of din like the noises in a hollow cave. Under my body, fathoms down, throbbed the organ-pipes of the sea.

Another moment of deep fear, loneliness, and confusion swept over me with a cold splash like spray. But I dared not hesitate. If this were not he, I might be too late. I must try a hail now. . . . But, if it were not he . . .

Then I saw it, unmistakably, and near. A boat, a dim shape, dark against darkness, the froth running white from her slowly-dipping oars. No light; no sound, save for the rattle of rowlocks that had caught my ear. She was seaward of me, standing across the bay towards the outer fangs of the rock-ridge. Lambis was coming in after all, without the signal; no doubt to reconnoitre the ridge before finally turning for the open sea, and Athens.

I put my head down, made a diving turn, and went at my fastest crawl back towards the ridge. My hand touched rock, I surfaced, clung, and turned, with my body held against the stack by the lifting water.

I had crossed the boat's course with plenty to spare; she was still slightly to seaward of me, but closing in, bearing for shore. And now she was level with me, looming between me and the stars. I shook the water out of my eyes, tightened my grip on the rock, and hailed her.

It came very breathlessly: "Ahoy there! Sailor!"

Silence. She bore on her way. The wind must have caught my voice and eddied it away in the rush and lap of the water. She was passing, soon to be lost again in the darkness. I could feel her wash lifting me against the rock.

I let myself go with it, hauling on my hand-grip as I did so. The wash carried me back, and up, against my rock-stack; a crevice gave me another handhold, then a slippery foothold. I reared myself up out of the water, and let it hold me there, spread by it against the rock, where my body would show paler. I dared not leave the rock, for fear of being run down. I called again, not caring how loudly, and heard how this time the rock caught the cry, and echoed it uncannily across the black water.

"Ahoy! Ahoy! *Náfti!*"

The jerking clack of wood on wood, and she came up as sharply as a checked horse. Then the high prow slanted, swung, and she had veered head on to me.

I gave a little sobbing breath of relief. It was over. And of course it was Mark. I had had time, now, to realize that no other boat would have put into this bay, along this perilous ridge, in this unlighted and stealthy silence. Only a few minutes more, and Frances and I would both be safely aboard, and that would be that. . . .

He was looming right over me. The faint line of frost under the bows seemed to brush my thighs. Then he swung broadside again, within feet of me, and the oars bit water. The boat halted, slid a little, backed water. I heard an exclamation, half of surprise, half of what sounded like fear.

I called softly, "It's all right. It's me, Nicola. I was swimming out."

There was silence. Feet away, the boat loomed.

"Mark—" I said.

Then, suddenly, a light flashed on; an enormous, blinding light; a pharos of a light. Straight above my head twin massive lamps were suspended in nothing. The beams, converging in a glaring ring, stabbed down onto the water, onto me. I was blinded, pinned down, held, dazzled, and helpless to move or think, in that appalling light.

I believe I cried out, cowering back against the rock, and, at the same moment, I heard him shout. It was a rough voice, and it spoke in Greek, but there was no time for this to register with me. Fear stabbed through at a purely instinctive level, and already, before he had moved, I had dived away into the dark beyond the floodlit pool.

I heard an oar strike rock, as he thrust against it, and the nose of the boat turned with me. The light followed. I had seen, in that sharp, immediate flash of terror, what this was: it was a light-boat, too small (but the dark had hidden this) for an inter-island caique; too furtive—surely—for one of the *gri-gri*. And I thought I knew whose light-boat.

A moment later, I was proved right. Noise ripped the night open, as the motor started. No, this wasn't one of the harmless *gri-gri* that the caique had towed out to sea; this was a boat with an outboard. Like Stratos'.

Stratos' own. I heard him shout: *"You? I knew it! And Josef?"* He was standing there now, brilliantly lit beside the lanterns, and the six-pronged trident flashed as he drove it down, straight at me.

CHAPTER : NINETEEN

It was that fatal and perfidious bark. . . .

Milton: *Lycidas.*

No TIME TO THINK, certainly no time to cry out through the choking swirl of water; impossible to shout to him, ask what he was doing, what danger I could be to him, now that the others were safely away. . . .

The harpoon went by me with a hiss; bubbles ripped back from the blades in a sparkling comet's-tail. I twisted aside, kicking my way frantically out of the merciless light.

The spear reached the bottom of its run, jerked the rope tight; then he hauled it back, as the boat swerved after me. The rope touched me as he dragged it up; the small graze, even through the rip of the water, touched the skin with terror, like a burn. I had a glimpse of him, towering beside the lanterns, hauling in the glittering coils of rope with rapid, practiced hands. Momentarily, he had had to let the tiller swing, and the light swerved away. Dark water swirled in the shadow of the boat, hiding me. I jack-knifed away again, towards the deep, black water. But *Psyche* came up to the tiller with a jerk, and turned with me, as if locked to my wake by radar. . . .

For a split, crazy second, I thought of diving under her; then I knew it would be a dive to certain death: if the screw didn't get me, I would be a sitter for Stratos and the light as I came up. As it was, this could only have one end, and that a quick one. . . . He needn't even risk another miss with the spear; another half-minute of this dreadful, uneven hunt, and I should be done, gasping on the surface, ready to be spitted. . . .

Full in the glare, I turned to face the spear, and threw an arm up towards him. I was trying, I think, to get my breath to shout; to gain a little time in which his crazy anger might be checked, reasoned with. But even as I turned, he swung his spear-arm up again. The long shaft gleamed golden, the barbed blades glittered; the light beat me down, hammered me into the water, held me there, like a moth frying on a flame. His other hand was on the tiller. If the spear missed this time, the boat, swinging on that radar-beam, would run me down, and plough me back into the sea.

I gulped air, watching for the first flash of metal as his muscles tensed for the throw. The flash came: I turned and dived for the darkness. Nothing followed, no blades, no rope; he must have missed. I held myself under as long as I could, thrusting down and away, steeply, into deep water. . . .

The moment came when I had to turn upwards. I was rising towards the light . . . it was everywhere . . . the sea paled to a luminous green, to a wavering of blue and gold, barred with the ripples of the boat's passage, blocked with the formidable shadow of her keel.

The turquoise and gold thinned, lightened, fizzed with sparks as the foam ran from her screw. . . .

Just before I broke surface I saw him, a shadow towering above a shadow, tall on the thwarts, huge, distorted, wavering like a pillar of cloud. He was up there, waiting, the spear still poised. I don't pretend I saw anything except the moving shadows above the light, but I knew, as surely as if the sea were clear glass, that he still had the spear. He hadn't thrown it before, it had been a feint. He would get me now, as, gasping and exhausted, I surfaced for the last time.

Then something touched me, drove at my outstretched hand, breaking my dive, and sending me sprawling untidily to the surface. The boat rocked past, her bow-wave piling. The spear drove down at the same moment, a flash among the million flashing and glittering points of light; stars, water-drops, splashing foam, the dazzle of my water-filled eyes. There was a crack, a dreadful jarring, a curse. The world swam, and flashed, and was extinguished, as a massive shape of blackness surged up between me and the light. I hadn't even known what had knocked me to the surface, but the animal in me was already clinging, gasping and sobbing for air, to solid rock. That last, long dive had taken me into the wake of one of the stacks of the rock-ridge. The spear, striking prematurely, had hit it, and the prow of Stratos' boat, following me too closely, had taken it with a jarring graze, and was even now, roughly headed off by the rock, swerving fast away.

The moment's respite, the solid rock of my own element, were enough. My mind cleared of its helpless terror as the air poured into my body, and I saw that I was safe, as long as I kept among the rocks.

Psyche turned again, wheeling for my side of the stack. I dropped back into the sea, and plunged round into the darkness at the other side.

I reached out for a handhold, to rest again until she could come around.

Something caught at me then, holding me back from the rock; something under the water. . . . It was thin and whippy as a snake, and it wrapped round my legs, dragging me down like the weight roped to the feet of a man condemned to die by drowning.

I fought it, with the new strength born of instinctive terror. I had forgotten the other danger; the light and the spear were of the upper air, this horror came from the world below. This was the swimmer's nightmare, the very stuff of horror; the weed, the tentacle, the rope of a net. . . . It held me fast, pulled me down, choking. And now the light was coming back.

My flailing hand met rock again; clung, with the thing dragging at my knees. I was done; I knew it. The light was coming.

Then it vanished, switched off. The sudden darkness, printed with its image still, roared and dazzled. But the roaring was real, the night suddenly shaking with a confused uproar of engines, a medley of shouting, the sharp crack of a backfiring motor—and then I saw other lights, small and dim and moving wildly across the water. The darkened light-boat hung between me and the stars, as if hesitating, then, suddenly, her motor was gunned, and the jet of white foam that shot from her stern almost dragged me off my rock. Her wake arrowed away, to be lost under the dark. In its place, came, gently, a biggish shadow, with riding-lights steady at mast and prow.

Someone said, "Hang on, sweetheart," and someone else

said, in Greek, "God protect us, the sea lady," and Colin's voice said breathlessly, "She's hurt."

Then a boat-hook ground into the rock beside me, and the boat swung in gently. Hands reached, grabbed. The side of the caique dipped, and I managed to grab it and was dragged half inboard, to hang gasping and slack over the side until the hands gripped again and lifted me in, and whatever it was that had twined round my legs and tried to drown me, came too.

I was down in the well of the caique, hunched on the thick rope matting, gasping and shivering and sick. Vaguely I was aware of Mark's voice and hands; something dry and rough rubbed me smartly into warmth, something sharp and aromatic was forced down my throat, while the caique swung and ground against the rock, and Mark cursed steadily under his breath in a way I hadn't thought he was capable of. Then came the dry roughness of a tweed coat round my bare shoulders, and another mouthful of the heady Greek brandy, and I was sitting up, with Mark's sound arm round me, feeling the warmth of his body comforting my own, and clutching his coat to my nakedness with numbed and flaccid fingers.

"Stay quiet; it's all right, just stay quiet." It was the voice he had used to comfort Colin.

I shook, clinging to him. "The spear," I said, "the weeds."

"I know. It's all right now. He's gone." Reassurance seemed to flow from him in tangible waves. "It's all finished; you're quite safe. Now relax."

"It was because of Josef's knife. I took it out of Lambis' pocket in the church, when we held him up. I forgot it. It was in my pocket. They saw it. H-he must have come after us."

A moment or so, while he assessed this. "I see. But it still doesn't explain why he—"

"*Mark!*" A shadow that I recognized as Colin dropped down to squat beside us.

"What?"

"This stuff that came up with her. It isn't weeds, it's rope."

"Rope?" I shivered again, uncontrollably, and the protecting arm tightened. "You mean a—a *net?*"

"No. It's a length of rope, with a float, and a sort of lobster pot at the other end."

The *schǎros* pots; of course. It seemed like a memory from another life.

I said, "He has pots laid along there. I forgot. That was all it was, then. It felt horrible, like weed."

208

"Chuck it back in," said Mark.

"But there's something inside." Colin sounded suddenly excited. "Not fish. A sort of package."

Mark let me go. "Send a light down, Lambis." He got down on his knees beside Colin. The wicker pot lay between them, a dark stain of water spreading from it. Gingerly Mark thrust his fingers in, and brought out a package, which he laid on the boards. Colin leaned close. Lambis, from his place beside the engine, peered in over their shoulders. The three faces were grave, absorbed, tense with a curiosity that was just about to break into excitement. The caique throbbed softly, swinging away from the rocks in a long, gentle drift seawards. We had all completely forgotten Frances.

Mark unwrapped the package. A layer of oilskin or polythene; another; a third. Then a bag of some soft species of skin, chamois-leather, I supposed, drawn together at the neck. Its coverings had kept it quite dry.

Mark pulled the drawstring loose, then up-ended the bag. There was a glitter and a coloured flash, a gasp from Colin and a grunt from Lambis. Mark picked up a kind of chain, very heavily ornate, and worked in gold; as he ran it through his fingers, red glowed and burned among the gold. Colin reached out, gingerly, and picked up something—it looked like an eardrop—with a hoar-frost glitter round a flash of green.

"I said it was jewels," he said breathlessly.

"This is the loot?" Lambis' voice, over our shoulders, was deep with satisfaction.

"This is the loot, the highly identifiable loot. "Mark let the gold and ruby necklace trickle back into the mouth of the bag. "It begins to make sense now, doesn't it? We wanted evidence, and oh boy! what evidence we've got! If this isn't what that poor blighter Alexandros was murdered for, then I'm the Queen of the May!"

" 'The London job,' " I quoted.

"Big deal, eh?" Colin still sounded almost awe-stricken. He was turning the emerald drop from side to side, letting it catch the light. "I wonder how many pots he's got?"

"That's a question that can wait for the police. Let's put these things back. Drop that in here, will you?" Mark held out the bag for the earring, then pulled the drawstring tight, and began to tie it.

I said slowly, "He must have thought that's what I was after. The knife made him suspicious, but he thought we were safe under his eye for a bit. Then he came out here to check

209

over his pots, and found me beside them, in the water. I'm not surprised, after all that's happened recently, that he saw red, and went for me regardless. I wonder if he even thought Josef might be double-crossing him? With me, I mean. He did shout something about him, and of course he must be wondering like mad where he is."

"What *were* you doing in the water?"

"We broke the torch, so we couldn't signal. I was coming for you. I—*Mark!*" I put a hand to my head, which was only just beginning to clear of the sea-noises and the confused terror of the chase. "I must have gone crazy myself. Get Lambis to put back to the rocks! There's—"

"You're hurt?" Lambis interrupted me sharply. "That is blood, no?"

"No. . . ." I must have looked at him with vague surprise. I had felt nothing, was feeling nothing even now; my flesh was still cold and damp to the touch, and too numb to feel pain. But as Mark snatched up the lantern, and swung its light round to me, I saw that there was, indeed, blood on my thigh, and a dark line of it creeping down onto the deck. "He must have got me with the edge of the spear," I said, faintly, because I was beginning to shake again. "It's all right, it doesn't hurt. We'd better go back—"

But I was interrupted again, this time by Mark, who leaped —no, surged—to his feet. "The bloody-minded *bastard!*" Colin and I—crouched at his feet like famine, sword and fire at the heels of the war god—gaped up at him, dumbly.

"By God, I'll not stand for this!" Mark towered over us, possessed, apparently, by one sudden, glorious burst of sheer, uninhibited rage. "I'm damned if we cut and run for Athens after this! We're getting after him, if it's the last thing we do! Lambis, can you catch him?"

I saw a grin of unholy joy split the Greek's face. "I can try."

"Then get weaving! Colin, throw me the first-aid box!"

I began feebly, "Mark, no—"

I might have known they would take no notice of me, and this time it was three to one. My feeble protest was drowned by the roar of the caique's engine, as she jumped forward with a jerk that set every board quivering. I heard Colin shout, "Man, oh *man*, Lambis, cool it wild!" as he dived into the cabin. Mark dropped back to his knees beside me, saying, simply and rudely, "Shut up. We're going back, and that's that. Hell's teeth, do you think I'd have sat there and let them do all they've done, if they hadn't had Colin to hold me to ransom with? What d'you take me for, a bloody daffodil? Now I've got you and Colin safe under hatches, I'm going to do what I'd have done in the first place, if I'd been fit, and the pair of you hadn't been a sitting target for them. And now shut up, and for a change you can sit quiet and let *me* bandage *you! Colin!* Where the—oh, thanks!" This as the first-aid box hurtled from the cabin door. Mark caught it, and pulled it open. "And find the girl something to wear, will you? Now, keep still, and let me get that tied up."

"But Mark, what are you going to do?" I sounded infuriatingly humble, even to myself.

"Do? Well, my heaven, what d'you think? I'm going to hand him over to the police myself, personally, and if I've got to paste the living daylights out of him to do it, well, that'll suit *me!*"

I said meekly, "Do you have to be quite such a sadist with the Elastoplast?"

"What?" He stared at me quite blankly. He really was looking very angry indeed, and quite dangerous. I smiled at him happily, well away now (as I was aware) on what Frances would have called Stage Three. Then the black look faded, to be succeeded by a reluctant grin. "Was I hurting? I'm very sorry." He finished the job quite gently.

"Not so much as I hurt you, I expect. Look, do you really think this is a good idea? I know how you feel, but—"

A quick look up, where, even in the lantern-light, I could read irony. "Darling, I admit I lost my temper, but there's more to it than a simple desire to clobber this thug. For one thing, this is the chance to connect him here and now with the jewels and Alexandros' murder—if we can catch him and identify him before he gets the chance to run home and cook up alibis with Tony. What's more, if we don't get straight back and alert the village elders, what's to stop Stratos and Tony lifting whatever other lobster pots they've got, and being a hundred miles away, with bulk of said loot, before we even sight Piraeus?"

"I see."

He shoved the things back in the box, and clipped the lid shut. "Mad at me?"

"What on earth for?"

"Because when my girl gets hurt, I've got to have another reason for hitting the chap that did it."

I laughed, without answering, and slipped painlessly into Stage Four—a stage Frances wouldn't have recognized, as it was new to me, too.

"Will these do?" Colin emerged from the cabin, clutching a thick, fisherman's knit jersey, a cotton-mesh vest, and a pair of jeans. "You can put them on in the cabin, it's warm there."

"They look marvellous, thanks awfully." I got up stiffly, Mark helping me, then Colin put the clothes into my hands, and retired modestly aft into the shadows.

The cabin was warm after the smartly-moving breeze on deck. I took off Mark's jacket. The wisps of nylon which—I suspected—had been almost non-existent as garments when wet, had now more or less dried on me, and were ready to reassume their functions as clothing. I rubbed my cold flesh again vigorously with the rough towel, then wriggled into the jeans. They must be Colin's; they would be tight on him, and were even tighter on me; but they were warm, and fitted comfortably enough over the Elastoplast. The sweater—Mark's, at a guess—was wonderfully warm and bulky, and came fairly well down over the jeans. I pushed open the cabin door, and peered out.

A rush of starry wind met me, the roar of the motor, the slap and race of water. . . . We had swerved, close in, round the second headland, and were tearing across the mouth of the bay towards Agios Georgios. I could see, low down, in few dim lights, and a yellow gleam that must mark the harbour mouth. Our own riding-lights were out. Lambis, at the tiller, was hardly visible, and Mark and Colin, standing together in the well, were two shadows peering intently forward. The caique jumped and bucked like a bolting horse as the cross-wind met her round the headland.

I opened my mouth to say, "Can I do anything?" then shut it again. Common sense suggested that the question was a purely rhetorical gesture, and therefore better unasked. Besides, I knew nothing about boats, and these three were a team which, freed now of everything but a single purpose, looked a formidable proposition enough. I stayed quietly in the shelter of the cabin door.

To seaward of us, the light-boats bobbed and twinkled. Some had worked their way in-shore, and one—probably the one that had passed so close to the Bay of Dolphins—was barely fifty feet from us as we roared past.

I could see the faces of its two occupants, open-mouthed and curious, turned towards us. Lambis yelled something, and their arms shot out, pointing, not towards Agios Georgios, but at the inner curve of the bay, where the hotel lay.

Lambis called something to Mark, who nodded, and the caique heeled till she lay hard over, then drove towards the looming crescent of cliff that held the bay.

Colin turned and saw me, and flashed a torch. "Oh, hullo! Were the things all right?"

"Fine, I'm as warm as anything now. The pants are a bit tight, that's all, I hope I don't split them."

"They don't look it, do they, Mark?"

Mark turned, looked obediently, and said, simply, "Boy, oh *boy!*"

Colin, laughing, vanished past me into the cabin.

"Well, well," I said, "something tells me you must really be feeling better."

"Sure. Try me. Just one hundred per cent—*there he is!*"

I dived after him to the side, peering to starboard. Then I saw it, too, barely a hundred yards ahead of us, a small shape, a dark tip on an arrow of white, hurtling into the curve of the bay.

"They're right, he's making for home!"

"Nicola!" Lambis hailed me from the stern. "What is it like? Is there a landing place?"

"No, but there's flat rocks right to the edge of the water. It's quite deep, right up to them."

"How deep?" This was Mark.

"I can't say, but deep enough for a caique. He takes the *Eros* in himself, and it's bigger than this. I've swum there; I'd say eight feet."

"Good girl." I must be far gone, I thought, when this casual accolade from an obviously preoccupied man could make me glow all through. Stage Five? Heaven alone knew —and heaven alone could care, because I didn't. . . .

Next moment a more substantial warmth met my hands, from the mug which Colin thrust into them. "Here, it'll warm you up, it's cocoa. I'd say you've just time, before we waltz in to clobber the bastards."

This got through. Mark half-turned, but at that moment the note of the caique's engine changed, and Lambis spoke, urgently and quietly:

"Here, we go in now. See him? He will make fast in a moment. Colin, light the lamp again; he must have seen us now. When we get in, you make her fast; I will go to help Mark. Take the boat-hook; you know what to do."

"Yes." But the boy hesitated a moment. "If he has a gun?"

"He won't use it," said Mark. "He can't know who we are, for a start."

This was undoubtedly true, but it had already occurred to me that Stratos might be making a fairly shrewd guess. In any case, whether or not he guessed whose caique was pursuing him, he must know that its owners had rescued me from his murderous attack, and were bound on an errand, if not of violent retribution, then, at the least, of angry inquiry—which would lead to the very uproar he wanted to avoid. We were, in other words, hard on the heels of a man both angry and involved to the point of desperation.

"Anyway," Mark was saying, "we've got one too, remember. Now, don't worry, here we go."

I pushed the empty mug back into the cabin, and shut the door. I half expected to be told to go in after it, but nobody even noticed me. Lambis and Mark were both leaning out, watching the dim rocks of the shore rush to meet us. Colin, on the prow, held the boat-hook at the ready. The caique heeled more sharply still, then drove in.

Stratos had seen us, of course. But even at the cost of helping us, he had to have light. As the light-boat ran in to the landing, he switched on the huge lamps, and I heard Lambis give a grunt of satisfaction.

Stratos cut his engine, and the boat lost way abruptly, slipping alongside the rocks. I saw him, the figure of my nightmare, rope in one hand, boat-hook in the other, poised beside the lights. Then his boat touched, kissed stone, and jarred to a rocking halt as the boat-hook flashed out and held her. I saw him glance back, and seem to hesitate. Then the lights went out.

"Ready?" Lambis' voice was almost inaudible, but it affected me like a shout.

"Okay," said Mark.

The three of them must, of course, have worked together at berthing the caique many times before. This time, done fast, and in semi-darkness, it was a rough berthing, but still surprisingly slick.

The engine accelerated briefly, and was killed. The caique jumped forward, then skidded sideways against the moored boat, using her as a buffer. I heard poor *Psyche* grind against the rock as the caique scraped along her sides. She was empty. Stratos was already on shore: I saw him, caught momentarily in our lurching lights, bending to fling a couple of rapid loops of rope round a stanchion.

214

Then Mark, in a standing leap from the caique's bows, landed beside him.

As the Cretan swung to face the challenge, Mark hit him. I heard the blow connect, sickeningly, and Stratos went staggering back. Mark jumped after him, and then they were beyond the reach of our lights, a couple of plunging, swearing shadows, somewhere in the scented darkness under the tamarisks.

Lambis pushed past me, scrambling ungracefully on the thwarts to leap ashore. Colin said urgently: "Here, *you* tie her up," shoved a rope into my hand, and jumped after Lambis, belting across the gravel into the darkness, where the roughhouse of the century was now playing havoc with the peaceful island night. Tables hurtled over, chairs went flying, someone shouted from a nearby house, dogs barked, cocks crew, Stratos was shouting, Colin yelled something, and then a woman cried out from somewhere, shrill and frightened. Stratos' homecoming could not have been more public if he had had television cameras and a brass band.

A light flashed on in the hotel.

I could hear a babel of other shouts, now, in the village street, and running footsteps, and men's voices, curious and excited. They were bringing lights. . . .

I suddenly realized that the caique—with me in it—was beginning to drift away from shore. Shaking like a leaf with cold, nerves and reaction, I managed somehow to find the boat-hook, pull her in, and crawl out onto the rock. I went stiffly to my knees, and began to wind the rope round the stanchion. I remember that I wound it very carefully, as if the safety of us all depended on how neatly I curled the rope round the metal. Four, five, six careful turns . . . and I believe I was even trying solemnly to knot the thing—all the while straining to see what was happening out there under the tamarisks—when the shadowy melée grew dimmer still, and I realized that the light in the hotel had gone out again.

Feet came running, lightly. I heard a quick tread on gravel, then he was coming, fast, along the rock towards me, dodging through the shadows. A glimmer of light from one of the advancing lanterns touched him. It was Tony.

I was full in his way, sitting there numbly, holding my rope. I don't even remember being afraid, but even if I had been, I doubt if I could have moved. He must have been armed, but he neither touched me, nor turned aside for me—he simply jumped straight over me so lightly that one almost expected Weber's long harp *glissandos* to pour spectrally from the wings.

"Excuse me, dear—" His voice was quick and high, and only a little breathless. Another leap landed him in the frantically rocking *Psyche*. There was a jerk at her rope as he cut it, the engine burst raucously into life, and *Psyche* lurched away from the rock so sharply that she must have shipped water.

". . . high time to leave." I thought I heard the light, affected voice quite plainly. "Such a *rough* party. . . ."

Then lights everywhere, and men shouting, and the dog-fight was coming my way.

Here was Mark, with a stain spreading across his shirt, reeling backwards from a blow, to trip over a chair, which, collapsing, crashed with him to the ground. Stratos aimed a kick at his head, which went wide as Lambis, charging through a tangle of metal tables, knocked him aside; and then the pair of them hurtled, furniture flying, through a crackling fog of tamarisk-boughs, to fetch up hard against a tree trunk. A *píthos* of carnations went rolling wildly: Stratos, who must know, even in semi-darkness, the hazards of his own territory, side-stepped it, but it struck Lambis full in the legs, just as the Cretan managed, at last, to pull his knife.

Lambis, plunging for the knife-hand, trod on the rolling pot, missed, and went down, tangled with carnations, and swearing lamentably. And now Mark, on his feet again, was lurching forward through the cheval-de-frise of tables, with behind him a crowd of milling, shadowy figures responding enthusiastically—if blindly—to Lambis' shouts.

Stratos didn't wait. He must have seen Tony, heard *Psyche's* engine, and thought the boat was ready there, and waiting. He swept aside the tamarisk branches with one powerful arm, and, knife at the ready, came racing for the edge of the sea.

He had suffered a good deal of damage; I saw that straight away; but it didn't seem to affect the speed of this final, express-train rush for freedom. Then he saw me, crouching there over the stanchion, full in his path . . . and, in the same moment, he must have seen that *Psyche* had gone . . . but the caique was there, and he hesitated only fractionally before he came on.

The knife flashed as he lifted it, whether for me or the rope I was never to know, for Colin flew yelling out of the dark like a mad terrier, and fastened on the knife-arm with—apparently—arms, legs, and teeth combined.

It hardly checked the Cretan. He stumbled, half-turned, brought his free hand round in a smashing blow which brushed the boy off like a fly from a bull's flank, then, a mad bull charging, he hurtled towards me down the last stretch of rock.

I lifted the rope I was holding, and it caught him full across the shins.

I have never seen a man go such a purler. He seemed to dive forward, full length, towards the rocks. The breath was driven out of him in a gasping cry, then, out of nowhere, Mark plummeted down on top of him in a sort of flying tackle, rolled over with him, then let his arms drop, and got rather unsteadily to his feet.

"One more to you," he said, and grinned. Then he pitched down on top of the Cretan's unconscious body, and went out like a light.

CHAPTER : TWENTY

Tho' much is taken, much abides. . . .

Tennyson: *Ulysses.*

THE CABIN of the caique was very full. There was Mark, rather white, and newly bandaged; myself looking, in Colin's pants and Mark's enormous sweater, like a beatnik after a thick night; Lambis, looking tough and collected, but still smelling exotically of carnations; Colin, with a new bruise on his cheek, silent, and rather close to Mark's side. That was the crew. With us, at the tiny cabin table, sat the headman of Agios Georgios, and three of the village elders, old men dressed in the savage splendour of Cretan heroic costume, which I suspected (from the speed with which they had arrived on the scene with every button in place) that they slept in. These were our judges—the Lord Mayor and all the Commissioners of Assize—while outside, in the well of the deck, and sitting on the engine coamings, and along the rocks, sat the whole array of jurors, the entire male population of Agios Georgios.

Four men had taken Stratos up to the hotel, there to watch over—and watch—him. Tony had, in the general confusion, got clear away. Although by this time most of the light-boats—attracted by the bedlam of noise and lights at the hotel—were converging on us across the bay, none of those near enough had had an engine, so Tony had dodged his way to freedom with the utmost ease and—it was reported —all the loose cash from the hotel, together with a sizable number of his own portable possessions. But it should be simple, they said, to pick him up. . . .

Myself, I rather doubted this. The cool-headed Tony, with his genius for disassociating himself from trouble, at large in the Aegean with a good boat, and the coasts of Europe, Africa, and Asia Minor to choose from? But I said nothing. We ourselves had need of all the sympathetic attention we could command.

It had not taken long for the four of us to tell our story. We had omitted nothing, down to the smallest detail of Josef's death. Over this there were grave looks, and some head-shaking, but I could see that the main climate of opinion was on our side. It seemed obvious that the actual acts of violence which Stratos had committed meant little, in themselves, to these men, and it might have gone differently with us if we had killed Stratos himself, whatever he had done in the course of his own private feud. But the death of Josef the Turk—and a Turk from Chania, at that—was (one gathered) quite a different thing. And in the matter of poor Sofia Alexiakis, who would have enough to bear when her brother's story came to light, it could be seen as the mercy of heaven that now, at last, as a widow, she could once more be a free woman, and a Christian. She could even—Christ be praised—make her Communion this very Easter Sunday. . . .

The rest was to be as easy. When Stratos later recovered consciousness, to be confronted with the discovery of the jewels in his fishing-grounds, the body of Alexandros (which was in fact found buried in the field by the mill), the guilty defection of Tony, and, finally, the death of Josef, he took the easiest way out for himself, and told a story which, in essentials, seemed to be an approximation of the truth.

He and Alexandros were not (as Colin's theory had had it) thieves, but had for some years been partners as "fences," or receivers of stolen goods, with Tony as a kind of assistant and liaison officer. Stratos, running an honestly profitable little restaurant in Frith Street, had provided unimpeachable "cover," and he and Alexandros had apparently had no connection other than a friendship between compatriots. Even this friendship had a perfectly natural explanation, for Alexandros was a Cretan, too, a native of Anoghia, the village which lay in the heights beyond the ruined Byzantine church. So things had gone on prosperously for a time, until the affair of the big Camford House robbery.

But Stratos had the good businessman's instinct for getting out of the deal at the right moment, and, well before the robbery at Camford House, he had set about realizing his assets at leisure, and in good order, ostensibly to retire with his "pile" to his native village. Alexandros—who could see only that a highly lucrative partnership was packing up in the moment of its greatest prosperity—bitterly opposed Stratos' move. Argument after argument supervened, culminating in a violent quarrel on the very eve of Stratos' departure, when Alexandros was driven to utter threats which he almost certainly had no intention of carrying out. The inevitable happened; tempers snapped, and knives were drawn —and Alexandros was left for dead in a back alley at least two miles from Frith Street, while Stratos and Tony innocently embarked that same night on the flight for Athens, for which their bookings had been made at least six weeks previously.

Recovering slowly in a London hospital, Alexandros held his tongue. Possibly he realized now—in the hue and cry over the disappearance of the Camford jewels—that Stratos' withdrawal had been opportune. The only thing was, Stratos had taken the lot. . . .

As soon as he was fit, and was sure that the police had not yet connected the obscure stabbing affair in Lambeth with the Camford robbery, Alexandros in his turn retired— armed—to his native land.

If it could ever be said that stupidity rated a punishment as final as murder, it would seem that Alexandros asked for what he got. Stratos and Tony received him—understandably—with a certain wariness, but soon, somehow, the affair was patched up, and there followed a scene of reconciliation and apology, made more plausible by the presence of Sofia and Josef. Stratos would, in good time, divide the spoils, and the three men would go their separate ways, but meanwhile it was only reasonable for all three to lie low for a period, until the jewels could, in some form or other, find their way gradually onto the market. This agreed, the family party (well wined and dined, Soho-fashion, by Tony) set out to escort Alexandros over to his own village, but on the way an argument had arisen, over the disposal of the jewels, which had sprung almost immediately into a quarrel. And then, Alexandros had laid a hand to his gun. . . .

It is probable, even, that Alexandros was not quite so stupid or credulous as the story made him. Stratos swore, and continued to swear, that he himself had never intended murder. It was Josef who had killed Alexandros, Josef who had shot at Mark, and who had gone, on his own initiative and without orders from Stratos, to make sure of Mark's death. As for Colin, who had been dragged off in a moment of panic-stricken and drunken confusion, Stratos swore that it was he himself who had given the order for Colin's release, and here (he said, and nobody doubted him) his sister would bear him out.

And, finally, the attack on me. . . . Well, what did anyone expect? He had gone to make a routine check of his spoils, and had found a girl whom he suspected of some connection with Josef's mysterious absence, diving after his pots. He had only done what any man would have done in his place— and here, it was obvious, the meeting rather agreed with him —and in any case (he vowed this, repeatedly) he had only been trying to frighten, not to kill me.

But all this was for morning. Now, the first explanations over, our story pieced together, weighed, and at last accepted, someone came across from the hotel with coffee for everyone, and glasses of spring water. By the time dawn broke, Agios Georgios had settled happily down to the greatest sensation since the Souda Bay landing.

I sat, weary, drowsy, and warm, with the cut in my thigh throbbing painfully, and my body relaxed into the curve of Mark's arm. The air of the cabin was slate-grey with smoke, and the walls vibrated with the noise of talking, and the clash of glasses as emphatic fists struck the little table. I had long since stopped trying to follow the thick, rapid Greek. Leave it to Mark, I thought sleepily; leave it all to Mark. My part in it was over; let him cope with the rest, then, soon, we could all sail away, free at last to salvage what remained of our respective holidays. . . .

A memory cut through the smoky cabin like a knife-blade of cold air. I sat up abruptly, out of the circle of Mark's arm.

"Mark! *Mark,* wake up! There's Frances!"

He blinked. "Do you mean to tell me—dear heaven, of course, I'd clean forgotten! She must be back there in the bay!"

"Well, of course she is! She's sitting there on a rock with

220

a twisted ankle. Frances, I mean, not the rock. Oh dear, how could we? That's twice I've remembered—at least, forgotten, but—"

"Pull yourself together," said Mark kindly. "Look, sweetie, don't start another panic; she'll be all right. Believe it or not, it's barely an hour and a half since we picked you up. If we go straight back there now—"

"It's not that! She'll be wondering what happened! She must be half out of her mind!"

"Not she," he said cheerfully. "She'd see us haul you in. She was yelling for help while you were in the water with Stratos after you. It was the noise she made that brought us in—that, and the odd way his light was behaving, so near our rendezvous. Then once we got near enough there was too much to do, and I clean forgot her. Oh, and she threw a rock at Stratos."

"*Did* she? Good for her! Did she hit him?"

"Did you ever know a female hit anything? That she aimed at, I mean? She hit me," said Mark. He got to his feet, and addressed the concourse in Greek. This was to the effect that there was another English lady to be rescued, some way westwards along the coast, and that they would have to trust him and his party not to run away, but we must immediately go and fetch her.

Instantly every man present was on his feet. I am not quite sure what happened, amid the passionate babel of Cretan Greek, but in a very few minutes, as the caique swung away from shore, she was as well attended as a Cunarder edging her way out into Southampton Water. Not a man in Agios Georgios but would have died on the spot sooner than stay behind. Those light-boats that possessed engines had now caught up with us, lights blazing. Those that had not, bobbed valiantly in our wake. Astern of us loomed the bigger mother-shapes of the *Agia Barbara,* and the innocent *Eros.* It was a noble procession.

To Frances, sitting nursing her sore ankle on her lonely rock, we must have been a brave sight, a pack of lighted boats swinging round the headland, our lamps yellow against the growing dawn.

Our caique drew ahead of the rest, and slid alongside the rock-ridge. Colin shot out the boat-hook, and held us fast. Mark hailed her, cheerfully.

"Ahoy, there, Andromeda! Perseus here, with apologies, but there was a little matter of a dragon."

221

I ran to the side. "Frances! Are you all right? I'm most dreadfully sorry—"

"Well," said Frances, "I can see *you're* all right, which is all that matters, though I did have information to that effect. How nice to be rescued in style! I'm glad to see you, Perseus. You're a little late for the other dragon, but, as you see, he did me no harm."

Mark's brows knitted. "The other dragon?"

I put my hand to my mouth. "Tony? You mean Tony? *Here?*"

"As ever was."

"What happened?"

"He came to collect the remainder of the jewels. The Camford House robbery, I understand." Frances was bland. "How well I remember the fuss when it happened."

"But he didn't know where they were," I said blankly. "I *know* he didn't. Colin said—"

"Yes, he did." Mark's voice was grim. "Fool that I am, I heard Stratos tell him tonight. He shouted out something about the *scháros* pots, when we were crashing around in the hotel garden like demented buffaloes. I don't know whether he was just cursing me, or whether he was letting Tony know, so that he could pick them up. But Tony heard, and it seems he didn't waste any time." He looked at Frances. "Do you mean to tell me that while we've been sitting jabbering like monkeys in Agios Georgios, he's just calmly walked away with the rest of the jewels?"

"Not all of them; only one pot-full. I don't know how many there are, and neither did he. He didn't even know where the pots were laid, and of course, even with the lights, it wasn't easy to find them. He hauled up four in turn, and only one of them had what he was looking for. The rest were fish pots, quite genuine. He was quite—er—picturesque about them. Then we heard the flotilla coming, and he cut his losses, and went. He said he'd got quite enough to make the whole thing worth while."

" 'He said'? You mean he saw you?"

"He could hardly avoid it, could he? At least one of the pots was almost at my feet. Don't look so horrified, my dear, he was very polite, and quite amusing. He simply kept nicely out of range—not that I could even have begun to try to stop him—and told me all about it. He really did seem pleased that Colin had got safe away."

"Small thanks to him," I said tartly.

"So I told him. But I gather you've quite a lot to thank

Sofia for. Apparently she refused from first to last to take anything from Stratos, because she thought it was all the proceeds of crime. She wouldn't have given him away, but it seems she did threaten to turn the lot of them in, Josef and herself included, if they hurt Colin. Master Tony passed that on to me, so that I could put in a word for her. And he sent you his love, Nicola; he was sorry to have to pass out of your life, but you'll get a picture post card from the Kara Bugaz."

"From the what? Where on earth's that?"

"I doubt if it need worry you. I've a strong feeling that we'll never heard of Little Lord Fauntleroy again, from the Kara Bugaz or anywhere else. Oh yes, and I was to tell you how much he approves of your trousers."

"Well," said Mark, "that's one thing over which he and I see eye to eye. Aren't you coming off your rock? I know we're pretty crowded, but I can guarantee Lambis to get you back without foundering, and Colin makes a smashing cup of cocoa."

Frances smiled at the three of them. "So that's Lambis . . . and this is Colin. I can hardly believe we've never met till now, I seem to know you so well." She put out a hand, and Mark jumped to the ridge, and helped her to her feet. "Thank you, Perseus. Well, Nicola, so this is your Mark?"

"Why, yes," I said.